KING OF H

"We are destined to be lovers, Charlaine. Go on now, run and hide. Or try to."

Every urge she possessed bade her do exactly that. Instead, she stood her ground and said icily, "I will not give you the satisfaction. You are no threat to me, least of all to my heart."

The words he spoke were as devastating as his mesmerizing touch. Each one pierced the last of her tattered defenses.

"One day, very soon, I will live with you. We will dine together. I will eat on your golden plate, and share your silver spoon." His voice went even softer, brushing against her like the velvet promise of a long, moonless night. "And I will sleep in your soft bed, and touch your silken skin. Then, when you know me, you will see me as I really am. The only man for you."

Her breath caught. She felt her will toppling. She felt herself teetering toward him. And precisely because she wanted his touch so much, she forced the words out. "You are nothing but a frog. A French rogue who wants only my money and position!"

Other *Love Spell* books by Colleen Shannon:
THE GENTLE BEAST

COLLEEN SHANNON

Prince of Kisses

LOVE SPELL   NEW YORK CITY

LOVE SPELL®
May 1997
Published by

Dorchester Publishing Co., Inc.
276 Fifth Avenue
New York, NY 10001

Printed in the United States of America.

Chapter One

Devlin Rhodes jumped down from the ten-foot-high stone wall, landing lightly on his feet. The mastiffs trotted up to greet him, their fierce wrinkled faces set in adoring expectation. As he had for the past week, he pulled two steaks out of the knapsack on his back.

He unwrapped them, letting the great hounds smell both the meat and the hand that offered it. After allowing them a tantalizing bite, he tossed the steaks behind a tall bush. Tails wagging, they padded after them.

"Eat hearty, *garcons*." He'd trade one of his jewelry stores to see the so-rich, so-snobbish Lady Charlaine Callista Kimball's face if she saw her vicious hounds literally eating out of the hand of her most detested rival. What a pity she'd never know he'd been there.

If everything went as planned.

Shrugging with the Gallic fatalism that was one of the few things he'd inherited from his French mother,

Devlin continued across an immaculate garden that Queen Victoria herself would envy. But then, rumor had it that the queen had asked her own gardener to help plan this masterpiece. Rumor also had it that Charlaine Kimball was one of her favorite subjects, with a puritanical bent similar to Regina Victoria's own.

Devlin grinned to himself. He loved nothing more than shocking the aristocracy. Tonight's work would ease some of the pain this particular class had caused him and his mother.

Clad in black from head to toe, Devlin moved with the night. He slithered from a stately linden tree to bushes trimmed to resemble forest creatures. Here an owl watched him with big eyes; there a stag seemed poised to take flight from a pursuing huntsman. At another time, Devlin might have paused to enjoy the clever blending of stone statue with blooming flora.

However, Lady Charlaine was also known to be a very private individual. She had several night watchmen about the place. Had Devlin not made it his task to learn their schedules, he would not have known that he had exactly five more minutes to scale the mansion before the early morning watch came on.

He moved with a stealth unused for some years, but the soft-footed sureness easily returned. His eyes, startling blue in his tanned face, constantly darted, looking for movement, or a twig on the ground. Anything that could reveal his presence—or his purpose.

He'd missed the old game since he became respectable. Store by store, he was slowly gaining acclaim even against competition such as the likes of Kimball's and Tiffany's. He had too much to lose to continue this delightful, but dangerous, sport. Tonight would truly have to be the last time.

When he came to the fountain centered on the vast

grounds, he paused to rinse his hands, dry them on his breeches, and then pull on his black kidskin gloves. He contemplated the statue in the fountain with an ironic smile.

Most appropriate. Diana stood there, her tunic slipping off her shoulders as if she'd just exited her bath. But her bow was held at the ready, her eyes trained severely on the all-too-human man kneeling at her feet, gazing up at her.

Devlin had come by his education the hard way—book by book. But his memory was retentive, and he recalled the story of Diana and Actaeon, who had spied the virgin goddess in her bath. She had turned him into a stag; then he was ripped apart by his own dogs.

"Charming," Devlin muttered, turning away with a shiver he could not squelch. He'd have to go into Diana's private quarters. That was where the safe was.

He continued on his zigzag path to the house. Though he was as alert as ever, his mind was filled with curiosity about the woman who had challenged him.

If she'd known him better, she would have realized that, like his older cousin, Devlin Rhodes never shirked a challenge. Even if it meant endangering the comfortable existence he'd at last won, he would prove to the noble Ice Princess whom no man could win that her estate was not burglarproof. Besides, he wanted to see what his dear cousin had sent her in the last shipment so he'd know what he was up against.

Why did she hate men so? She surrounded herself with women, and probably did business with Cecil Rhodes only because she had to. He had the best diamonds, after all.

Bitterness burned the backs of his eyes. The familiar vow returned to him. Someday Cecil Rhodes would

9

regret refusing to acknowledge his first cousin, born of his uncle's youthful indiscretion with a young French girl.

Devlin slipped into the shadow of the ivy-covered wall. "Someday, *cousin*, has arrived," he whispered aloud. Devlin plunged his hand into the thick ivy, found the rope and pulled it out. Slapping the rope against the wall to free it from the ivy all the way to the fourth-story tower at the top, where it was anchored, Devlin gripped the rope with both hands. He set his feet flat against the wall and began to climb.

The ivy made it tricky. Still, his rubber-soled shoes found purchase every time he slipped. The spring night was cool, but his back was trickling with sweat by the time he finally reached the casement window high at the top of the round tower.

Partially resting his weight on the ledge, he shoved the window gently. It resisted, then swung inward before the heavy curtains stopped it. He released his pent-up breath. So far, so good.

Devlin eased the curtains aside and dropped, sure-footed, into the room. Moonlight streamed through the crack in the curtains, revealing the plush flower-patterned carpet smothering the floor. As he tiptoed forward, he saw that the flower motif was repeated in the silk wallpaper scattered with orchids. Hothouse orchids, their pearly petals so perfect they looked carved, filled an exquisite cut-glass vase. They nodded their regal heads from a long table behind the couch before the vast marble fireplace. Lamps glowed with muted colors even in the dim moonlight. The exquisite stained-glass art pieces could only be of Tiffany's manufacture.

Devlin scanned the room but, oddly, saw no pictures. A huge gilt mirror covered one wall, but it would be too cumbersome to give access to a safe. Devlin advanced another soundless step, but he couldn't see past the middle of the room, so he tugged the curtains a bit wider.

Bookcases lined one wall. He crept nearer to examine them. A sound made him freeze.

A sigh, soft as the breeze whispering through the open casement. Devlin had assumed this was a sitting room, but now he saw the dim outline of a vast fourposter bed. He glanced at the shelves, at the bed, hesitating.

Curiosity won. Surely he had time for one glimpse of the woman all London buzzed about, the woman who, like the queen she consorted with, ruled her empire with a feminine but iron hand.

Devlin crept over the carpet, but the pile was so thick his tread would have been muffled even if he'd worn boots. As he rounded the bed, moving away from the moonlight, his eyes adjusted to the darkness. Two steps away, he froze. The air left his lungs in a whoosh.

A goddess did indeed slumber in the moonlight, but she was no huntress. She was Aphrodite herself.

Long hair fell over the side of the bed in shimmering waves to the floor. The red tresses caught every stealthy ray of moonlight and cast it back; he could only wonder what her hair looked like at noon. Her eyes were closed, but her lashes were sable fans against her flawless ivory skin. Her dark brows arched wickedly above, flying away to her temples with a reckless disregard for fashion that he found enchanting.

She slept on her back, one leg half out of the covers, bare to the knee. Her ankle was slim but sturdy, a pleasing segue to the shapely calf and hidden thigh that must complete the stunning limb like the crescendo to an aria. He couldn't see her breasts, but the covers mounded over her chest in a way that proved

11

she was very much a woman, in spite of her attempts to live—and act—like a man.

Devlin swallowed, mastering the stirring at his groin, and tore his gaze away. Despite the fact that they both owned jewelry stores, they were as far apart socially as the moon and the stars. He'd learned at an early age that wanting what he couldn't have only made his desire hurt more. Besides, he wore no mask. Not that she'd recognize him. But if their mutual contacts should one day bring them together . . .

Quietly he searched the bookcase, nudging at corners, carvings and books. Finally, when he pressed on a medallion on one end, part of the case slid open on well-oiled springs.

A safe gleamed behind it. Devlin took his glove off with his teeth, pulled a stethoscope out of his pack and slipped it around his neck and in his ears.

Turning the dial in his sensitive fingers, he listened to the teeth ticking off each number until a distinctive hollow click sounded. Mentally filing the number, he proceeded, working left and right, until he had all four digits. In ten minutes, he had the safe open.

Quickly now, for he heard the covers stirring, he pulled out the contents, the familiar solid feel of stones and gold comforting him. Then his fingers felt something unexpected. He pulled out a wrapped, rectangular object. Deftly he opened the oilskin rag. A book? What book could be so valuable that it had to be stowed with a king's ransom of jewels?

Devlin barely had time to glimpse an exquisite binding inset with jewels before a hiccup came from the bed. Dropping all willy-nilly into his pack, he buttoned the knapsack closed and shouldered it. He pulled his glove back on and latched the safe. The bookcase slid home just as quietly as it had opened.

He'd almost made it back to the window when a

cold feminine voice said, "Stop right there or I'll shoot you where you stand." Lady Charlaine Callista Kimball came forward into the moonlight, her thin gown revealing a voluptuous form.

However, Devlin's appreciation was somewhat spoiled by the incongruous accessory she bore. The tiny pearl-handled pistol glittered with a gimlet eye in the moonlight.

He let his gaze linger insolently on all the shadowy curves and valleys he itched to discover with his hands. What he wouldn't give for a blazing noon sun. Still, she was intimidated enough to hunch her shoulders, but she merely succeeded in emphasizing her lissome curves.

Grinning, Devlin leaned against the wall beside the casement and crossed his feet at the ankles, hoping she couldn't see the pack on his shoulders. "You really don't need to threaten me, you know. I'll gladly stay in your bedchamber with you as long as you like, *chérie*."

"Do not call me that," she said through her teeth. "Doubtless you will not find me dear when I throw you to my dogs."

A lesser man might have backed away at the threat that so closely fit his earlier whimsical speculation; Devlin Rhodes merely raised a well-defined black eyebrow. "Please do. I have not found the time to play with them today."

That set her back for a moment, but he had to admire her aplomb when she said coolly, "Indeed? This I must see." She started to wave him downstairs, noticed her bare feet poking from beneath the hem of her gown, and abruptly seemed to recall how she was dressed. Even in the moonlight he saw her blush. Savagely she jerked up a dressing gown from the foot of her bed.

She looked at it, then at him, and finally down at the gun in her hand.

He had to smile at her dilemma. Indeed, it would be difficult to put on such a heavy garment while trying to hold a pistol on him all the while. He bowed gallantly. "I shall be delighted to hold the pistol for you."

She glared at him. She nibbled that full, sensuous lip.

"That, too, I shall be even happier to do," he said softly, his gaze caressing her mouth. "I have a feeling you do not utilize the gifts God blessed you with so richly."

"Ooh!" She held the dressing gown over her form and backed to the door, the pistol still leveled at his chest. Awkwardly holding the gown over her with an elbow as she fumbled for the knob, she opened the door, backed outside and locked it. He heard her light steps hurry down the hall; then she called, "Henrietta! Fetch my watchman!"

That was the only encouragement he needed. How fortunate that she thought he'd entered through the door. He would just go out the way he'd come in.

To his dismay, by the time he'd got in position to climb, several moving torches were bobbing around in the gardens far below. Devlin heard footsteps tromping upstairs farther down in the hall.

Trapped. He gave a last desperate look at the room, but all the obvious hiding places were too small. Unless . . . He eyed the bed. It was doubtful even her own men would search the Ice Princess's reputedly virgin bed. Quickly, before he could change his mind, he picked up the heavy glass bowl filled with flowers and water, carried it to the window and threw it outside with all his might.

A satisfying thud sounded as the heavy weight hit

the ground. One of the torches bouncing nearby stopped. "There he be! This way!" a man called. The torch leaped toward the sound.

Devlin shoved the casement window wide, pulling the rope out of the shielding ivy. For good measure, he tossed one of his gloves at the foot of the tower. Then, pushing the pack beneath the bed, he dove beneath the down covers. The feather bed was so soft that his form barely made an impression under the mound. He settled back, alert for the tiniest sound.

He was not scared; he was not tense. In fact, the rakish grin that lingered in the minds of all who saw it stretched his mobile face.

The emotion tapping against his ribs was far more heady than fear.

And far more dangerous . . .

In the hallway foyer, Lady Charlaine Callista Kimball tapped a small, bare foot impatiently on the priceless black and white Carrara marble floor while her men searched her room. Her head watchman came back down, respectfully tugging his cap.

"Sorry, ma'rm, ain't a whisker sign 'o him. From the looks o' things, he climbed out the same way he come in. One of my men heard him land, but couldn't find no sight o' him." The grizzled man was obviously a veteran of the class war between gentry and poor working sod, for his words grew faster the longer she took to respond. "I thinks we should fetch the bobbies."

"Never mind. I do not want this insolence bandied about. I shall find the scoundrel myself. Now leave me." Charlaine waited until the man scurried out before venting her anger. She kicked a chair leg, sending a priceless gilded chair skidding across the marble, leaving a deep scratch in the shining floor. She turned away disdainfully, knowing her army of workmen would have the marble replaced before the sun had set. The fact that her toe ached only added to her rage as she tromped back upstairs. Doubtless her father would castigate her for losing control, but she'd long since stopped caring what he thought. At least she'd learned to vent her rage in private.

Charlaine almost tripped, so intent was she on vowing retribution on her intruder. She grabbed the banister with a most unladylike curse that would have shocked the queen.

A robbery! Why, in all the years the Kimballs had owned this estate, no one had ever dared to break in. Who was this fellow of the dancing eyes and the nimble fingers, who could sprout wings and fly? For surely that was the only way he could have escaped.

She slammed the door to her suite behind her, threw aside her robe and turned up the gaslight beside her bed to appraise her haven with jaundiced eyes. No man had ever set foot in here, including her own father.

Until tonight.

Again, the image of those flashing white teeth and laughing blue eyes haunted her. The man's thick black hair tumbled with abandon across his broad, intelligent forehead. His brows were untidy accents to the rest of a perfectly symmetrical countenance. Handsome nose, not too big, not too small; wide, perfectly shaped lips. And his physique! His formfitting clothes gave her active imagination plenty to work with. Odd that she could picture the scoundrel so vividly. What he lacked in breeding he made up for in boldness; part of her had to admire his audacity. She seldom found men attractive, in fact avoided eligible young bachelors when she could, despite her queen's urging to the

16

contrary. But then, she seldom came across men so handsome.

For if she should fall in love and marry, according to English law, she would lose all she'd sweated and sacrificed to build. To distract herself, she stirred the dying coals in her fireplace to roaring life, pausing with an arm on the mantel to again appraise the only place that ever saw the real Charlaine Kimball.

Here she let down the cold mask she displayed to most of the world. She laughed and played cards with her few friends, and her trusted maid, Henrietta. She read on wintry evenings, feet tucked under her, before the roaring fire. She sewed her exquisite embroidery designs. Her latest had been a heart-shaped pillow with her name at the bottom.

If, on occasion, she sighed in her self-imposed isolation, well, that was the cost of carrying on the Kimball legacy. It had taken her many years to accept, but she finally knew that she was truly her father's daughter, the only Kimball left to carry on an old, proud line. In her twenty-five years, she'd learned that, in the business world at least, the ruthless won; the compassionate lost. Durwood Arthur Bryant Kimball, her father, had taught her that lesson well, by both example and design. To his constant reminders that she should have been a boy, she responded by doing her best to become just like him.

If, at times, she hated her own metamorphosis, well, of that she told no one.

She straightened with resolve. If ever again she saw the man who had dared invade her privacy, he would rue the day he'd caught her at such a disadvantage. And tomorrow she would set her workmen to ripping out the wallpaper and the carpet, and carrying the furniture to the attic. When the room was once more pristine, all trace of him would be obliterated.

Colleen Shannon

As she pulled the screen over the fire, dusted her hands off and turned toward her bed, a rogue thought crept under her guard: Could she obliterate her memory of the scoundrel as easily? She scowled at her own weakness. Girlhood longings were for the poor and the weak. She was neither. Indeed, she was the great-great-grandaughter of a pirate.

As she moved to the bed, she glimpsed herself in the mirror. That creature there, all soft curves and smooth skin, was the antithesis of her image of herself. She should be tall, with a deep voice and muscular build, the better to rule her empire. How she wished she could have been born in an earlier time as a boy, to learn at the side of her revered ancestor, the former pirate, Drake Kimball. Since she was in leading strings, she'd heard the stories of how he'd bested his enemies, restored the family fortune with no advantage but his wit, and founded a dynasty with one of England's boldest ladies, Callista Raleigh.

What would her legacy be? She stared at her too-perfect features a moment longer in disgust, and then she flounced away to the bed. She was beginning to doubt that she would ever have heirs to give her immortality in their own family tall tales. Would she have a grand romance to add to the family—

She drew in a sharp breath and rushed to the hidden safe. The jewels were insured, but the precious illuminated book passed down from great-great-grandfather Drake Kimball, where her grandfather and father had added stories of their own stormy courtships, was irreplaceable. Her fingers trembled as she spun the dial and swung open the safe. Her vision swam before her. She reached inside, as if her eyes deceived her. But no. The safe was empty.

"Blast and damn his black, thieving heart! You shall pay for this, and richly, I vow on the blood of my ancestors!" She slammed the safe shut and kicked the bookcase panel closed so hard that half the books fell out. She had to jump back to avoid their falling on her feet. She would tear London apart, send her best detectives to every hellhole and fence in the city until she found one rather ordinary jewel thief. They would bring him before her, and he would bow on bended knee, begging for mercy.

She made a scoffing sound. Mercy? Indeed, she would treat him just as gently as men had treated female captives through the ages. She kicked a few of the unoffending books, and then threw a Dresden shepherdess against the wall for good measure. The satisfying crash made her feel better for all of five seconds. She was still breathing heavily when she finally returned to her bed, turned up the gas lamp and prepared to read the night away, as she often did when she had trouble sleeping.

She stuffed the pillow behind her head and tried to pull the covers over her legs. Odd. The heavy down seemed caught on something. She tugged harder, but the down pulled taut and did not budge. Most odd. Come to think of it, the bed did not feel quite right. She got up on her knees and leaned toward the end of the bed to see what the covers were stuck on.

She felt the opposite side of the bed move and turned in that direction, her eyes wide with shock, but she was too late. The covers themselves seemed to take life, rising to envelop her in a crushing hold. She found herself sprawled flat on her back in her own bed, the intruder she'd thought long fled now master, where only she had been mistress a scant few seconds earlier.

No man had ever been so close before. She felt every inch of his tall, muscular frame weighing her down into the soft bed. Oddly, the pressure was not unpleas-

19

ant. Something about his planes and angles seemed to fit her curves just right, but the primitive feeling horrified her conscious mind. As did the odd stiffness pressing into her lower abdomen.

Innocent she might be, but she knew what that meant. He must have watched her standing before the fire in the thin gown. The fact that he found her as physically pleasing as she secretly found him only added to her frustrated rage.

She was so stunned and still, staring up at those bold blue eyes, that his big hand eased its pressure over her mouth.

"Promise me you won't scream, and I will let you up."

She nodded slightly. He eased his palm away and started to move aside. She took a deep breath, but the scream had barely started before that tough, capable hand swallowed it. His grin made her quiver deep inside. He settled on her comfortably, pushing her deeper into the bed.

"Your choice, *chérie*. I much prefer this position over a chilly spring night." He squirmed atop her, grinning wider when her eyes fluttered closed. He cocked his head to one side and raised his torso so he could contemplate her pleasing shape. With his free hand, he flicked at the high neckline of her sweeping nightgown. "Even your choice of bed attire is cold and proper." He leaned to whisper in her ear, "Save when you stand in front of the fire. There, I suspect, is the real Charlaine Kimball. Your hair tumbles down your back like liquid flame, but it is still cold compared to the passion you suppress within."

The things he was saying to her were horrible, unthinkable. Why could this scoundrel, on their first meeting, see so easily beneath the mask others accepted at face value? She began to buck beneath him, frantic to get away, to be safe again.

Holding her chin in one strong hand, he drew his muffling palm away. She had no time to scream, for another substance, softer, warmer, immediately latched onto her mouth.

She had been kissed before, but those were furtive affairs ended coldly by her. This time, when she tried to draw back, she had nowhere to run. She could only lie still, captive to him and the feelings he aroused. Those lips were so warm, so sweetly gentle. She would have expected a rough-and-tumble man like he to be brutal, to demand her surrender.

Not he. He assayed, testing her like a prospector seeking something far more valuable than gold. And he seemed to find it, for he slanted his head for a deeper angle and rubbed his lips against hers, growling his own pleasure. She felt his heart rate accelerate, and her own heart followed, as if he led her in some pagan dance.

She gasped into his mouth, but that only urged him to greater trespass. The tip of his tongue dipped into her open mouth like a hummingbird seeking life's nectar. As if only she could supply it, only he could take it. *Share with me*, he seemed to say. *We will each be the richer for it.*

Her defenses slowly crumbled under the persuasive assault. His skillful mouth aroused in her such feelings as she had never known, no, nor even dreamed of. No one would know if just this once she were weak, if she explored the great unknown of what it meant to be a woman with a man.

When the teasing tip of his tongue retreated, she struggled her hands free and cupped the back of his head to slant her mouth under his. She was a fast learner. Boldly she followed his example, dipping her tongue into his warm mouth scented of brandy and peppermint. When she was limp beneath him, her head swimming with his scent, his touch, his taste, he drew away slightly.

Murmuring French endearments, he lowered his mouth to her throbbing neck and stabbed his tongue into the scented hollow of her throat. And then his hands, his big, capable hands, skillfully worked at the buttons of her bodice.

A niggling doubt winnowed through the pleasant fog of arousal. Something was wrong. If only she could think.

"Mon cœur," he whispered into the vee of skin he was slowly exposing.

The realization hit her like a blast of winter air: He spoke French so well because he *was* a damned frog; she was not the first—no, nor would she be the last— to wilt under his expert seduction.

She was a Kimball, not some harlot to play a light-skirt beneath a French libertine!

He'd reached the fifth tiny button. He was taking his time, as if he were not a hunted thief, but a welcome guest. As if she were not the favorite of royalty, but a common chit he could have his way with and discard.

Gall at his arrogance revived her formidable will-power. She caught his big hands as they moved to pull her bodice aside. He paused and looked down at her. *"Ma chère,"* what is amiss?"

So tender his tone, as if she really were his dear. She flung his hands aside and caught his wide shoulders to push him away. He balked, catching her wrists in his hands and holding them above her head. He was gentle, but inexorable.

Like the tide. Like the sunrise. Like the seasons. The thoughts came unbidden, but she squelched them. A force of nature he might be, but she was a creature who liked her comforts civilized.

Her tone was cool, as if her voice alone could master her own fevered flesh. "An experiment, mainly. Quite pleasant, but in the final analysis, you fail. You may let me up now, if you please."

He froze, obviously surprised by her calm. Then he smiled. A crooked, knowing smile that acknowledged her secret battle with herself. "Ah, but what if I do not please?" He tilted her chin back and lowered his mouth.

"Then I shall scream loud enough to shake the rafters," she said into his lips. She turned her head aside. But the breath to scream would not come—only because he was on top of her, pressing her into the feather mattress with his heavy weight.

Or so she told herself even as he eased away, as if challenging her to do as she threatened.

Nothing stopped her from screaming. Nothing save those sultry blue eyes that made icy composure impossible.

"One day, *ma chère*, you will scream beneath me with a different emotion." The soft words had the nature of a vow, all the more troubling since she didn't understand his meaning. He glanced around, tugged the velvet cords off her bed curtains and proceeded to tie her to the bedpost. He used a strange knot that held her but gave slightly when she pulled at it.

Still, to be tied up in her own bedchamber, to the bed she'd unwillingly shared with this bold stranger . . . Outrage gave her strength.

He stifled her scream with a large hand. "Promise me you will not call them for five minutes, and I will not gag you." He eased his hand away.

"Frog!"

Back came the hand. That long length of sheer masculinity settled back atop her. "As you wish. I will stay." His eyes filled half her world, then three quarters, and finally she saw nothing but him, felt nothing but him.

When he pulled his hand away to kiss her, she said breathlessly, "Very well. I promise not to scream for five minutes."

The kiss landed on her neck, blending with a heavy male sigh that sounded like regret. "Pity. Never have I enjoyed a battle of wills more."

Finally his weight lifted. She heard him rummaging about, even though she couldn't see him.

She had to wound him somehow. "How do you know I will keep my word?"

"Because you are a woman of fortitude and honesty, or so say all who do business with you." His voice was muffled, as if he had bent over something.

How could he know so much about her, when she had never seen him, or heard of him? Was he involved in the jewelry trade somehow?

While she speculated, he came into her field of vision again. That maddening smile stretched his expressive, sensual lips. "Besides," he added softly, "the Ice Princess will never admit to the world that she was bested in her own chamber by a mere, ah, what was it you called me? Ah, yes, a frog." He cocked his head and appraised her. " 'Tis you who looks a bit green about the gills, my sweet. But fear not. We shall meet again."

At the window, he turned. With only the moon to bless his parting, he threw her an airy kiss that landed like a brand. He'd stuck something else in his bulging pack, but she couldn't tell what it was.

Even as she glared at him with fury, part of her knew she would never forget the sight of him at this moment. His black hair blew in the breeze from the open casement. His brilliant blue eyes sparkled in the moonlight.

He stepped over the sill and paused astride it, surveying her as if he were master of this domain, she, its mistress only until his return. "You are wasted alone up here, my Ice Princess. But not for long. Two things I promise you: When the time is right, I shall return your treasure to you. And one day you will melt beneath my kiss, and beg me for what we almost shared this night. Until then, I will not kiss you again, no matter how much you beg."

"You arrogant frog, never, ever will I beg you for anything! Not in your dreams—"

"But in yours, yes?" He had the temerity to wink. And then, with a lithe twist of his fit body, he had dropped out of sight.

But not out of mind. Even as she stewed, pulling at her silken bonds, part of her knew she would never forget him.

He had not tied her tightly, and she was free within minutes. She hesitated, torn between the window and the door.

A last sight of him, perhaps? Or a shout to warn the household?

Again, her baser instincts won, to her shame. She ran to the window.

The garden below was brilliantly lit by the moon. At first she saw nothing unusual. And then a breeze rustled the hedges. There, where her statue of Cupid stood, his bow and arrow on the alert, was her heart-shaped pillow.

Her mouth dropped open as she stared.

The blighter had stuck it on the end of Cupid's arrow!

Charlaine threw on her dressing gown and ran down the stairs, so anxious to fetch the pillow before anyone else saw it that she didn't pause to put on slippers. Her tender feet barely felt the rocks gouging them. She lunged for the pillow, almost falling in the pond. The delicate silk tore, but not before she saw the message he'd scrawled on the fabric.

"*Adieu*. But not good-bye. Dream of me, *chère*, as I will dream of you."

Even as a thrill ran up her spine, her eyes narrowed in fury. She marched to the trash pile behind the storage shed and buried the pillow beneath a mound of garbage.

Then, her pride assuaged by the symbolism, she returned to her sanctuary.

But somehow she knew it would never feel the same. He had spoiled it for her. She touched her tingling mouth, the rogue thought coming: When she saw him again, would she kiss him or call the guards on him, as he deserved?

Chapter Two

Devlin yawned as he climbed the narrow stairs to the flat above his largest jewelry store. He was dressed respectably now, in the black frock coat, striped maroon-and-gray waistcoat and intricately tied ascot so much the rage in this grand year of Queen Victoria's Golden Jubilee, 1887. Devlin hung his top hat and gloves on the hall tree beside his door, then turned up the gas chandelier centering the living area. The room was spare, decorated with a few genuine Louis XV chairs and tables rather than cluttered with bric-a-brac and heavy rococo furniture, like so many rooms in the current mode.

In one way he had succumbed: he'd created a cozy Turkish corner in the side of his living area. A plush medallion backed couch squared off with a marble table; the new morris reclining chair sat intimately next to an overstuffed armchair. Only a brilliant Tiffany dragonfly lamp poised on the center table lit the intimate scene. The ladies loved his little indulgence, often initiating intimacy themselves.

His mouth twisted sardonically. Ladies? They were a rare breed, indeed, especially in his stores. Most of his clientele consisted of working class women purchasing their first extravagance, or of men acquiring gifts for their mistresses. Of true ladies, he had known exactly two. His mother, and now Charlaine Kimball. And, if he knew what was good for him, he would give her a wide berth. Doubtless she was vowing retribution on him this very moment.

His smile deepened. He could hardly wait until she descended on him. Like her colleague, Cecil Rhodes, she would acknowledge him soon enough. If only to curse my name, Devlin vowed.

He carefully laid his pack on the vast four-poster bed, the only inheritance he had from his mother's people. Despite their own impoverishment, they were still aristocrats too fine to acknowledge the foolish younger daughter who had gotten herself with child by a married man, then run off to America.

However, when he'd arrived in Europe a couple of years ago, wealthy at last from the diamond mines of Africa, he immediately went to Nice. He was curious about the family his mother never criticized, even on her deathbed, when tuberculosis finally claimed her. He found the grand seaside estate sold to a wealthy Spaniard, the French aristocrats long since moved to the America they'd once scorned. An old family retainer sold him the bed.

Devlin ran his hands over the intricate carving. The scalloped posts soared almost to the ceiling. The headboard was topped by a grand pediment in the ornate style of Chippendale. Devlin closed his eyes, trying to visualize his mother being born in this bed, but he was haunted instead by his last sight of her. She had been so gaunt, and her sapphire eyes were bloodshot and crusted with the fluid slowly filling her lungs. He had been eighteen then and an accomplished thief. He had taken her skeletal hand, trying to impart some of his own wild strength into her.

Weakly, she wiped his tears away. "*Mon fils*, do not cry for me. Always I will be with you. Here." She touched his closed eyelids. "And here." She touched his heart.

He forced the bold smile she so loved. "*Maman*, do not speak so. Why, in a week you will be up and about, scolding me again." They both knew he lied, but she did not chide him. She struggled to remove the locket he had never seen her without. She was so weak he had to help her. She pressed it into his hand.

"Go to England one day, and find your father's family. I gave you their name, though I could not wear your father's ring. This locket will prove who you are." He slipped it uncaringly into his pocket. He had hated her obsession with the diamond-encrusted locket, for on many occasions they'd gone without food because she refused to sell it. On one side was a miniature of her as a beautiful young girl; on the other was a miniature of his father, a stern-looking man with a kind mouth and a shock of luxurious black hair.

However, even at eighteen, he understood that she had saved the locket not only because it had been given to her by the man she loved shortly before his death in a barroom brawl, but because it proved her union had been more than one of the flesh. And finally, it was the only thing of value she had to leave to her son.

As if the ritual of inheritance ended her tenure on earth, she leaned back, sighed, and died. Her wasted face was peaceful as the angels bore her away from him.

Now, tears in his eyes, Devlin went to his own hidden safe, opened it and took out the locket. He cradled it, knowing that this one possession had been his lodestone for the past ten years. He'd never held it in his hand until that sad day, but even then, in his grief, he'd been struck less by its symbolism than by its beauty.

The heavy, cool smoothness of the gold. The brilliance of the diamonds. The fine hinges and tiny lock that clicked with such precision when he closed it. How did one acquire the skill to make something so beautiful? There and then, he resolved to stop his thieving and pursue an honest trade, the first trade he'd ever found as exciting as theft.

After his mother's funeral, he besieged the diamond brokers and jewelers in New York. In his tattered best suit, he begged for a job. Most looked at his frayed clothes and bruised knuckles and firmly showed him the door. Finally, on a dingy side street in a tiny shop, a Jewish bachelor by the name of Mordecai Levitz looked at him through thick eyeglasses that magnified his steely gray eyes.

"And why should I hire a *putz* like you, boy?"

Devlin lived in the Irish section of Hell's Kitchen, but he didn't need a translation to realize he'd been insulted. A hot response trembled on the tip of his tongue. Instead, he followed his instincts. Pulling the locket from his pocket, he handed it over to the small, wiry man who could have been fifty or eighty. "I want to learn to do this," he said simply.

The ease with which the pudgy hands handled the locket told Devlin all he needed to know of Mordecai's ability.

Mordecai handed it back, looked Devlin up and down and said sourly, "I'll try you for one week. Cleaning and running errands."

Devlin opened his mouth to protest, but shut it under that imperious gaze. "Yes, sir."

A bare month passed before he was helping at the gold bench. By the following year, he was beginning to design. And when he was twenty, Mordecai began calling him by name instead of "boy" and financed him on the journey to South Africa that was to change both their lives. And Devlin's nocturnal ventures grew fewer and fewer. In truth, he'd never intended to steal again until Lady Charlaine offered her challenge.

Devlin put the locket back in the safe and had opened the pack to stash his heist away when his door knocker sounded. He slammed the safe closed, pressed the hidden spring that made the corner washstand rotate back out, hiding the safe, and stuffed the knapsack beneath his bed. "Who is it?" he called.

"Mordecai."

A delighted grin stretched Devlin's face. He swung open the door, hauled the little man in by the shoulders and pumped his hand enthusiastically. "Damn, it's good to see you. But you're early. I was not expecting you until tomorrow."

Mordecai was a man of great intellect and deep reserve, and he had always been uncomfortable with Devlin's voluble expressiveness. He waited to respond until the door was shut. Even then he only replied, "One thing I will say for English packets: they are more reliable than our American ones." He looked about with veiled curiosity.

Devlin smiled as Mordecai mentally calculated the value of every pot and every chair, which he had, after all, helped pay for. Devlin waited with bated breath, but Mordecai gave a short nod, as if he approved of Devlin's taste, and got right to business. He pulled a black cloth, rolled and bound, from his capacious inner frock coat pocket. Putting the cloth on Devlin's

31

oak dining table, he untied it and pushed it open with the dexterity of experience. Devlin stuck his long fingers in the tiny pouches and pulled out the stones, turning them this way and that in the light of the chandelier, carefully putting each back in its proper place before removing more.

"They look good." He fetched his best loupe and appraised a half-carat diamond. "One inclusion, and look at this color! It's almost perfect."

"Look at this one." Mordecai reverently pulled out a large pink stone cut in a teardrop shape.

Devlin blinked and touched the rosy pink fire dancing on Mordecai's palm. The stone looked at least five carats in size. It was too brilliant to be a tourmaline, nor would Mordecai hold the stone with such care if it were the more common mineral. "A pink diamond?"

"Yes. I had to outbid the buyers at Tiffany's and Kimball's to get it, so set it well."

Devlin drew the loupe to his eye and turned the diamond beneath the magnifier. "I don't see a single inclusion."

"It was cut and polished in Amsterdam. I was told they got four smaller, less perfect stones out of the original rock."

Devlin looked up eagerly. "And are they available?" A necklace, harmonious in its simplicity, was already shaping in his mind, but it would require the other stones to be balanced perfectly.

Mordecai's little mouth set primly. "No. I couldn't afford to outbid Kimball's after winning the largest stone."

Devlin ducked his head to hide his smile. He hadn't yet had time to go through his cache, but if he were lucky, the jewels would be among the stones he'd taken from her safe. Of course, this made the horns of his dilemma all the sharper. How could he set them with the central stone and display the necklace in his window? Even he was not quite so bold—or foolhardy—as to blatantly proclaim his theft. Besides, he had not planned to keep her jewels. He'd only meant a lesson for the Ice Princess.

And to get an edge up on the competition, he admitted with his usual cutting honesty.

He'd intended to anonymously leave a pouch with the jewels inside in one of her stores, near closing time. Maybe he could just retain the rose diamonds, claim they were not there or something. He closed his eyes to the glorious refraction of the huge diamond, struggling with temptation.

Mordecai watched him shrewdly. His tone took on that sharp edge that he had not used with Devlin in years. "What have you done now?"

Devlin stuck the rose diamond back in its niche. "Nothing that cannot be rectified."

Scratching his balding head, as if he missed the cap he seldom wore in public, Mordecai moaned. "Tell me you have not been stealing again."

Devlin shrugged his expressive shrug, another remnant of his mother. "Not with ill intent." How could Mordecai read him so well? Of course, the little bachelor had long since become more a father to him than a mentor. Even before they became close, Mordecai had been able to look at him with that arrow-straight gray gaze and pierce to the heart of Devlin's vanities.

Mordecai rummaged frantically in his satchel. He pulled out his yarmulke and settled it on his head, as if he needed its comforting weight to think clearly. "No man ever broke one of the commandments with anything but ill intent, no matter the pretty face he puts upon it. I am disappointed in you, boy."

Devlin blushed with chagrin to hear himself addressed so for the first time in years. "I intend to give

33

them back. I only wanted to see what Cecil had sent her."

Mordecai plopped back in a chair, obviously too shocked to stand. "You actually breached Charlaine Kimball's estate? Every jeweler in the world knows she guards her possessions as does the queen herself."

The mix of chagrin and awe in Mordecai's voice tickled Devlin's wicked sense of humor. "I did more than that. I also breached her bed."

A rare sight treated Devlin: words actually failed Mordecai Levitz. His gaping mouth quivered, but nothing came out.

Devlin decided he'd best put his friend's misconception to rest before the little man had an apoplexy. "With no intent but to hide from the men she called to apprehend me." At least, not in the beginning. Memory of that soft, warm bed, and its softer, warmer occupant, caused an instinctive reaction that made him glad he was sitting down.

What a woman she would be when she learned to bend a little—if she did not break the man who tamed her.

Mordecai interrupted his fantasy by wiping his brow. "They obviously did not find you." A spate of Yiddish escaped him, another sign of his distress.

Devlin didn't understand the words, but the meaning was plain enough. Something along the lines of, *You idiot, we both have too much to lose. You will be the death of me if you—*

Devlin stopped the tongue-lashing with a succinct, "Don't you want to see my loot?"

Curiosity and morality warred in Mordecai's clear gray eyes. Before the winner could surface, Devlin fetched his pack and dumped its contents on the table. He could no longer wait to see his haul himself.

Mordecai gasped as rainbows danced on every wall.

Devlin ripped back the curtains to the living room windows that faced only an empty back alley. The rainbows deepened in color, gyrating like gaudy dancers as Mordecai couldn't resist running the king's ransom of jewels through his fingers.

A sapphire-and-diamond necklace with matching bracelet and ring flowed from one of his palms to the other, flashing like sacred fire.

Precious, warm and heady. So heady, men would kill for what Mordecai held in his hands.

Devlin pushed aside a heavy diamond choker that must have held at least a hundred carats of stones, and found the velvet roll in the bottom. He pulled it out and opened it. Every stone was of the best quality, but he found nothing unusual until he rolled a loose yellow diamond into his palm. The size of a bird's egg, it was of the old-style rose cut. It nestled there like a flower forever captured in its unfurling glory.

Devlin held the loupe to his eye. One tiny inclusion on the side, and nothing else. He'd never seen a canary diamond this large that was so perfect. Strange that it was unset. It was obviously very old.

Feeling an odd tingling, as if the stone had a story it longed to tell, Devlin put it back. Finally, in the last pouch, he found what he was looking for.

Mordecai pushed the pile of jewels out of his reach, shoved his glasses up and said firmly, "You will take them to her store early in the morning."

Devlin was too busy to answer. He set the four smaller pink diamonds, all of which were cut in the round shape, out in a half circle on the table, with the large pink diamond in the middle. He cocked his head at the mock-up of a necklace. No, that wasn't right. He moved to rearrange them, but Mordecai caught his wrist.

"No! They do not belong to you. Devlin, listen to me."

Reluctantly Devlin tore his gaze away from his creation. Somehow, in their icy purity with a secret heart of fire, the stones reminded him of Charlaine. The necklace taking shape in his mind, all pink and perfect, could only look right on someone with her red hair and long neck.

Mordecai insisted, "These stones are too distinctive for you to claim you bought them somewhere else. Do you want to end up in jail and ruin all we've sacrificed for?"

The accent stones would have to be teardrop and round dia— His head popped up. "What did you say?"

Mordecai stuck his sharp nose into Devlin's face. "Charlaine Kimball is, by all accounts, both shrewd and unforgiving. If she can prove you took these stones, she will not rest until she sees you jailed."

And I will not rest until she sees me as I really am. The thought popped into Devlin's head. He bent his head to hide his flush. Angrily he shoved her possessions back into the pouch and wrapped the pouch tight. "You are right, of course. Unless . . ." His gaze lit on the last object on the table. It was too bulky to be jewelry. Ah, yes, it was some type of book.

He unwrapped it curiously. Mordecai's dressing-down stopped midspate as they both got their first good look at the beautiful object lying on the table. Mordecai ran a fingertip gingerly over the ornate embossing on the front of the book. The entire soft leather surface was gold-leaved except for the central painting. It depicted a beautiful woman with red hair reaching out for a yellow rose, watched by a man in a dragon mask.

The miniature had been painted with such skill that the dragon's intent desire and the woman's strength

36

and innocence leaped from the page. Each corner of the book was set with different stones: diamonds, rubies, pearls and sapphires.

Reverently, gently, Devlin opened the book. In a striking masculine hand, the words leaped off the page, "I will never forget the first time I saw you. . . ." Quickly, feeling like an intruder, he flipped the pages until the writing ended. There, in a bold hand, it was signed, *Durwood Alistair Kimball*. And underneath, *Your Drake*.

Obviously an ancestor of Charlaine's. Before he could object, Mordecai wrapped the book back up.

He scowled at Devlin, his thick spectacles magnifying his disapproval tenfold. "This is quite obviously a priceless heirloom. How would you feel if Charlaine invaded your chambers and took your mother's locket?"

Devlin frowned. He fetched an innocuous-looking brown sack and stuck everything inside, including the rose diamonds. "Point taken. I accede to your greater wisdom." He glanced sidelong at Mordecai. "Due, no doubt, to your mysterious advanced age."

Mordecai did not accept the bait. Size, in his case, did not equate with intellect. He was the smartest man Devlin knew—too smart to be goaded into admitting his age. In all the years they'd known one another, Devlin had never been able to weasel it out of him. It was the only concession to vanity Mordecai made.

Devlin went to his small kitchen and turned on the kettle. Since arriving in England, he'd taken up the ritual of tea. "I went to a kosher bakery and got you some bread and soup. Would you care for an early lunch? Then we'll tour our new stores. I believe you'll like the changes I've made. You can put your things in the second bedroom, the one on your left."

Mordecai stood. "Very well. But I will not leave your

side until you've done your penance." He carried his satchel into the bedroom Devlin indicated.

Quickly Devlin grabbed the book out of the sack and hid it inside a large pot in the kitchen. He had a suspicion that of all he'd taken, the book was the most valuable to Charlaine. It wouldn't hurt to keep it as a bargaining chip.

Just in case.

If his conscience tweaked him a bit, he assuaged it by telling himself that he did not intend to keep the book. Once she cared for him, he'd give it back.

He paused in stirring the soup. Why was he so determined to make her see him as more than the thieving frog she'd called him?

True, she was lovely.

True, he admired her strength and her head for business.

She was also willful, spoiled and snobbish.

He grinned. Nothing in life, even hearing Cecil Rhodes accept him as a relative, would give him more pleasure than making the spoiled girl into the passionate woman he'd glimpsed so briefly.

The next morning, Charlaine controlled her urge to toss her cup of tea at the detective's grizzled head. She'd hired an American Pinkerton detective because they were rumored to be modern in their methods, unlike England's aging Bow Street Runners. She certainly did not want to involve Scotland Yard and have the press catch wind of this. "What do you mean, you can find no trace of a thief of his description in the London underworld? A thief as efficient as he is has plied his trade long and well."

Lewis Temple, a man as burly and stalwart as the aged oak he resembled, twiddled with the bowler hat he'd respectfully removed when the butler had ushered him into Lady Kimball's immense salon. "We've only been at it a day, miss. Please be patient."

Charlaine stifled the urge to remind him that she was a lady. He was just a brash American, after all. She waved him off. "I will double your fee if you bring me word of him this week."

The steady brown eyes didn't flicker away from hers. In fact, his large mouth tightened, as if he were insulted at the bribe, but he only replied, "My methods have been successful in the past, but they will take some time in a city the size of London. If you want faster results, contact Scotland Yard. And good luck to you."

Charlaine squelched her impatience. The rose diamonds would be difficult to replace, but it was the illuminated book she was most concerned about. "Very well, go on. But please send me word daily. And I will have my own sources making inquiries of every fence in London."

He rose, settling his hat on his head. "Don't worry. We'll run him to ground." He strode off, stolid and insufferable.

She was beginning to doubt he knew what he was doing. She shoved her cup and saucer aside, nibbled at a scone, then surged to her feet. She could not, would not, sit still and wait for her nemesis to be brought, sobbing and remorseful, to kneel at her feet.

Her little smile faded. As much as the image pleased her, she knew it would never happen. That bold frog was more likely to flash his detestable smile and dare her to do her worst. If or when she found him.

She called for her carriage. She needed occupation or she would go mad. Perhaps she'd try some clerking at her newest store. It didn't hurt to keep her hand in every aspect of the business, despite her father's protests. Yet again, she blessed her great-great-grandmama Callista Raleigh Kimball, for leaving in trust such a large fortune to the females of the family.

No man would ever get his hands on it. Not while she drew breath.

Straightening his top hat, Devlin settled his gold-tipped cane over his arm and opened the door to the new Kimball's. The door was an impressive affair, made of the heaviest, costliest mahogany inset with one of Tiffany's famous grape arbor stained-glass designs. Mordecai's little hand trembled as he straightened his sober frock coat, and he glanced askance at Devlin's anticipatory smile.

"You should at least have the grace to be a bit nervous," he hissed, walking inside London's largest jewelry store.

Devlin held the door for a modishly dressed couple, tipping his hat, then let it swing shut on silent hinges behind him. "Why? I am quite looking forward to this. If I'm lucky, she'll be here."

Mordecai's agitated color drained from his face. He looked around like a hunted animal at the brightly lit cases and primly uniformed salesmen.

Devlin whispered in his ear, "You can wait outside, you know. If you see the bobbies arrive, run along home. But I'd bet my rose diamond that Lady Charlaine Kimball will keep this theft quiet. She's a snotty little thing. She'd never have it bandied about that her sacred tower had been invaded, or that a mere thief had gotten the best of her."

Devlin strode forward, jauntily swinging his small satchel. He had to admit that the new store, with its soaring dome inset with a stained glass window and priceless Venetian chandeliers, was a study in elegance that his own simpler stores could not hope to compete with. As for the merchandise, well, that varied from mundane jet necklaces to ostentatious diamond rings the size of shooter marbles. And just about as tasteful, he concluded with a disdainful sniff.

He stopped at a case that held fobs and watches, plopping the satchel at his feet. Mordecai stopped beside him, guarding the satchel like a small but ferocious guard dog.

Smiling at a dour young man in a conservative uniform, Devlin said, "I am looking for a pocket watch made by Fabergé. Do you have any?"

The man's expression thawed to an obsequious smile. Devlin found it more distasteful than the former hauteur as the man said, "We have none at present, but we can certainly commission one for you."

Of course they had none. Peter Carl Fabergé was already gaining renown as Europe's most talented goldsmith. Only the wealthiest aristocrats could afford the prices he charged to be torn away from his favorite clients, Czar Alexander III of Russia and the members of his royal court.

Having curried the man's interest, Devlin asked to see one of the watches in the bottom tray. He intended to whip the sack out and leave it on the counter as the man bent low, but a stir at the entrance distracted him.

The red-suited doorman had bowed so low his nose almost touched his knee as he held the door wide. Every clerk in the store stood straighter as an elegant figure in maroon velvet swept inside as if she owned the place.

Which she did.

"Lady Charlaine, it's an honor to see you this fine morning," said the conservatively suited manager, rushing forward.

She nodded regally, the swansdown on her maroon hat swaying. It was a small, side-perched affair of

Colleen Shannon

matching maroon velvet adorned only with gold braid and the feathers. Her dress was likewise tastefully plain, with the same gold braid at the high neck, the bosom and the tight waist. The velvet was pleated in a vee to her tiny waist. The pleats widened again to the skirt hem trimmed with the same gold braid. Unlike so many women of the time, she seemed to hate bustles, for her own was barely visible.

Not that her attributes needed the help, Devlin decided, his fingers itching inside his white gloves at the memory of those attributes. What to do?

The manager rushed forward. He kissed her maroon-gloved, dainty little hand when she extended it. "Lady Charlaine, we are honored at your visit. May I be allowed to show you our new merchandise?"

"Certainly. I wish to see the new pearl necklace we designed for the queen's Golden Jubilee."

"It's over here." He led her to a case near the door.

A queer choking sound came from Devlin's right, but he paid Mordecai little heed. He turned back to study the watches, wondering what to do. She hadn't noticed him yet, but if he tried to flee, he'd have to walk right by her.

He considered himself a good judge of character, the female temperament in particular, but she was a volatile, strong personality. Then, as he so often did, he staked his all on a bold gamble. She was too prideful to cause a scene in her own store, or to fetch the authorities and have to admit he'd bested her.

Firmly, Devlin handed back the watch the man had tendered. "Not quite what I'm looking for, my good man, but I thank you." And he sauntered off, carrying his satchel.

After one look at that anticipatory grin, Mordecai clenched his teeth over a moan. But he stayed rooted in place, only his darting eyes testifying to his panic.

Devlin stopped at Charlaine's shoulder, respectfully waiting for her to notice him. She ran the black and white pearl necklace between her fingers, watching the light play off the round diamonds interspersed with the pearls.

"I like it v—" She noticed the shadow over the case and turned toward him with the polite smile she doubtless showed to all her clients. It froze on her face. He savored the widening eyes, the white teeth that showed in her gasp. The pearls slipped from her fingers to the floor, but she stayed frozen, staring up at him as if she could not believe her eyes.

He made an elegant bow. "Lady Charlaine, my felicitations on your new store. It is most impressive."

"You, you . . ." she finally managed to gasp.

"I confess I am a competitor." He bent, swept up the pearls and offered them to her. "But I know beautiful things when I see them." His eyes never left hers. Limply, she accepted the pearls. But she was beginning to recover her composure. She looked frantically around for her guard.

Luckily, the manager distracted her by saying, "You're Devlin Rhodes, aren't you?"

No doubt the man had visited Devlin's own stores to study his competition. Devlin nodded. "The same."

Charlaine slowly turned to face him again. "*You* are Cecil's scoundrel of a cousin? The owner of the Rhodes jewelry stores?"

The manager reared back in astonishment at her rudeness.

Devlin hid his chagrin with a wide smile. At least he was riling her. She never would have been so rude otherwise. "I'm flattered you have heard of me, though it's obvious where you got such a description."

She waved a dismissing hand. Again she looked about, but he forestalled her by opening his satchel

43

and glancing inside. "I have a gift for you, my lady. May I give it to you in private?" He rattled the satchel until she could hear the clinking jewels.

Her breath caught. She nibbled at her lip, but when his gaze latched on her mouth, she stopped. Finally she spied her guard. She motioned him over. "Guard the door," she said grimly. Then, like a force of nature, she swept forward, her expression making all who stood in her way part like leaves before a gale.

She threw open the office door and snapped at a frightened secretary, "Out!" He all but ran out, leaving the door ajar. Devlin closed it gently, watching her with that bold smile that he could see infuriated her.

"How dare you come here, bold as brass—"

His smile widened. "Or bold as a man smitten by your charms?"

That gave her pause, but only for a second. "You did not even know I would be here. If you had, you would not have dared to show your face."

"Oh, yes? Then why didn't I scuttle out the back, or hide in a corner until you moved away from the door?"

Bewilderment chased away her black scowl. "But . . . why? Surely you know I will set the law on you the first chance I get?"

"For what?"

Her mouth dropped open.

While she fumbled for words, he pulled the sack from his satchel and dumped its contents on the desk.

She looked from him to the desk and back. When she just blinked at him, as if he had two heads, neither with a brain, he led her gently to a chair and seated her. "I have a feeling you are seldom at a loss for words. May I tell you why I did it?"

She nodded eagerly.

"Your estimation of my background was not far wrong. I am both half French and, shall we say, not exactly respectable. At least, not in the way I grew up, though my mother's family consisted of French aristocrats. It is rumored, actually, that Marie Antoinette is one of my direct ancestors." He smiled grimly. "Though, to be honest, I care not a fig. My only knowledge of my royal association is with the French aristocrats who refused to acknowledge my mother, or her by-blow."

He watched her as he said it, but she did not look disgusted. If anything, she seemed intrigued. He took a relieved breath, then finished, "She emigrated to America and worked at what she could until I was old enough to support us both. Her health was not good and she died when I was eighteen. I admit thieving was easier for me than the book-learning she tried to instill in me. I resisted it then, but in later years I've made up for my earlier laziness.

"As for the thefts, well, as I prospered after making my fortune in Africa, they grew less frequent. But I missed the excitement of them. And when I heard that you had vowed that your estate was impregnable . . ." He spread his hands expressively. "I only intended to see what my inestimable cousin had sent you. I always intended to give the jewels back."

"What an odd perception you have of excitement," she said, rising to check the top of the desk. He knew from her tone and expression that she was still not appeased.

"I suspect we both agree where the sweetest excitement lies." His voice softened seductively as he ran his fingertip up her back, following the line of one of the pleats.

She stiffened and turned back around, gripping the desk with both hands. "Where's the book?"

He clasped the desk next to her, trapping her in the

circle of his arms, but not quite touching. Yet. "In a safe place."

She gritted her teeth together. "It is mine. Give it me immediately."

"I've never seen anything like it. Would you care to tell me its history?"

Now her mouth clamped tight over her teeth.

He raised one hand to run a fingertip over her lips, lowering his head to whisper, "Such a luscious mouth was never meant to be prim and proper. Come now, show me again the woman who lurks beneath your high-necked dress and high-handed hauteur." He lowered his head until his lips hovered above hers, but he did not try to kiss her.

Heat flared within her at the taunt, but she told herself it was anger. She said fiercely, "No. Never again will I let you kiss me, you . . . you frog." She shoved him away.

He sighed. "Really, the insult gets tiresome. I am only half French, you know."

"Perhaps. But you are all scoundrel."

He bowed his head slightly, as if she had complimented him. "Indeed. But I can give you recommendations from several, uh, ladies of my acquaintance if you wish to see what kind of lover a scoundrel makes."

Her eyes widened, then darkened to the green of a dangerous sky before a hailstorm—or a tornado. "You will regret speaking to me like that!" She stalked toward the door.

He leaned back against the desk and appraised his well-manicured nails. "Pity. I guess you shall never see your book again."

She stopped. Slowly she turned. "I will not be blackmailed."

That was all the encouragement he needed. He pounced, shoving her back against the wall and pressing into her with his whole, long length. "Persuasion is so much more pleasant. For both of us." Again he lowered his tempting mouth. She stared at it.

Inwardly he groaned. Why had he made that stupid vow? He'd dreamed of her kisses day and night since that delightful interlude in her bed. Perhaps he should just give her a quick kiss. . . . He mastered his own yearning to know that forgetfulness again. He already knew her better than that. Her affections could be won, but never coerced. Dimly, he was aware that something momentous had happened to him, but for now he had to concentrate on the curvaceous virago writhing to escape.

He stepped back, saying simply, "One day, I promise, you will beg me to kiss you. But I will not until you admit that I am the only man for you."

She scrubbed her arms with her hands, as if to erase his touch. "I'd as soon kiss a frog! A real one, because you will be in prison."

"And you will never see your book again."

Impasse. They glared at each other. She looked as if she might explode with anger, but finally she blew a brittle laugh. "You win." She reached for the doorknob, but threw a darkling glance over her shoulder. "For the moment."

He was not intimidated. "I promise not to sell it, and to keep it safe. When the time is right, I will give your pretty little bauble back to you. You have my word."

She muttered something uncomplimentary he could not quite catch and again turned back around. The gist of her meaning was plain enough. He hid a smile and took the rose diamonds out of the pouch. "In the interest of friendly competition, may I propose that we jointly design a rose diamond necklace for Her Majesty's Golden Jubilee?"

A flicker of interest chased more of the green clouds

out of her eyes. "You have the large diamond, then?"

"Yes. And neither your stones, nor mine, will be complete unless they are joined into one beautiful entity, as they were meant to be." He held her gaze.

She blushed to a shade that complemented the stones. "We can never work together felicitously."

An arched eyebrow preceded a male snort. "Now you're talking like an angry female rather than a hard-headed business woman. We have a common goal: winning the jewelry competition. We have a common means: rose stones that were meant to be set together. And we have a common benefit: if we win, excellent promotion for our stores."

And working closely with you won't hurt my goal any, either. But he kept his manner brisk as he said, "Well? Shall we try it?"

"I shall think on it. But I have your word that you will give me my book back if I agree not to pursue charges against you?"

He bowed. "My word as a fellow lover of jewels." He dragged the sentence out to a luxurious finish, "and other beautiful things."

This time, when she went to the door, he swept it wide for her. She ignored the curious, scandalized looks she received from the patrons in the store as they exited. It simply was not done for two unmarried people to be in the same room for such a long time unchaperoned, business rivals or not.

Devlin had to admire the way she scorned the curious. When Mordecai looked at him, his eyes huge behind his thick spectacles, Devlin nodded, certifying that all was well. Mordecai took a deep breath, then watched Charlaine as she marched up to her guard at the entrance.

The burly fellow glanced between her and Devlin,

looking sorry when she said, "You may go about your business."

When the man was gone, and no one else was in earshot, she told him stonily, "Invade any of my properties again at your peril."

He swung the empty satchel idly. "Is that in the nature of a challenge?"

She blanched, but rallied with a firm, "No. A warning. I will not be merciful twice. And if I catch wind of a certain illuminated fairy tale on the black market . . ."

He gave her a mock salute. "I shall expect to hear from you soon regarding my proposition."

"Which one?" The words had obviously escaped her before she could think better of them. She looked as if she wanted to strangle herself.

He grinned. "Both." He beckoned to Mordecai. When the little man had joined them, he said, "My Lady Charlaine Kimball, meet Mordecai Levitz. The most talented goldsmith I have ever worked with, and my business partner."

Mordecai nodded. "Your ladyship."

She curtsied slightly. "Mr. Levitz, it is a pleasure."

Mordecai stepped on Devlin's toe, but his civil smile never slipped as he said, "A most impressive store you have here, my lady. We would be pleased to have you visit us as well."

"Indeed. So I have been made to understand." She glanced at Devlin, her eyes darkening with an emotion he couldn't read. "Now, if you will excuse me, I have business to attend to. Good day to you both."

"Good day, *chére*." Devlin waited to see how she would react. He knew her full name, but it wouldn't hurt to call her as he saw her.

She stopped and glared over her shoulder, then hurried on.

When they were safely outside, Mordecai muttered, "Someday your propensity for danger will land you in jail. I cannot believe she let you go."

"She not only let me go, but we may work together on a design for the rose diamonds."

Mordecai shook his head. "And you expect me to believe you persuaded her with the sheer force of your personality?"

Devlin strode faster. No need to tell Mordecai about the book. He would not approve. "Something like that. Now, about the new store . . ." He distracted Mordecai as he usually did, with business.

But late that night, long after Mordecai slept, Devlin wandered the flat. Finally, he turned up a gas lamp and pulled out the book. He did not mean to pry, but damn it, he wanted to know everything about Charlaine Kimball. Only then could he win her.

He began to read.

Chapter Three

After Devlin left, Charlaine did her best to concentrate on business, she truly did. It wasn't her manager's fault that the pearl necklace and its matching bracelet seemed insipid compared to the rose fire dancing on Devlin's rough palm. She could get neither his words, nor the image they conjured, out of her mind . . . *joined into one beautiful entity, as they were meant to be.*

And she saw him, leaning over her on her own bed, his wide, imposing chest bare, as he admired the rose diamond necklace he'd draped over her nakedness. The stones fit so well together. . . .

"My lady? My lady!"

Her manager's concerned voice made her blush and snap to attention. She was mad, to be tormented by that wastrel's empty taunting. "Excuse me, Mr. Foster. I did not sleep well the night prior. You were saying?"

That, at least, was true. She stifled a yawn as he

Colleen Shannon

continued explaining the difficulty they'd had finding enough black pearls of the same size to make up the necklace and the bracelet. She finally interrupted his tale with a mild, "It's a fine set, but do you believe it distinguished enough to win the jewelry exhibition?"

Foster looked crestfallen. "Her Majesty is reputed to be ever fond of pearls."

She set the pearls firmly back on their prominent pedestal in the main display case. "Nothing prevents us from entering more than one item, surely?"

"No, of course not, but we do not have a lot of time—"

"Leave it to me. Now, I am pleased with the look of the store, and our people seem polite and well trained, but . . ."

As if tensed for a blow, he stood rigid when she finished, ". . . we seem to have precious few clients."

"It is early days yet, my lady. And that Rhodes chap down the street is consistently pricing his stock beneath ours."

Her eyes kindled at the complaint. She suggested gently, "Then I suggest you adjust our own prices slightly below his."

A wide grin sweetened his sour expression. "I have been wanting to ask your leave to do that very thing, but I feared His Lordship might be unhappy if we cut our profit margin so low."

"Leave my father to me. Just do as I say." Charlaine drew on her gloves and tilted her hat at a more rakish angle. "Keep up the good work, Foster." She smiled and waved at the rest of her employees, calling loud enough for them to hear, "You can all consider the day of the queen's Golden Jubilee a holiday."

An excited burst of thank-yous followed her to the door, which Foster held for her. Charlaine opened her matching parasol and strolled down the street, grimacing as she pictured her father's reaction to her latest generosity. England was in the midst of a growing debate over working hours and just compensation, and given the increasing competition of her fellow jewelers, it behooved her to keep her employees happy.

Or so she would put it to her father.

Durwood Alistair Bryant Kimball scowled at his daughter when she entered his imposing study. Late as usual. The child positively enjoyed infuriating him. Like her mother, and her grandmother before her. And doubtless the matriarch of the entire Kimball clan, Callista Raleigh, had given his revered pirate ancestor, Drake Kimball, an equally merry chase.

He sighed wistfully, remembering his own stormy courtship and his all too brief happiness with Hanna before she died birthing Charlaine. He settled back in his plush leather chair to regard his only progeny. He'd done his best with the girl, but doubtless he'd been too indulgent. She was a termagant of the highest order despite his best efforts to teach her control and breeding.

The thought that they did not get on well because he was equally stubborn did not occur to him. He had inherited more than his dashing dark looks from Drake Kimball. "And where, pray, have you been?" His striking blue eyes looked even harder than usual.

Charlaine stiffened in the act of removing her hat. "Do I not warrant so much as a good day?" She tossed the hat neatly on the stack of papers before him.

He stifled the urge to toss it back, recognizing one of her petty acts of defiance. With measured control, he moved the hat aside, taking great care not to crush it as he longed to. "When we have a meeting scheduled, I would appreciate your timeliness. Now. What was in the new shipment from Rhodes?"

Colleen Shannon

Charlaine slumped in the chair before his desk, slouching down in the manner she knew he detested. "The agreed-upon number of high-quality diamonds."

"And did our agent get those rose diamonds we heard about?" He wondered why she suddenly looked away.

"Yes, most of them."

"How did the pearl set for the Golden Jubilee turn out?"

"Adequately."

One thing in her he trusted implicitly—taste. If she was not enthusiastic about the pearls, the judges would not be either. He tapped his fingers on the desk. "Do you have any ideas as to a new jewelry design?"

Again she acted strangely. Normally she was pleased when he asked her opinion, but now she seemed sullen. He turned up the gas lamp on the wall beside his desk. Indeed, she was slightly flushed. She did not answer.

He sighed. "Well, I shall speak to our best designers and see what they can contrive. I want to see the new rose diamonds immediately. Would you bring them to me, please?" He stood, signifying the interview was over.

She did not stir. "I took them to the new store. They're in the safe there."

Again, something odd in her tone alerted him. He'd just returned from a business trip to Amsterdam, but he had noticed that workmen were once more banging away upstairs in her suite. She only redecorated when she had to crush her natural nesting instinct. Some suitor must be getting too close.

His heart lurched in hope. She was five and twenty, well on the road to spinsterhood just to spite him. He'd presented her with countless suitable young men and she'd spurned every one of them. She had the queer notion that every man was secretly a despot at heart.

Where, he wondered, had she formed that idea?

Somehow, some way, he would find someone willing to wed his little shrew.

And, willingly or not, she would give him the heir they needed to carry on the Kimball dynasty.

Preferably a male heir.

He sat back down and pulled a bill up to study it. He was careful to keep his eyes lowered when he said casually, "And what did you do while I was away?"

"Nothing of interest." She stood, now that he was content to let her remain. "Father, I prefer to retain the rose diamonds. I am considering a new setting for them and entering them in the jubilee."

Interesting. She had not actually designed anything herself in some time. He shrugged. "As you wish."

She turned to leave. He shoved the bill aside. "Charlaine, will you not attend the grand ball with me?"

She halted. "You know I despise affairs like that."

No, what she despised was her natural reaction to dancing with all the handsome young men thronging to sign her card. He stood, rounded the desk and took her strong shoulders in his hands.

"My dear, do you not see that you are denying the natural order of things by refusing to consider marriage? Not to mention assuring the death of our dynasty." He rarely spoke of his disappointment in her, for she merely became more obdurate when he did. But he sensed a change in her that he had to investigate.

She pulled away and turned to face him. That sneering half smile he despised twisted her lovely face. "Natural selection has a way of equalizing everything, as you have often stated yourself. You are such a proponent of Darwin in all you say and do. Well, consider this—the male may be faster, stronger and at the top of the food chain. But he will not survive long as a species without the female to bear his young."

He reared back as if she'd slapped him, but he recovered quickly. "When you know the joy of a lover's touch, you will not speak of the act so analytically."

She ran to the door and swung it open violently, only to be blocked by their surprised butler. He stood there, his hand raised to knock. She slipped past him, but halted when she saw the man standing in the hall.

"Er, I was coming to fetch you, my lady, to tell you—" Jeffries, the butler, began in his dignified way. He was a small, wiry fellow with the remnants of a Scots accent and a balding pate. His prominent Adam's apple acted like a bouncing ball, bobbling furiously when he was nervous. Charlaine shook her head at him, anxiously glancing over her shoulder at her father. Durwood stared through the open door at the man in the bowler hat.

"In here, please," she said evenly, flinging open the parlor door. The tall gentleman, who had much the look of an American to Durwood, peered curiously between the study and the parlor, but complied without complaint.

Jeffries turned to continue his duties, but Durwood called, "Wait, Jeffries!" The master of the house rose and approached his servant. "Who is that fellow and why is he here to see Charlaine?"

The butler assumed a bland expression. "I believe he is an American with the Pinkerton Detective Agency, sir."

Durwood's deep blue eyes kindled to dancing flames. "Indeed? And who is she investigating?"

"She has not seen fit to tell me."

Durwood leaned his broad shoulders against the doorjamb. Charlaine had twisted the family retainer about her dainty little finger since she was in leading strings. Durwood knew exactly where Jeffries's true loyalty lay, but this time the head of the Kimball family would not be denied. "Come now, Jeffries, we both know a mouse doesn't scurry in this household that you don't ferret it out. Come clean, old chap. I shall find out anyway."

Jeffries pried at his tight shirt collar. "Well, Lady Charlaine's maid did tell me that her mistress is determined to find and punish the rascal who stole from her the other night while you were away."

Slowly Durwood pushed away from the door. "What?"

Jeffries swallowed, his Adam's apple fairly vibrating. "That is all I know, my lord. I swear."

Tight-lipped, Durwood waved him away. Then, partially closing the study door behind him, he peered through the crack and waited for the American to exit the parlor.

Inside the parlor, Charlaine crossed her arms and tapped her foot impatiently. "It is none of your concern why I am discharging you, my good fellow. Suffice it to say that I have recovered my property." Most of it, anyway, she added to herself. For some reason she could not—dared not—name, she trusted Devlin Rhodes to one day return her precious manuscript, as he had promised.

The Pinkerton man shrugged. "It's your blunt." He glanced at the check she handed him and stuck it inside his jacket pocket. "But I can't say I'm fond of leaving this rascal to terrorize someone else. I always get my man."

Charlaine wiped away her slight smile when he eyed it suspiciously. "Your conscience need not trouble you. He will not steal from anyone else, I assure you."

He made a scoffing sound. "I presume he told you this balderdash himself?"

She merely stared back, but he apparently found her silence damning.

"I warn you, ma'am, you know nothing of these sorts. He'll lead you a merry dance and steal you blind if you let yourself be bamboozled by him."

She marched to the door. "For the last time, your services, my good man, are not required. Good day to you." She swept the door wide, her back to it. She didn't see the widening crack of the door across the hall, but the Pinkerton man's mouth, obviously open to protest, shut abruptly as he glanced in that direction.

"And good day to you. Do not think to hire me again when you find out how wrong you are." He stomped out.

She slammed the door behind him. She thought she heard the murmur of her father's voice in the hall, but when she peeked outside, the hall was empty, the study door firmly closed.

For the rest of that day, she tried to ignore the brash fellow's comment. Still, that night, as she tossed and turned in the shambles of her room, his words haunted her. *He'll lead you a merry dance. . . . lead you a merry dance.* She crushed the pillow over her head to deny her own thought.

It had been an age since she had danced.

Devlin tossed aside the paper in disgust. "Damn him! Rhodes just bought the last claim, so he's almagamated all of De Beers under his control. The bastard will end with a monopoly on the entire diamond trade if he gets his way." Devlin shoved aside the papers on the desk in his office and propped his feet on the blotter.

Mordecai placidly continued his inventory. He paused in counting the tiny five-point diamonds to say, "Someone should have done it long ago. It's the only way to make the mines productive now that they're collapsing." And he continued counting without missing a stone.

Devlin gave him an irritated glance. Mordecai's unerring sense of practicality annoyed him at times, never more than when they discussed Rhodes.

"I never would have sold out my claim if I'd known it would end up in Rhodes's hands."

"And we would not be here now."

Devlin leaped to his feet. "You know how I feel about that man! I should think you would show a little sympathy."

"Why? You have enough for both of us." When Devlin glared at him, Mordecai glanced up, his gray eyes huge behind the magnifying glasses. "I should think Barney Barnato will put a check on Rhodes's ambitions. As he is so fond of saying, he's never engaged in a speculation that failed."

The Jewish owner of the diamond and mine brokers Barnato Brothers was the strongest claimant in the Kimberley mines, De Beers's chief competitor. In fact, it had been Devlin's experience that the quality of the Kimberley diamonds was actually sometimes better than those found at De Beers.

Devlin slumped back in his chair. Depressed, he briefly debated selling his half interest to Mordecai and returning to the diamond fields. Sometimes this stuffy English air that always carried the scent of soot, and the equally stuffy English society that barred his entrance, made him long for the uncomplicated filth of the African "blue ground," the bluish breccia composite that hid a fortune in diamonds.

His nostalgia was interrupted by a knock at his office door. "Yes?"

The door opened to a sharp-nosed young clerk who resembled a penguin in his black frock coat and bulging waistcoat. "Sir, there's a detective here who wishes to speak with you."

Near the end of his count, Mordecai started and dropped the last of the small diamonds on the wrong pile. He gripped the edge of the table, staring at the mess he'd made of his work of the past hour.

Devlin ignored him. He rose leisurely, his interest piqued. "I shall be right out."

Persistence was another quality he could add to Charlaine's growing list of damnable virtues. No wonder she got on so well with the queen.

His swagger was a bit more pronounced than usual when he exited to his small but tasteful shop. Austrian shades of the finest silk covered his windows; his expensive crystal lighting fixtures sparkled almost as brightly as the gems inside the glass cases.

The second he saw the man awaiting him, Devlin's Hell's Kitchen instincts shouted a warning. Detective this tall, burly fellow might be now, but he had *copper* written all over him.

Devlin held out his hand. "Welcome to my humble shop, sir. May I help you?"

The man eyed Devlin's hand and shook it as quickly as he decently could. "Lewis Temple here, sir. Pinkerton National Detective Agency. May I have a word with you privately?"

"This is regarding . . . ?"

"A recent jewel theft."

Devlin held the steady brown eyes with his own. "I shall be delighted to do what little I can to serve justice."

Temple covered what might have been a snort with

a cough. He followed politely enough, however, as Devlin led him to the office.

Mordecai was counting laboriously again, but when Devlin flung open the door, he looked up. His mouth, moving silently in the count, froze half open as he, too, recognized the danger this man posed to Devlin. Muttering to himself in Yiddish, he swept the diamonds back into their pouch, obviously opting to count them on another day. A calmer day.

Devlin waved Temple to a seat before the massive oak desk and sat behind the desk like the affluent proprietor he was. "Now, what do you wish to know?"

Temple took a small notepad from his pocket and flipped it open to peruse it. He let the silence drag, then said mildly, "Your whereabouts on the evening three nights ago."

The intimidation tactic was familiar to Devlin, so he answered steadily enough. "In my rooms. Reading. Am I to suppose that you suspect me of this crime?"

Temple flipped the notebook shut and pocketed it. "I know who you are, Mr. Rhodes. I know where you came from and why you moved to London. I know what you formerly did to survive."

"Ah, but do you know the price of tea in China?"

The flippant response made the stolid detective stiffen. "Your charm will not work with me, you scoundrel. I am not an impressionable young girl."

Perhaps I should have *scoundrel* tattooed into my forehead, Devlin reflected. He leaned back at his ease in his chair. "Thank you, kind sir. I could not believe that Charlaine set you upon me. Which leads to the even more interesting question—who hired you?"

The detective reddened. "Am I to understand that you admit your crime?"

"I admit nothing—save that I can find out the price of tea in China if you wish to know it."

Colleen Shannon

Temple surged to his feet. "You will regret mocking me."

Devlin rose to face him. "I am not a man who lives by regrets. And threats have the opposite effect on me to intimidation."

Temple searched for words, apparently couldn't find any crushing enough, and stalked out. The glass in the door rattled as he slammed it.

Mordecai moaned and cradled his head in his palms. "You will end up with a noose about your neck if you are not careful."

"To coin your earlier criticism of me, you are careful enough for both of us." Devlin sat back down, folding his hands placidly before him.

Apparently Mordecai recognized that contemplative expression, for his hands dropped. He sat straight in morbid expectation.

Devlin's striking blue eyes cleared. "I have it! Her father must have hired him."

Mordecai cradled his head again. "We are doomed."

"No, not at all. It is well known that Durwood Kimball encourages all suitors for his daughter's hand. I have made an impression upon Charlaine, I know it. He must see that also." Devlin rose. "Well, I may have to introduce myself."

The Kimball dinner table was a glum place that night. Charlaine pushed her spring asparagus in Hollandaise and leg of lamb with mint sauce about her plate. She truly wished her father would quit studying her as if she were a particularly vexing puzzle. How many times had she longed to tell him that the qualities he most disliked in her she'd learned at his knee? However, since that would only alienate him further, she held her tongue. If, just once, he would praise her, she could die happy.

He eyed her over his burgundy, then set the exquisite crystal glass down precisely by his plate. "Must you submit me to these sullens night after night? I declare, you quite put me off my food."

"Since you seem to believe everything I say is inane or argumentative, I find silence serves our relationship best." She speared a piece of asparagus stalk and forced herself to eat it.

He sighed and shoved back his full plate. "What has led us to such a pass? I was so close to my own parents."

Her throat tightened as she recalled the many times he'd read her the story of his parents' dangerous, tumultuous relationship. They had gone through hell for one another, endured a decade-long separation, and finally emerged on the other side into a happiness few married couples ever find. Their only sorrow was the loss of their first born son in a riding accident, but they'd achieved peace of another sort when their late baby, Durwood, was finally born to them. Lacking a female heir, the Raleigh estates had been held in trust until Charlaine achieved her majority.

She did not remember her grandparents well, as they had been quite old when she was born, but she vaguely recalled a small woman with silver and black hair, unusual grace of limb and movement, and the most distinctive lavender eyes she'd ever seen. Durwood's father had been a man of medium height with a soldierly bearing and kind blue eyes. Other than the story of their unusual courtship, that was all Charlaine knew of her grandparents. Durwood would never tell her much of her grandmother's ancestry, only that she had been a happy wife and mother.

It was certainly a happiness Charlaine would never know. Unbidden, a handsome face with a reckless grin and laughing eyes popped into her head. Firmly, she shoved back her own plate, as if putting temptation out of reach.

"If I had not seen at an early age how marriage should be, I probably never would have married your mother," Durwood said, still turning his wineglass about, as if the deep red drew out of him confidences he rarely allowed. "I, too, was determined not to wed. But my brief time with your mother was the happiest time of my life."

Her throat closed with emotion. One could not doubt his sincerity. Again, the longing for the mother she knew only in pictures almost overwhelmed her. His next words brought tears to her eyes.

His stern face had grown soft with a tenderness she rarely saw. "I only want the same happiness for you, my dear daughter. You are a passionate person, with much to give to a man and a family. Why deny yourself only to spite me?"

She looked down at her lap, twisting her fingers together. When she could speak steadily, she answered, "You, above all others, should understand how much the family business means to me. I can never wed and relinquish control of all I've worked for to a man who would doubtless marry me for wealth and position anyway."

Again, he showed uncommon interest in his wineglass. "And what if you should find a person with the same interests? A man experienced in the jewelry trade, perhaps. Someone you could trust."

She was too busy trying to deny that persistent face to notice his sly, sideways glance. "There is no such person." She rose, tossing her napkin beside her plate.

At that moment, a discreet knock sounded at the door. At Durwood's assent, their butler entered.

"Sir, a Mr. Devlin Rhodes requests an audience."

She covered a telltale gasp with the back of her

hand, but Durwood merely smiled, looking intrigued. "Tell him to come in."

Briefly she looked as if she might bolt, but under her father's steady appraisal, she forced an iron control. If he ever caught the slightest hint of her damnable attraction to this bold fellow, he would move heaven and earth to throw her at him, despite Devlin's questionable morality. He was experienced in the jewelry trade, successful in his own right, handsome and well off. And, most important, unquestionably virile. A perfect match, in her father's opinion. In fact, recalling his words of a few minutes ago, she had to wonder if somehow Durwood already knew of the younger Rhodes. Her eyes narrowed on her father's face. Had he somehow planned this?

As firm footsteps sounded outside, Durwood said softly, "There's my girl. Chin up."

When the door opened, she was still trying to decide if that was pride or prejudice in his voice.

Devlin's gaze swept the room, lit on her with a kindling that struck sparks deep inside her, then settled on her father. He strode up to Durwood, his hand extended. "Sir, I am honored to meet you at last. Devlin Rhodes at your service."

Durwood shook the hand firmly, appraising the younger man. In his cutaway coat, top hat and pinstriped breeches with a maroon velvet waistcoat, Devlin looked exactly like the gentleman he most assuredly was not. Charlaine sat down at the table again, telling herself no, she was not weak at the knees.

She was angry at this brash invader. That was it. How dare he march boldly through her front door? This thief had climbed her tower and invaded her haven, stealing her most cherished possession.

Not to mention her peace of mind.

After the one comprehensive glance, Devlin had not looked at her again. Somehow that only made her stew more.

"Sir, I appreciate the audience, and would beg your patience about an idea of mine. May I acquaint you with it?"

Durwood waved him into a chair. "Certainly."

"It has come to my attention that you recently bought several fine-quality rose diamonds."

When Charlaine made a strangled sound, both men turned to her politely. Come to his attention indeed! An image of his knapsack dangling from his capable hand almost made her pick up a water glass and toss it at him. *The bounder.* But she contained herself and pretended an interest in the elaborate floral centerpiece.

Devlin turned back to the older man, who watched him with keen attention now. "I hold the largest stone that was cut from the original rock. I believe it would match your diamonds exactly."

Believe, do you? Balderdash. She kept her mouth shut by biting her lip so hard that she tasted blood.

"Might I suggest that we combine our assets in one magnificent necklace? It would do both our shops a world of good to win the jewelry competition."

Now that bright blue gaze found her, pinning her to her chair with unerring accuracy. It was obvious which of her father's assets he really coveted.

Get up. Walk away. Tell him to go to hell.

She did none of these things. She sat there, remembering the touch of his lips on hers, her bones turning to a glue that kept her in place despite herself. She felt her father's fixation on their silent battle of eye and mind, but the warning bells ringing in her mind still couldn't stir her to action.

66

Her father said, silky smooth, "Do you have a design in mind?"

Why did every word these two deceitful men spoke have a double meaning? Charlaine dragged her gaze to her father, but he was turned away, facing Devlin.

"Indeed I do. I am not at liberty to divulge it yet, however. When the time is right."

Somehow Charlaine knew both men actually discussed her, despite the seemingly businesslike topic. She felt silken cords slipping about her waist, preparing to bind her to him. And her father, her blasted supposed protector, would do all he could to tie them tight.

Durwood pulled a card from his vest pocket and handed it to Devlin with a flourish. "Meet me at my club tomorrow for lunch. We shall discuss this further."

"I would like to be present, Father." She lifted her head proudly under Devlin's curious stare.

"You know that is impossible, my dear," her father said. "Women are not allowed at my club."

"Meet him elsewhere, then."

He patted her arm in that condescending way that made her teeth grind together. "Trust me to know what's best. Now, Mr. Rhodes, would you care for a cigar and a brandy?" Durwood stood.

Devlin also rose, rushing over to Charlaine to pull back her chair. "I should be honored, sir."

Another male ritual she would not be allowed in on. Charlaine's instincts were on full alert now. She had been wilting at the knees, thinking of this blasted frog and his blasted French charm. No more. If he allied with her father, he automatically became her deadly enemy.

Her spine was ramrod straight as she marched to the door. "Enjoy your strategy, gentlemen. But this citadel will not fall to blandishments, flattery or co-ercion."

"No, but one day it shall open its doors gladly."

Her firm steps faltered at that smooth promise. She waited for her father to make some comment at the brazen familiarity, but Durwood said nothing. Charlaine flung the door open so hard it banged against the wall, knocking a picture askew, and slammed it equally hard.

"Whew." Devlin whistled, long and low. "What a temper." He straightened the bucolic landscape.

Durwood appraised him. What manner of man was this? He was a bold one, all right, to march in here and make suggestive remarks to the virginal daughter of one of the richest men in the realm. Especially if the American detective was right and this man had truly climbed Charlaine's tower and stolen everything from her safe. If so, he had returned them quickly, for Durwood had found all the jewels at their new store, save for the family manuscript. Doubtless Charlaine had that squirreled away. It was the one possession she was fondest of, having heard the stories of their ancestors on his knee.

Durwood sniffed. He'd long ago stopped encouraging her in her foolish romanticism. He'd be happy to see her wed to virtually any healthy, successful man who could sire heirs. A great love, such as he and her mother had experienced, was rare in their social circles. Charlaine was too willful and independent ever to melt in a man's embrace, in his opinion. Fine. After the children were born, she and her husband could go their own ways. What use was a family dynasty if it died with its last female progenitor?

Would this be the man he'd been looking for? Devlin Rhodes glanced around the study with interest, but none of the avarice Durwood usually saw. He did not seem intimidated, frightened or even angry at Charlaine's spoiled behavior, a great plus in Durwood's eyes. Too many of Charlaine's erstwhile suitors had been put off by that snooty air of hers, which was exactly why she cultivated it. In fact, Durwood would have sworn from the gleam in the young rascal's eye that he was eager. Much as Durwood had been in courting his own sweet but hot-tempered bride.

Durwood opened the door. "We shall be more comfortable across the hall in my study."

Devlin followed politely, waiting for the older man to sit behind the desk before flipping his coattails aside and seating himself.

Durwood's striking blue eyes watched his pen doodle on his ink blotter. Charlaine would have stiffened at that studied casualness. "I never enter into a business relationship with anyone I know nothing of. Tell me about yourself, young man."

Devlin's mobile lips lifted. "I see where Charlaine gets her directness. I grew up in America, raised by my aristocratic French mother until her death when I was eighteen. All I have, I earned, first as a gold apprentice, then as a jewelry designer, and finally in the diamond fields of Africa."

"A self-made man. Admirable."

Devlin shrugged. "You should also know that I am a by-blow of the black-sheep brother of Cecil Rhodes's father." Devlin watched proudly, as if awaiting condemnation. "He is, in fact, my cousin, though he will not acknowledge me as such."

That didn't surprise Durwood. Despite his great business acumen and basic decency, Cecil Rhodes was something of a snob. Durwood's estimation of Devlin rose another notch. Most of the social-climbing young men of his acquaintance never would have been so frank. But despite his many failings, Durwood was not a prig. How could he be, when he numbered a pirate and a highwayman among his direct ancestors?

"I see. Since we are being frank, might I ask what your interest is in my daughter?"

Devlin cocked his head to the side, as if he had not expected such an odd question. "You mean aside from her beauty, her wit, her intelligence and her spirit?"

"Not to mention her money," Durwood said dryly.

A wooden expression descended like a panel over Devlin's expressive face. "She would interest me equally were she a pauper."

Durwood stared into those blue eyes that were several shades lighter than his own. When he realized Devlin was sincere, his last doubt dissipated. "You mean to wed her, then."

"Yes, sir. With or without your permission."

Durwood smiled wryly. "It is Charlaine's permission you will find difficult to get."

"I am counting on it. Nothing easily won is ever highly valued. If I have learned nothing else in life, that I know. And it is a lesson she, too, will learn."

"Did you truly steal from us?"

Devlin blinked, then responded without hesitation, "Borrowed, rather. She had issued a challenge, you see, and I love nothing more than a challenge. I have returned all the jewels to her."

He stopped rather abruptly, but Durwood didn't notice it since his own thoughts were careening along tortuous paths. "Very well, I give you leave to court my daughter. And I wish you the greatest luck. You shall need it."

"Thank you, sir. Might I ask a few questions now?"

Durwood nodded.

"Did you send that Pinkerton detective to me?"

"In a roundabout way. I told him to look among the

new jewelers in London because I figured that only someone in the trade could have disposed of such distinct stones."

"Do you intend to call him off?"

A satisfied gleam appeared in Durwood's eyes. "Alarmed you, did he? Well, you have had some small punishment, then."

"It will be rather hard to court Charlaine from jail."

"I shall dismiss him directly. It was my daughter who hired him initially, then dismissed him, apparently when you returned the jewels. I rehired him mainly to find the man who had so stirred her interest."

Devlin nodded his satisfaction. "I suspected as much, which is why I barged in here tonight."

"Hmmm, well, since you seem to enjoy, er, barging, would you care to barge in on a ball at Buckingham Palace?"

For the first time, the young man seemed taken aback. "Me, meeting the queen?" He started to shake his head, then paused. "Is Charlaine attending?"

"If I have to hog-tie her and take her there."

"Then I accept." Devlin rose. "And I promise not to blow my nose on my napkin."

"If I thought you a bumpkin, I would not have invited you. As for your jewelry design, I think it an excellent notion. I shall order Charlaine to work with you on it."

Devlin opened his mouth, shut it, then nodded. "Thank you, sir."

The unspoken criticism of Durwood's arrogance hovered in the air. Durwood's mouth tightened as he opened the study door, waving Devlin outside into the hall. "You shall find, young man, that the only way to deal with my daughter is with a firm hand."

"Or a loving one. My own mother . . ." Devlin trailed

71

away as light footsteps descended the stairs.

Charlaine's lovely green eyes were curious as she descended to the hall, her firmly upswept hair gleaming, a symbol of all the passion she tried to control. She had obviously caught the end of their exchange, but when both men stopped speaking, she wrinkled her pretty little nose. "Father, Cecil has arrived. I saw him from the upstairs window." She spoke to her father, but it was Devlin she watched.

Durwood, too, appraised the black sheep son of a black sheep. Aside from a tightening of his mouth, Devlin showed little reaction to the arrival of his apparent enemy.

"Do you wish me to leave by a back door, sir?" he asked.

"Nonsense. Not unless you are ashamed to meet him."

"Not at all. But we do not get on well. We once came to fisticuffs in Kimberley."

When the knock came, Durwood himself answered the door, waving the butler away. "Lay out our best crystal in the study, Jeffries, along with the brandy and sherry. Then you may retire." The butler disappeared to do his bidding.

Durwood opened the door. "Cecil, old chap, it is good to see you again."

As Rhodes entered, Charlaine stared at Devlin. He leaned casually against the wall near the study, crossing his gleaming half shoes at the ankle. She knew him well enough by now to realize that his nonchalant pose was a mask for stronger emotions. The brilliant azure eyes were the keys to his soul.

She turned firmly away, wondering why she should think such a thing, or even care if he had one. She stifled the urge to hold her hands out to Cecil just to prove to Devlin that she found other men attractive too. Cecil was not a demonstrative man, and none too fond of women, either.

Cecil Rhodes, now in his mid-thirties, was a big man, with a broad face and a cleft chin that, allied with his gray eyes, always reminded Charlaine of sunlight on granite. He could be worn down, raindrop by raindrop, but never moved. Yet, when he pleased, he could be charming, and his rare smile lit up a room. He was one of the most complex men she had ever known, and she did not understand him well. One thing she knew, however: he made a better ally than an enemy. The door closed behind him. And for the first time she noticed the handsome young fellow behind him. She groaned inwardly. Not him, again.

Cecil waved the man forward. "You both remember Henry Dupree, my secretary of business affairs in London."

Henry kissed the air above Charlaine's hand. "Enchanted, as always, my lady." His eyes were blue, his hair as black and vital as Devlin's. His features were, if anything, more handsome. Almost, she wished she could form an attachment to him, but there had always been a supercilious air to his manner, as if he felt the world owed him more than he'd hitherto received, that repelled her. She had to forcibly withdraw her hand, for he would not release it.

Cecil scowled at him. "Get your notebook out, Henry. We've a deal of business to cov . . ." Cecil's firm tone faltered as, for the first time, he looked around the foyer and noticed Devlin. For once Charlaine had no trouble reading him.

Recognition flared in his eyes, followed by intense dislike. Then he stared at a spot over Devlin's head. As if Devlin were part of the wall, not only insignificant but invisible. "Shall we proceed to the study, Durwood?"

Durwood started, as if he had just remembered his other guest. Charlaine knew better. He loved to stir up trouble, stand back and watch. She wanted to slap that charming smile off her father's face as he put a hand on Devlin's back and urged him forward. "Cecil, this is Devlin Rhodes, a new business associate of mine. I understand you know each other slightly."

"Very slightly." Cecil nodded once, brusquely, then shoved past Devlin into the study.

Henry stared curiously at Devlin, then followed.

When the door had closed behind them, Devlin said, "He doesn't change much."

"Why does he dislike you?" asked Durwood. "It seems to be more than your, ah, family connection."

"That is a very long story, one I do not have time to tell."

"Or inclination," inserted Charlaine.

Devlin gave her a sardonic salute with one finger to his forehead. "Astute of you, *cherie*." He strode up to her, so close she could feel the heat of his body. "But it will be so much more interesting for you to wonder."

She backed against the doorway to evade the hand that tenderly tucked a loose tendril of hair behind her ear. She almost fell backward when the study door opened inward.

Cecil stood there, taking in the scene in one comprehensive glance. He scowled at Devlin, his bold chin uncannily like his cousin's. "Be off, my good fellow. We've a deal to cover and precious little time to do it in."

"Ah, yes, everything is on a schedule with you. Bechuanaland today, Matabeleland tomorrow?"

Charlaine didn't understand the reference, though she recalled accounts of Cecil's decisive actions in the past year or so that had helped gain Bechuanaland as a protectorate of the Crown. She assumed the other territory must be farther north.

Cecil's dislike glistened in his gray eyes like a newly honed knife blade. "How can you have lived in South Africa and not realize that Bechuanaland is the gateway to the north? And if we do not take Matabeleland, the Boers will. Besides, would you have the interior remain under the control of those savages?"

Devlin opened his mouth, but Durwood said firmly, "Gentlemen, we cannot carry on such a lively discussion of politics in the hall." He shoved the study door wide and waved both men in. He tried to close the door in Charlaine's face, but she shoved it wide and gave him a challenging look, marching past him. She did not see his slight smile of satisfaction, for when he sat behind his desk, his expression was neutral.

Henry snapped open his notebook when they entered, but his sideways look at Charlaine's low bodice was anything but businesslike.

Cecil didn't bother shoving aside the tail of his wrinkled frock coat as he sat down across from Devlin. His ascot was askew, and his starched cuffs had wilted. He was well known for the carelessness of his dress. Devlin, however, looked as if he had just stepped out of a shopping spree on Bond Street.

The two men had other differences as well.

Cecil continued angrily as if they had not been interrupted. "The chief of the Matabele is a tyrant, and there are rumors that he is about to sign a treaty with the Transvaal. Every man in his tribe is fed entirely on beef, which kills the weaklings of dysentery and leaves the rest strong and hostile."

"Yes, yes, I know. And the young men are not allowed to wed until their thirties, only after they have bled and been bled in war. You forget, I lived with them for a year. Does their savagery give us the right to be ruthless in an altogether different, but equally reprehensible way?"

Cecil made a scoffing sound. "No wonder you left. You don't have the stomach for what it takes to succeed there."

For the first time Devlin looked angry. "For every one of your successes, another man loses. Yes, I sold my claim for a considerable sum so I could follow my true love of jewelry designing. But quite frankly, had I known my rich little patch of earth would end in your grasping hands, I would have kept it."

Cecil leaped to his feet so quickly that his chair overturned. "You ruddy blighter! No one speaks to me like that."

Devlin rose too. "Then they should. Your dreams of empire have already ruined the South Africa I knew, for me at least. You can become rich as Croesus, but you will still die a lonely man."

Cecil stabbed a finger into Devlin's modish waistcoat. "How dare you sit in judgment upon me? Why, the queen herself has thanked me for my efforts on behalf of the empire."

"When your ambitions are shielded in philanthropy. What was that little homily you coined? Ah yes, 'Pure philanthropy is very well, but philanthropy plus five percent is even better! There, in that one comment, we sum up the life and times of the great Cecil Rhodes. God preserve me from your generosity."

While Cecil went red, obviously searching for a response cutting enough, Devlin turned to Charlaine and made a neat bow. "My lady, it has been a pleasure, as always. I shall be delighted to escort you to Her Majesty's spring ball this Saturday hence."

Charlaine collected her scattered wits. "I do not attend."

"We shall see. Sir, good evening. I shall see you

shortly at your club." To Rhodes he said not a word.

Finally, as Devlin opened the door, Cecil said through his teeth, "You have not heard the last of this, you, you . . ."

In the doorway, Devlin turned. "It's Mr. Rhodes to you." And then he was gone, the door closing quietly behind him with a sound more definite than a slam.

Cecil sprawled back in his chair, fury hanging over him like a thundercloud. He ran his big hand through his graying hair, leaving the already tousled mass even rougher.

Durwood poured a glass of brandy into an exquisite snifter. "Calm yourself, Cecil. The rogue would be delighted to see you so put out." Cecil accepted the glass and took a tiny sip. His puritanical bent was well known.

Henry sipped his with more appreciation. Charlaine took her sherry with good grace. Brandy was yet another abomination those heathen Frenchmen had forced upon the civilized English, in her opinion. And yet, as she recalled Devlin's cutting remarks on this very subject, her conscience asked a simple question: Who was more civilized, the man who forced his will upon an inferior people, or the man who tried to live with them side by side?

The conclusion made her uncomfortable, so she changed the subject. "Have you brought us anything new, Cecil?"

Broodingly, he set his glass down and reached into his jacket pocket. He pulled out a black pouch and dumped its contents on the blotter. Diamonds of every hue rolled like light incarnate across the dark leather. Pink, blue, yellow and brown sparkled among the clear ones like exclamation points, accentuating the beauty of all.

Durwood fixed a loupe to his eye and turned up the

gas lamp. He picked up the largest pink one. "Good quality, but not as good as the ones we bid on from Barney Barnato." His eye, magnified by the loupe, fixed on Cecil's reddening face.

Charlaine peered into her sherry, wondering if the ruse would work.

Apparently not. Cecil scooped the diamonds back in the pouch and held out his hand for the rose one Durwood still held. "Go to him as your main supplier, then."

Durwood clutched the diamond in his fist. "I did not say I didn't want to bid on it."

Charlaine stood. "If you will excuse me, gentlemen, I believe I shall retire." They scarcely looked up, these two warriors of commerce, so intent were they on their eye duel.

Henry leaped up to open the door for Charlaine. His perfect white teeth sparkled even in the dim light. "Might I be so bold as to ask you to reserve a waltz for me at the ball?"

"Why not? You might as well be like every other male who sets foot in this household."

The smile slipped.

She sighed. "Forgive me. Certainly, if I attend, I shall be happy to dance with you."

The smile brightened again. "Jolly good."

A surly voice called out, "Henry, come here and record the bids." Henry's handsome nose wrinkled as he closed the door.

Thoughtfully, Charlaine climbed the stairs. She would not like being at Cecil's beck and call, either, but he doubtless paid young Henry very well.

But, as she reclined upon her deep feather mattress and looked about her newly designed room, it was not of Cecil that she thought.

* * *

The next morning, the Pinkerton man folded his check and slipped it into his pocket, but his expression was glum for a man who had been paid his usual fee plus a bonus. "Might I ask, sir, why are you relieving me?"

"You might." Durwood did not look up from recording the check in his account book. He said nothing else.

The Pinkerton man squashed his bowler hat upon his head. "If you let that rascal in your good graces, you will regret it."

Durwood gently set his pen down. "You are dismissed."

The detective strode out, slamming the door behind him.

Durwood tapped his pen thoughtfully upon the blotter, pulled up an expensive piece of vellum paper and began to write.

A couple of hours later, Devlin read in Durwood's extravagant, flowing hand:

> *You have a positive facility for making dangerous enemies. Beware of Lewis Temple. He is determined to see you jailed. Under the circumstances, it's best that we not meet today at lunch. I give you carte blanche on your designs. Both of them. Yours, etc.*
> *Durwood Kimball.*

Devlin folded the paper thoughtfully and stuck it in his drawer.

Mordecai's eyes narrowed on his face. "What's amiss?"

Devlin smiled slightly. "Do I seem nervous? I'm losing my touch."

Mordecai snorted. "That legendary light touch of

79

yours has landed us in the soup more than once. This time, my hotheaded young friend, I suggest you concentrate on what's yours, not what you want to be yours, for a change."

Devlin propped a lithe thigh on the desk. "Why? It's in my blood. Like my esteemed cousin, I follow Napoleon and Alexander. *Veni, vidi, vici.*"

"Indeed. You came, you saw, you conquered—and I'd advise you to remember how Napoleon and Alexander ended."

Devlin wrinkled his nose at his mentor. "You take all the fun away. Now, what do you think of this? The proportions are not quite right."

While Mordecai pored over the latest drawing of the rose diamond necklace, Devlin looked out the window, feeling a sudden longing for the blue dirt of his old claim. Despite the faulty pumps, the crumbling reef, the unreliable workmen, that time of his new beginning had been one of the happiest of his life. Devlin Rhodes, pickpocket, pauper son of an aristocrat, had become Devlin Rhodes, miner, jeweler, businessman. Above all, simply man.

The nostalgia was a strong pull, but not strong enough. A winsome face, green eyes vibrant with life and wistful with a longing she didn't understand, drew him even more strongly to stay.

He would woo her, win her and wed her. When she saw him not as a French frog, but as the prince she'd dreamed of in her lofty, lonely tower, he would be at peace.

He looked over Mordecai's shoulder, listening as his friend suggested changes in the design.

Buckingham Palace resembled a gigantic illuminated triptych, with its three pedimented false fronts and numerous windows, each ablaze with light. This icon was not a monument to the holy Trinity, however. It celebrated one thing, and one thing only.

The power of Britain's monarchs.

As his carriage rumbled to a stop before the huge rectangle, Devlin swallowed his unease. He hated these hoity-toity affairs, where decorum ruled. Not that he'd ever attended a social function so grand.

As his carriage pulled away, leaving him flotsam in the tide of humanity flowing up the steps, Devlin checked the ornate pocket watch in his gold-embroidered white silk vest. Durwood had asked him to meet them out front promptly at eight, rather than call to collect them. They were late.

A lovely young brunette gave him a sly peep as she flounced up the steps on her father's arm. Devlin smiled at her. She blushed, looked away and joined the long receiving line into the palace.

"You never change, do you?" asked an all-too-familiar caustic voice.

Devlin stiffened and turned to meet his cousin. For once, Cecil was immaculate, wearing the same black cutaway coat, shiny dancing slippers and formfitting gray silk trousers as his enemy. Devlin tipped his silk top hat to the party of four: Durwood, Charlaine, Cecil and Henry.

"Good evening, all. A sense of purpose runs in the family, cousin, wouldn't you agree?"

He turned to Charlaine, who was staring after the winsome young brunette with a tightness to her mouth that gave Devlin hope. He offered his arm. "May I escort you inside, my lady?" She wore a pink silk cloak trimmed in chinchilla that covered her dress. Her upswept hair was dressed simply with only a diamond diadem as accent. She looked regal, gorgeous and aloof, the Ice Princess come to life.

She glanced from his proffered arm to Cecil's. A

blank expression descended over her lovely face. Taking Henry's arm, ignoring his surprised look, she said, "Well, gentlemen? Do we dawdle on the steps or join the procession?"

At her slight tugging, Henry strutted up the steps at her side. Devlin smiled wryly at her masterful put-down and followed. At the entrance to the vast foyer, with its magnificent chandelier twinkling high overhead, they handed their wraps and hats to the cloakroom attendant.

Devlin turned from offering his hat to freeze at the sight of Charlaine. He'd seen her barely dressed in her nightgown, he'd seen her dressed for a formal dinner at home, and he'd seen her dressed as the businesswoman she was.

But she had never been more desirable than at this moment. The pink silk dress was scattered with brilliants from the heart-shaped décolletage to the skirt swept up at the sides and tied with small bow pins. White lace peeped at the bottom of the hem and at the vee of the low bodice, where another, larger bow pin was attached. Unlike the other women at the ball, she wore no profusion of fake roses, bows, braids or puffs and flounces. Save for the brilliants and the pleasing form of the wearer, her dress was almost plain.

He took a closer look at the bows and smiled. No wonder they sparkled so—they were diamond brooches. Tiny bow ear bobs bounced with every movement of her head, those, too, no doubt real. He wondered if she'd designed the set. Her graceful arms in the white gloves were unadorned.

She carelessly brushed back a loose strand of hair inside her diadem, but other than that, she obviously gave little thought to her appearance. That, too, he had to admire in her. Most beautiful women of his acquaintance were vain, staring at themselves every time they passed a mirror. The receiving hall was lined with mirrors, yet she merely smiled courteously, sweeping a graceful curtsy to the heads of state lined up to greet the guests.

When they were through the line, he elbowed Henry aside and caught up to her to offer his arm. She hesitated, but he was blocking the exit line, so she wrapped her fingers about his arm and swept inside the ballroom beside him.

In the center of the main wall, a tiny but commanding figure held court from an ornate chair on a pedestal. Devlin resisted when Charlaine headed in that direction. She stopped to look at him.

"Have you never met the queen?"

Devlin swallowed. "No."

"She's a very kind woman, once you get to know her. Come along. I shall introduce you." Her beautiful mouth stretched into a delighted smile as they joined the line awaiting the queen's pleasure.

"What's so amusing?"

She looked around to be sure no one could hear. "I am thrilled to see that some things, at least, make you nervous."

If she only knew. He was glad she couldn't feel how sweaty his palms were. He glanced behind them and met Cecil's unsmiling eyes. He looked quickly back around. He would have wished for a more understanding audience to this milestone in his life, but he'd be damned if Cecil would see him sweat.

When the tall man in front of him bowed deeply, he got his first close look at Regina Victoria. She was a tiny, plump woman, garbed in the finest black silk. He had heard it said that she still mourned her beloved Prince Albert, even though her consort had died over twenty-five years ago. He had doubted the truth of

Colleen Shannon

that, but her choice of color at so festive an occasion offered its own proof.

Her simply upswept gray hair was accented by a diamond tiara. Her plump, wrinkled neck was circled by a diamond-and-pearl necklace that matched the two bracelets on her wrists. Her dress was too fussy for his taste, but one could hardly deny that she looked, sounded and acted like the queen of the world's greatest empire.

At her turn, Charlaine swept to the floor in a curtsy and bowed her shining head. The queen drew her up and pinched her subject's cheek. "Enough, child. You must not dirty that lovely dress. Why have you not joined us at Osborn for my last house party, as we requested?"

"Forgive me, Your Majesty. The press of business—"

"Business, pah! When will you leave off this business nonsense and join our court as a maid of honor?"

"Ah, well, that is . . ."

The queen sighed. "Very well, child. I will pester you no more." Her eyes sparkled in the lights. "For the moment. Now who is this young man?"

"Your Majesty, may I present Devlin Rhodes? He is the owner of the Rhodes chain of jewelry stores."

Devlin swept so low in a bow that his nose almost brushed the floor. "I am deeply honored, Your Majesty," he said, aware that his voice trembled slightly, despite his best efforts.

The queen glanced from him to Cecil, who stood in line behind them. "Rhodes, eh? Any relation, Cecil?"

Was it Devlin's imagination, or was there a lull in the orchestra music? Those close enough in line to hear watched avidly as Cecil opened his mouth, then shut it.

Devlin straightened, like a man waiting for a blow, knowing that his scant social aspirations would stand or fall with his cousin's response.

84

Chapter Four

Cecil Rhodes, for once in his self-contained, confident life, looked nonplussed. He glanced from Victoria's curious expression, to the people in line behind listening, all agog. He even looked at Charlaine. However, he avoided eye contact with Devlin. He cleared his throat and drew himself up to his full, formidable height.

Devlin braced himself, for he knew what was coming. He was a by-blow, a bounder, no relative—acknowledged anyway—of the great Cecil Rhodes.

A soft voice said, with a charming laugh, "And so I have wondered, Your Majesty, on more than one occasion. They delight in keeping me in the dark. These men and their secrets!" Charlaine caught Devlin's arm. "Whatever his ancestry, Devlin designs absolutely exquisite jewelry. I would recommend him highly, competitor or not. Our two houses have allied in designing a parure for the exhibition celebrating

Your Majesty's Golden Jubilee. If we win, we shall be delighted to offer the set to the Crown."

Successfully distracted, Victoria said, "And where is your establishment, young man? We shall definitely visit it sometime."

Devlin gave her the address of his shop. Victoria glanced at one of her hovering ladies in waiting, who pulled a small book from an exquisite beaded bag and wrote down the address. Then, nodding regally, Victoria waved them on, saying only to Cecil, "Make an appointment, Cecil. I wish to speak with you in private."

Cecil nodded gravely. The minute they were through the line, he hurried in the direction of the Oxford crowd. Devlin watched as he was enthusiastically welcomed by members of his old alma mater. It was rumored that Cecil had made considerable remuneration to Oxford in his will.

Devlin said under his breath, "I am most grateful, my lady. I would not wish to look the fool on my first meeting with the queen. And I am delighted that you have agreed to work with me on the jewelry design."

Charlaine pulled her arm away. "I don't know what possessed me." And she flounced off, ignoring his call to remain.

I know who will, he vowed to himself as he watched her enticing hips sway in an agitated stride. Unable to hide his grin, Devlin took himself to the buffet table, suddenly ravenous. He was filling his plate with the feast of partridge, stuffed goose, peas in cream sauce, Duchesse potatoes and flaky rolls when sniggering caught his attention.

Cecil and his cronies looked his way, openly laughing. Devlin glanced down to see if his fly was open, but no, dignity was intact. He stared at his plate, pretending he neither saw, nor heard, their snobbery.

One young man who looked vaguely familiar said loudly to Cecil, "Damn, even in court dress, he looks like what he is: a poor boy working his own claim. Do you suppose he still has dirt under his fingernails?"

That was why the bastard had seemed familiar. Stewart Snipes had purchased several of the claims neighboring Devlin's, but he'd hired workers. He was too high-and-mighty to dirty his own hands.

Cecil seemed a bit uncomfortable as Devlin passed by carrying his loaded plate. Devlin paused as he drew even with the clique. "Evening, Snipes. I say, do you always dribble your pabulum?" Devlin stared pointedly at the greasy spot on Snipes's shirtfront.

Snipes looked down at himself and went red.

Devlin balanced his heavy plate on his fingertips and squeezed between an overweight dowager and her equally heavy young daughter. He didn't spill a drop as he tossed over his shoulder, "You should try a little manual labor. It makes one extremely nimble. Ask your friend Cecil."

For a moment, blue eyes met gray over a sea of faces. Cecil had dug for diamonds himself before he made his vast fortune, when he was just a poor clergyman's son with great ambition and grander dreams. Devlin would have sworn there was reluctant admiration in Cecil's eyes, but the roiling humanity bore Devlin away on the tide. Devlin found a seat against the wall and sat down to eat. Pity Cecil had such a dislike for him. They were similar in many ways.

Durwood plopped down next to him, wiping his brow. "Whew! Decidedly hot in this crowd, despite the cool air outside. But Her Majesty has recently had a cold, so they will not open the windows. We shall just have to suffer."

When Devlin didn't answer, Durwood eyed his future son-in-law severely. "Why are you stuffing your

Colleen Shannon

gullet instead of circulating? Why, half the wealthiest people in England are in this room. Go make yourself known. Offer your card."

Devlin finished his last bite of goose. He wiped his mouth with the heavy cloth napkin, folded it intricately over his empty plate, and offered both to a laboring waiter. Then, leaning back, he said, "The only person present I wish to impress has retired to the ladies' lounge. To escape my filling up her dance card, I expect."

Durwood cocked his head curiously. "You would really rather dance with Charlaine than win new, wealthy clientele?"

Devlin shrugged. "I have all the money I shall ever need. I have no lack of customers, even if they are from the working class. Besides, growing up poor makes one learn to enjoy the best things in life. They cost nothing."

Rolling his eyes, Durwood scoffed, "Now you're going to extol the sunset, and the moon, and—"

"Not at all. I speak of even nobler things." Devlin rose. "If you'll excuse me, I believe I see Charlaine peeking around the corner. Time to pounce." Devlin strode unhurriedly through the crowd.

Durwood stared after his ally with a confused expression.

As she tried to melt into the crowd, Charlaine's heart tapped nervously at her ribs. She knew Devlin watched for her. She knew he'd filled his plate, stopped to banter with Cecil and his cronies, then sat down against the wall. She knew because her eyes, curse them, seemed to be drawn to his movements by some mysterious magnetism she couldn't name, much less explain. She'd finally disappeared to the ladies' retiring room to get herself together after that narrowly averted scene before the queen.

Why had she come to his defense? She owed him nothing, much less loyalty. Rather the reverse, in fact, given the way they met. It still stung that he withheld her most cherished possession. Yet every instinct she possessed told her he could be trusted, that he would keep her treasure safe, and never willingly hurt her.

She'd never felt this deep confidence in a man before, not even her father.

Especially not her father.

What was different about Devlin Rhodes? He was a frog, his own mother hailing from that nation that she, along with most good Englishmen and -women, despised.

She was still remonstrating with herself when a male voice said intimately into her ear, "My lady, you are in stunning looks this evening. May I beg the favor of a dance?"

Charlaine looked into Henry Dupree's pale blue eyes. They regarded her steadily, but there was a calculation in them that not even his handsomeness could disguise. The same instincts that told her to trust Devlin bade her beware of Henry.

When he reached for the dancing card dangling from her wrist, she pretended to step abruptly aside from a laughing couple on their way to the ballroom. The orchestra could be heard tuning up. When they had passed, she smiled sweetly. "I do not intend to remain long. I have promised the first dance to Cecil. Perhaps later, if I do not become fatigued."

Charlaine turned away from his chagrin to come face-to-face with the man she'd been avoiding. Devlin looked so quintessentially male in his severe attire, the tight pants clinging to him in just the right places, that she almost went weak at the knees.

Charlaine gave him a polite smile and tried to sidestep. He moved obligingly—in the same direction. Charlaine tried the other foot. Again, he blocked her. She froze, glaring up at him.

The rogue had the gall to bow deeply and offer his arm. "I humbly request your favor in the opening dance."

Charlaine flaunted her dance card, where Cecil's bold hand had signed the top line.

Devlin lifted an eyebrow. "Oh, yes? We shall see about that. Come along." He caught her arm and urged her near the wall, where Cecil still stood with his cronies.

Charlaine considered literally digging in her heels, but curiosity overcame her. Cecil seldom allowed anyone to get the better of him, much less a man he apparently disliked.

Her first partner broke off midsentence when he saw them approach. He checked his solid gold pocket watch studded with diamonds, snapped it closed and said, obviously embarrassed, "Forgive me, Lady Charlaine. I did not realize the dancing was about to start. Excuse me, gentlemen." And he walked forward.

Not once did he look at Devlin or acknowledge his cousin's presence in any way.

When he drew even with them, he offered his arm to Charlaine.

Politeness dictated that she honor her promise. Especially here, where decorum was not only expected, but demanded by the woman who lived an example for each of her subjects. Charlaine looked from Cecil to Devlin and back. Why was the choice so difficult?

Slowly, reluctantly, her fingers relaxed on Devlin's arm, but before she released him, he spoke.

"I challenge you for the right to claim the first dance with this lady."

That caught Cecil's attention. His gray eyes narrowed. "Do I apprehend that you are actually challenging me to a duel?"

"If you wish to name it such. Though the weapons I had in mind require something more deadly than brute force." He emphasized the words *in mind*.

"And what are those?"

They were beginning to claim attention. Charlaine cleared her throat. "Gentlemen, now is not the time or the place—"

"Our wits." Devlin released Charlaine when she struggled to be free.

Cecil blinked. "What?"

Devlin smiled slightly. "Shall we both pose a riddle? The one who answers correctly wins the first dance with Charlaine."

"I believe I have something to say to this," Charlaine asserted, but neither of them was listening now.

An old rivalry was taking new shape before her eyes—and other prying ones.

The Oxford crowd had angled closer. Charlaine sensed another presence. Henry Dupree hovered in the rear. Her father pushed through the crowd to take her hand. She gave him a pleading look, but he shook his head.

May the best man win, his look said. Charlaine longed to stomp her foot and throw something, but since that would only draw even more unwanted attention, she could only watch helplessly.

Cecil glanced down to brush a careless hand over his waistcoat, as if flicking away lint, but his little smile was still apparent. It was obvious he did not consider Devlin a threat intellectually, and equally obvious that he welcomed the audience that would witness his rival's humiliation. "Who goes first?"

Devlin pulled a sixpence from his pocket and tossed it in the air. Cecil won the toss. Devlin made a show of slipping the sixpence back in his pocket, drawing out the suspense while Cecil collected his thoughts. Cecil ran a hand through his hair. Snipes whispered something in Cecil's ear.

Cecil grinned. "What creature walks in the morning on four feet, at noon upon two, and at evening upon three?"

Only someone with a classical education could answer this riddle. Charlaine swallowed. Somehow she couldn't bear the thought of Devlin being humiliated by the legendary trickery of the Sphinx.

Devlin rubbed his chin. He tapped his foot. When the ever-growing crowd about them had gone quiet, he said, "Why, could it be man? As a babe he crawls on his hands and knees, as an adult he walks upright, and as an ancient he uses a cane."

Something treacherously similar to pride washed over Charlaine. Her father squeezed her hand triumphantly.

Snipes's mouth dropped open. Cecil quickly hid his chagrin. They had not expected a boy who'd grown up on the streets of one of New York's meanest districts to know the riddle that Oedipus had solved, thus winning a kingdom.

The buzzing crowd quieted again when Devlin waved a silencing hand. "My turn. Are you ready, Cecil?"

Cecil nodded, standing to his full, formidable height.

Devlin smiled slightly. "What cannot be seen, heard or touched, but has done more to alter the course of human history than any war ever fought or any sovereign who ever reigned?"

Again, Cecil ran a hand through his hair as he often did when he was distracted or thinking deeply. His brow cleared. "Why, ambition, of course."

An odd expression flickered in Devlin's eyes. For a moment, Charlaine wondered if that could actually be pity. Surely not. He waited so long to answer that Snipes had slapped Cecil on the back in congratulation by the time Devlin shook his head.

"No, I'm afraid not. The answer is love."

"What sort of riddle is that?" Cecil growled. "I've never heard of it."

"Of course you haven't. I made it up."

Admiring whispers circled the goggling crowd. Cecil reddened.

"Unfair," muttered Snipes.

"I did not say that we could not use our own imaginations."

"This little incident says much of your values," Cecil snapped. Then he stiffened under the curious glances, obviously trying to rein in his chagrin.

Devlin's little smile faded. "No, my dear Cecil, it says more of yours. Ambition is your guiding star. I knew you would never come up with the answer."

"Why you—"

Snipes grabbed Cecil's rigid arm.

A regal little figure was walking through the crowd. The group parted before her like waves before the ship *Britannia*—which she was, in a sense.

Devlin walked up to Charlaine and flourished an arm. "Would you care to dance, my lady?"

Charlaine glanced from Cecil's quiet, waiting expression to Devlin's unreadable one, and finally, at the queen.

Victoria watched the two men curiously. "What is amiss, my child?"

Charlaine took a deep breath and grasped Devlin's arm. "Nothing, Your Majesty. A slight misunderstanding about my dance card."

With a deep bow to the queen, and a curt, "Good

evening, Your Majesty. I shall call shortly, as you directed," Cecil strode off.

Victoria watched him go. "Nothing, eh?" Her full mouth trembled in a smile that she quickly stifled. She cocked her head slightly to one side as she appraised Devlin. A lady-in-waiting rushed up and whispered something in her ear. Victoria waved a dismissing hand, and then bent piercing blue eyes on Devlin, moving so close that he towered over her. With a glance, the queen sent the crowd scurrying off, leaving the three of them an isle amongst a sea of humanity.

"Do you want this young miss, sirrah?"

Charlaine studied the wall, wishing herself back in her tower haven. She resented being discussed as if she were on the marriage mart, and the queen the broker. But she could hardly say so to Her Majesty.

Devlin shifted his feet, but that was the only sign of his nervousness as he responded steadily, "Yes, Your Majesty."

Victoria's plump face stretched into an approving smile. Her opinion of the role of females, young females in particular, was well known. Charlaine grimaced inwardly, but she held her tongue.

"We approve, young man. 'Tis high time this young filly was reined in." The queen tapped Charlaine's mutinous face with her fingertip. "You do not know it yet, but the happiest part of your life will be serving your husband and children. Now be off with you to the dance floor. We are fatigued." And she turned and waddled away.

Devlin bowed. "Thank you, Your Majesty." He led Charlaine away. "You can stop grinding your teeth now. She's gone."

Charlaine took a deep, calming breath, but it didn't help her composure much.

94

"Why does her good sense upset you so?" he whispered.

Since it would definitely not do for them to be overheard, she hissed back, "Good sense! If that is not just like a man. Like her, you probably think that because I wear a skirt, my only destiny in life is to dress extravagantly, be parsimonious with household funds, to fawn over my husband and to pretend stupidity in the presence of men with intellect."

When he arched a wicked eyebrow, she braced herself.

He leaned so close that his breath tickled her neck. "You forget the most important requirement, which Her Majesty has fulfilled many times."

She knew she'd regret falling into his trap, but she was too angry to care. "And what is that?"

"Why, procreation, of course. As talented, strong and intelligent as you undoubtedly are, even you cannot manage that on your own."

She gaped at him even as a queer tingle started in the center of her body and spread to her extremities. How dare he speak to her like that, especially in such company.

The ballroom, a blaze of lights, gilded molding and mirrorlike dance floor, made a queer battleground, but Charlaine felt attacked on all sides. First her father, now the queen, pushed her at this thief who masqueraded as a gentleman. If they only knew how she had met him . . . As Devlin swept her onto the floor in a waltz, she wished she could say she found his touch distasteful. Or that she felt no secret flush of pleasure to hear him imply that he wanted her. Charlaine had to admit, at least to herself, that her panic stemmed from the attack of her most perilous enemy: her own instincts.

And those instincts were not quelled by the touch

of his firm hands at her waist and palm, or at the way his legs brushed against her as he swirled her expertly around the floor. "How does a thief learn to waltz so well?"

His steps never faltered, but his hand tightened on hers until she looked up into his gorgeous blue eyes. "Like he learns everything else: one day at a time. I do not spend my days in idle pursuits, alone in a tower dreaming of what could be. I try to accomplish something worthwhile every day of my life. That credo has brought me from Hell's Kitchen, New York, to Buckingham Palace, dancing with the most beautiful woman in England."

That soft, traitorous glow spread at his words. Those eyes, so clear a blue that she felt invited to swim in them, lapped at her warmly. She tried to tell herself that he was like all the rest, that he really wanted her fortune, but the catechism did not ring true. The hostility was even more forced this time. "And where did robbing me fall in your day's accomplishments?"

His mobile lips spread in an intimate smile. He dipped his head to whisper in her ear, "Pitiable, compared to the wealth of my memories of a certain soft bed and its softer, warmer occupant."

She gasped, stumbling. He caught her up against him, breaking the rhythm of the dance for a more primitive beat. For an instant, they were most improperly positioned, chest to chest, thigh to thigh. Charlaine's heart surged a response to the thumping of his. Dimly, she realized people were staring. Fascinated, she watched his Adam's apple bounce as he swallowed harshly, set her back and caught her again in the proper waltz stance.

Could it really be true? Did he really want her as much as he claimed?

The rest of the dance passed in a blur. Amongst the

august gathering, they somehow made their own little haven. Never had she danced so well, felt so light, or regretted the end of a dance more when the music ended with a crescendo.

Leading her to the sidelines, Devlin bowed deeply over her hand. "Thank you, *chère*. I shall call on you soon to discuss the parure." His cheeks were flushed, and he adjusted his jacket as he walked away.

Charlaine stared after him. She blinked when Henry appeared at her side for his dance. She nodded at the right moments, followed the right steps, but the gay, glittering scene had suddenly gone gray and lifeless.

By the time he reached his flat, Devlin's arousal had finally softened. Grimly, he realized he played a dangerous game. Awakening Charlaine to sexuality would require more control than he had anticipated. In the glittering ball gown, she did indeed seem as exquisitely untouchable as the Ice Princess her rejected suitors had dubbed her. Yet, when he danced with her, felt the heat of her body, the thump of her heart, he knew her frigidity was as much an illusion as his own aping of a gentleman. At heart, he would always be a boy from Hell's Kitchen.

Or, more apropos of her insult, a frog out of water.

His slight smile faded when he opened his door to find Cecil in his living room. Mordecai, his yarmulke askew, sat warily on the edge of a plush seat. He had obviously thrown on his clothes, because his waistcoat and stockings were rumpled.

Devlin slammed the door behind him and leaned against it. "Hello, cousin. I did not know that this was a proper hour to call." Pointedly, he snapped open his pocket watch. He peered at it and tapped the crystal as if it could not really be one in the morning.

Cecil towered to his feet. "You can stop the acting

now. I do not appreciate your theatrics."

Devlin unhooked his fob and tossed the watch on a table. "Pity. I do so enjoy yours."

Cecil's big hands clenched into fists. "I came here to tell you that, even if you have no care for the name we regrettably share, you should have a care for the young lady we both admire and not make her the butt of jokes again."

Devlin's grim mood turned pitch black. "No one was a butt tonight but you."

Cecil took a stride forward, then caught himself. "You humiliated me in front of the queen. For that I will never forgive you."

"That will keep me up nights." Devlin took a challenging step forward himself. "Now we come to the true reason for your visit. It is your own reputation that concerns you, as usual. Might I make a suggestion? If you cannot bear to lose, do not accept challenges. Now be so kind as to take yourself off."

A queer sound came from Cecil. His eyes glittered, gray and lethal as steel. He gathered himself to lunge. Devlin turned squarely to meet him.

Mordecai stepped between the two men and put a firm hand on each broad chest. "Enough! Schmucks, that's all the pair of you are. Two bantam roosters thinking they're peacocks."

Cecil's ire increased. "How dare you, sir?"

The look on Mordecai's face made Devlin take a step back. Mordecai seldom lost his equanimity, but when he did . . . Devlin started removing the breakables from Mordecai's reach.

Mordecai said mildly, "Dare? Why, it was me, sir, whom you disturbed from a sound sleep. It was you, apparently, who brought shame to the name Rhodes this night. Now please leave, before you shame yourself more. For a mature man, you certainly can act juvenile."

Cecil's florid face paled. His head lowered on his shoulders, but before he could move forward, Mordecai's gray eyes narrowed into slits. He took two steps back, picked up the bowl of fresh flowers on the table and tossed the water and flowers over Cecil's fulminating head.

Gasping, Cecil blinked in shock and froze where he stood.

"Open the door, Devlin," Mordcai ordered.

Devlin swept the door open.

Mordecai caught Cecil's arm and marched him out to the stoop. Cecil's befuddlement came alive. He turned on the little man, catching him by the collar and shoving him against the wall. "Why, you—"

Mordecai didn't struggle. His own gray eyes zeroed in on Cecil's livid ones. "No wonder you're such a big man in Africa. You don't reason with opposition. You manhandle it, stomp it into the ground and trample on it. You must fit in very well there."

Cecil released him as if burned. He looked from Mordecai to Devlin, who had quietly come to the door. "You will both regret this. That I promise you." Cecil drew his tattered dignity around himself and stalked into the darkness.

Devlin put a hand on Mordecai's still rigid shoulder. "I'm sorry, old friend. Had I known he would come, I would have returned earlier."

Mordecai stomped back inside. "Put that schmuck in his place, Devlin. No matter what it takes." His bedroom door slammed.

Wearily, Devlin took off his coat and slung it over a chair. Cecil's vague antagonism had just hardened into something far worse. Somehow, at this moment, Devlin could not look forward to this new challenge.

*　　*　　*

Once back in his study in his suite of rooms at a luxury hotel, Cecil went straight to his desk and unlocked it. Part of his mind noted that his things were not as neat as usual, but he was still too infuriated to pay the disorder much heed. Finally he found what he was looking for. He pulled out the card, tossed it on the desktop and left a note for Henry.

Get me an appointment with this man, Henry. As soon as possible. Cecil.

Then, his expression still grim, he sought his bed. But, as had been the case all too often lately, he found little comfort there. Time to go home. Home to Africa. The momentary vision of bright sun, exotic scents and rugged mountains made him recall that disgusting little Jew's insult. Cecil smiled grimly in the darkness. Fine. Let them find out just how ruthless he could be.

Two days passed before Charlaine saw Devlin again. During that time, she wavered between relief and longing. He was bad for her. He was addictive. He drained her will and her soul.

So why was it that, every time she saw him, she recalled the erotic touch of his mouth on her own, and on certain other forbidden places?

She tried to occupy herself at the stores, but the hustle and bustle as they began to decorate for the upcoming Golden Jubilee was hardly conducive to calm. And that night, when she arrived home, her father presented her with the rose diamonds. He opened the black velvet pouch with a flourish.

"I understand from Devlin that he has a design almost ready. I suggest you meet him tomorrow to—"

"Finalize things?"

At her honeyed tone, Durwood stood back warily.

"I might as well construct a noose about my neck as this cursed necklace. Do you think I am unaware of his designs on me, and of your own encouragement of him?" Her voice gathered volume with each word.

Durwood pulled out the chair next to her and tried to take her hands. "My dear, please—"

She jerked away. His rare patience only made her angrier. He should be defending her against this . . . this frog, instead of throwing her at the Frenchman's head. "Do you want an heir so much that my own well-being is of total unimportance to you?"

"You may not recognize it yet, but it's your happiness I'm thinking of." When she laughed harshly, his dark blue eyes narrowed. "It's in your blood to love once and well, Charlaine, as the Kimballs always have. And I see your attraction to this man in your eyes whenever he's near. Why not give him a chance?" Gently he caught her chin and turned her to face him.

She pulled away like a restive filly evading the bridle. "I have too much to lose." She rose and hurried to the door, but his quiet retort would disturb her sleep that night.

"And everything to gain. Deny it all you wish, but he will be the making of you, my willful, spoiled darling."

Thus, when the butler announced Devlin the next morning, Charlaine was in no mood to see him. She debated denying him entrance, but instinctively realized that avoiding him would only incite him.

Indeed, they had met precisely because she had unknowingly challenged him by bragging about the impregnability of her estate. She told the butler to admit him, then went to the long mirror above the sofa in the salon. She was glad she'd worn her ice blue silk this morning, along with her best diamond earrings.

Colleen Shannon

The heavy fabric was draped to the small bustle and trimmed with swansdown at hem and mutton sleeves. It was a fussier gown than she normally wore, but she'd intended to call on the Dowager Duchess of Kensington, an old family friend, at that lady's request. Anything to get out of this increasingly drab and quiet prison. She was already late, but she had time to put this rascal in his place.

When the butler closed the door on Charlaine's request, Devlin bowed deeply. "You are in looks this morning, milady."

She could have said the same of him. But she didn't. She nodded regally.

He added with a sidelong look, "And the Ice Princess reigns today, I see."

"Today and always, whenever you are around." She ignored the challenging arch of that black eyebrow. "To what do I owe the, er, honor of this visit?" She was rather pleased with herself at the polite snub.

Until he approached on silent tread. Until he stood so close she could feel the heat of his body. He did not touch.

Yet. The promise of his hands on her was even more tantalizing. Cool, stay cool, she remonstrated with herself as she forced her eyes to meet his unwaveringly.

He pulled something from his pocket and held it up to her cheek. "Ah, I knew it would complement your flawless skin. I cannot wait to see you wearing our necklace, with nothing between it and your skin." He cocked his head to the side in that teasing manner she was beginning to recognize and turned the huge rose diamond from side to side. "It's an even better match when you blush."

She willed the heat in her cheeks away and took a step back. "I have decided not to work on the necklace with you."

102

He shrugged. "Your father will be surprised. I am not."

She stiffened. Whatever did he mean?

He spanned the short distance she'd put between them and leaned so close that his clean breath stirred the upswept hair at her temples. "Coward. But it will not work, you know. . . ."

He trailed off, still leaning over her.

Goaded, she snapped, "What will not work?"

"Denying your feelings for me. The harder you push me away, the more I will torment you in your dreams."

She stumbled back three steps this time. How could he know? She went to bed thinking of him and rose thinking of him, but no living soul knew that.

He slipped the diamond back into his pocket, those bright blue eyes pinioning her to the spot. "I know that, you see, because it is the same for me. We are destined to be lovers, Charlaine. Go on now, run and hide. Or try to."

Every urge she possessed bade her do exactly that. Instead she stood her ground and said icily, "I will not give you the satisfaction. You are no threat to me, least of all to my heart." She wanted to bite her tongue off when he stiffened like a hound on the scent. Dammit, she'd challenged him again!

This time, when he stalked her, she retreated. Only when she was pinned against the secretary against the wall did he stop. Still, he didn't touch her.

Not because he didn't want to.

And most certainly not because she didn't want him to.

The words he spoke were as devastating as his mesmerizing touch. Each one pierced the last of her tattered defenses.

"One day, very soon, I will live with you. We will dine together. I will eat from your golden plate, and share your silver spoon." His voice went even softer, brushing against her like the velvet promise of a long, moonless night. "And I will sleep in your soft bed, and touch your silken skin. Then, when you know me, you will see me as I really am. The only man for you."

Her breath caught. She felt her will toppling. She felt herself teetering toward him. And precisely because she wanted his touch so much, she forced the words out. "You are nothing but a frog. A French rogue who wants only my money and position!"

For the first time, anger stirred in those gorgeous eyes. He put both hands beside her head and trapped her between them. "*Chère*, you know that's a lie. I—"

A dry female voice said, "I deduced you had a good excuse for your tardiness, Charlaine. I am pleased to see I was right."

At a less stressful moment, Charlaine might have laughed at the dismay in Devlin's face. She was delighted to watch a dull flush color his high cheekbones. He stepped back and turned to face the formidable old woman standing in the doorway.

The Dowager Duchess of Kensington propped one age-spotted hand on her generous hip and drew a lorgnette to her eyes with her other hand. She was dressed modishly, as usual. From the wide hat trimmed with lace and flowers to the hem of her frilled dress, she defined taste and refinement. She still had a figure a woman half her age might envy, and her discreetly powdered face was youthful for a dowager on the wrong side of seventy. She had been best friends with Charlaine's fraternal grandmother and was the closest thing to a mother Charlaine had ever known. She had been a scandalous person in her youth, Charlaine had heard, but she had married well twice, and her form, her speech, even her morals, were all that was proper.

Except when she wished it otherwise.

Gleefully, Charlaine leaned against the secretary and crossed her ankles. Aunt Elizabeth would put this rascal in his place for his familiarity.

A gilded mesh reticule set with brilliants flashed on Elizabeth's wrist as, still eyeing Devlin, she steamed down the long salon toward him like a luxury liner bent on running a rusty barge aground.

Charlaine was not surprised when Devlin, far from dodging her, sailed forward to meet her. "Your Grace, what a pleasure it is to see you again."

Just you wait, Charlaine thought. *She'll squash you like a bug.*

She blinked when, with the familiarity of long company, he took that lady's hand and kissed it.

To Charlaine's astonishment, Elizabeth's lorgnette fell back upon her generous bosom on its string. "Oh, is that you, Devlin, my boy?" She peered up at him from beneath her wide hat brim. "I can see it is, now that you've come out of the confounded shadows." Nothing would ever make the duchess admit that she could see nothing clearly unless it was within six feet of her. "What are you doing here, fawning over my gel?"

"Same as you, I expect. Prostrate with affection and admiration." He made a show of putting a weak hand to his brow, but the wicked wink he dropped at her was a truer clue to his nature.

Slowly Charlaine uncrossed her ankles. Not Aunt Elizabeth too? Was no one immune to this rascal's overblown charm? "Ah, do you known this man, Aunt?"

"I should say so. I was one of his first clients."

Thunderstruck, Charlaine opened her mouth, but nothing came out.

The duchess tut-tutted. "Psaw, get that betrayed

105

look off your face. The goods you and your father carry are too stuffy by far. And you are hardly wanting for business." The duchess shook the reticule. "He found me this bauble, and set it with diamonds when I complained it was too plain. He is a most talented jeweler."

Charlaine's eyes kindled at the word *bauble.* "Indeed," she agreed sweetly, "he does have a fondness for baubles." *And he'd better keep mine safe.*

The duchess drew the lorgnette to her eyes again. They were a curious hazel that took on whatever color she happened to be wearing, which, at the moment, was green. Appropriate, since even her formidable willpower could not disguise the flash of envy in her eyes as she watched the two young people. The thrill of the chase radiated from Devlin; Charlaine longed to run—but to him or away from him? It was obvious she did not know herself.

An old, old story, but one that was new to those involved every time it happened.

"So, that's the lay of the land, is it?" the duchess said softly to herself, too softly for them to hear. "About damn time. You lucky girl."

Louder, she said, "Well, Miss Priss? Do you join me for nuncheon, since you have already missed breakfast?"

Charlaine dragged her gaze away from Devlin's. "Uh, yes. Indeed."

"Fetch your wrap. It is chilly this morn."

As Charlaine turned to leave, Devlin said, "We shall continue our discussion this evening. Over dinner at my flat."

Charlaine froze. "I am engaged for this evening."

"Break it. I do so need your help in understanding a certain manuscript."

She whirled. "You read it?"

"Yes."

"You had no right."

"Perhaps. But I've never let that stop me."

"I shall not come!"

Devlin appraised his perfectly manicured finger-nails. "Then I shall just have to take it to a bookseller. Perhaps a professional can help me with the difficult passages."

She paled at the very thought of some stranger reading her intimate family history. Desperately, she cast about for an excuse. "Father will not let me visit a bachelor's residence."

"Mordecai will be there."

"I can go with you, child," the duchess offered.

Charlaine gritted her teeth. Was all of London in collusion with this dashed frog?

Devlin's mobile lips twitched but straightened quickly under her fulminating glance. *The harder you push me away, the closer I will come,* his eyes promised.

She read them clearly, and was so furious at his temerity that she snapped, "Very well! What time?" She would show him how the Ice Princess earned her nickname.

"Shall we say seven?"

She waved a dismissing hand and flounced out.

Her generous bosom shaking with repressed laughter, the duchess gasped out, "Seven, indeed! You have that child at sixes and sevens, all right! I declare, if I did not think you would be good for her, I would set the law on you!"

"For what?"

"For wielding a dangerous weapon with reckless disregard for vulnerable young women." She sobered abruptly, eyeing the dashing figure he cut in his calling costume.

He shrugged, obviously catching her meaning. "I very much hope she finds me as, ah, enticing as you believe. But I will never hurt her. On that you have my word."

An indelicate snort bespoke her opinion of that. "Male arrogance! Doubtless Romeo used that very line to Juliet right before she killed herself out of love of him." She stalked up to him to stab a finger at his waistcoat. "But I warn you—hurt this child and you will answer to me. I promised her grandmother at her deathbed that I would watch over her, and I always keep my promises."

He made her a short bow. "Warning taken." He straightened. "Do you really intend to join us this evening?"

Light footsteps warned of Charlaine's return, but the duchess's gleeful smile still had charm enough to light the dim room. "I would not miss it for the world!"

When Charlaine entered, the duchess strode up to take her adopted niece's arm. "Come, child. Let us fortify ourselves." As they exited, she sent a sly wink to Devlin over her shoulder.

He grinned back at her, obviously aware what a powerful ally she would make.

Or an equally powerful enemy.

And he already had enough of those. . . .

Some distance away, at one of London's nicest hotels, a man in a bowler hat knocked on the best suite door. Henry Dupree answered. "Good morning. He will be with you shortly." Dupree went back into the adjacent room, closing the door softly behind him.

Lewis Temple might have twiddled nervously with his hat as he was forced to cool his heels in the exquisite salon. He might have moistened his dry mouth at the thought of being hired by such a famous, wealthy man. And he might even have paced to stave off his nervousness.

Lewis Temple seldom did what he might; he was more in the habit of doing what he ought. And seeing that young Devlin Rhodes paid for his easy way with women was more than a devotion to duty.

It was a mission.

Temple waited calmly, one ankle propped on the opposite knee, for the great man to appear. This veddy proper suite in this veddy proper city would have made the young man he'd once been sweat. That was years ago. Before he fought in the Indian wars. Before he became a detective.

Before Sally died.

The opening door was a welcome distraction. Temple rose and followed Dupree's beckoning hand. Cecil Rhodes looked up from his vast mahogany desk and shoved a weighty stack of papers aside. "You may go, Henry."

Henry went.

Cecil eyed Temple under beetling brows. The industrialist was known for his mercurial temper, dour one moment, merry the next. Temple wondered what had set him off.

"I am told you are one of the best detectives in the Pinkerton agency. Normally I would hire an Englishman, but since the man I want you to investigate is American, perhaps this will be best. I also understand that you have already been hired to track this fellow by an associate of mine, and that you were abruptly dismissed."

Undoubtedly this industrialist had thoroughly done his own investigation, through his many sources, of one Lewis Temple. Temple's estimation of the Englishman rose a notch. "I can hazard a guess as to who you might wish me to track. A certain wastrel, half

French, half English, who grew up in America."

Rhodes leaned back in his chair, eyeing Temple even more sharply. He was obviously not accustomed to being so predictable. Finally, he shrugged. "I confess to a hearty dislike of Devlin, er"—he swallowed, and his tone was like gravel when he added—"Rhodes. But I do not want him weaseling his way into the good graces of a young and innocent girl, then leaving her ruined."

"He excels at that." Temple snapped his teeth closed on the remark.

His new employer stiffened. "Eh? What's that? He's done this before?"

Temple hesitated, then said softly, "Yes. To my younger sister."

Silence prevailed in the small study for a moment; then Rhodes bestirred himself. "And you know this for a fact?"

"From her own lips, before she died."

"You consider him responsible?"

"Indirectly. He rejected her affections, spreading himself like manure over all the attractive young women from our neighborhood. She was so unhappy that she wandered into the street in a daze and was hit by a dray." Of the fact that his sister had already been an opium addict, Temple said nothing. Devlin could have made her happy enough to leave off the foul stuff, if he had not put his own ambition first and gone haring off to Africa to make his fortune.

Temple smiled inwardly. Devlin's money would do him little good in prison, while he served time for theft. Eventually the Kimballs would come to their senses and press charges against him. Or he would steal again. His type always did. And Lewis Temple would be waiting.

"However," Temple said baldly, "I am not in the

110

habit of taking anyone's money under false pretenses, sir. I should warn you that with or without your fees, I will hound this degenerate to hell and back until I find enough dirt to bring him in. Here or in America, it matters not to me."

"But it matters to me. If you take him back to America and get him off the soil of my mother country, I will triple your fee." Rhodes opened a drawer, frowned down at its contents. He rearranged things. "That's funny. I would have sworn I left this on the other side. Well, no matter." He pulled out a heavy leather book, flipped it open and wrote out a check. He blew the ink dry and handed the check to Temple. "That should be more than adequate to get you started. I will pay you an equal sum weekly, plus expenses, until you bring me evidence enough to put this man behind bars. And as I said, I will triple the entire sum if you take him back to America with you. Fair enough?"

Temple looked at the amount on the check, whistling softly. Rhodes must hate his black sheep cousin very much. He pocketed the check. "More than fair." He stood, uncertain whether or not to offer his hand.

Rhodes decided for him, offering his own. Temple shook it, noting that, even after all these years, the man still had calluses on his palm. "Thank you, sir. I will not disappoint you."

Temple strode to the door. He heard a slight rustle on the other side, but when he opened it, Henry Dupree was primly seated on the settee, reading a paper. Temple gave him a suspicious look. He knew when a man listened at a keyhole. Still, it was none of Temple's concern.

Nodding brusquely, Temple exited. His steps were firm, his shoulders thrown back in a posture that other detectives would have recognized.

111

Temple, as righteous as his name, was on the trail again.

The flat near Grosvenor Square was ablaze with lights that night. When a fancy carriage pulled up and disgorged two sophisticated ladies, the neighbors peered from behind their curtains. A phonograph could be heard playing a Strauss waltz when the door was opened, but then the ladies entered and all was quiet again.

Disappointed, the neighbors returned to their own boring meals.

Inside, Devlin took the ladies' wraps. His warm gaze lingered on Charlaine's bare shoulders above the heart-shaped bodice of the black silk dress. The dark color set off her skin and flaming hair, having the opposite effect of the severe one she had obviously hoped for. Her passion was displayed against the silk like a jewel sparkling against a satin background, awaiting only the right setting to show its true glory.

She nodded coolly as he folded her fringed shawl carefully over his arm. "Good evening," he said. "Welcome."

"Good evening," the two ladies echoed.

Her obvious resolve to play the Ice Princess to the hilt melted a tad under the heat of her own curiosity as she looked about. The duchess watched the byplay between them indulgently, handing over her own silk-and-fur wrap.

She nodded approvingly at the Tiffany lamp and expensive but spare furniture. "You have good taste, my boy." She sniffed. "And what is that enchanting aroma?"

"Mordecai's specialty." Devlin hung the wraps on a coatrack.

"Is Mordecai in the kitchen?" The duchess rushed toward the source of the aroma. They heard a pot lid clatter as she entered the tiny kitchen, then a deeper rumble as Mordecai welcomed her.

Charlaine stared after her. "Odd. I have never seen her move so fast."

"She and Mordecai have shared many an argument at the shop, during his visits over the years." He cocked his head on one side. "Why, do you think them too old to know what attraction means?"

"Of course not! I merely meant that she seldom gets out anymore, and when she does little seems to thrill her."

"Living by her example?"

Her mouth still open, she stared at him. "I am not some recluse who disdains company."

"No, only men in general. Or so you tell yourself in your lonely tower." He reached out to trace the seductive lines of her soft mouth. "But the woman I first met will never let the Ice Princess rule for long."

She reared back from his touch. "If you are going to continually bait me, I will leave right now."

"Why, are you tempted?" he asked softly.

When she stalked toward her wrap, he threw his hands up in surrender. "Very well. We shall be light, gay and happy." He caught her arm to formally escort her to the small table that was set for four. Elaborate silver candlesticks held tall candles. Fresh roses exuded their own subtle scent as he handed her a box of matches with a flourish.

"Be my guest. I have lit enough fires for one evening." And he smiled.

If her hand shook slightly as she lit the candles, he did not remark on it. And it might have been the heat from the candles that put the flush in her cheeks.

But the gooseflesh trailing up her spine as he accidentally brushed against her when he seated her could have only one source.

Devlin sat opposite her, glad for the shielding table-cloth. What a dual-edged sword seduction is, he mused.

Chapter Five

The duchess bustled in from the kitchen, her hand possessively crooked in Mordecai's arm. Mordecai, too, was dressed more richly than usual. He actually sported a striped waistcoat and white spats that covered his shoes. His intricate cravat was spotless, but it was the look on his face that made Devlin stare.

Moonstruck might have come to mind if it were any other man. But Mordecai Levitz? Mooning over a woman? Impossible. To Devlin's knowledge, his old mentor had never had a serious relationship with a woman. Devlin knew for certain that he'd never been married.

Charlaine peered over her shoulder to see what held his attention.

The two older people were of a height, for Mordecai was short for a man, and Elizabeth was tall for a woman. As they walked, her hip brushed against him. He paused, looking down at her. With the blaze of

Colleen Shannon

lights forming a nimbus around them, their expressions stood out. Elizabeth stared into Mordecai's gray eyes as he said softly in a voice Devlin knew he was not intended to hear, "Lizzie, watch yourself unless you want to embarrass us both."

Devlin's eyes widened further. *Lizzie?* And that intimate smile that flashed across the duchess's face could have only one meaning. But she released Mordecai with a last proprietary pat and sat down in the chair he pulled out for her. She smiled benignly into Charlaine's shocked face.

Charlaine stammered, "L-Lizzie? I thought you detested the shortening of your name, Aunt."

"It all depends on the way it is spoken. A certain . . . panache is required. Now, what are we to be served this evening?"

Mordecai glared at Devlin and jerked his head at the bell. Devlin blinked out of his daze and rang the small silver bell. A serving maid, complete with lacy apron and mop cap, left the kitchen with a heavy tray. They had hired her for the evening.

She carried in the first course of matzo ball soup. Devlin watched Charlaine sip it gingerly, then more eagerly after the first bite. Next came the slow-roasted rosemary-and-thyme chicken with spring vegetables and challah bread. And lastly they ate the delicious apple kugel Mordecai had prepared himself.

The conversation began as lightly as the soup, but grew heavier with each course. Charlaine and Devlin stared curiously at the older couple, who held hands under the table. The duchess's mouth lifted wryly, but she did not remark on their obvious shock. Instead she brought up the Golden Jubilee.

"It will be a deuced nuisance, I know, but one must be present at the abbey for the ceremony. After all, it is not every English sovereign who can celebrate fifty years of reign. I daresay Victoria herself wishes not to attend."

Charlaine protested, "I have not received that impression. I am certain Her Majesty most appreciates the devotion of her subjects."

"I have heard she fears assassination." Mordecai patted his mouth with his napkin.

The duchess sighed grimly. "Indeed. She is not popular in some quarters, particularly among the Irish. She will never support home rule, despite Gladstone's feelings about the matter."

"Do you attend the jubilee, Mr. Levitz?" Charlaine asked politely.

"I have not been invited, ma'am."

"Oh, I can finagle you an invitation if you wish one, Mordecai," the duchess said. "But why would you wish one? It will be a sad crush. We shall be lucky to get a seat for the whole dreary affair."

"Dreary?" Devlin inserted. "Why, all of London is abuzz with the preparations. Half the royalty of Europe will be there."

"Do you plan to go, Devlin?" Charlaine asked. She took a small bite of the comfit she'd judiciously selected off the treats tray as a finish to her meal.

Despite her feigned indifference, Devlin felt her acute interest in his answer. "I have not been invited either."

Charlaine swallowed hard, but delicately wiped her hands with her napkin as if wiping her hands of the matter.

This time it was the older couple who stared at them.

Devlin, too, paid uncommon attention to the comfit tray to hide his hurt. He shouldn't have expected her to invite him, but when she'd brought it up . . .

Elizabeth leaned close to whisper in Charlaine's ear,

"Well, child? Where are your manners?"

Charlaine said nothing.

With a frown at her charge, the duchess turned to Devlin. "Please, Devlin, be my guest for any and all events you wish to attend. Mordecai will wish for male company, I know, and people will talk if we attend by ourselves."

Devlin gave her his boldest smile, determined not to let Charlaine see how she'd hurt him. "I thank you, Your Grace, but I would not wish to intrude."

"You scapegrace, think you I'd ask if I found you an intrusion?" The duchess selected a piece of Turkish delight, took a thoughtful bite and added, "Now that's settled, if you wish to show your gratitude, you can give me a discount on that emerald ring I've been eyeing."

The laughter at the table dispelled the uncomfortable pall that had settled over them. Even Charlaine giggled.

Mordecai sighed. "Lizzie, you are shameless."

Lizzie winked at him. "Indeed. Aren't you glad?"

The tablecloth rustled slightly. Mordecai jumped and went red.

Devlin wiped his mouth to hide his grin. He knew when a man had been grabbed. He glanced across the table. Charlaine was puzzled as she looked from Mordecai's tense expression to her aunt's mischievous one. Devlin clenched his hands under the table to deny his own longing to explicitly, slowly and thoroughly educate the innocent Ice Princess in what it meant to be a woman with a man.

Patience, he counseled himself. His body did not listen. It was only when they had finished the dregs of their coffee that he was composed enough to say, "Shall we retire to the seating area?" He held Charlaine's chair for her.

The duchess rose as Mordecai did the same for her. "Later. For now I wish to speak to Mordecai privately. Where?"

The kitchen and bedrooms were the only other rooms in the small flat. Mordecai looked wary, but he led the duchess into the kitchen and closed the door. They had dismissed the serving maid some time ago.

Charlaine folded her hands in her lap and stared after them.

Devlin crossed one long leg over the other one and bounced his shiny evening pump.

Charlaine shifted sideways in her chair to stare out the window.

Devlin switched legs and bounced the other foot.

Be damned if he'd break the silence. If she wished to treat him as if he had the plague, let her. It would not avail her long. He felt her attraction to him. The longer she denied it, the stronger it would grow. But he did not deny his eyes. They wandered, touching her where they willed.

Finally, as if she could not bear his silent stare any longer, she said hastily, "I thought you wanted to ask me about the book."

"I wanted you to bring it up. It is your family history, after all." When she bit her lip, he leaned forward to emphasize his words. "Truly, I do not wish to intrude. I have not breathed a word of what I read to a soul, even to Mordecai. If the truth be told"—he trailed off until she looked up at him—"I am envious that you have such a rich history to be proud of. I know little of my own family."

"You know Cecil."

He smiled bitterly. "Indeed. One of the richest men in England is my cousin. And he despises the sight of me."

Colleen Shannon

"What did you do to give him such a distaste of you?"

"I wouldn't sell him my claim. I wouldn't join his grandiose schemes to bilk the natives of yet more land, and more land, to satisfy his ambition, all in the name of empire." He sighed heavily. "That said, it is also true that he has done much for Africa, and he truly loves the land and even, I suspect, in some regard at least, its people. But his goals can only be achieved by ruthless means, and this I cannot support, as I said volubly and often in Kimberley, to his dismay."

"Is that why you left?"

"Partly. Mordecai wanted to open the London store, and I was weary of the dirt and work. My goal was always to be a jewelry designer. Little excites me more than to take a rough diamond out of the ground, dirty and cloudy, wash it, cut it and polish it to a thing of beauty that can only know its full potential when complemented by an equally beautiful wearer."

She swallowed hard, but this time she didn't look away from his intent stare. "Is this why you are so determined to have me help you design the necklace for the exhibition?"

He leaped at the excuse. "Partly. I cannot get the image of you wearing the parure out of my head." Naked. In my bed. "Is it such a bad thing to be an inspiration to a fellow?"

Pleasure at the thought flashed in her lovely green eyes before she veiled them with long, dark eyelashes. "I confess I have never been such, to my knowledge."

He smiled ruefully. In any other woman, he would have considered the claim artifice. But she truly did not know that she was the subject of many a private club conversation around London. Ah, what a bundle of contradictions she was. Spoiled but sweet. Intelligent but gullible. Willful but innocent. He had to

120

clench his fingers around the arms of his chair to avoid the impulse to grab her, to keep her for himself alone.

With an air of resolution, she said, "Very well. I will help you with the design. Do you have a sketch of it?"

He offered her his hand. She accepted it and joined him at a small card table beneath a bright gas lamp suspended from the ceiling. He went to his secret compartment, opened it beneath her interested stare, closed it and returned with a black pouch, a drawing . . . and an oilskin-wrapped book. She looked from it to him, then at the wall where he hid his safe. "You trust me with the location of your safe?"

"I trust you with my life." His hand covered hers on the table.

Wondering green eyes softened to velvet, wrapping around him. "But . . . why?"

Because you are my love, though you do not know it yet. Because we were fated to meet, marry and mingle all we have been and all we can be. He had to clear his throat to steady his voice. "I pride myself on my judgment of character. You are a fine person, and I think you are beginning to understand that in my own way, so am I. If I had any doubts about your opinion of me, you set them to rest when you defended me before Her Majesty."

While she digested this, he briskly opened the wrapping over the book. "Are you willing to answer some questions about the book?"

She blinked. Then she smiled, a sweet seductive smile that hit him like a blow to the gut. "Perhaps. If you agree to give it back."

"Minx. You know I cannot do that."

"Why not?"

"Because we agreed that I could keep it safe until you, ah, change your mind about me."

121

"And what if I have? You yourself said that you trust me implicitly." Possessively, she traced the ornate embossing on the cover.

His breath quickened. Slowly he turned her chin toward him, his fingers burning even at that slight contact. "Will you marry me, my Ice Princess, and turn to fire in my arms?"

She drew back abruptly, that seductive half smile going cold. "I will never wed. Anyone."

Sighing, he pulled the book away from her. "Then the book stays with me."

He wrapped it up just in time, for the kitchen door swung open. The duchess and Mordecai came back into the room. If Mordecai's cravat was a bit crooked, and the duchess's ornate coiffure a bit mussed, neither Devlin nor Charlaine was so crass as to remark on it. Devlin hid the book beneath his chair under Charlaine's watchful gaze.

Mordecai's acute gray eyes took in the situation at a glance. As he always did, he came to Devlin's aid by trying to defuse the tense atmosphere. He picked up the piece of art paper and spread it wide, beckoning to Elizabeth. "Look at Devlin's design for the jewelry competition. Is it not unique?"

The duchess peered over his shoulder. She drew in her breath sharply. "Magnificent!"

Charlaine's sullenness eased enough for her to lean forward and look at the drawing. Her mouth fell open.

Devlin smiled wryly and used his forefinger to close her mouth. "I am not flattered at your shock. Did you think me too untalented to create something worthwhile?"

She traced a graceful fingertip over the design. "The way you have the stones suspended . . . are they on springs?"

He nodded. "Yes. They should move and shimmer with every step you take."

She froze. Mordecai and Elizabeth looked at him sharply.

Mordecai reminded him, "But you know the winning parure is to be donated to the Crown."

Devlin tried to visualize his creation about the queen's plump, wrinkled neck. Instead he saw a long, slender neck rising to a clean, stubborn jawline and an exquisitely passionate mouth. He cleared his throat. "Then we shall just have to hope we take second prize, won't we? This parure was designed for one woman alone." And he wrapped the drawing up, as if that were the end of the matter.

The duchess appraised him shrewdly. She looked at her confused charge. And she smiled. Knowingly, gladly, as if Devlin had just presented her with an invitation to a wedding.

No designer, no matter how talented, could create such splendor without caring for she who had inspired it. From the heart shape of the necklace, to the pink tinge of the stones that would complement red hair so beautifully, to the delicate, delicious dance of fire as the jewels shimmered and moved, the work suit her perfectly.

Mordecai and Elizabeth shared a warm glance. Then the duchess patted her confused niece's cheek. "It is late, child. We should let these gentlemen rest after the delightful evening they have given us."

Devlin pulled back Charlaine's chair, bending to whisper for her ears alone, "I shall come to your store tomorrow, where we can work on the design together. All right?"

Dumbly, she nodded. She sent a wistful look at the bundle under the table that almost made Devlin fetch it and offer it to her. But he didn't. Some primitive instinct warned him that the book would do more than a prize in a competition, or even blackmail, to tame her to his hand.

If he lost the book, that symbol of love and heritage and happiness, he lost her. He didn't know why he felt that so strongly, but he had learned at a young age that sometimes cool, clear logic simply did not serve one as well as instinct.

Gut instinct had brought him great advantage on more than one occasion. It had showed him which claim to purchase in Africa, and when to sell it. It had helped him found his first jewelry store.

It had led him to Charlaine.

And it would win her in the end.

After they escorted the women to their carriage, Mordecai promptly went to the table to fetch the parcel. Over Devlin's protests, he unwrapped the book. He turned it wonderingly in his hands, read the first page, and snapped the book closed.

"You should not have kept this, and you know it. She will never forgive you for stealing it."

"Until the day I give it back to her along with my heart and hand."

Mordecai did not look surprised, but he did show all his years as he sagged into a chair. "You delight in a challenge, Devlin, but this time you may have set a goal you cannot reach. From what Lizzie says, no man has ever melted the ice around Charlaine Kimball's heart. Besides, Durwood Kimball would never allow his daughter to wed you, a man of—"

"Dubious background and morals? Perhaps you don't know Durwood as well as I do. Their family heritage is full of rascals. I shall fit right in." Devlin picked up the book and cradled it for a moment, dreaming of adding their own story to the other three. That bold smile flickered on his generous mouth. "Besides, have you not heard the fairy tale about the princess who kisses a frog and turns him into a prince? And what woman can resist a prince?"

Mordecai gave him a look that would have put a lesser man in his place.

Devlin Rhodes dropped a sly wink. "But I have a different ending. I shall turn an Ice Princess into a woman when I kiss her again. You shall see." Devlin carried the book back to his safe.

Mordecai stayed where he was, but his worried look only deepened.

The conversation in the splendid carriage was equally spirited.

"No, Aunt, I will not discuss him further. I will help him with the jewelry design, but that is all."

Elizabeth threw her hands up and stared out the window.

Charlaine bit her lip, but the question spilled out of its own accord. "How long have you known Mr. Levitz?"

The duchess cocked her head. "Nigh on two years now, I suppose. I met him at Devlin's store. Why? Do you disapprove?" Elizabeth tone made it plain she cared not a farthing either way.

"Me? No. But others will."

"Why?"

"But, Aunt, he's, ah, you know—"

"Jewish? And what, pray, does that have to do with anything? Would that we could all claim to be God's chosen people." At Charlaine's troubled expression, Elizabeth's affront subsided. She patted her adopted niece's hand. "Never you mind, child. We are discreet, as we would be at any age. Mordecai doesn't want it bruited about that his inamorata is a duchess who was considered scandalous in her youth. Indeed, I suspect he's a bit more embarrassed about my past than I am about his. He's a prudish old chap—during the day-time."

Charlaine blushed when her dear aunt smiled wick-edly. Would she ever be so bold and free about private matters? A handsome face and a soft feather bed came to mind, causing a reaction in rather lower quarters, so Charlaine blurted the first thought that came into her head to distract Elizabeth—and herself. "But, Aunt, he's an American!"

She said it as if that were the most heinous crime of all.

Elizabeth turned up the carriage lantern. Her wicked smile grew to a grin; then she began laughing so hard that her rich bosom trembled. "Spoken like . . . a loyal . . . subject," she finally gasped between chuckles. When she'd composed herself, she turned Charlaine's chin in her direction. "But if you are truly so anti-American, why are you so interested in that young rascal? He's about as American as they come in his ideals and values."

Charlaine debated evading the issue, but she knew Elizabeth would worry the question until she broke down. "Indeed, he does tend to aspire to high places," she agreed dryly, remembering him climbing out of her tower, his knapsack bulging with her possessions. "And he is exceedingly democratic in his notions of how wealth should be distributed." She didn't expect Elizabeth to understand her references, but Elizabeth, as usual, surprised her.

As the coachman drew up before Charlaine's estate, Elizabeth waved a dismissing hand. "Poppycock! He gave everything back to you, and only did it because you challenged him." As Charlaine gathered her wrap about her shoulders, preparing to step out, Elizabeth caught her niece's hand. "My dear, you should despise neither his American, nor his French side."

Elizabeth nibbled at her lip, then said quickly, "You are part French yourself."

Charlaine's fingers froze in arranging her shawl. "What?"

"Durwood made me promise not to tell you, because he has always disapproved of the French so, but your grandmama Kimball was half French. And a ballet dancer to boot. That's how we met, actually. She was the prima ballerina and I was in the corps de ballet. So you see, I am not one to stand in judgement on anyone. Nor should you, given the fact that you count a pirate and a dancer among your ancestors."

Charlaine's mouth worked, and finally she gasped, "I will never forgive Father for not telling me!"

Elizabeth tapped her cheek. "Never mind. I suppose I should feel guilty for breaking my promise to Durwood, but he never should have kept this from you because of his own silly prejudices. I just want you to recall this fact the next time you are inclined to berate Devlin for being a frog."

Charlaine gathered her shawl tightly about her shoulders, wishing she could draw on indifference to their subject as easily. "Perhaps. But this entire argument is moot anyway. It is actually not his background I despise as much as his manner. He is a scoundrel, English, French, American, or Hottentot. I will not be his latest conquest."

"Take it from one who knows—there is sometimes much joy in surrender. Besides, surely his own good business head and love of jewels should appeal to you—"

Charlaine flung open the door as the coachman touched it, sending him stumbling back. "I passionately wish every person of my acquaintance would not push this fellow at me! I do not wish to discuss this again, Aunt." She stepped down. She bypassed the coachman, who had regained his balance and held the door wide for her, wooden faced, and hurried inside the home that was no longer a haven.

Even when she gained her rooms, she looked about with jaundiced eyes. He was spoiling everything for her. She used to cherish her time alone. Now, despite the decorating changes she'd made, she couldn't be in her own chambers without remembering the touch and feel of that . . . invader.

Angrily, Charlaine tossed off her shawl. How was she to get this man out of her life, out of her dreams, out of her—She squelched the last rogue thought. Never, ever, would he invade her heart.

Rubbing her elbows, she paced up and down. Mayhap she'd handled him wrong from the start. Her usual tactics with suitors were ineffective against Devlin Rhodes because the more she pushed him away, the more interested he became. It was the chase he relished. Doubtless once he caught her, he'd lose interest.

She froze, her brow crinkling. Why not? Such tactics were dangerous, but they didn't call her the Ice Princess for nothing. She could pretend to respond to him while keeping her true feelings inviolate. She smiled slowly. The next time he blandished her with that charming grin, she'd simper back. The next time he leaned close, tormenting her with his scent and warmth, she'd melt against him. The next time he tried to kiss her . . . her mouth went dry at the thought.

To herself she had to admit: more than food, more than drink, even, God help her, more than she wanted her father's respect, she wanted to feel those warm, soft lips tugging at hers again. And damn him, precisely because he'd vowed not to kiss her until she cared for him, she was determined to make him kiss her. Doubtless this time he would leave her unmoved. That was it. Like the closet romantic she was, she'd built that first kiss into a cataclysmic event that had changed her life. Once she kissed him again, she would be able to banish him like the phantom of her dreams that he truly was.

The real Devlin Rhodes was a thief, a bounder, not the charming descendant of Marie Antoinette he claimed to be.

Feeling as if a weight had been removed from her shoulders, Charlaine prepared for bed. Her sleep was peaceful, but when she awoke the next morning, a dampness between her thighs told of her erotic dreams.

Angrily, she ripped off her nightclothes and tossed them at the feet of her suprised maid. "Burn them," she said curtly.

She hoped to slip out without seeing her father, but he stepped from the study into the hall, speaking to someone over his shoulder, as she passed.

"Tell him that I— Good morning, my dear." Durwood offered a tentative smile. They had not spoken since their last argument.

She nodded, smiling politely at the man who followed her father. "Good morning, Mr. Dupree."

He hurried forward to pick up her hand and kiss it. "You are in looks, as usual, my lady."

Her deep green silk dress with the small bustle and wide straw hat with a matching silk ribbon complemented her flawless complexion and green eyes. She'd chosen the ensemble precisely because it was so flattering. If ever she needed confidence, it was now. However, it was not Henry Dupree's admiration she wanted. She eased her hand away. "Thank you, sir. If you will excuse me, I—"

Colleen Shannon

"Do you go to the store this morning, Charlaine?" her father asked.

She didn't glance at him, afraid he'd see her new ire. Why he should deny her the truth about her own grandmother out of some peculiar fastidiousness, then push her at a man from the same background, she could not fathom. And they said women were fickle! Her only response at the moment, however, was a bland, "Yes, for a while. I've some things to attend to."

"Do you mind if I accompany you?" Dupree asked. "I have a gift to purchase. I should be very grateful for your advice."

Charlaine could hardly refuse a new customer. "Certainly."

Durwood walked them to the door. He glanced at Dupree's hired coach. The coachman stepped down to open the carriage door, but Dupree walked right past without a word, whipping open the door of Charlaine's barouche with a flourish, then getting in behind her.

They were off by the time the coachman ran into the drive after them, shaking his hat. Charlaine didn't see the man, who was obviously upset at not being paid. However, Durwood sighed and pulled out his wallet, sending a resigned look after Henry Dupree.

Inside the carriage, Charlaine drew her skirts aside from Dupree's leg. Why had he chosen to sit beside her instead of across, as was proper? The answer was, unfortunately, soon evident.

"Miss Kimball, may I be so bold as to call you Charlaine?" When she said nothing, he took one of her gloved hands, ignoring her gentle effort to draw away. "Charlaine, you must know how you affect me. You are a song on my lips, a throb in my heart, a—"

130

She jerked away, just managing to stifle her urge to snap, "And you are a pain in my . . ." But even in her thoughts she could not be so crude. "Please, Mr. Dupree—"

"Henry."

"Please, Mr. Dupree," she repeated. "I cannot encourage your, er, admiration." *Whether it be for me, or my fortune.* "I do not wish entanglements."

When he looked stricken, leaning back, she said hastily, "But I shall be happy to help you select a gift. May I ask for whom it is?"

His high cheekbones were dull red, but his voice was steady. "My mother."

"And do you have a price in mind?"

He named a figure that surprised her. She would not have thought a clerk, even one who served one of England's wealthiest men, could afford such largesse. "I see. Well, for that sum, you should be able to acquire something very nice indeed. What do you want to buy?"

"A ring."

Charlaine tapped a gloved fingertip against her chin, mentally reviewing their latest acquisitions. She did not notice Dupree's clenched hands, which he hid next to him on the seat, or his wandering eyes.

She smiled as they drew to a halt in front of the store. "I have an exquisite Kashmir sapphire we just set very simply, so one notices the unusual clarity of the blue. It should be pleasing to an older lady." As the coachman opened the door and put down the steps, she scooted over to descend again unaware of Dupree's dark gaze.

An even more basic emotion flickered in his eyes as he watched her hips sway when she descended, but by the time he exited to hold the mahogany door open

131

for her, his expression was benign. "After you, my lady."

Charlaine swept inside, going straight to the jewelry case that held the sapphires. She took the key from a hovering clerk and opened the case, pulling out the small velvet box and handing it to Dupree. "What do you think?"

He pulled the ring out and turned it toward the light. When the clerk offered a loupe, he held it to his eye and focused in on the ring with a practiced air.

This, too, surprised Charlaine. Perhaps he came from a wealthy family. If so, why was he working as a clerk?

He set the loupe on the counter and handed the ring back. "Do you like it yourself?"

"I think it's lovely."

"I shall take it, then. Will you accept my bank draft?"

"Certainly."

While he dealt with the delicate matter of payment, she herself wrapped the little box in their best paper. What a devoted son. She felt a stab of melancholy that she would never bear such loyal progeny, but she quelled it.

Her course might not be the easiest, or even the best, but it was one she had set for herself and would never waver from.

At that propitious moment, Devlin Rhodes swept into the store. She felt him before she saw him. The very air seemed to take on a different quality, growing heavier, sweeter, like the aroma of fine wine.

Her fingers fumbled as she tied the gay ribbon. She watched the female clerks simper as he walked into the store like the man he was: confident, handsome and aware of both. He apparently did not see her in the corner, for he went straight to the counter where they'd set the rose diamonds on tiny stands.

They glittered, unset diamonds of the first water.

"May I see them?" she heard him ask the clerk.

The male clerk eyed him suspiciously. He looked toward Charlaine.

She handed the package to the person taking Henry's bank draft and walked toward Devlin. She did not see Henry's expression as he watched her approach Devlin.

Her competitor's eyes lit up in welcome. "Ah, so you did keep our bargain."

She scowled at him. "A bargain with the devil hardly has to be honored. I am here because I choose to be." She bit her tongue under the curious gaze of the male clerk. Why did this damned frog always rile her so easily?

For her ears alone, he leaned over to whisper, "I do tend to sprout horns whenever I look at you."

She stared at him blankly, wondering what had incited that wicked grin.

He turned back to the ogling clerk. "I promise not to steal the diamonds if you let me look at them."

Under the clerk's inquiring glance, Charlaine nodded shortly. The man pulled them out, giving Devlin an admonishing look. He apparently recognized their rival and did not trust him.

Charlaine made a mental note to give the perspicacious fellow a raise.

Reverently Devlin laid the jewels out on a black velvet square. Taking a tiny instrument from his pocket, he measured their size and drew a sketch of their shape on a piece of paper.

Charlaine jumped when a smooth voice said behind her, "Somehow you look quite adept fondling something that is not yours."

Devlin straightened slowly to face Henry Dupree. "An attribute you obviously share." Devlin glanced at

Colleen Shannon

Charlaine before adding, "Perhaps you get it from your master."

Henry frowned. "No man is my master."

These men and their petty squabbles! Charlaine said, "Gentlemen, I—"

They both ignored her.

"This lady deserves better than to be importuned by a . . . a . . ." Words scathing enough apparently failed Henry.

"Scoundrel?" Devlin suggested silkily.

"That and more."

"Your own intentions are the best, of course."

"Yes." Devlin snatched the box from Henry's clenched fist, turning the distinctive shape over in his hands. "And this? It's obviously a ring. Let me guess. You had her help select it, but said nothing about intending to offer it to her—along with your eager heart and loyal hand."

His high cheekbones taking on an unattractive red, Henry took a threatening step forward.

People were staring. Charlaine stepped between the two men, snatched the ring from Devlin and handed it back to Henry. "Please, sir, don't let this . . . this"— under Devlin's challenging glare, she continued— "scoundrel, as he himself admits, embarrass you. I am certain that your mother will wear this for the rest of her . . ." She trailed off as something in Henry's expression alerted her. Could Devlin be right? Surely Henry had not tricked her into selecting a ring, hoping she would wed him?

Why, she hardly knew the fellow. She was so flustered that Devlin's actions took a moment to register.

Plucking the bill from Henry's jacket pocket, Devlin rudely appraised it. He whistled, handing it back to Henry with a mocking bow. "My compliments. Clerking must pay better than I thought."

134

Charlaine gawked at him in disbelief. Not even his upbringing could excuse such bold and uncivilized behavior.

Apparently Henry agreed with her. He stuffed the bill into his inside jacket pocket this time, his face beet red now. "Kindly come with me outside so we can settle this as men should."

Devlin looked from Henry to Charlaine and back. A strange smile stretched that handsome face. "A challenge, is it? Lady Charlaine can tell you how I react to them."

It was Charlaine's turn to blush under Henry's suspicious gaze. Turning a haughty shoulder to both of them, she said, "Please, both of you, be about your men's sport. I wish you the joy of bloodied noses and broken knuckles." And she marched into her office, slamming the door behind her.

All was quiet in the store. She knew because, despite herself, she stood with her ear to the door, listening for an altercation. Nothing but a quiet murmur, then the sound of the huge exterior door opening and closing, equally quietly.

His footsteps were so silent that the door shoved her off balance before she realized it was opening. Devlin came into the room in time to catch her hand and save her backside from the carpet. He grinned, but stifled it when she ground her teeth together. Solemnly, courteously, he seated her in the chair behind the desk.

Then, with a graceful flip of his formal tailed coat, he sat down opposite her and pulled a black pouch from his pocket. "Now, as to why I've come, what do you think of this?" He set the pouch on the desk and started to open it.

She tried, she really did, but finally she had to burst out, "Well? What happened?"

He blinked at her. "To what do you refer?"

"To Henry, of course." *You dolt,* her tone said.

He shrugged. "Nothing of consequence. Now, about the necklace . . ."

Her suspicion that he was goading her turned into certainty. "If you think to humble me into asking you again, you mistake the matter. Do not slam the door on the way out."

He *tsk*ed with his tongue. "My, what a temper you have. You flounced off in such a hurry that I assumed you were uninterested in whether we, ah, now how did you put that so charmingly?" He snapped his fingers. "You wished us joy of broken noses and bloodied knuckles."

"That rankled, did it?" She leaned back in her chair with satisfaction. "Good. If you act like a brute, I shall treat you like one."

He was dangerously still. Then, in two seconds flat, he was beside her and hauling her out of the chair into his arms. "And if you act like a hellcat, I shall treat you like a hellcat." Lightly he patted her rear. "Pity I can't bear to see my property marked."

She shoved him away. Or tried to. "How dare you! I belong to no man, nor ever shall."

Those mesmerizing lips came closer until they filled her world. Her own mouth tingled with her need to feel their contact again. Damn him, why did he make her so weak? Her struggles slacked off, then ceased as every nerve tingled to his seductive whisper.

"Belong you shall. To me. Body and soul. As I will belong to you. Not because I make you, or even seduce you. But because you will one day see that I am your best, indeed, your only chance for happiness." He planted a gentle kiss on the side of her neck, then released her.

Her knees failed and she sank back into her chair.

Her heart thudded so hard against her ribs that she had to force herself to listen to him.

Only his dilated pupils gave evidence of her own effect on him. "As to the altercation with Henry, why, we ended it as gentlemen should. I apologized to him for my boorish behavior. He snarled at me and stomped off."

When she heaved a sigh of relief, he added, "I could not embarrass you in your own store, you see. But a word of warning. Henry Dupree is not to be trusted. He stops at nothing to get what he wants." He smiled wryly. "Cecil must have recognized in him a kindred soul. However, stubborn as he is, my cousin is an honorable man. I doubt that of Henry Dupree."

"A family trait, it would seem."

Devlin cocked his head in that charming, inquisitive manner that always reminded her of his French heritage. "The honor or the determination?"

Charlaine was tempted to goad him by referring to the latter, but she had to admit, "Both. At least I can say that unreservedly once I get my property back."

He nodded gravely. "Understood." But he did not offer to return the manuscript. "Now, do you wish to see the sample design of the necklace?"

"I have already seen the sketch."

"This is not a sketch." Like a magician, he pulled a thing of life and beauty out of the velvet pouch.

Devlin had used piano wire and wax molds for his preliminary creation. Even the coarse setting could not disguise the exquisite beauty of the design. Charlaine could not hold back a gasp, despite her growing fears of this necklace.

The central stone was perfectly balanced by the smaller ones, following the heart-shaped curvature of what would be solid gold. The huge middle diamond was set at the apex of the peak on a spring that made it shift with every movement. The smaller rose diamonds were set at intervals along each curve, and smaller round white diamonds of perfect clarity and color had been set between each. Two square-cut diamonds were set on the springs with each of the smaller diamonds, but the ones in each interval were flat. The overall effect was one of exquisite beauty.

Charlaine was both drawn by the necklace and repelled by it. She instinctively realized that he intended her to wear this design, and that his professed hope that they could win the competition was false. He was molding this symbol of love for her, and her alone.

And what that said of his true feelings made her even more uncomfortable. Part of her wished to consign his creation to the trash heap. An even stronger part made her long to wear it.

"It is lovely," she said in a colorless fashion. "I can add nothing to it."

"May I have the stones to finish the design, then?"

"Certainly." Relieved, she opened the door and went back among the lights, the people—and safety.

From him, or from her own feelings? Feverishly she went to the clerk and had him make out a receipt—on loan—for the unusual rose diamonds.

He pocketed the receipt. "Thank you, *chère*."

She blushed as that same suspicious male clerk gasped. "Ah, now if you'll excuse me, I have pressing business." She hurried across to appraise the huge floral centerpiece they'd set up on the table where they invited guests to sign in. She fiddled with the flowers until the room took on proper proportions again. By that, she knew he was gone.

But not forgotten, damn him.

Devlin's spirits were lighter as he strolled back toward his own store. He was making definite progress.

If she only knew how much she reminded him of his creation. Come hither, go away. Tempting, but set firmly in her own way.

He smiled to himself. And he certainly had designs on her . . . his smile faded as he shoved open his shop door.

He'd recognize that rigid back and bowler hat anywhere. Lewis Temple turned from appraising the estate jewels in one of Devlin's cases. His dark scowl turned even blacker. Without a word, he turned back to his perusal.

Looking for stolen goods, no doubt. *And good luck to you.* Devlin intended to stalk past him without a word, but the gibe slipped out of its own accord. "A bit above your class, isn't it, Temple, old chap?"

Temple turned. "We all want things above our station. Some more than others." He drawled the last comment.

The man was a bit too complacent as he awaited Devlin's reaction to the insult. Devlin bit back an even nastier response, since goading him was obviously Temple's goal. Instead Devlin offered his banal proprietor's invitation. "If you see anything you like, we shall be glad to assist you."

"Do you have receipts for all this stuff?" Temple asked abruptly when it was obvious Devlin was about to turn away.

"That is none of your concern."

"Oh, but it is. And I can make it Scotland Yard's concern as well."

Devlin leaned back against a case, crossing his ankles casually. Charlaine would have stiffened at the pose. "Are you threatening me?"

"Not at all. Unless you have something to hide, of course."

Devlin tapped his fingers against the glass top to the

case, but finally he decided that, in this case, prudence was the better part of valor. Neither his ambitions nor his courtship would be served by continuous surveillance by this man and his ilk. Better to set their suspicions at rest, no matter how it might gall him.

Striding to a locked cabinet in his office, he opened it and pulled out a bulging file marked ESTATE JEWELRY PURCHASES.

Returning to the store, he slapped the file down before Temple. "Enjoy yourself."

He smiled sweetly as Mordecai bustled in, his arms laden with packages. "Hello, Mordecai. Would you assist Mr. Temple in matching the receipts to the estate jewelry? We should certainly not want any of our records to go missing."

Mordecai dropped his bundles in a chair, wiped his brow and nodded glumly. He pulled his keys out of his pocket to open the case.

Devlin returned to the office to work with the necklace, confident that Mordecai would keep his usual eagle eye on the predator loose in their nest.

Still, as he worked, the thought occurred to Devlin—why did this man take such a personal interest in seeing him humiliated at best, jailed at worst? To Devlin's knowledge, he'd never met the fellow. He'd known only one other Temple in his life, and that had been in his teens, shortly after he went to work for Mordecai. Sally Temple had been a lovely young girl with an unfortunate addiction to opium. She had also initiated Devlin into the rites of love from her greater experience of one year. However, she had been the kept woman of the owner of an opium den and saloon. Despite her feelings for Devlin, and his attempts to help her, the addiction had been too strong for her. Shortly after he went to Africa, Mordecai had written that she'd been killed crossing the street.

He'd grieved his first inamorata as every young man did, but he'd been too ambitious and too tired to mourn her long. In fact, he'd not thought of her in years.

Could Temple be related to her? But how? The man was too young to be Sally's father and too old to be her brother. Besides, they looked nothing alike.

No, Temple must have something else against him. It would be interesting to find out what. Unconcerned, Devlin went back to work.

However, in the shop, Mordecai's gray eyes had deepened to worried slate as he watched how doggedly, how efficiently, Temple slogged through every receipt. Occasionally the investigator made notes to himself in his little book.

The day was long and night was approaching before he left. He nodded shortly. "Thank you for your assistance, Mr. Levitz."

Mordecai locked the door behind Temple and the last exiting clerk.

Then, his expression grim, he sought his young partner.

"Devlin, are you certain that you got rid of all the merchandise from your last, er, expedition?'

"Hmmm?" Devlin's steady hand didn't shake as he carefully set one of the stones Charlaine had given him in place with tiny tweezers.

Mordecai slammed the door.

Devlin started and dropped the stone. It rolled across the desk to the floor. He bent to pick it up and go back to work, took a good look at Mordecai and paused. "What's the matter with you?"

"That man is intelligent, determined and absolutely obsessed with finding something in your past, or present, that will get you jailed. Have you not wondered who hired him?"

Colleen Shannon

Devlin shrugged. "Cecil, most likely."

"And that does not give you concern?"

"I've done nothing wrong. Not for years, anyway."

Mordecai shook his head in despair. "And robbing Charlaine Kimball is not wrong?"

"You know I gave everything back."

"With one exception."

"That will be hers, too. On the day she weds me. Besides, neither she nor her father will ever press charges against me." Devlin picked up the tweezers again. "Let Temple look. Poor fellow obviously needs occupation."

Mordecai watched as Devlin grew engrossed in his creation again. But as shadows danced on the wall in the gaslight, he twiddled with his skullcap nervously.

Abruptly he rose. "I shall be out this evening. Do not wait up."

Devlin nodded vaguely.

Outside, Mordecai hired a cab. "Take me to the Duchess of Kensington's." Lizzie would help him with her own little investigation. She had sources that would make Cecil Rhodes blush. Since Devlin was so blithely unconcerned, it would be up to the two of them to discover who Temple was, why he hated Devlin, and who had hired him.

Then, and only then, could they take the proper defense.

This time Devlin's calm assurance would play him false. Doubtless he'd still wear that bold grin as they marched him off to jail.

But not while there was breath in Mordecai Levitz.

Chapter Six

Mordecai approached the imposing portico of the largest house in Grosvenor Square. Once, in his youth, he would have been intimidated by the ornate pillasters, the exquisite wrought-iron balconies and the massive front door with an unusual dragon-head knocker.

However, he knew Lizzie had wed often and well, prospering by sheer force of will and personality, as he had. One thing he had learned in life: a short Jewish diamond dealer and a blue-blooded aging duchess could, and did, wear the same natures in different skins. They sought one another's company because they had much in common and they pleased each other. It was as simple as that.

The rest of the world did not feel the same, a fact vividly brought home to him as the heavy door swung inward. The toplofty butler stared down his long, thin nose from his long, thin height. Mordecai gave as good

143

as he got. "Kindly tell the duchess that Mordecai Levitz wishes to see her."

Reluctantly the butler opened the door just wide enough for Mordecai to squeeze through. Mordecai gave the gap a dismissive glance, crossed his arms, and waited. The butler inched open the door.

Mordecai didn't budge.

The door opened a bit more; then finally the man, with a disgusted snort, pulled it wide. Mordecai strode in as if he trailed ermine cloak behind.

"I will see if Her Grace is in," the butler said, his tone dripping icicles as it echoed off the three-story foyer and massive curved marble staircase. With measured tread, he climbed the stairs.

Rudely left standing in the hall, Mordecai quelled the urge to twiddle with his skullcap. He debated barging into the adjacent salon, where Lizzie had entertained him many times, but he was too polite to repay rudeness with rudeness.

A door slammed above; then came a familiar, irascible voice. "You old snob, I've told you before that Mr. Levitz is to be admitted at any time, day or night. One more insubordination, and I swear I will relegate you to the kitchens."

The duchess hurried down the stairs, graceful and swift as a woman half her age. But she squinted, her nearsighted gaze sweeping the hall, and apparently didn't see his dark suit against the deep mahogany door. She turned toward the salon.

"I'm here, Lizzie," Mordecai said.

She stopped and swung back toward him, sending a fulminating glance up the steps. "He did not even have the courtesy to let you wait in the salon?" She took his arm and guided him into her elegant salon.

"I have not quite figured out if it's my nationality or my religion he detests more."

She sat next to him on a tapestry-backed settee. "Both, my dear friend. I would turn him out without a reference if he had not served my late husband's family since they were both in short coats."

Mordecai patted her agitated hand as she tapped the settee arm. "Never mind, Lizzie. I am not unfamiliar with such behavior, even in America. It speaks more ill of him than it does of me." But his color was still a bit heightened, and this close, she could see it clearly.

She curled her fingers into his in sympathy. "And England." She sighed. "Prejudice may become a dull sword after a while, but it still cuts."

Mordecai shrugged. "We have more important things to discuss. Lizzie, I need your help."

Her fingers squeezed tighter. "I confess I never thought I'd hear those words from you." She leaned close to whisper in his ear, "Though even better would be, 'Lizzie, I need you.' "

His color deepened. "Yes, well, it is not for me that I ask this. It is for Devlin." Quickly Mordecai explained about the Pinkerton man, and how he seemed determined to catch Devlin in some illegal act. "I do believe he bears a grudge against Devlin, though why and how, I cannot divine."

Lizzie frowned thoughtfully. "Are you certain Devlin has not been up to his old tricks?"

"He swears he will never steal again."

"Hmm, well, in my experience a tiger may change its stripes, but only when it turns into a house cat. And Devlin Rhodes will never be content sitting at any woman's feet. Even my lovely adopted niece will not succeed in taming him, though she secretly hopes to."

"Does she? I confess I have not figured her out yet. She seems torn between pushing Devlin away and holding him close."

With a droll rolling of her eyes, Lizzie said, "A trait

145

she shares with many of her gender, poor child. She has not figured out herself what she wants. Yet."

A smile played about Mordecai's stern mouth. Only now, softened by humor and warmth, could one see how sensual his prim little mouth truly was. "Unlike the lady present. To say you are direct is . . ." He trailed off with a delicate cough.

Lizzie's hand wandered to his knee. "Mincing words? Putting too fine a point upon the matter? Come now, Mordecai, admit it. That is precisely why you find me so fascinating."

Mordecai sent an uneasy look at the open door and moved away a proper two feet down the settee. "Now, Lizzie, you know this is not the time."

Lizzie scooted closer. "Nonsense. At our age, every moment is the time. If we so wish it."

He was so uncomfortable that she desisted with a sigh. "Oh, very well. I shall wait for our next little rendezvous. But I tell you plainly, Mordecai Levitz, you make me feel alive again, as nothing has for a very long time, and I do not intend to let you get away. For now, I shall allow you to evade plans for our future and live in the moment, at least until we get our exasperating young people settled. If you insist?" She put a question mark on her last comment, along with a suggestive squeeze of his knee. When his breathing quickened, but he stared rigidly at the wall, she sighed and desisted.

Lizzie rose to her full, imposing height and crossed to the bell rope, tugging it firmly. "Coffee and sandwiches," she said to the mobcapped maid who entered. Then, shoving the silver cigar box, ornate lighter and inkwell to the side of the large writing desk in a corner, she pulled up a chair next to the other one. "Sit. We shall strategize."

Rising, Mordecai stepped gingerly toward the desk,

146

hoping his long coat hid her effect upon him. At the moment, he only hoped he had done the right thing, turning her loose upon Devlin's problems. Once Lizzie got the bit between her teeth, nothing stopped her until she had run her race, first over the finish line. Luckily, she was busily writing down a list of people she intended to contact, so she didn't see the look in his eyes.

Blindly, he stared at her list, lecturing himself. This was but a pleasant interlude. Why, anything lasting between them was impossible. He was a Jew from New York; she was a duchess from London. Anything more than a brief intimacy was . . .

Inappropriate.

Impossible.

Heavenly.

He gripped the desk—and his control—firmly. He was too old to act like a moonstruck calf. The business at hand was more important.

Nothing more remained to be said.

Still, as he sat next to her, took in the heat of her body and the subtle scent of her perfume, a great deal remained to be felt.

Up, down and around the study Charlaine strode. "I am sick and tired of the heat and congestion. Whether you think it appropriate or not, I am leaving for Monte Carlo within the week. I shall stay for the summer."

"But you will miss the jubilee and the jewelry exhibition," her father protested. "You know Her Majesty will be offended if you are not there."

"She will be too busy even to notice."

Durwood scowled his disagreement. "She notices everything; you know that."

"Then I will make every effort to return in time for the coronation, but afterward I shall leave again."

Durwood walked around her until he could see her face. "Running, child? That is not like you."

Her head reared back in affront. "Hardly. But I am heartily sick of unwanted suitors vying for my hand."

"Do you want me to tell Cecil to send Henry away on business?"

She shook her head. "No. I would not get him in trouble with his employer. After the summer, he will be infatuated with someone else, in the male way."

An ineffable sadness chased the calculation out of Durwood's deep blue eyes. "Poor child, have I been such a terrible father as to make you think all men are unreliable?"

Charlaine played with the letter opener on the desk, but she owed him the dignity of a response, so she shoved it away and stood tall to face him. "No, quite to the contrary. To my knowledge, you have never shown more than a passing interest in any woman other than Mother."

"Indeed. But I have too often let business take me away from time I should have spent with you."

She shrugged. "To my ultimate benefit. Few of my gender are so lucky as to help run a family business, much less own property."

"But at what price?"

She thought about pretending obtuseness, but his next words cut her to the quick.

"What if Devlin Rhodes tires of your rejections and returns to America?"

She whirled and went to the window to pull up the shade so he couldn't see her expression. Pain pierced her at the thought of never seeing Devlin again, but the cool, logical mind she'd inherited from her father warned that it would be best for both of them.

That soft voice would not be denied, any more than the pangs in her heart.

"Charlaine, I am certain your great-great-grandmama Callista Raleigh would not have wished her legacy on you had she known you would deny your own destiny—"

"Do not speak to me of my ancestors in that lecturing manner, when you have kept the truth of my own heritage from me."

Durwood sighed. "Elizabeth told you about my mother, didn't she?"

"Yes."

He spread his hands. "I merely wanted to protect you from the gossips. They never approved of Chantal. Not that my father cared a whit. But, in a way, I am glad that you know you have a great deal in common with Devlin, right down to your heritage."

"That cannot change my feelings."

"You mean your fears. If only I could help you see how misplaced they are." His tone grew softer and more tender than she had ever heard it. "You cannot know the sheer joy of sharing everything with your chosen mate. Your bodies, your thoughts, your dreams, your very essence with the person God has decreed for you as you create new life together."

Charlaine's hand shook as she snapped the shade back down. The glorious summer day was too bright, too tempting, and she had temptations enough to deal with. Every forbidden instinct she possessed bade her listen to her father's wise counsel. If she could only believe in Devlin Rhodes, believe her own longing to be his was not a betrayal of all she'd worked for, perhaps this panic would cease.

But the little girl who had learned to depend on servants because her mother was dead and her father was always gone had followed a different path. A path that had been lonely and long, but safe. The high walls protecting her worked both ways, however. They kept her secure, but they kept others out.

She swallowed back the traitorous tears as an image formed in her mind. With each tentative step, the walls grew shorter, until, far at the end, she saw a tall, proud figure, a man who looked more like a prince than a frog.

No, that way lay disaster. Turn back, or flee, but she could not walk to the end.

"No, Father. My mind is made up. I leave in the morning." And she walked out of the study to pack.

With an expression on his face that made him the image of his piratical ancestor, Drake Kimball, Durwood fetched his hat and cane and called imperiously for his carriage.

The two men stared grimly at one another. "Dammit, I know the cursed fellow hides a larcenous soul behind that smarmy grin," Cecil said. "You have not looked hard enough or far enough yet. Somehow I want this vermin out of my country."

Back in mine, with the other vermin, eh? But Lewis Temple held his tongue. Cecil Rhodes was not unique among his countrymen. There was no greater snob than a self-made English millionaire. "I spent most of a day comparing his estate jewelry holdings to his receipts. He could account for every one. But I'm not done with him yet. I have a tail on him at this very moment. Something will turn up."

"What I cannot understand is why Durwood Kimball cannot see through the scoundrel. He is usually quite an astute judge of character." Cecil tossed his gold-tipped pen aside in disgust.

"I believe, from what I have gleaned, that even Devlin Rhodes is better than no son-in-law at all. Apparently the girl is quite attracted to him."

"Which disappoints me as well . . ." Cecil trailed off.

Absently he picked up the pen and twirled it in his fingers. "Durwood Kimball is very sensitive to the honor of his name. If Devlin should, er, encroach on that honor, Durwood would send the dashed frog packing. Literally."

Temple's eyes narrowed. "What do you mean?"

Cecil told him.

"You want me to do *what*?" Devlin stared at Durwood Kimball.

Durwood hung his gold-headed walking cane on a chair back and sat down opposite Devlin's desk. He eyed the necklace Devlin was working on, but even the stunning design could not distract him. "I know my daughter, Devlin. If you let her run away now, she will grow such thorns and hedgerows around her feelings that you will never be able to reach her. She's fleeing precisely because you are, ah, affecting her, though a band of angels would never make her admit that."

Devlin rubbed his eyes and turned up the gas lamp above his desk. He peered at the regulator clock on the wall, and then looked surprised at the time. "I hope to spend the rest of my life getting to know your daughter, but one thing I do understand about her: coercion makes her dig in her heels."

"I do not dispute that. But I warn you that your suit will best be served by, er, daily contact with her." Durwood held Devlin's eyes, hoping his expression would say more than his words.

A flicker of surprise, then longing, flashed in Devlin's eyes before his long, thick lashes covered them. "I am flattered that you trust me that much on such short association."

Durwood smiled humorlessly. "You misunderstand the matter. It is not you I trust, but my daughter that I love. She does not know it, but when she looks at

151

you, it is her mother come to life again looking at me. If she succeeds in driving you away, she is doomed to a loneliness she has no comprehension of." Melancholy turned down the corners of Durwood's mouth as, for the fifth time that day, he missed his wife. Would that he could love another woman, but he had too much of his father's steadfast heart in him. There was only one woman for him, and he'd lost her. There was only this man for Charlaine, and by hook or by crook, he would make her see that.

"And you will never have an heir."

The astute comment made Durwood's smile genuine. "You cannot blame me for wanting to sustain the legacy that was so hard-won by so many of my ancestors."

Devlin shrugged. "It's my opinion that these generational things are overrated. I am a descendant of Marie Antoinette, but I am treated like the baseborn scoundrel that I am by most people. In America, it is not your birth that matters, but your ability."

"In that case, you are a veritable prince that I should be happy to name my son."

Devlin peered at Durwood, as if seeking sarcasm. He apparently found none, for he blushed. "Should Charlaine honor me by becoming my wife one day, I hope you will continue to see it so."

"You won't do it, then."

"It may not be blatantly apparent, but I do have my own code of honor. I will, however, follow her to Monte Carlo."

Sighing, Durwood rose. "Very well, I accede to your scruples, misplaced though they are. Now, how much longer before the necklace is complete?" And for the next half hour, they indulged in their mutual passion.

Had Devlin known Durwood better, he would not have been so relaxed. But he was too busy showing off his best design to notice the other man's calculating look.

The next morning, the train station was a hurly-burly scene of travel, that international equalizer. The English were known for three things: the quality of their tea, the inclemency of their weather and the promptness of their train schedules. From the wealthy lord in his silk top hat to the miner in his dirty clothes, each and every person had to be aboard at the appointed time or be left behind. Every ticket holder kept a wary eye on the eminence presiding over all—the huge clock ticking its inexorable tyranny.

General chaos reigned impartially over rich and poor alike. Hurrying businessmen on their way to the continent yawned as they dodged families leaving for holiday, the mothers anxious as they squired their progeny, the fathers irritable. Pickpockets plied their trade amidst preachers herding their flocks. The vast, vaulted station echoed with barking dogs trotting before their masters, and unattended children shrieking as they played ball.

Their ball bounced off the head of a fat woman in an expensive dress, sending her wide-brimmed hat askew. She glared at them as feathers molted over her broad face. "Hooligans."

Porters scurried everywhere, carrying bags to and from the train, which lay panting like a giant, exhausted beast. When its belly was full, it would take on new life, only to disgorge it again and start the process all over.

Into this mob, from different directions, came three people. The lady was stunning in an emerald green pelisse, brown kid traveling boots and dashing hussar-style hat. A close observer, however, might have noted the shadows under her eyes. A porter labored at her side under three large cases, but not even his usual wooden expression could hide his awed admiration as he watched her masterfully dodge the fray on the way to the end of the train.

A tall man in a bowler hat straightened from his position against a shadowed pillar and moved into the throng after her. He paused behind a mound of bags and swept the train platform with an eagle eye.

An even taller, more athletic man watched the lady enter the private train car, then went to the window and purchased a ticket. He joined the general queue lining up to board the train, which had started to wheeze with renewed vigor.

Lewis Temple watched Devlin climb the steps before he purchased his own ticket and became one of the last to board.

And just as the conductor started to pull up the steps, a man with a gold-headed walking cane escorted an elderly lady up to the train.

She was twittering to him, "So kind of you to pay my fare, Durwood. My daughter will be so surprised to see me."

Durwood handed her small bag to the conductor, who eyed his pocket watch, then closed it with a snap to take the bag disdainfully. "Think nothing of it, Imogen. Just remember that you promised me you would have nuncheon with Charlaine about ten this morning. I know she will be delighted to see you."

Durwood stepped back, waved and watched as the conductor pulled up the steps. The train gave a last belch, then bestirred itself. Only when the train had rounded the corner track did Durwood Kimball permit himself a smile. "Do not hate me, my darling. This is for your own good. You shall see."

As the train whistle blew a final lament, he disappeared into the mass of humanity.

*   *   *

In her private car, Charlaine yawned and said to her hovering attendant, "I am exhausted. Do I have time for a brief nap before we reach Calais?"

The maid checked the pretty silver watch pinned to her imposing bosom. It had been her last Christmas present from Durwood Kimball. "Yes, ma'am. We are due into Calais at eleven. Do you wish me to wake you?"

"Yes, at ten-thirty. You may leave until then. Please lock the door behind you."

The maid nodded and left. Charlaine did not notice that she hovered outside the car in the connecting chamber for a long time, watching through the glass. When a certain gentleman pulled a newspaper up to read it, she dodged out quickly, sat down in the closest seat and pulled her hat down over her face to nap.

Charlaine debated unpacking one of her night-gowns, but decided she was too tired even to do that. She would sleep in her shift.

Yet again this morning, during breakfast, her father had tried to dissuade her from leaving. She'd been too tired to argue, but she had left without eating, which only contributed to her tiredness now. She'd scarcely slept a wink, a fact her father had obviously noted, and she was in no mood for his machinations.

The bleak cloud that had settled on her was not scattered by her exhaustion. Even as she pulled a scented sheet over her shoulders and lay back in her comfortable feather bed, the image that had haunted her for days on end lurked behind her closed eyes.

Sensuous lips filled her vision, smiling at her, kissing her, loving her. No matter how she tried to tell herself that she didn't want him, she didn't want his kisses, the part that had kept her pacing the floor most nights knew she lied.

Which was precisely why she was here. Once she had some distance from him, she would own herself again.

She told herself that to the rhythm of the rails until she finally fell asleep.

In the adjacent train car, Lewis Temple watched Devlin Rhodes fold up his paper and then check his pocket watch for the third time. He checked his own. Nine-thirty on the dot. Temple hunched down in his seat as, rising, Devlin looked around the car. When Devlin went to the door between the last two cars, Lewis peered after him, easing closer so he could see into the small glassed anteroom. To his astonishment, Devlin pulled out a key and unlocked the last private train car, entering quickly.

Lewis plopped back down in his seat, thinking feverishly. Then he noted that an elderly lady had watched with equal interest as Devlin exited. Almost as if she knew Devlin, or the owner of the private car. Lewis sat down next to her in the empy seat and tipped his hat. "Morning, ma'am."

Inside the private car, Devlin paused. He wasn't certain why, but he felt vaguely uneasy. Durwood had assured him that Charlaine had agreed to have a late breakfast with him.

"Just go on in," Durwood had told him. "She and her maid may not hear you, what with all the rattling of the rails and such."

Devlin had frowned. "Are you sure this is proper?"

"Her maid has been with us since Charlaine was a baby. She is an adequate chaperon."

Surely Durwood knew etiquette better than he did, Devlin had decided. Besides, they'd know no one on the train. For all the passengers knew, they were married, and most would think nothing of him entering her private car.

Yet now, as he looked about the opulent little moving home, his heart began to thud at his ribs. How easy it would be to send the maid away on a long errand and do as Durwood bade. He knew Charlaine would not resist him long.

He also knew she would hate him afterward, almost as much as he would hate himself.

Devlin took a deep breath. "Charlaine, excuse me, but I'm here for our breakfast."

No response. Only the rattling rails, marking time and distance.

Time's awastin', they seemed to say. Devlin took several tentative steps forward and knocked on the thick door in the rear wall that divided the small car. "Charlaine, I have your key."

Nothing. Devlin knocked harder on the door. It swung inward. He peeked inside. His breath left his lungs in a whoosh, just as it had on that night that was only a few weeks ago, but seemed like years.

As she had then, she slept on her side. One lovely limb poked out of the covers, bare to the frilled end of her knickers, which came just below her knee. Her batiste shift had come untied as she slept, and her breasts were bare almost to the aureole, pressing together in a luscious display that scattered every thought from his head.

A niggling little voice tried to warn him that something was amiss. The maid had disappeared somehow without his seeing her, he conveniently had the key—too conveniently—and Charlaine was obviously not expecting him for breakfast as Durwood had claimed.

All these things he could recall clearly later.

Later is just another word for regret, his baser instincts trumpeted over the still, small voice. *Live in the moment, as you always have.*

For so long he had wanted her. He could not remember a time now when he had not awakened every morning hard for her and gone to sleep every night thinking of her. No woman had ever affected him this way. He tossed his coat over the end of the bed and sat down beside her. He traced a fingertip over the arching eyebrows, down the perfect nose to that mouth that was more sensual than she knew. He had to bite his lip against the desire to kiss her as they both wanted—and needed—but a vow was a vow.

However, no power on earth could have kept him from touching her. His fingertip wandered from her mouth, down the lovely arch of her neck, to the deep vee and lower. His breathing quickened at the feel of that voluptuous, silken skin. Sleepily, she swatted at his hand, as if thinking an insect tormented her. Her hand touched his, wrapped around it. Her eyes fluttered open.

Proof that she was indeed deeply attracted to him was apparent in her own soft intake of breath and in her unguarded expression. Joy glowed at him for the barest, heady moment. "Devlin," she whispered. Her hand tugged his, pulling him close.

It was obvious that she was still half-asleep, wondering if she were dreaming. It was equally obvious that she meant to kiss him. God, how he longed to show her yet again the sweet forgetfulness of kisses. But determination was stronger.

Not yet. Not yet. Holding her luminous gaze, he leaned closer, closer. Their lips were a whisper of hope away when he turned his head slightly and kissed her earlobe. Her sweet scents, of lilacs and woman, made his head swim. He suckled her ear, smiling into it when her heart leaped against his breast. Slowly, tenderly, he cupped a breast. Blood surged to his already aching loins as she cupped her hand over his to encourage his exploration. Her firm flesh overflowed his hand, offering a bounty that made him ravenous.

Just one kiss? His lips trailed over her cheek, hovered above her mouth. He stared at it, ripe for his picking. A trembling fingertip traced its seductive contours. She kissed his finger. "Ah, *chérie*, you shake my resolve as no one ever has," he whispered. "Tell me that you love me, that you will be mine, and I will kiss you into tomorrow."

The glazed green eyes blinked, then focused on his. She tried to turn away.

Idiot. Before she could barricade herself again, he turned her fully into his arms. Murmuring endearments, he scattered kisses from her eyelids, down the bridge of her nose, down her pointed chin, tracing the graceful curves of her neck, and downward.

Gradually her stiffness eased. He buried his hungry lips in the deep vee above her excuse for a bodice. The soft batiste slipped further. A breath, a sigh, a dream, and it would fall.

He took a deep breath; she sighed. And if they both dreamed forbidden things, neither would admit it. Not yet. The moment was enough, for with the bodice went their last resistance.

He drew back to eat her with his eyes. She blushed to match the red velvet curtains, but she did not try to cover herself.

"*Incroyable*," he said on a breath. Gently, reverently, he clasped a perfect globe, learning its weight and exquisite texture. "It is fitting that you work among precious, beautiful things. You are ivory"—he ran his lips around the perimeter of her breast—"and rubies." He sweetly, gently, kissed her nipple. But when she hardened against his lips, he groaned, arched her over his arm, and suckled.

159

The small mantel clock in the adjacent sitting area struck ten, but neither of them noticed. Nor did they hear the light rap against the door, much less the twin footsteps approaching.

Their thundering hearts were the only sounds they heard, the touch of lips to skin all they felt. A closer rap sounded against the bedchamber door.

"Charlaine, my dear, I am here for our nuncheon," twittered an elderly female voice.

Too late they heard; too late they moved.

The two inquisitive gazes took in the scene for exactly what it was: an aroused man making love to an equally aroused woman. The sexual flush left Charlaine's face in a rush, leaving her ghostly pale. Devlin's healthy tan took on a greenish hue, but even in his distress, he leaned over Charlaine, hiding her bare flesh until he could pull the sheet up.

Imogen Harrigan, the worst gossip in the realm, stood in the open doorway with her mouth agape. Next to her stood Lewis Temple.

Devlin set Charlaine against the covers and eased the sheet over her bare torso, but he was too late. Slowly he turned. He rose to face the woman. He did not know her. But the man—the man he knew all too well.

Triumph gleamed in Lewis Temple's eyes. "Are you all right, Lady Kimball?" he asked solicitously.

Charlaine swallowed, clenched her fists about the sheet and answered with admirable aplomb. "Quite. As well as I can be expected to be after suffering such a rude invasion of my privacy."

Imogen stiffened. "How dare you! Why, I was inv—"

Devlin swept her a deep bow. "Hush, Charlaine, this charming lady could not know we were, er, engrossed when she decided to pay her respects." Pointedly, after the one darkling glance, he neither spoke to nor looked at Lewis Temple. "Do I have the honor of knowing your name, ma'am?"

Imogen relaxed slightly, but there was an avid slant to her narrow mouth that spoke the same volumes she would shortly spout. "Imogen Harrigan."

He kissed her hand. "Devlin Rhodes." Then, finally, he looked at Lewis Temple as he said softly, "And I believe you both know my bride, Charlaine Kimball, do you not?"

Three gasps sounded in the little chamber, but the one from the bed was loudest. Devlin arrowed a warning glance over his shoulder at Charlaine before the protest obviously trembling on her tongue could fall.

Lewis sniffed. "A likely story."

"By special license. Only yesterday. If you contact Mr. Kimball, I am certain he will confirm our story."

Imogen blinked, her short, thick lashes fluttering her disappointment. "May I be one of the first to congratulate you?"

"You may." Devlin made a show of sitting back down beside his "bride" to take her hand and kiss it. "Now please excuse us." When her nails bit into his hand, only he knew it. He managed not to wince.

Imogen reluctantly backed out, but, as usual, it was Lewis Temple who had the last word. He spoke so the woman in the next room could not hear, but the venom of his words was no less potent for their softness. "This is a bald-faced lie, which I will shortly prove. You will be hounded out of England by this scandal, you unregenerate scoundrel. No one will buy your jewels or accept you into their homes before I am done with you." Temple stomped out, slamming the chamber door.

Devlin did not relax his pose until the outer door also slammed.

Charlaine jerked her hand away. "I never thought

161

to find myself in agreement with such an arrogant man. But he's right. You are an unregenerate scoundrel to do this to me."

The hair rose on the back of Devlin's neck. She did not scream; she did not even rise in high dudgeon. She merely lay like a queen against the covers and whispered, "You will be sorry you did this to me." And she turned her face away, but her icy pose was almost spoiled by the trembling of that luscious mouth.

A thousand excuses Devlin could have offered, none of which she would believe save the most damaging one, which was the truth. He opened his mouth, but the words would not come.

Better she think him duplicitous than know the truth. It would only feed the fire of her conflict with her father. Besides, he had suspected Durwood was planning something, but he had listened to the lower half of his body rather than the upper. And, as his devout Catholic mother had so often told him, if one practiced the deadly sins, eventually one had to pay.

However, he had one saving grace: the emotions Charlaine inspired in him were incited by much more than lust, but that was a truth she was not ready to hear, and he was certainly not ready to speak. He stood. "Perhaps we will both be sorry. But not today. Today there is too much to do. Like it or not, you must wed me."

She shook her head weakly. "No. Perhaps she won't say anything . . ." But she trailed off, and it was apparent she did not believe her words either.

"Indeed. Even in the unlikely event she stays silent, Lewis Temple will not care if he wrecks your reputation along with my own. We have no time to waste." As if cued, the train blew its whistle and began to slow. Devlin raised the shade to see the outskirts of Calais. "I will make arrangements to have us taken back to

London." He turned to leave, but with his hand on the knob he said almost inaudibly, "I will be good to you, Charlaine. I swear it." His footsteps retreated.

Only when the outer door had closed behind him did the sound of soft sobs echo through the rail car.

By the time London finally peeked over the horizon, Charlaine found it hard to believe that it was only noon. The sun shone between the clouds, the wild-flowers nodded and the birds sang. It was as if the whole world celebrated her misery.

He had trapped her, good and proper. For an unguarded instant of, of . . . what was it he made her feel when he kissed her breast? she asked herself. Lust, sheer and simple.

But as she peeped at her fiancé's handsome profile outlined against the carriage window, she knew her feelings for him could never be described as simple. Still, for that brief pleasure, whatever its source, she would pay with the rest of her life. She had no illusions about her world or his place in it. She had to wed him or be shunned. She might as well flee England for parts unknown, but even there, somehow the scandal would follow her.

As for Devlin, he would take to his new position in society, like, well, like a frog to water. With her ruin came his triumph.

For that, she would never forgive him.

Durwood scowled at Devlin. "You did what? How could you, young man?" But as Charlaine stared out the study window, he dropped a wink to take the sting out of his words.

Devlin glared coldly back. He bit his tongue over a retort, for this man's damned Machiavellian nature had made his task doubly hard. The walls around the

163

Ice Princess had been crumbling, but this humiliation and coercion would make them so high that he might never scale them.

"Can you arrange it or not?" Devlin demanded. "Even if we can get a special license for today, Temple will investigate. What do we do about the date?"

"Leave that to me. Not that I'm happy about it, you understand."

From the window, Charlaine said, "Oh, please, Father, spare me the act. You are tickled pink, and we both know it. I honestly believe you care not who does the deed. As long as I bear your heir, your legacy is assured. But I may have something to say to this."

Uh-oh. Devlin held his breath as she turned. Save for a whiteness about her mouth, she was calm.

Icy calm.

Her tone was mild. At first. "Sometimes I wonder how men and women inhabit the same earth, much less propagate it together." She glanced between the two men as if she found each of them equal—equally lacking.

"Never have I wanted solitude more, nor deserved it less. I have no one to blame for this imbroglio but myself."

Devlin frowned. What on earth was she talking about? All too soon he understood.

She continued, "The first day you set foot in my hallway, Devlin Rhodes, I should have fled for parts unknown. I should have realized my father would become your ally because you are two of a kind. To wit, selfish, arrogant and uncaring of whom you hurt as long as you get your way. Know this: Today, if I speak the vows you both want to hear me say so very much, it will be the last time either of you get your way with me."

Warily Durwood approached his daughter, his arms

up to embrace her. "Child, I know you are upset, but truly I have y—"

She sidestepped him neatly. "If you tell me you have my best interests at heart, I will hit you, Father." Her composure cracked a little.

The torment in her lovely eyes, hidden behind the sheen of ice, almost made Devlin leave her to her doubtful peace. Almost. But that deep instinct he always trusted told him that there would not be peace, or happiness, for either of them unless they found both together.

"Then speak your mind, my dear daughter." Durwood was obviously losing patience. "As if you need encouragement."

Charlaine did not dignify his sarcasm with even a glance. "I will wed this man on two conditions."

Devlin braced himself.

"One, he signs papers eliminating himself as heir to either my property or my fortune."

"That is grossly unfair! Why—" Durwood interjected, but she cut him off.

"And two, he will not consummate our marriage unless, and until, I give him leave."

Durwood's eyes bugged out. Speechless, he stared at his son-in-law-to-be.

The first condition didn't bother Devlin; the second concerned him vastly. Slowly he approached her. She did not stiffen, or try to pull away as he took her hand. It remained limply in his. For her ears alone, he whispered, "Is it me you fear, *chère*? Or yourself?"

Her proud head did not bow an inch. She might have been stone deaf for all the heed she gave his seductive whisper as he continued, "Deny me pleasure and you deny yourself. Surely you want to get something out of this union you obviously abhor. But this you shall discover on your own."

He released her hand and stood back. "I accept your conditions."

He waited until she relaxed slightly before adding, "But we must be fair. If I am to be banned from your possessions, then you are banned from mine."

Charlaine shrugged indifferently—until he leaned against Durwood's desk and idly fingered the book of poetry Durwood had left there.

"It is not yours!" she spat at him.

"Yes, it is. On the day you come to me and tell me you love me, I will give it to you."

"This is blackmail!"

It was his turn to shrug. "If it pleases you to name it so. But the fact remains. I possess it currently. You do not."

Durwood darted his eyes back and forth between the pair. "What on earth are you talking about? What is this possession?"

Neither answered him. With a curt bow, Devlin stomped to the study door. "Please excuse me. I will change and return shortly with my best man."

The door closed quietly behind him. Charlaine frantically searched the room, picked up a Dresden lady in a ball gown and hefted it experimentally. Durwood tensed, getting ready to duck. His mouth dropped open as, with a visible grinding of her teeth, his headstrong termagant of a daughter slowly set the figurine back down.

"No. This time I remain calm. He cannot seduce a stone." And with exaggerated poise, she glided from the room.

Exhausted, Durwood plopped down in a chair. He wiped his brow, seriously wondering if he shouldn't make his own continental tour.

But then he grinned. No. He couldn't bear to miss

the fun, especially after he'd started this comedy of errors.

The atmosphere at the wedding was anything but convivial. The bride wore puce to match her skin tone, and the groom wore black, to match his mood. Mordecai's gray eyes were cloudy as he watched Devlin take Charlaine's stiff hand. Only the Duchess of Kensington and Durwood seemed to find any pleasure in the proceedings.

They watched with proud smiles as this day each had doubted would ever dawn finally came to pass. Charlaine Kimball was getting married. No matter if she hated the groom, had vowed to ban him from her bed, and had even made him agree to give up all claim to her estate.

She would have the ring on her finger and, one day, the babies to tug at her skirts. Nature would win, as it always did. One day Devlin Rhodes would make their girl happy despite herself.

That day seemed far removed as lightning flashed outside the small chapel. Brilliance briefly put the candleglow to shame, illuminating the expressions of the bride and groom. This stalemate of stubborn wills and proud hearts was just beginning.

The minister seemed to understand this, even if Charlaine's family did not. Curiously, while he recited the old, old words, he appraised the living embodiment of an old, old conflict. The bride was not willing, and the groom was not happy.

Inwardly he shrugged. It would not be the first time he'd wedded a reluctant couple, and doubtless it would not be the last. He only hoped Durwood was right about the feelings these two young people had for each other.

They were certainly not apparent to him.

He and Durwood had been friends since boyhood, and so he had agreed to "accidentally" slip the date of the nuptials back by one day. If challenged, he could claim that he had been forgetful of late, and that the participants had been so eager to wed that they had charmed him into the hasty ceremony. The special license was perfectly legal, after all.

But, as he was a pious man, he hoped no one would catch him in such bald-faced lies, especially if this union ended as badly as it had begun.

The bride's response as she repeated the words was almost inaudible. She stumbled over "To honor and obey," and ran through the rest of the solemnity as if eager to get it over with.

The groom, on the other hand, was firm and loud, especially as he said, "With my body, I thee wed." He squeezed his bride's hand, holding it closer when she tried to pull away.

The minister found himself rushing through the rest of the ceremony and ended with a veritable gasp. "You may kiss the bride."

The couple froze. Lightning flashed again, striking so close that the little chapel shook.

"I said, you may kiss the bride," the minister repeated, thinking they had not heard him. Slowly the groom lifted the bride's chin. Her eyes seemed very dark in the gloom as his mouth lowered toward hers.

Her lids fluttered shut just as his lips seemed about to brush hers. Her mouth opened slightly.

The minister relaxed a bit at her reaction. She obviously wanted to be kissed. Then, to his utter astonishment, the groom seemed to lose his way. His lips brushed her cheek, and the tip of her nose, then withdrew. He pulled her rigid hand into his arm and led her up the aisle to their small group of well-wishers.

Charlaine accepted Durwood's hug but did not return it. "Come, darling, smile for me. You are so lovely when you smile." Charlaine's lips moved, but the movement could hardly be termed a smile.

Elizabeth elbowed Durwood aside. "Don't badger the child. Today, of all days, she can be as weepy as she pleases." She pressed a powdered, scented cheek to her niece's, whispering in Charlaine's ear, "But don't let them see you are upset. Buck up, my girl. We shall rout their male arrogance in the end."

Charlaine's smile became genuine as she met Devlin's suspicious glance. "Thank you, Aunt. You make me feel much better."

"Now why does that make me nervous?" Devlin asked dryly. "Should I employ a food taster?"

She cocked her head as if considering the notion. "No, poison is too fast." And she flounced out of the church.

Mordecai chuckled at Devlin's disconcerted expression. "Now that you have her, do you know what to do with her?"

Devlin barreled after his errant bride.

The duchess shook her head at her friend. "Don't tease the poor boy. He has enough to contend with."

"Aided and abetted by you, no doubt."

The duchess sniffed. "Downtrodden and dominated as we of the female gender are, we are not helpless."

Settling his yarmulke firmly on his head, Mordecai gave her a speaking glance and hurried after the bride and groom. The duchess glanced over her shoulder at Durwood, who stood talking with his friend.

"I know who the true author of this match is, my dear Durwood," the duchess said in a silky whisper. "And when the time is right, Charlaine will know too."

And she followed the others.

* * *

The nuptial dinner that followed was a gay affair. For everyone but the bride and groom.

Charlaine picked at the elaborate meal, feeling far removed from this day and this reality. She watched the three-carat diamond Devlin had given her sparkle on her hand. It was a lovely thing, but it was as cold and distant as she had resolved to be. Something about the sardonic tilt to his mouth when he gave it to her warned that he felt the same. Now why did that pain her? she asked herself as she squashed her peas together.

Silent beside her, Devlin did the same.

"Of course they will go away," Durwood said. "My gift to them will be a monthlong tour of the continent. They will get back just in time for the jubilee."

Devlin looked up. "That is up to Charlaine."

Her hackles, which had risen, fell back at his consideration. "I do not wish to leave London at this time."

Durwood glared at her. "But just yesterday you could not wait to get away."

That was before the wedding. The thought of spending a month alone with Devlin made Charlaine so nervous that her hand trembled as she picked up her water glass to take a fortifying sip. "We still have the jewelry competition to get through."

"I am finished with the necklace." Devlin, too, sipped his water.

"Then there's nothing to stop you, what?" Durwood insisted.

Nothing but her own fears. But Charlaine could hardly admit that. While she was still searching for a reply, a gentle knock came at the dining room door.

The butler peeked in at Durwood's call. "Mr. Cecil Rhodes, Mr. Lewis Temple and Mr. Henry Dupree are all here to see you, sir."

A fork clattered against the gold-rimmed china. The little color in Charlaine's face fled at the news. She didn't need to be told why they'd come. And, at the moment, playing the blissful bride was beyond her.

Durwood hesitated, but finally he said, "Show them in."

Solicitously, Devlin wet his napkin in a finger bowl and wiped Charlaine's hand, which had been dotted with pea juice when she dropped her fork. "We can play the happy couple, just this once. Please, Charlaine."

His eyes, dark blue as skies beyond sunrise, held hers. For just an instant, she longed to believe the fidelity and promise of protection they gave. She swayed toward him as the door opened.

Chapter Seven

Lewis Temple led the way in. He stopped cold at sight of the banquet. Cecil was hot on his heels. He avoided barreling into him only because Temple dodged. The two older men stared at the streamers hung from the lights, the elaborate meal, the towering cake and the bouquet beside Charlaine's place at the table. For once, they seemed beyond speech.

It was left to Dupree to remember the niceties. "Please excuse us. We did not know we interrupted a, er . . ."

Smoothly Durwood rose to approach the three with extended hand. "Wedding banquet?"

The discomfiture in Cecil's eyes faded. "I knew it. Your daughter was not wed yesterday, as this fellow claimed on the train."

Devlin started to rise, but Durwood waved him back into his seat. "To the contrary. We didn't have time for this dinner yesterday, they were so eager to wed, but

172

I insisted on it as soon as they returned. Would you care to see the wedding license?"

"I would." Cecil crossed his arms over his broad chest and stood waiting.

This time Devlin ignored Durwood's subtle signals. He stood, rounded his bride's chair, and then paused with his hands on her shoulders. "I would that you did not. By your own choice we are not family, so why should you concern yourself with my intimate affairs?"

"Oh, your welfare is of supreme indifference to me. But I consider this girl almost like a younger sister. She needs protection from you and your sort."

The duchess and Mordecai gasped at Cecil's rudeness.

Only a flicker of his eyelashes betrayed Devlin's brief hurt as he shot back, "There speaks the envy of a man who has never known, nor ever shall, the joy of loving a woman."

This time the gasps sounded even louder. Durwood tensed on the balls of his feet, as if preparing to block the imminent fisticuffs. The pair were literally old sparring partners, but from all reports, they were quite unmatched. A couple of Durwood's friends had been present at a fight in Kimberley between Devlin and Cecil a number of years back. Apparently the fight had started over that second most volatile of subjects after women—politics. Durwood had no interest in repeating that particular history today. Decisively, he moved forward.

Henry Dupree closed his eyes, cringing at the impending explosion.

For an instant it did indeed look as if Cecil Rhodes would blow apart with rage; then he gave a brittle laugh. "I deserved that, by God. If the girl married you, she must see something in you that I do not. Accept

173

my apologies for ruining your celebration, my dear." He bowed to Charlaine.

She nodded numbly.

Lewis Temple was looking at Cecil Rhodes as if he'd never seen him before. "But the marriage license—"

"In all our years of business together, I have never known Durwood Kimball to lie to me," Cecil said, leading the way to the door. "Good day, and forgive the interruption."

Temple glanced back from Devlin to the others who watched with interest to see what he would do, and then finally followed Cecil without another word.

Henry Dupree swallowed harshly. "Congratulations, Lady Kimb—Uh, Mrs. Rhodes." He hurried off, but the distress in his expression made even Mordecai's eyes soften in sympathy.

Once their audience was gone, Charlaine wrenched her shoulders away from Devlin's loose grip. She tossed her napkin down and shoved back her chair, smashing into his elegant pump. He grunted, stepping back.

She fled, tears coming to her eyes, ignoring her father's plea to wait. Devlin stared, confused, at the empty doorway.

Durwood started after her, but the duchess put a gentle hand on his arm. "I will go. It's only hearing herself referred to as a 'Missus,' you see. It will take some time for her to grow accustomed to that appellation." She hurried after her niece.

Devlin fell back into his chair, massaging his smashed toes against his pants leg. Abruptly he seemed weary, like a bridegroom with one long night behind him and another to look forward to. Except he did not seem like a man looking forward to anything. For the next half hour, he picked at his food, answered in monosyllables when either of the older gentlemen spoke to him, and started at every sound. His gaze remained glued to the doorway.

Finally Durwood said in exasperation, "And the queen will dance naked in Trafalgar Square at midnight while I play a harmonica."

Devlin nodded. "That's nice."

Durwood grimaced at Mordecai and twirled a finger next to his ear. Mordecai shook his head and tapped his heart.

That appeased Durwood as nothing else could. What father did not want his daughter to wed a man who loved her?

More gently, Durwood said, "She will come about; you will see."

Devlin looked at him. "What did you say?"

"My daughter is a typical Kimball—stubborn, strong-willed, intelligent, but also fair-minded. Treat her well, and she will grow to care for you."

A loud clatter of fork to plate bespoke Devlin's opinion of that little homily. "Is that why you engineered this day?"

Carefully Mordecai wiped his mouth and watched Durwood's reaction.

"What do you mean?" Durwood asked, calmly sipping his champagne.

"I thought it peculiar that Charlaine had agreed to breakfast with me, since she fled to get away from me. And when I entered her train car, it was exceedingly strange that her maid had already left her unchaperoned at precisely the time I was due to arrive."

"An odd confluence of circumstances, I agree," Durwood said. "But you can hardly blame them on—"

"And then an old harridan who is one of the worst gossips in the realm just happens to arrive for nuncheon at a most inopportune moment."

"Next you will blame Lewis Temple's presence on me."

"I would not put it past you, if it served your ends."

Durwood slammed down his champagne glass so hard that the liquid sloshed over the exquisite lace tablecloth. "Are you implying that I planned for you and my daughter to be caught, er, in . . ."

"Compromising circumstances?" Devlin grimaced as if his memories of that moment were both more intimate and more emotional than the euphemism could relay. "In a word, yes."

Durwood shoved back his chair. "Well, I never would have thought my new son-in-law would speak to me so at my own table when I've only offered him hospitality and honor."

Devlin, too, rose. "You, sir, are a liar."

Mordecai gasped.

Durwood blinked.

Leaning his palms on the table, Devlin skewered his new father-in-law with an arrow-straight blue gaze that struck the bull's-eye of Durwood's hypocrisy. "I have a good friend who works in the ticket office at the station, you see. When we returned to London, I stopped by for a casual little chat. My friend remembered Imogen, who was the last person to board, and he also remembered the 'tall swell' who purchased her ticket. The man carried a distinctive dragon-headed gold cane." Devlin glanced derisively at the cane leaning in the corner. "Care to regroup and come at me from a different direction?"

Durwood made funny sounds, as if he would strangle with rage; then, with a bitter laugh, he plopped back down in his seat. "Hoisted on my own petard." He cocked his head with interest, appraising his new relative as if he'd only now noticed him: Devlin Rhodes was an interesting personality in his own right, not just a healthy stud to sire a new line. "You'll fit into this family very well, my boy."

"You'll excuse me if I don't take that as a compliment," came the dry response.

Durwood's admiring gleam faded. "Do you intend to tell Charlaine?"

Mordecai, too, seemed very interested in Devlin's response.

Devlin turned toward the door. With his hand on the knob, he finally answered, his voice almost inaudible, "No. Not to protect you, but to . . . Tell her I'm going to work. If she wants me, she knows where to find me." The door closed quietly behind him.

Mordecai shoved back his plate and rose. Attaching his skullcap firmly, he stomped toward the door.

"Now what have I done?" Durwood complained. "Why is everyone leaving?"

"I suggest you enjoy your wedding banquet. It may turn to crow in your mouth soon enough." And Mordecai slammed the door behind him, the thud muffling his muttered aside: "Putz."

Upstairs, the atmosphere in Charlaine's sitting area was even grimmer. "But you cannot hide up here forever," Elizabeth protested for the umpteenth time.

"Why not?" Charlaine stared blindly out her tower window. She saw Devlin hurry outside as if the hounds of hell pursued him and stride rapidly up the street, not even bothering with a carriage. For the first time she had to wonder if, just perhaps, he had wed under duress, as she had. *No,* she told herself. *He only wanted to get his hands on your person and your fortune.*

Both of which she had put firmly out of his reach. She squelched the thought. Husband or no, this frog would never get the better of her. Unless . . .

Unless he won the best of her. Even as she whirled away from the window to change her clothes, deep inside she knew that part of her yearned to put aside this contest. When he kissed her, when he touched her breast, some primitive response changed them from male and female combatants to lovers striving for a common bliss.

Which was precisely why she had to be firm and do what was best, or lose all she'd fought for. Once she succumbed to him, the Ice Princess would become another docile, servile, sniveling little woman, a baby factory, not the heiress to a long line of proud, independent women. With a martial straightening of her shoulders, she tied the bow to her demure bodice. "I shall come down now, but only to go to the shop. Today is no different from any other day."

Elizabeth raked an agitated hand through her elaborate coiffure. Several pinned-up curls came loose, cascading onto her shoulders. "I swear you know better than that, my child, but flee if you must. The horns of your dilemma will only grow longer while you ignore them."

Charlaine hurried downstairs and scrambled into her carriage. Elizabeth watched from the front door, the other half of her coiffure now disarranged.

Still nursing his champagne and his wounded pride, Durwood joined her. "Where is my errant daughter off to?"

"Forgetfulness, she hopes. She will be disappointed." Sighing, Elizabeth crooked a finger at a footman, who hurried off to the stables. "As I am. In you."

"Not you too, Elizabeth." Durwood braced himself.

The barrage of criticism trembled on her lips; then, with a little *humph* of disgust, Elizabeth went to a hall mirror to rearrange her hair. "Your mother would be disappointed in you, Durwood." As if that were the worst condemnation of all, she stalked down the steps, dignity and hair firmly affixed. "As I am. And as a former dancer, the daughter of a coachman, I can safely say that I am shocked by your behavior. You weary me. I'm leaving."

Durwood watched her step up into the coach, agile as a woman half her age. Then, scowling, he slammed the door closed and stalked into his study.

He was right. They'd all see.

Proximity would offer an olive branch to the feuding young couple. They were too strongly attracted to each other to battle for long. He knew, because he'd been there, felt the same conflicting emotions during his stormy courtship and early marriage with Charlaine's mother. The Kimball heirs loved once and well, but their happiness was always hard fought and harder won, all the way back to his great-grandfather, Drake Kimball.

Charlaine would accept her destiny, eventually. He was certain of it. Complacently Durwood cut himself a huge piece of the untouched wedding cake, dreaming of bouncing his grandson on his knee.

Destiny took an unkind turn over the next few days. To Durwood's dismay, Devlin decided to stay in his bachelor flat for the time being. Over Durwood's protests, he said, "I have never cared a fig what other people think. Tell the curious and the condemning that I have to pack my things and prepare my affairs. Charlaine has my name, and that will have to suffice for the moment."

"But Charlaine will never soften toward you if you persist in this lunacy."

Devlin leaned back in his office chair to affix a cool azure gaze on his new relative. "My only lunacy was in agreeing to wed an obviously unwilling woman.

Had your scheme not worked so wonderfully well, I would by now be close to winning Charlaine's affections. Now that she believes me so duplicitous, she will probably never come to me. If she changes her mind, she knows where to find me." And once more, he bent over his accounts.

"Then I shall tell her who was the true author of her, er, incentive to wed you."

Devlin's head popped up. "I would not recommend that. Better she hate just me than both of us. The fact that you arranged that little scene will not affect her feelings. She was still forced to wed me. And nothing either you or I say or do can ever force her affections."

"Then what do you intend to do? Sulk in your office until all of London is abuzz?"

For the briefest instant, pain and frustration flashed in his blue eyes before Devlin looked back down at his entries. "Our entire relationship began with me coercing her in one form or another. I will not have our marriage begin the same. When she wants me to come to her, I will come."

Two days later, Durwood had no better luck with his daughter. He slammed her office door against her wall and stalked inside, shutting it with equal force. "You are making a laughingstock of our name all about London," he growled by way of hello.

Her pencil stopped briefly as she sketched a design for a set of earrings with a most unusual clasp that made them wearable either as bobs or as a pin. "You forget. My name is no longer Kimball. It must be your own name you refer to." And she used her eraser to touch up a line.

"That is where you are wrong. Until your marriage is consummated, you are not legally wed," he tossed back. At the flash of interest in those green eyes, he bit his tongue, but it was too late.

"Thank you for reminding me of that. As if I needed another reason to stay away from that . . . that . . . lying scoundrel."

Durwood's mouth worked as if he might say something, but at her steady gaze, he snapped his cane down and pivoted, slamming the door again on his way out.

Unfortunately no one was there to see the wistfulness in Charlaine's eyes as she twisted her wedding band. Then, resolutely, she returned to her design.

And so things might have proceeded, if an unexpected source had not intervened.

Or, more aptly, a force to be reckoned with.

The next morning, the fifth day of her wedded bliss, Charlaine was once again hard at work, trying to occupy her wandering thoughts, when a stunned clerk burst into her office without knocking. "My lady, the queen is here to see you!"

The pencil slipped from Charlaine's fingers. She leaped to her feet, straightened her severe bodice and smoothed back her tight chignon. She had decided that if she was to have the name, she would play the wifely game. And if she secretly hoped that dressing like a prude would make her into one, well, it was as good a defense against her husband as any. Of her pique that he had made no effort to see her, she told no one.

The queen, who had once been a strong-willed bride herself, was not so easily fooled. She took one look at Charlaine's appearance, waved her hovering entourage away and said, "Back into the office with you, my girl. We shall have a quiet coze."

Charlaine's unease heightened. For the queen to take time out of her busy schedule for a private audience boded ill for Charlaine's hope to keep her private affairs private.

The queen took Charlaine's chair and waved her subject opposite. She wore a white shawl about her plump shoulders and her usual black silk. "Now, what is this nonsense I hear that you refuse to live with your new husband?"

"He has made no effort even to see me."

"Is this distasteful gossip true?"

"What gossip, Your Majesty?"

"Do not try to fadge me off, Charlaine. I have known you too long. This rumor that you had to wed because you were caught, ah, *en flagrante delicto*."

"And who told you that?"

"Cecil Rhodes. But only when I asked about you."

She should have known. Charlaine clenched her hands in her lap, wondering what the penalties were for lying to one's liege. "Yes, Your Majesty." She reddened and looked away from that condemning gaze.

"So now you compound your sin by refusing to live with your husband? This is not done, Charlaine. It is simply not done. The only thing that will stop this unpleasant gossip is for you to take your rightful place at your husband's side. As I recall, he's a handsome lad, so it should not be too difficult for you."

Difficult? Impossible, more like. But Charlaine could only nod humbly. "As Your Majesty pleases."

The queen rose. She tapped Charlaine on the cheek. "I have your welfare in mind, child, though it may not seem so at the moment. We will expect to hear from our emissary that all is well in the Rhodes household." And with a nod, she swept back outside.

Charlaine eyed the glass paperweight on her desk. She picked it up, gritted her teeth, and set it back down. Though it would give her temporary satisfaction to break the cut-glass ship, she would need all her energies for a more apocalyptic battle.

For surely her entire existence as she knew it was at stake.

Devlin was no happier at the royal decree than Charlaine. When he opened her note, he scanned it eagerly, hoping she'd missed him at last. Lord knew, he'd missed her.

The breath left his lungs.

The queen commands us to cohabit. I prefer to live in my home. Please apprise me of your decision forthwith. Charlaine.

Nothing else. Not a bit of warmth or longing. Devlin crumpled the note and tossed it across his office. He had a good mind to respond in kind.

I do not care to sleep with an icicle. We have made our bed. Now we shall lie in it. Separately.

Mordecai came in. "Devlin, the new diamond shipment is . . ." He trailed off at Devlin's expression. He followed Devlin's gaze to the crumpled note. "May I?"

Devlin waved an uncaring hand.

Mordecai uncrumpled the note. Relief flickered in his gray eyes, but Devlin was too busy staring blindly at the wall to notice. "You will obey, of course?"

"I have not decided."

A spate of Yiddish expressed Mordecai's opinion of this obduracy, the meaning clear despite the language barrier. Finally, when Devlin did not react, Mordecai took a deep breath. "You will never win Charlaine from afar. You have no choice."

I can run back to America. Or even Africa. Dirty hands and an aching back sound good at this moment. Make my dear cousin Cecil happy, at least. And my blushing bride. But he had never been a coward. She wanted a battle? He was in just the mood to give her one. So he responded, "I may have to live with her, but I don't have to be happy about it. I am finished trying to make love to an iceberg."

And even as he packed, he tried to keep that resolve as steady as his hands. Her silence since they wed had hurt him deeply. He had never done anything to warrant this treatment. Well, aside from that first little transgression. His guilty eyes strayed to his hidden safe, but the pang didn't last long.

After all, he had been forced into this marriage as well. A less honorable man might have left her fodder for the gossip mill. Especially when she put those unconscionable conditions on the union. Inwardly he knew it was that final condition that infuriated him now. By his own vow, he could not kiss her; by hers, he could not bed her.

How would he ever win?

More to the point, did he even want to anymore?

The next morning, the delusion did not survive his first look at her. His knees went weak with desire when, as the butler reluctantly let him in, he caught his first glimpse of her in almost a week.

She was dressed in an emerald silk dressing gown, and her hair flowed down her spine like liquid copper shot through with gold. She had her feet curled demurely under her as she sat in the salon reading. He tilted his head to see the title: *A Tale of Two Cities*.

"How apropos for my arrival." When she looked up, he said silkily, "A far, far better thing you do than you have ever done before."

Calmly she glanced back at her reading, retorting, "No, that part comes when you depart."

Devlin had to school his expression to indifference. Damn, the Ice Princess knew how to thrust at a fellow's vulnerable spots. Suddenly he could not bear this. Indeed, it might be a far better thing to do to annul this mockery of a marriage here and now. "Oh yes? Well, there's no time like the present." He turned on his heel. His hand was on the knob when she tossed the book aside.

"Please."

He waited, his back still turned.

"Please don't go."

"Why?"

"Because . . . because the queen commands that you stay."

But the betraying catch in her voice, and the hesitation, spoke as eloquently as her choice of reading material. His shoulders lifted in a deep sigh, but his expression was neutral when he turned back around. He propped one foot behind him on the door and rested an arm on his raised knee. He was pleased to see her betraying glance as the pose put his male attributes on display in the tight breeches. "That is a sorry reason. You shall have to give me a better one."

Her chin tilted high. "I have none."

He pushed off with his foot and approached her.

She wavered, as if she might give ground, but then she caught herself and stood tall. Waiting.

For what? Was that fear or longing on her face behind the ice?

When he was close enough to touch her, he stopped. "You seemed to feel differently on the train."

"Do not torment me with that! It is my weakness that put me in this imbroglio!"

She was so tempting in her defiance, all glowing green eyes, fiery hair and ivory skin, that it took all his control not to sweep her into his arms and kiss her senseless. That was her problem: she thought too much. And distrusted her feelings. That too he had Durwood to thank for. "Does it not occur to you that this 'weakness' is not the sole provence of the weaker sex?" He grimaced at the truism, for the "weaker sex" actually ruled the world from the cradle to the grave, though men were too dense to see it.

Devlin hesitated; then he held his hand out, palm down before her eyes. It trembled slightly. "Do I seem a pillar of strength at this moment?"

Dumbly, she stared at the betraying quiver.

"I long to hold you, to love you, with all my being, but I know you too well, *chère*." His voice softened. "When you love, you will do so for the rest of your life. I can wait for that day."

She swayed toward him, started and then took an alarmed step back. "You merely dress up lust with a pretty word!"

"Lust? I admit that I lust for you. It is a healthy, natural emotion, especially between man and wife. But I adhere to your command. You notice I do not say that I adhere to your wishes—for we both know what those are. Soon enough you will come to me."

She did not hurry to the door; she ran. Ran as if her very life were at stake.

As it doubtless was, in her eyes. Almost, he felt sympathy for her. Panicky little virgin, too innocent and willful to know that the "lust" they shared was both natural and beautiful. He would delight in proving both to her, sooner rather than later, he hoped.

When she opened the door he said, "I shall join you shortly."

She stopped dead. "You will sleep in the tower opposite mine."

"I will sleep in your chamber, or I will leave."

Slowly she turned. "No."

"Yes." He had to admire her control. The slings and arrows of misfortune had certainly made her more mature. A longing to throw something flashed in her eyes, but she crossed her arms over her lovely bosom and stared at him calmly.

"When the queen said we had to live together, she only meant in the same house. She does not approve of the gossip about us."

"And don't you think the servants might remark on the newlyweds living in opposite sides of the house?"

A frown disturbed her composure. She had obviously not thought that far. "We shall just have to let them talk."

"I will not be made any more of a mockery than I already am. I did my duty by wedding you. Now you can do yours by letting me share your chamber." When she began to protest again, he held up a hand. "Your chamber only. As I recall, you have a comfortable couch. Only we need know that I sleep on that."

Her distrust of him peeked from her eyes. She hesitated.

He contemplated his fingernails. Proximity was his only hope, as wise old Mordecai had said. He felt better, now that he was here. She was still deeply attracted to him. She was just too cursed proud to show it.

Finally she whispered, "All right. But if you try to . . . become too forward, I will ask you to leave."

He swept her a mocking bow. "As her ladyship pleases." She hurried out. It was a good thing her back was turned.

She saw neither the hungry, predatory look of the prowling Frenchman, nor the iron resolve of the Yankee. Devlin Rhodes, American expatriate, defined both in that moment.

The Ice Princess's virgin days were numbered.

Devlin carried his own baggage up the stairs, to the dismay of Jeffries, the butler.

187

Colleen Shannon

"But, sir," that worthy protested, certain of his duty despite his disdain for Devlin himself. "That is our job."

"Your job is to see to this household's comfort. I am more comfortable carrying my own baggage. Now butt out." Devlin hefted his large portmanteau over his shoulder and carried it up the stairs without visible difficulty.

Offended, the butler stomped back into his pantry to take his frustrations out on an underling. When the cowed young maid scurried off to do his bidding, he so forgot himself as to take out a rag and actually polish the silver. This brash young man would have his orderly household at sixes and sevens, unless he much missed the mark.

As usual, Jeffries was correct.

He started in Charlaine's bedchamber. Devlin knocked with his foot, then burst in without waiting. Her robe half off her shoulders, Charlaine just had time to duck behind a dressing screen and glare at him.

He stopped, eyeing her bare shoulders. She hunched down. He arched an eyebrow, then stomped in, tossing his case down next to the couch. "Where should I put my things?"

She pointed at an armoire against the wall. He opened it and began unpacking, ignoring her.

Quietly she dressed.

While he pretended supreme indifference, in actuality every rustle of fabric brought another tormenting image. By the time she left her haven, demurely clad in bronze taffeta with a high neckline, he was sweating and irritable. This "cohabitation," as she had put it so coldly, would be harder on him than on her.

He glared down at himself. Quite literally.

"I am going down to breakfast. If you need more

188

room, tell my maid. She can clear some of my old clothes from my closet."

"This will suffice. Thank you."

She nodded regally. Only when she was gone did he allow himself a French curse. In his most emotional moments he reverted to the tongue of his birth. What a farce this entire situation was. Two healthy young people who wanted one another, legally wed, sharing a chamber but not a bed at the command of an aging queen who knew her own way about a bed, given her considerable progeny.

The only question remaining, Devlin brooded, was which would break first.

The bride's will or the groom's control.

"He moved in this morning," Lewis Temple said baldly, setting his bowler hat on Cecil's desk. "So much for their marriage being a sham. I told you we should have demanded a look at the license."

Henry folded up his notebook and made to rise, but Cecil waved him back. "Given your feelings for the girl, Henry, you should be privy to this." Henry's cheeks reddened as he took the rebuke for what it was, but he said nothing.

"I know Durwood well. He was not bluffing about the license. The pair either wed when they said they did, or he had the license doctored. In either event, we have something of more note to be concerned about. Namely, the queen has taken an interest. She visited Charlaine yesterday, I hear," Cecil continued. "I should have kept my mouth shut. But she asked me about them, and I could hardly lie. I suspect this is her doing. She is quite fond of the Kimballs. Pity, but she seems to like this detestable frog, though God knows why."

"Do you wish to discharge me?" Temple asked.

Cecil looked at him as if he were crazy. "No, I need you more than ever now. If the frog succeeds in wheedling his way into the Kimballs' good graces, I shall never be rid of him."

"He's obviously already succeeded in bamboozling Durwood, given the man's defense of his new son-in-law at the wedding banquet."

Waving a dismissing hand, Cecil stood. "Durwood would accept the devil himself into his family as long as he acquires an heir in the bargain. It is Charlaine we must worry about. If she truly grows to care for this fellow, she will stand beside him through thick and thin."

A certain wistfulness crept into Cecil's expression.

Temple looked away. He suspected it was not Charlaine Cecil longed for, but similar loyalty and love. Curiously he looked at Henry, to see if the secretary agreed with his appraisal.

That handsome young fellow paid no attention to either his boss or to Temple. He stared at the wall. Temple frowned. He knew obsession when he saw it, and the sheer hatred that flared in the lad's eyes as they discussed Devlin surpassed even Temple's own.

Temple had to drag his attention back to Cecil. ". . . and that is the way we shall catch him."

"How's that?"

"Rumor has it that she made him give up all claim to her fortune. But I believe he still holds some of Charlaine's possessions. Hostage, as it were, until she bows down to him. If we can prove he stole from her, we can still see him jailed."

"It is doubtful she will let him remain there."

"I suggest we search his flat, now that he's gone."

"That Jew is still there."

Cecil frowned. "Well, he must leave to go to work. Search the premises then."

"As you wish. Good day, Mr. Rhodes."

"Good day. And good hunting."

As Temple rose and put on his hat, Henry Dupree bestirred himself. He stood and led the way to the door. When the door was closed, Henry said, "I shall be glad to offer my services to help you prove this bastard for what he is. He does not deserve Charlaine Kimball."

Temple nodded noncommitally. "If I need your help, I shall let you know."

Not likely. Temple distrusted pretty boys and their ugly ways. They were too used to winning ever to be content with losing. No wonder Dupree hated Devlin Rhodes.

They were two of a kind.

Charlaine, poor lady, would have a miserable time married to the bounder. It was up to him to rescue her. And Lewis Temple went on his sanctimonious way, planning how to break into Devlin's flat.

Indeed, during those early days, Charlaine would have agreed with Temple's appraisal.

The great Cervantes might have best described her marriage: "Love and war are the same thing, and stratagems and policy are as allowable in the one as in the other."

And, as Charlaine was to learn shortly, Devlin had far more experience and skill on this particular field of valor. A full frontal assault she might have overcome, but not his secret forays into her sacrosanct territory.

How could she expel an intruder who lived with her?

The routine that had formerly been Charlaine's salvation became a battleground fraught with obstacles.

Male obstacles.

Her resolve to ignore her new husband until he conceeded defeat and went away proved impossible, given their constant proximity. She awoke to the sight of him, went to sleep to the rhythm of his soft breathing, breakfasted with him, supped with him. Even without his daily physical presence, his accessories would have been a formidable reminder of the subtle, pleasing differences between the sexes her father was always lecturing her about.

His shoes, twice the size of hers, sat neatly at the foot of the couch, but somehow she always managed to stumble over them.

His subtle male cologne wafted on the rarefied air of her bedchamber. Despite heavy use of her own perfume, she could never block the evocative scent that inspired primitive memories she was resolved to forget.

And he took positive delight in undressing before her. He seemed to sleep only in his underdrawers, a habit she found scandalous.

Why, only men of questionable morals slept so. But then, who could expect more of a Frenchman, and one born on the wrong side of the blanket at that?

No matter how she lectured herself, however, her instincts were neither prudish nor prudent. They avidly reminded her that, by-blow though he might be, Devlin Rhodes was also a descendant of that scandalous queen, Marie Antoinette. Generations of breeding showed in every proud line of him.

Charlaine always took advantage of the screen to change, but Devlin didn't bother. Her first intimate lesson came that very first night, after a dinner at which her father and Devlin conversed amiably about everything from the ship of state to the latest stock exchange offering, ignoring her.

Wearing her heaviest nightgown, she slipped into

her feather bed, trying not to remember the last time he had been in this room. She'd had nightmares ever since.

Well, dreams, maybe.

All right then, evocative transports to a shadowy world where Devlin Rhodes was not a frog, but a prince who transported her to heaven with the power of his kiss.

And with what followed the kiss.

All these thoughts flitted through her brain as she lay tensely in the bed, fearing, hoping, wondering. If he got into bed with her, would she really scream?

He stood in the dark watching her. Moonlight drifted through the gauzy curtains on the wings of a summer breeze. Honeysuckle grew up her tower wall, scenting the air with its rich promise of life anew.

Still, he did not move, but his eyes glittered in the soft light. Was he, too, remembering that encounter that had changed their lives?

When he finally moved, she started against her sheets. The quivering in her knees spread throughout her body. The breeze stopped; the moon ducked behind a cloud.

Tension almost suffocated her as he took two long strides toward her. But then, with a soft French epithet, he dragged back the cover she'd spread neatly over his couch and began to undress. Now she could see nothing, but she heard the tantalizing rustle of clothing.

For a minute or so she saw nothing as the moon played hide-and-seek with the clouds. But then its lovely glow smiled into her chamber again.

She gasped. Devlin stood there wearing only his tight drawers. They ended above the knee, and were such a tight woven cotton that he might as well have been naked.

193

Hide, run, he will ravish you, whispered the Ice Princess.

Invite him to your bed, clamored the woman he'd awakened. Greedily her gaze ran over him as he stood there staring out the window as if he, too, longed to flee.

From his tousled black hair to his perfect toes, he did indeed seem more prince than frog.

His strong neck supported a graceful head that she had never realized was so well proportioned. Against the moonlight, as he turned his head, his perfect profile might have been one of the silhouettes touted in the ladies' magazines as the personification of manhood.

His wide shoulders looked as broad and powerful as those of the strong man she had once seen in a circus, but he had none of that man's bulging muscles. Devlin's musculature, from biceps, to forearms, to chest and legs, was defined but not overwhelming. He looked as if he'd earned his strength precisely as he had: with backbreaking labor. She wondered how he maintained that perfect physique given his current cerebral occupation.

Her eyes skimmed over the mysterious bulge between his legs. She had felt him against her, been curious to touch him, but this most obvious proof of his manhood was a threat to the way of life she had chosen.

Virgins should not find such images so pleasing. So, with a grinding of her teeth and the exercise of all her formidable willpower, she turned on her side away from him. She heard him slide between his own sheets and pull up the cover. Then all was quiet.

But all was not still.

The very darkness was alive with forbidden thoughts and scandalous desires.

The victory on this field of valor was yet to be decided, but that first night set a pattern that affected both of them.

Did either of them really win when both lay there aching to lose?

Devlin awoke early, when sunlight just brushed the room with roseate strokes. He was hard again. That state was not unusual for him these days, and instantly he realized where he was. Angrily he tossed back his covers, but even his offended male pride could not control his straying gaze or his restive urges.

She lay as he had first seen her, sleeping on her side, with one leg half out of her down duvet. This time her high-necked gown covered her breasts, but since he had seen them, his mind could picture them clearly. Her hair fell almost to the floor, picking up the feeble light on hues of gold and red. Her softly parted mouth was as great a temptation as he had ever faced. His body throbbed with a will of its own, urging him to make her his, as she longed to be, whether she knew it or not.

This was ridiculous. They were legally wed. He should be in that bed, awakening her as a bride should be awakened, instead of standing before the Ice Princess like a supplicant.

He took a step toward her, clasped his hands into fists, took a deep breath and did the only thing left to him.

He fell to the floor and did push-ups. He'd reached a hundred by the time she stirred. He was sweating with effort, but was still glad his hips pointed down when she blinked at him sleepily.

Her eyes widened. She sat up. "Is that how you stay fit?"

He stood, turned his back and began running in place. "Fit for what?" Certainly not for her ladyship, no matter how many exercises he did.

He felt her fascinated gaze, and knew sweat gleamed on his back and torso, but he was beyond caring. He either worked his instincts to exhaustion or let them claim him—and her.

After five more minutes he stopped, his chest heaving. Grabbing a towel from a stand, he slammed the water closet door behind him. When he came out thirty minutes later, the towel was around his loins and water gleamed in his clean hair. He was resolved to throw off his surly mood and charm her.

She was gone. Dressed and fled. Devlin picked up the robe she'd tossed across her bed, brought it to his face and inhaled deeply. Her scent made him hard again. He flung the robe against the wall and began to dress.

One thing was certain. The softness creeping up on him since moving to London would not progress. He would do so many calisthenics that he'd be as fit as he had been in the diamond fields. He smiled at himself in the mirror, his teeth gleaming.

And when the time was right, she would find his stamina astonishing.

After a hasty breakfast, they did not see each other again until dinner. Both worked in their own stores, tending to the usual business. Pretending that their lives had not changed.

The delusion did not survive the week. They were intimately bound now in every way, in all but body. His clothes took up her armoire; her books shared table space with his.

It was as if the mingling of their things was the first sign of a deeper union.

The second morning, she found a shaving set at her water basin. She picked up the elephant-headed ivory brush and ran it over her face. The bristles were surprisingly soft, and they reminded her of the hair on his chest that she had felt all too briefly during their train ride. She closed her eyes, and when she opened them, he was watching her in the mirror. Blushing, she set the brush down and tried to flee, but there was no room in the small closet.

He blocked the exit. "Would you care to help me shave?" he asked.

"No, of course not. I . . ." She trailed off with a gasp as he came in and closed the door.

She shrank against the basin as his formidable presence seemed to fill the tiny space.

He reached around her, picked up his shaving cup, poured some powder in it, added a dab of water, and began to mix, all the while keeping her pinned in place with his arms about her.

Her nose twitched at his scent, fresh but masculine. "I'm hungry. Let me go."

"So am I," he said throatily, smiling at her.

She swallowed, aware, as he had taught her, that some appetites were even stronger than the need for food.

He swiped the lather-laden brush across his face, making his eyes appear a deeper blue than ever. They sparkled at her wickedly as he picked up his straight razor and drew it down the side of his face. Smooth skin gleamed in a tempting path that broadened with every stroke. Witnessing this peculiar male ritual made her tingle in all the strangest places. He was so pleasingly male, so strong and different, that she longed to explore those differences.

Which was exactly his intention, she realized as she saw his pleasure in her fascination. She was about to give him a tongue-lashing when he held the razor out.

"Would you care to shave my neck?"

197

"I've never used a razor. I could hurt you."

"That's the difference between us, *chérie*. I do not spend my life trying to protect myself from hurt. Without pain, there is no pleasure." He leaned close, so close that those blue eyes consumed her world. "Besides, I trust you. You will not hurt me. Any more than I will hurt you."

He held up her right hand and put the handle of the razor in it. He grinned ruefully. "On the other hand, if you truly wish to be rid of me, here is your chance." He tilted his head back.

Charlaine stared at the strong angle of his throat, down at the razor, and back. *Put it down, this is ridiculous, it's another trick.*

But something stronger made her slowly, carefully, gently, stroke the razor over his vulnerable skin. The pleasure that suffused her in assisting in this intimate grooming made a mockery of all her fears. He trusted her. This was right. Perhaps, in a way, she should trust him too. Dimly aware that this simple act had a complicated significance, she set the razor in the basin and peeped up at him shyly.

His neck and cheeks gleamed. Drying his face of the residue, he sighed his pleasure and ran his hand over each smooth contour. "Smooth as a baby's bottom. Here, feel." And he brought her hands to his face.

She gasped. Their gazes met. The tiny mirror above the basin fogged over as they stared at one another.

Her fingers explored each pleasing curve and minuscule crevice. His face softened under her touch. His eyes closed. He cradled his cheek into her palm and made a sound that reminded her of a cat's purr.

A very large, dangerous cat's purr. She longed for nothing so much as to drink that sound from his lips. Charlaine glimpsed her fascinated expression in the mirror. She pulled her hands away, shoved him aside and fled down the stairs, so agitated that she forgot she wore only her dressing gown.

Her father caught her at the foot of the stairs. His eyebrows rose. He smiled, delighted. "Sleeping late this morning, my dear?"

Chapter Eight

Charlaine blushed and stared down at herself. What excuse could she give?

Devlin materialized beside her. He put an arm about her and kissed her on the neck. "The night past has given birth to a new day such as I have never seen before," he said intimately.

But not so intimately that Durwood couldn't hear him.

Tipping his top hat, Durwood went on his way outside. "Have a good day together, you two lovebirds." And even the heavy door could not muffle his cheerful whistling.

Charlaine wrenched herself away. "If you pretend to please him now, he will only be more disappointed later." She marched back to her room, trying to close the door in his face.

A foot caught the door and effortlessly pushed it wide despite her attempts to close it on him. She stumbled back, thought about dashing behind the couch, but tilted her chin instead and gave him an icy stare.

He leaned back against the door and crossed his feet at the ankles. "Later, when? When you leave me? Or when you think you will force me out of your life by your coldness?" He pushed away from the door and took slow steps toward her. "You mistake your man, *chère*. Frog I may be, but we are adaptable creatures. We live well in chilly climes and in hot ones. I stay, and I thrive, no matter how cold you become. Do you know why?"

He stopped directly in front of her. He didn't touch her, except to tilt her obstinate chin to force her to look at him. She gritted her teeth, but damn him, he waited so expectantly that she had to bite out, "Why?"

Hot breath sent a frisson of thrill-fear through her as he leaned close. "Because you want me. You want my kiss, my touch, my passion, my presence. And soon enough, you will want my love."

Violently, she shook her head. "No. I will never love a man—"

He continued as if she had not spoken. "Until that day, in public, for my own honor and for yours, I suggest you play the part of blushing bride, and I will play the part of doting bridegroom."

She opened her mouth to protest, but he put a finger over her lips. "Do you want people to talk, to mock us more than they already have?"

Her lips tingling, she drew away. "No." *But I cannot bear for you to touch me. It makes me long for things I cannot even think of, much less do.*

"I promise we shall be as prickly as you please in private. My advances end at your bedroom door—until you want it differently."

She nibbled at her lip, and then stopped when his gaze dropped to her mouth and acquired a gleam she

201

was beginning to recognize. Anything to get rid of him, so she could get herself together. "Very well. I agree."

At his relieved look, she held up a hand. "But only if you do not become too . . . bold."

"*Moi?*" Big, innocent blue eyes blinked at her.

Making a sound suspiciously like a snort, she turned away to the screen. "Now if you do not mind, I wish to dress. In private."

"Certainly. As soon as I find my briefcase."

Warily, she watched him over the screen as she tossed off her robe and nightgown to pull on the layers of clothing every lady had to wear. How much easier to be a man, with but one undergarment and outerwear that could be put on without help.

She glanced impatiently at her door. Where was her maid? She rang the call button again, listening, but no familiar steps came up. Finally, tired of waiting, Charlaine pulled the dress over her head and tried to fasten the tiny buttons in the back. Impossible. She moved to the spine, and managed to fasten one, but it felt askew.

Frustrated, she didn't realize Devlin was watching until he said, "Need some help?"

"Not of your kind. I thought you were leaving?"

"I seem to have mislaid my briefcase. It must be downstairs. But I shall be happy to assist you before I leave."

"No, thank you." She struggled some more.

Smiling slightly, he leaned against the bookcase and watched her gymnastics.

Finally she scowled and said, "Oh, very well. You might as well make yourself useful, as my maid seems to have fallen off the face of the earth."

He was beside her before the words were out of her mouth. The commodious space behind the screen grew cramped and warm when he joined her. He twirled a finger at her. She turned obediently. He could see little but the back of her ruffled petticoats and chemise. She disdained corsets, all the rage or not. She did not need one anyway.

Capable fingers buttoned each tiny pearl button, but she felt his breathing quicken. She wondered why until she realized that her position, leaning slightly forward, allowed the dress to gape open at the front and showed her bosom in the low-cut chemise. She stood board straight.

His fingers stopped. "I cannot see what I am doing." When she stayed rigid, he sighed and bent down, finishing the task hastily. She pulled away so quickly that she knocked him off balance. He fell to one knee.

She turned to help him up. "I am sor—" She broke off with a gasp when she saw his expression.

His white teeth gleamed in a grimace. With a tormented sigh, he put his arms about her and hauled her close to bury his head in her abdomen. "Ah, *chère*, it is good that you are untouched. You do not know this constant, painful desire."

Did he really want her so much that merely buttoning her dress could arouse him this way? She looked down at the front of his breeches. Sure enough, a large bulge confirmed his need. Her pride screamed at her to escape, but deeper, truer feelings brought her hand to the back of his head. His hair was as thick and soft as that of the boy he had once been. Would he pass this glorious attribute on to his son?

For an instant she allowed herself an image of what a strong, fine son he would sire. Would that she were free to be the woman to bear the lad. She stroked Devlin's hair, liquid warmth flowing between her own legs as she contemplated the event that must precede the birth. She knew enough to realize that she too was becoming aroused. She pulled his arms from about her waist and stumbled out, ignoring his call to wait.

Her clerks found her agitated, demanding and altogether impossible that day.

Her new bridegroom was even worse. When Mordecai made the mistake of asking Devlin how Charlaine was, Devlin almost bit his head off.

Offended, Mordecai squashed his skullcap on his head and stomped out. "To seek more pleasant company," as he put it. Somehow the distance to Lizzie's mansion, which was not far, was covered before he even realized where he was headed. He paused outside the iron gates.

Every time he came here, he felt like an interloper. An upstart little Jew who didn't know when an aristocrat was above him. Or so her servants obviously felt. Lizzy herself had never made him feel unwelcome. But then, she was the most unusual woman he'd ever known. He couldn't even define what made her different.

He only knew she was just . . . Lizzie. And that he'd found her too late. He was too set in his ways, and her way of life was too different from his. He turned to depart when she appeared beneath her portico, preparing to step into her carriage. Her coachman, who had driven Mordecai on more than one occasion, saw him and said something to her. She stopped and waved. "Mordecai! Good morning. My errand can wait. Do come in."

Make an excuse. Go about your business. Instead he entered her gate and approached to give her a deep bow. "Good morning, Your Grace."

She scowled and tapped him on the arm with her fan. "Mr. Levitz, I'll not have you talking to me like that. It's Lizzie to you, and well you know it. Come along. We shall share a cuppa together. I have been wanting to speak to you anyway." And she hooked her arm in his and escorted him into her home.

Mordecai exhaled a sigh of relief when they made it into her salon without encountering the butler. Insufferable putz. Lizzie seated him on a settee and sat next to him. "Now, how are the children?"

Mordecai shrugged. "Like most married couples, apparently—at one another's throats, if Devlin's mood this morning is any indication."

"Hmmm, well, that does not surprise me. Charlaine will not give up her independence easily. She's too young to know that she can love and still remain her own person." Lizzie glanced at him sidelong.

Clearing his throat, Mordecai inched away on the settee. "And what of the plans we spoke of? How do those proceed?" He sipped the tea she'd poured him.

"Slowly. Cecil Rhodes is a very private man. None of my acquaintances know him well enough to do as I ask. But I shall prevail."

No doubt about that. "I am glad to hear it. I have a feeling our young friends are going to need all the help we can give them. Now, I must be on my way, and not take any more of your time." He made to rise, but she pulled him back down.

"Why have you not come to see me?" Her lovely eyes still sparkled, the crow's-feet only emphasizing the cheerful nature of one who lived well and laughed often.

He studied the leaves in his teacup, as if he could read the future. Depression descended over him. Indeed, he probably could. Devlin had a new wife, and would start a family soon enough. He would doubtless take over the larger Kimball store, and leave Mordecai Levitz alone. But then, Mordecai Levitz was used to that.

Lizzie's tone softened. "I have missed you."

I miss you too. Every morning when I wake up and you are not there. Those stolen hours with her had been so brief, yet he did not dare repeat them. Right now, when the time came for him to go back to New York, he could do so and forget her eventually. He hoped. But if their illicit affair went further . . .

Decisively he set his cup down on the sofa table and rose. "Well, I must be off. Thank you for the tea."

A proud expression descended over her face. "You are welcome." She rang the bell beside her settee. When a maid answered, she said formally, "Show Mr. Levitz out."

Nodding to disguise his hurt at her abrupt coldness, Mordecai followed the maid to the door. He walked away, determined not to look back.

He managed not to, but the image he carried in his brain made the glance unnecessary.

And so things went for a time. Mordecai and Devlin worked in their store; Charlaine worked in hers; and Elizabeth threw herself into a whirlwind of social activity. Devlin grew muscular beneath his clothes. Charlaine's tiny waist grew tinier still as her face became thin and hollow eyed.

Mordecai's clothes began to sag on his lean physique. And Elizabeth, well, she seemed in fine spirits, flitting from soiree to ball to garden party.

June drew nigh. All of London was in a nervous dither over the upcoming jubilee. Streets were repaved, lights cleaned, windows washed and garbage cleared. London might be an aged biddy, full of decay, but give her a party to look forward to, and the old dame perked up like a debutante.

As the great day drew near, London virtually sparkled with gaiety.

The stores stayed open later for the influx of people coming from all parts of the world for the grand celebration. The restaurants had to turn away diners. Hotels bulged at the seams, hastily furnishing storerooms as bedchambers. Caterers and couturiers worked around the clock, sewing for all of London and half the continent.

Business was brisk at the local jewelry stores. As she sat in her office approximately two weeks after her marriage, Charlaine was thankful for the extra work. She needed to be exhausted at night to have any hope of sleeping. Even in the dark, she could feel her husband's watchful eyes. And she was astounded at the number of exercises he did both morning and night.

Of late, it had become easier to think of him as her husband, though in truth they resembled roomates, and not very compatible ones at that, more than soul mates. By her choice, his reproachful eyes reminded her. Charlaine tried to force Devlin from her mind and concentrate on her work. Their jewel cases were becoming bare. She was even now appraising the offerings of companies she'd formerly disdained working with. She liked none of their creations, however. After viewing the necklace Devlin had almost finished, even the most exquisite diamonds seemed tasteless and bland.

A knock offered a welcome distraction. At her command, her manager peeked inside. "Mr. Cecil Rhodes requests an audience, my lady."

"Tell him to come in." Charlaine stacked the sketches in a neat pile and tossed them in the garbage. Better to have few offerings than to ruin their reputation as the queen's jeweler by selling this refuse. She rose and extended her hand to Cecil.

He bowed over it. He waited politely until she was seated, and then flipped his coattails back to sit down opposite her. "I have come to invite you to attend the jubilee with me."

Leave it to Cecil not to mince words. "I am flattered, but I must, of course, attend with my husband."

His brows lowered in that beetling scowl he was famous for. "But I have it on the best authority that you are not, ah, on good terms with your husband."

Charlaine leaned back in her chair and folded her hands on the desk. Better that than to slap him for his presumption. "And who told you that, pray?"

He waved a dismissive hand. "Never mind. Is it true or not?"

Charlaine rose, gracefully rounded the desk and flung open the door. "You are so good at forging new alliances and charting unknown territory, that perhaps you can revel in this new experience: you are not welcome here. We will in future buy our stones from Barney Barnato."

Cecil gawked up at her. "But . . . but . . ."

"The eloquent Cecil Rhodes stunned to silence? Amazing. Please leave."

His face red with humiliation, Cecil surged to his feet. "Durwood will hear from me about this indignity."

"Good. And he shall hear from me, as well."

As Cecil pivoted to stalk out, she added softly, "And by the way, Cecil. When you threaten my husband, you threaten me. Leave us be. For all our sakes."

With a last furious glare, he stomped out.

Charlaine closed the door and weakly leaned back against it. She reserved the right, as his wife, to speak to Devlin as she pleased, but no one else had that luxury. Especially a man who refused even to acknowledge Đevlin as his relative. Still, when she remembered Cecil's face, she had to giggle nervously. What had come over her, to speak to Cecil that way?

Thrill to the most sensual, adventure-filled Historical Romances on the market today...

FROM  LEISURE BOOKS

As a home subscriber to Leisure Romance Book Club you'll enjoy the best in today's BRAND-NEW Historical Romance fiction. For over twenty-five years, Leisure Books has brought you the award-winning, high-quality authors you know and love to read. Each Leisure Historical Romance will sweep you away to a world of high adventure...and intimate romance. Discover for yourself all the passion and excitement millions of readers thrill to each and every month.

Save $5.⁰⁰ Each Time You Buy!

Each month, the Leisure Romance Book Club brings you four brand-new titles from Leisure Books, America's foremost publisher of Historical Romances. EACH PACKAGE WILL SAVE YOU $5.00 FROM THE BOOKSTORE PRICE! And you'll never miss a new title with our convenient home delivery service.

Here's how we do it. Each package will carry a FREE 10-DAY EXAMINATION privilege. At the end of that time, if you decide to keep your books, simply pay the low invoice price of $16.96, no shipping or handling charges added. HOME DELIVERY IS ALWAYS FREE. With today's top Historical Romance novels selling for $5.99 and higher, our price SAVES YOU $5.00 with each shipment.

AND YOUR FIRST FOUR-BOOK SHIPMENT IS TOTALLY FREE!

IT'S A BARGAIN YOU CAN'T BEAT! A Super $21.96 Value!

LEISURE BOOKS A Division of Dorchester Publishing Co., Inc.

Get Four Books Totally
FREE – A $21.96 Value!

PLEASE RUSH
MY FOUR FREE
BOOKS TO ME
RIGHT AWAY!

Leisure Romance Book Club
P.O. Box 6613
Edison, NJ 08818-6613

The answer tugged at her heartstrings, but, for the moment, she stilled it with hard work.

Outside, Henry opened the carriage door for his master. "What did she say?"

"Never mind. Engage an immediate audience with Durwood Kimball for me." Henry climbed in after Cecil and banged on the carriage roof. It lurched away.

From a corner of the plush squabs, Lewis Temple looked at his employer's reddened face. "I tried to tell you that she would not betray him."

Cecil propped a long leg on the seat opposite his. "Yes, well, I had to see for myself how well he'd seduced her. If she'd accepted, he would have been so angry that a wedge would have been driven between them."

"Now what?" Temple asked.

"You found nothing in his flat?"

"No, but I was just beginning to search when the Jew arrived. I had to hide until he left, and by then the maid was due. I'm certain there's a safe somewhere on the premises."

Henry looked at the two older men with a frown. "But even if you find something, how will you make it known without, without . . ."

Cecil arrowed a glance at him. "The pot calling the kettle black, as it were?"

Expressively, Henry spread his hands, saying, *What else*?

"We will find a way. Give a fellow like that enough rope, and he will always hang himself."

Lewis Temple watched Henry carefully as Cecil made the statement.

*   *   *

That night, over dinner, Durwood appraised the silent young couple. They had a habit of playing with their food rather than eating it, and he was growing concerned about them. All was obviously not well in their bedchamber, despite their efforts to make him believe otherwise.

"Cecil came to see me today. To say he was offended at your comments, my dear daughter, is to put a light face upon a grim matter." Durwood sipped his wine.

Charlaine wiped her mouth delicately with her napkin. "He deserved every word. But I do not wish to discuss this now."

Glancing between them, Devlin frowned. "What happened?"

"Charlaine berated him for—"

"Nothing that concerns you." Charlaine set her napkin neatly beside her plate and rose. "Please excuse me. I am exhausted. I will leave you gentlemen to your port. Good night."

Devlin hurried to the door to open it for her. For a moment their eyes met. He tenderly traced the shadows under her eyes. He whispered, "Do you wish me to sleep elsewhere? You are looking ragged, *chère*. I hope it is not because of me."

She pulled away. "I am too busy at the store. That's all." And she fled up the stairs, as if hoping he would not notice that she did not reply to his generous offer.

But the little smile that flitted about his lips said that he did notice. That he found it most interesting that she did not take the opportunity to be rid of his presence.

Durwood observed their expressions, wondering what was said. Devlin's smile faded as he sat back down. "Now, what transpired between Cecil and Charlaine?"

Absently toying with his silverware, Durwood pretended not to hear. "Would you care for some port?"

"You know I don't like the stuff. Too sweet."

"Ah, yes. I have noticed that about you. Your tastes lean to the pert and piquant. In women and in wine." Durwood rose to pour himself a glass of port from the sideboard.

"Quit trying to distract me, Durwood. It won't work. I will find out what happened today even if I have to ask my esteemed cousin."

Durwood choked on a sip. "I should love to see his expression."

Such a black look clouded Devlin's face that Durwood took pity on him. "Oh, very well. I make no doubt Charlaine would prefer that you not know this, but I think you should. She came to your defense when Cecil invited her to attend the jubilee with him."

Perfect white teeth gleamed in Devlin's open mouth. Then he surged to his feet. "The bounder! How dare he—"

"Precisely the way Charlaine reacted. Though she might have her own quarrels with you, she would never subject you to such humiliation. I have the perfect ticket to silence all this gossip. A ball to celebrate your union. The invitations have already gone out."

But Devlin didn't seem to be listening. His rage had been replaced with something both quieter and more calculating. "Excuse me, Durwood. I shall see you in the morning." Devlin strode out of the study and up the stairs two at a time.

Durwood raised his wineglass in salute, smiling wistfully as he glanced at his wife's portrait over the dining room sideboard. "Soon, my dear. We shall have our heir. I hope."

A soft glow of gaslight filled her chamber with romantic shadows, but Charlaine barely noticed as she sat before her dressing table brushing her hair. She was not expecting Devlin for some time, so she sat in her chemise and stockings, a wrap carelessly thrown about her shoulders but not fastened. God help her if Devlin found out how strenuously she'd defended him. It would only be one more weapon to use against her.

As to why their relationship always seemed to be reduced to a battle of some sort, she could not, or would not, fathom. She only knew that the emotions raging within her at his touch, at his glance, at his mere presence, could best be described as her own personal Waterloo. Triumph over her own weaknesses and she won all she'd staked her life on; give in to this man who'd marshaled all his formidable skills against her and she would end a broken woman, dreaming in her tower of what might have been.

Lost in thought, she started when he appeared in the mirror behind her. His eyes, those gorgeous blue eyes that had seen much and knew all, devoured her in one gulp.

"If you knew how many times I have dreamed of you exactly as you are now," he purred. A wicked smile stretched those mobile lips. "Well, the venue was slightly different." He glanced at the bed.

Every hair on her neck stood on end. He had not been so bold in weeks. He knew. Her father had told him, the beast. She turned to the side, tied her wrap firmly about her waist and flipped her hair forward to brush it vigorously. Thus shielded, she was confident enough to bluff. "Dreams are such insubstantial things. They bear so little resemblance to reality."

The brush was gently pulled away. "Reality is what we make it." And he tilted her head back, brushed her long, lush hair away from her face and framed her cheekbones in his hands. "Reality is dawn held back by delight, a child's first cry at his mother's bosom, the helping hand we share as we grow old together."

Her eyes grew misty despite her best efforts, for the images he inspired with his eloquence were the same ones that haunted her dreams, the same ones that mocked her attempt to reduce their relationship to nothing more than a battle of wills. It was not pride that kept her still under his touch. She had no strength to resist when he bent and lightly, so lightly she barely felt it, brushed the tip of his tongue against the corners of her mouth. Her lips tingled so that she had to touch them, but she could not block out his words.

"Reality is a wife's loyalty and defense of her husband against his enemies." He caught her shoulders and turned her back around before the mirror. "And her husband can do nothing but show his appreciation." He tugged her wrap open.

She covered his nimble fingers with her own clumsy ones. "What are you doing?"

"You helped shave me. I am merely returning the favor in helping you with one of your own female rituals."

He slipped the robe off her shoulders, picked up the hairbrush and began to stroke it through her already brushed hair. But he did it in such a gentle, sensual manner that her shoulders lifted in a contented sigh. Her eyes drifted shut, so she did not see him take his free hand and adjust himself in his breeches.

When she was drowsy and unguarded, he quickly unlaced her chemise. Her eyes popped open when the fabric was pulled over her head, leaving her bare to the waist. She started to rise, but he gently pressed her back down with his hands on her shoulders.

"Reality," he whispered, "is the sheer pleasure of my hands on you, of our eyes meeting in a need that is greater than either of us separately. A need that can

213

be fulfilled only when we come together as husband and wife should."

Those mesmerizing blue eyes bathed her in flames that warmed but did not burn as slowly, slowly, he started at her shoulders, kneading with persuasive fingers. If he had looked at her bare bosom, she would have run. Instead he held her gaze. She so badly wanted to believe the devotion she saw there. Surely there was something behind the passion that she could hold for a lifetime.

And because abruptly, painfully, she had to know, she stayed still and let him seduce her.

The gentle touch lowered to her spine, tracing its perfect curvature from nape to tailbone. Gooseflesh marked his path. Only then, when her nipples were hard with pleasure, did he gently bring both hands around her to cup her breasts. Still holding her eyes in the mirror, he lifted the exquisitely sensitive orbs, cradled them, caressed them until her heart beat so hard against her rib cage that she trembled.

His lips parted over his white teeth as his own breath quickened. Finally he looked down at what he held. Helplessly, she looked too.

The sight of his tanned masculine hands cradling the essence of her femininity routed the last of Charlaine's forces. With a contented purr of her own, she surrendered. Waterloo be damned. Exile with him would be a happiness such as she'd never known.

He obviously saw the softening in her face, for he closed his own eyes. He made a little sound that was half groan, half prayer, and then he bent, his soft hair brushing her shoulder, and sampled her offering. The feel of his mouth on her, suckling, licking, was more than she could bear. She squirmed on her seat, crossing her legs to still the ache between them.

Sweeping her into his arms, he carried her to the

bed. She kept her eyes closed, for if she opened them, the dream would dissipate. Or would it be the reality he described so sweetly? She swore she did not know, even as he laid her on the bed and pulled her stockings off.

His lips traced the lithe curves revealed, teeth nibbling at the arch of her foot.

She bowed against the bed, astounded to find such a mundane part of her anatomy could bring such sublime feelings. His hands were at the waistband of her pantalets, preparing to pull them off, when his husky voice reached her through a sensual haze. "Do you want this, *chère*? Do you want us to truly wed this night in fact as well as name?"

Yes! Yes! screamed her senses. *Wait*, begged the Ice Princess. Charlaine opened her eyes and tried to focus on him. The gas lamps behind his head cast his face in shadow. His hands were still as he awaited her decision.

Had he not stopped to ask, she never would have stopped to think. But he had, and she must, or be hanged as a hypocrite, mouthing her protests even as she squirmed her pleasure beneath him.

"I . . . do not know," she finally managed.

The blessed weight that she wanted to feel throughout her length lifted. He towered by the bed. "When you know, I will be waiting." He straightened his clothes, gave a curse and stomped out.

Charlaine sat up to call him back, but she bit her tongue instead. This was best. Yet the tears came, not in a trickle, but a flood. She buried her head in her pillow to stifle them. She beat the soft mattress with her fists, but the tantrum could not drown the cool voice that taunted her.

Damn him, the last thing she'd expected from her

Colleen Shannon

French frog was such chivalry.

A prince, however, wore chivalry like his crown.

"Fool! Idiot!" Devlin castigated himself as he poured brandy with a shaking hand. His heart's desire had been his for the taking and he'd stupidly let honor interfere. He tossed back a snifter full, and a second, before the burning in his belly eased the pain at his groin. Much more of this and he'd have to seek out a lady of the night or go mad.

He was still growling at himself when Durwood came in wearing a dressing gown of plum silk with gold braid. The male frippery doubtless cost more than Devlin had made in his first year in the diamond fields. The contrast of his life then and now could not have been stronger. And yet he had been a happier man with a hungry belly and dirty fingernails than he was in this palace. Then, at least, he had been free to succeed or fail based on the efforts of his own strong back. Here he was trapped in a situation of his choosing but not of his design.

Devlin slouched back in his father-in-law's best wing chair and raised his glass. "To us. The frog and the Ice Princess." He drank deeply.

Frowning his concern, Durwood nudged Devlin's legs aside to take the other chair. "You quarreled?"

A harsh laugh was his only answer.

Durwood sighed. "Don't worry, my boy. The first year is always hardest."

Devlin spewed a mouthful of brandy back into his glass. "I am living proof of that, sir." He brooded down at himself.

Only then did Durwood notice the bulge in Devlin's breeches. Concern grew. If the pair had not been intimate by now . . . He tried to think of a delicate way of asking, but there simply was none. "Does she deny you her bed still?"

"Your daughter is a most stubborn woman." Devlin beat his head against the soft chair back several times. "And I am a fool."

Such information was not exactly elucidating, though the latter appraisal Durwood could not agree with. Durwood stood to pour himself a brandy. Then, sitting back down, he eyed his son-in-law. "Would you like to hear how Charlaine grew up?"

"Indeed I would." Anything that would help him understand her better, the better to slip under her weaknesses and into her bed. Past that, Devlin could not plan.

"She was an only child, lonely from the beginning because we lost her mother, God bless her soul. I did my best with nursemaids and such, but there is simply no substitute for a mother's love."

"Yes." Devlin could not imagine what would have happened to him if his mother had deserted him, as so many in her situation had. He had no way of knowing which was worse: growing up without a father or without a mother. "May I ask sir, why you never wed again?"

Durwood stared into the fire, a faraway expression in his deep blue eyes. "I never loved again. Nor shall I ever." He sipped his brandy. "It is a Kimball failing, my boy. One Charlaine shares. From the time of my great-grandfather, the pirate Drake Kimball who founded our fortune, we have always loved once, and only once."

A pang sliced through Devlin. What if he were not that man for Charlaine? If she were truly destined to care for him, as her father thought, wouldn't she have begged him to love her this night? It was obvious she wanted him. Yet something held her back.

Durwood's voice recalled him to the present. Reality. He smiled bitterly, remembering his passionate words to Charlaine. He had meant them at the time, but now they seemed as pretty and as empty as his life in this shell of good taste and refinement.

"Charlaine had few friends," Durwood continued. "Even when I sent her away to the best young ladies' academy, she kept to herself. She has always been a very self-sufficient child. Too much so. It began when I taught her to think for herself, like a man. By the time she was eighteen, she was helping me in the business, and running her own trust fund and the estate left to her on the distaff side of my family."

"What estate?"

"It's called Summerlea. A small Tudor mansion with lands not far from London. It's been in my family for generations." Durwood smiled ruefully. "Or I should say in the female side of the family. The Kimball women have left it to their female descendants, from the time Callista Raleigh bequeathed it to her daughter, and to her daughter's daughter, and so on. Even when there were no direct female descendants, as in my family, the estates were held in trust for the next female."

"Interesting. I begin to see why Charlaine was so determined not to wed."

"That's partially my fault. From the time I dandled Charlaine on my knee, she's heard of Callista Raleigh and her heirs. We even have a family heirloom, a most magnificent book of fairy tales, that recounts these stories. I shall show it to you sometime." Durwood drank deeply, and did not see the dull red that colored Devlin's cheekbones.

He went on, "With these examples to follow, Charlaine was determined never to wed for station, or for society, or even for wealth. She would wed only for love, and she was frightened of that. That end became increasingly unlikely as she rejected all suitors. She feared losing her independence to any man, even one who would care for her."

"So you forced her into my arms." Devlin set his glass down on a side table and rose. "Well, in my arms she may be, but in my bed she is not. And frankly, I am becoming so frustrated that I may soon ruin any chance we have at happiness if she does not change her mind."

Durwood hurried beside Devlin to the door. "Nonsense, Devlin. Persist and you will win her. Take it from one who knows: the love of a woman like Charlaine is worth working for, even suffering for. When you win her, she will never leave you. Why, this very day she defended you against a very powerful man—"

"For which I tried to show my gratitude tonight. She spurned me." Devlin held up a hand wearily when Durwood would have protested further. "I will persist for a while longer. But if something does not change soon, I am going back to my flat." And sanity. But this last Devlin did not say as he glumly climbed the stairs. He paused outside her chamber, staring at the door.

With a frustrated groan, he turned away to the first guest room he came to. Not tonight. No exercises, no furtive looks in the dark. Just sleep.

And forgetfulness.

Both came slowly, but eventually they came.

Not so for Charlaine. All through that long night she waited. And waited for him to come. At three in the morning, she finally admitted defeat, turned up her gas lamps and picked up the first book she came to. When she realized it was a book of love sonnets, she dropped it as if burned, buried her face in her hands, and wondered what in the name of heaven she was to do about this mess of a marriage.

At six she dressed carefully, resolved to speak to Devlin and work out some kind of compromise. How much longer he would remain so . . . forbearing, she could not say. But these close quarters without intimacy were difficult for him. She knew he wanted her. She did not have to be experienced about men to understand that. And if these past hours spent aching for him were a nightly experience for him, then she could not blame his short temper.

Feeling slightly better, she tripped down the stairs and burst into the morning room. "Good . . ." She trailed off when she saw only her father at the table. He lowered his paper to look at her.

"Good morning, my dear."

"Where is Devlin?"

"At his shop, I believe."

She glanced at the brooch watch pinned to her lapel. "At seven in the morning?"

"I believe he, ah, had a difficult night." Durwood watched her closely as she sank into a chair.

When he shoved a laden platter of kidneys, boiled eggs and kippers toward her, she blanched and shoved it back again.

"But you are not eating enough. You are growing positively thin." Despite her protests, he piled a plate with scones, fruit and one egg, setting it before her.

"I am not a child." She poured herself a cup of tea and nursed it, along with her wounded feelings. Though why she felt wounded, she could not say. For the past two weeks she'd hoped he'd sleep elsewhere, yet the first time he complied she felt betrayed.

"Then do not act like one. A mature woman knows her duty, and does it."

Charlaine systematically crumbled a scone. "Now

why do I have a feeling that we do not speak of food?"

Like a master of ceremonies, Durwood tapped his spoon against his egg cup. "But I have devised a plan for you to prove to the world—and to Cecil Rhodes—your devotion to your husband." He waited expectantly, but when Charlaine merely sipped quietly at her tea, he ground out, "A ball. This Saturday. I have even commissioned a new dress for you in honor of it."

Slowly, carefully, Charlaine set her teacup precisely in her saucer. "How solicitous of you. Pity I can't be in attendance." She stood.

Durwood surged to his feet and caught her arm as she rounded the table. "You will come, and gladly. You will play the part of devoted wife, or by God . . ."

She wrenched her arm away. "You invoke the wrong deity. Your plan, which Devlin and I are both paying the price for, was devilishly successful, that I admit." When he gasped, she said sweetly, "It was not hard for me to figure out. I merely went to see our dear acquaintance Imogen. She twittered on about how kind you were to buy her train ticket and even escort her to the train."

Durwood folded his arms over his chest, obviously not feeling guilty, or even disturbed. "It was for your own good."

Despairingly, Charlaine closed her eyes. Of course he would say that. "You do not know what is good for me any longer, if you ever have." She turned toward the door, but his quiet comment froze her in her tracks.

"Perhaps not. But one thing I do know." He stalked around until he faced her. "Devlin Rhodes is a prince among men, and you are a fool if you let him get away. No man, no matter how chivalrous, can take continual rejection and remain faithful. In short, my dear daughter, since you obviously believe yourself a mature woman: deny him your bed and he will find another."

The truths hit her like blows, but it was his last telling strike that had her running for the door.

"And I suggest you ask yourself why Devlin did not tell you at once who was responsible for your marriage. I forced this alliance, not he. He was as much a victim as you. Yet he would not tell you, and recommended that I say nothing. Why?"

Why? Why? The question taunted her even as she fled into her carriage, and then stared blindly at the gay scene outside her window as London reveled in anticipation of the jubilee. She jumped down without waiting for the coachman to lower the steps, ignored the chorus of hellos from her employees, and locked her office door behind her.

Her peaceful haven was no comfort that day. The stacks of special orders, the constant decisions of who to hire to help with the extra business, and even approving or disapproving her staff's designs, gave her no solace.

Why? Why? The question beat at her all morning long. Finally she rested her head against her chair back and gave in. She had to know, even if it meant swallowing her pride and going to the source. She rose and said curtly to her manager, "I will be out for lunch." She stalked out, pausing only to pick up her parasol.

"But, ma'am, there are so many undesirables about the streets," protested the guard who held the door. "Let me escort you."

"I am going only a few blocks," she said. "I shall be fine." And off she went, forging a way through the crowds with her lacy parasol that matched the lace at her sleeves and throat.

Indeed, she did receive many interested glances even in this respectable part of London, but none of the unattached males dared to approach, given her obvious breeding and wealth. She had made it to Devlin's shop when a familiar voice stopped her.

"Miss . . . uh, Charlaine, wait!" Henry Dupree hurried out from a shady awning covering a nearby haberdashery.

Charlaine stopped. "Good afternoon, Henry."

"It is so good to see you," he said, eating her up with his eyes. "I am glad you are looking well despite . . ." He trailed off.

She had to smile. "Despite my wicked incarceration? Is that what people say?"

"Some of them. All I know is that you did not wed this person willingly. That no one has seen you socially since your wedding. And I feel pain for your circumstances and a burning desire to help you in any way that I can." Pleadingly, he reached out to her. "Let me help you, my very dear lady."

Charlaine's skin crawled as he touched her bare forearm and caressed it with his palm. What was it about this handsome young man that gave her the shivers?

She was still wondering when a sardonic voice said, "Had I known you intended to visit me, I would have met you with bells on."

Her parasol sagged in her grip as she looked up and saw Devlin. He glared at Henry's encroaching hand until the secretary dropped Charlaine's arm, but Charlaine barely noticed. Her attention was focused on something else.

Or someone else.

A gorgeous creature with a head of blond hair too brassy to be real was hanging on her husband's arm. But the wench's china-doll complexion and long-lashed blue eyes were real enough, as was the curvaceous figure her daring gown emphasized rather than disguised.

Deny him your bed and he will find another, her father's voice insinuated in her ear. She ignored the wise counsel.

Gripping the parasol firmly, she cooed, "But what makes you think I was coming to see you?"

Aloof blue eyes glanced at the sign above her head. "I see. Mere chance brought you to my doorstep. In that case, I bid you good day." He tipped his hat to her, pulled the creature's hand more firmly into his arm and shoved open his shop door.

Bells tinkled, sending a pang through her as she recalled his sardonic comment. The only woman he angled to impress at this moment was certainly not his wife. But then, she could not really claim that title either, except in name.

Henry tilted her chin up to him and asked for obviously the second time, "Will you lunch with me?"

"Hmmm? Oh, I do not think so. I must get back." Blindly she pumped his extended hand. "Good to see you, Henry." She hurried off, her steps not so jaunty this time.

"I shall see you at the ball," he called after her.

She nodded, her throat too choked for speech. Willingly or not, she had to attend this ball and pretend to be a devoted wife. Henry's testimony to Devlin's choice of companion would be making the rounds by nightfall. And even if she had incited her husband to seek his pleasures elsewhere, the ton could not know that. They would be agog that her marriage, so hastily arranged, was also hastily regretted.

That she could not bear. She had her pride, after all. And if she also had her yearnings, and a smidgen of loyalty toward her husband, well, no one need know that.

As soon as he realized Charlaine was gone, Devlin eased away from Maybell. "Good to see you, my dear. But if you will excuse me, I have work to attend to."

"Lor', luv, is that yer missus? A cold 'un, she is." Maybell leaned close to whisper, "Come back to me, lover, and ye won't be regretful-like. I'm flush, and I'll even spring fer me own geegaw."

Devlin cleared his throat in embarrassment as his staff stared. Maybell had been his first mistress when he moved to London. Then, her ample charms had seemed fresh and appealing after the few women he'd known in the diamond fields. But their relationship had not lasted past the second lover he'd found in her bed. He cursed his luck at running into her on the street just as Charlaine had softened enough to come to him. What had she wanted?

Smiling weakly, Devlin backed toward his office. "Uh, my staff will be happy to assist you. It was good to see you again. Good day." And good riddance. Wiping his brow, Devlin leaned back against his office door.

Mordecai glanced around his shoulder as the door closed, smiled slightly, and looked back at his accounts. "Your past coming back to haunt you?"

Devlin glared. "In a manner of speaking. Damn the wench. She accosted me just as Charlaine was coming to see me. But that damned obnoxious Dupree was hanging on her arm. I've a mind to rearrange his pretty face."

"A sentiment he shares about you, no doubt." Mordecai shoved back his ledger book, his gray eyes sharp as honed steel. "But Charlaine is not interested in him. Put aside your petty jealousy and think about the real question—why is the fellow hanging about outside?"

"Watching me, no doubt. Hoping I will prove to be a fence of stolen goods." Devlin shrugged. "Let him watch until he turns into stone. That part of my life is over." With an effort, Devlin went back to work.

Mordecai watched him for a long time, fiddling with his yarmulke. He was obviously debating something, but finally he said, "Devlin, someone tried to break into our flat the other day."

That caught Devlin's attention easily enough. "How do you know?"

"Whoever did it was clever. Nothing was disarranged, except that a piece of paper I had put between the front door and the sill had dropped."

Devlin smiled. "Mordecai, I did not think you had such subterfuge in you."

Snorting, Mordecai retorted, "These London swells are amateurs compared to New York's jewel thieves, as you very well know. I have been expecting this. I suggest you move the book, which is all that remains of your last job."

"Temple, no doubt. He will never find my safe. Even if he does, I can say that my bride gave me the book. No, at this point Temple and Cecil are the least of my troubles." Unconcerned, Devlin returned to paying his bills.

But Mordecai played with his cap for a long time before he could force his attention back to the ledger.

Both of them would have been more concerned if they had seen Henry hurry after Maybell and offer his card with a smart bow. She simpered at him and willingly took his arm. They strolled down the street together.

The ball to celebrate the marriage of the last of the Kimball line was to be remembered long after the glow of the Golden Jubilee had faded. From the dukes, earls and lesser nobility in attendance, to the employees of the two jewelry stores, the event would be talked about for generations, adding to the Kimball legacy.

This part of the legacy, however, had more than a whiff of scandal.

That too was not new to the Kimballs. Or to the Rhodeses.

The night began appropriately enough. In Charlaine's chamber, Elizabeth twirled her finger before her niece. "Turn, my dear."

Charlaine turned. The gown was of gold silk so fine that it clung to every curve of her body. The low bodice was trimmed with black jet. Black satin ribbons tied beneath the bodice in a crisscross pattern to Charlaine's tiny waist, emphasizing the lush curve of her bosom. The skirts were narrower than the ones all the rage, with only the hint of a bustle at Charlaine's derriere. A big black satin bow embellished with jet decorated the fall of gold lace cascading from the bustle. More black jet studded the lace, which trailed behind Charlaine in a train. A black jet haircomb held Charlaine's curls atop her head. Gold lace gloves with a jet band at the top completed the ensemble.

Elizabeth nodded approvingly. "I never would have credited Durwood with such taste, but he chose well. You look like what you are—a woman grown."

And ripe for the picking. Elizabeth knew better than to add that aloud however.

Charlaine took a deep breath, nervous at the way her bosom pressed taut against the low bodice. She'd have to be careful, or she'd be most embarrassed. Odd that now she was wed her father allowed her to wear something so daring.

But then, maybe it wasn't so odd. This dress was for the delectation of one man. A man who had been most

227

remote of late. Charlaine had not exchanged three words with Devlin since that encounter outside his shop a week prior. Every time she saw him he was either on his way out, or in, up to the guest room he'd claimed for his own. For this reason only, Charlaine had decided to wear this dress. Surely even her strong-willed new bridegroom could not be indifferent to her tonight.

When she heard the orchestra tune up, Charlaine took a deep breath. "Are you ready, Aunt?"

Elizabeth, stunning in her own right in lavender silk and amethysts and diamonds, rose. "And able, my dear child." There was a martial slant to her jaw as she asked casually, "Have you heard if Mordecai attends?"

"No one has seen fit to share the guest list with me. But I assume so. He and Devlin are close."

The two women found the spacious hall and every formal room ablaze with light and flowers. For once Charlaine had let her father see to things, and he had planned amazingly well. The long table in the dining room had been cleared of chairs so guests could load their plates as they pleased and sit in the folding chairs against every available wall. The silver epergne in the middle of the table bubbled over with wine punch, while a music box in its base played *Claire de Lune*. A gold-plated bride and groom danced atop the epergne, rotating with the music.

Charlaine touched the pretty thing. She had never seen it before. But it was obvious her father had spared no expense. He'd bought new china and silver to accomodate the crowd he apparently expected. Orchids battled with roses for prettiest arrangement in every room. And her father had had hundreds of candles lit to add to the soft gaslight glow. From the sounds of the orchestra tuning up, it was one of the best in England.

Elizabeth looked around in delight. "This reminds me of my balls as a girl. Durwood's taste is impeccable."

Butterflies battled with hunger pangs in Charlaine's beleaguered stomach. As she turned to proceed to the next room, her heart leaped to her mouth. Devlin stood in the doorway staring at her.

It seemed that he too was starved. The look in his blue eyes as they swept over her was so hungry that her knees went weak and she had to brace herself against the wall. He was so striking in his black tails and severe white shirt that she almost burst with pride to think herself married to him.

How would she ever make it through this night, touching him frequently, dancing with him, laughing with him, and then return to her cold virgin bed?

Chapter Nine

Devlin appeared to swallow as he approached to bow over her hand. "I am honored to be at your side this night—wife."

"And you do me honor as well—husband. You are, um . . ." She trailed off at his wicked, tempting grin. This was the old Devlin, the Devlin she had missed. Still, this Devlin was much more dangerous to her peace of mind and willpower than the stranger who avoided her.

"Handsome? Debonair?" he teased.

Her lashes lowered. Once upon a time, she would have put him in his place. But at this moment, she could only nod shyly.

Devlin smiled at Elizabeth. "Would you leave us alone for a moment?"

"Certainly," answered that lady. She turned to the door, but tossed over her shoulder casually, "Does that old fussbudget, Mordecai, attend?"

"He is invited, but I do not know if he will come," Devlin responded.

The duchess nodded and departed, her sensual mouth as straight as her spine.

"It is heartening to see that love is still a great leveler, no matter what your age," Devlin said, staring after the duchess as if he could see into her heart. "Poor Lizzie. She will find Mordecai a sore trial, I fear."

"Do you truly believe they love one another?" Charlaine asked, skeptical.

"Yes. But whether a Jew who loves New York can be happy with a most English duchess . . ." He shrugged. Then, taking her hand, he led her to one of the chairs against the wall, seated her, and knelt before her on one well-clad knee.

Charlaine's eyes widened.

Taking her hands, he said solemnly, "This is weeks too late, but I want you to know, lady mine, that I pledge my troth to you and your happiness." He released one of her hands so his own could fumble in his pocket. Something gold as sunshine, sparkling as laughter, precious as love, danced at his fingertips.

Touched, Charlaine could not speak as he dangled the heirloom in front of her eyes. Although she would have recognized the stone in her sleep, it wore a new guise that flattered its natural beauty. The Yellow Rose, that legendary jewel that began a dynasty, had been recut to an even more perfect rose shape with modern tools that had been unavailable in the century long ago when it was set. Devlin had surrounded the large canary diamond with alternating teardrop and round diamonds. It was a rose forever new, symbol of love and . . . Charlaine looked away, unable to gaze into those tender blue eyes and pretend she could not see the devotion there.

231

His voice was husky as he fastened the simple chain behind her neck. "This is a wedding gift from your father. These are from me." And he pulled a tiny box from his pocket.

She flipped it open, her fingers shaking. She gasped. Large yellow diamond earrings, each a carat at least, matched the necklace perfectly, right down to the white diamond settings.

"Allow me." He pulled the ear bobs from the box and put them on her ears. They dangled, catching fire with every movement of her head. He leaned back on his heels, cocked his head on the side and whispered, "*Magnifique!*"

She wavered toward him, unable to resist his powerful spell any longer. She no longer knew if this man was a frog or a prince, but one thing was as clear as the diamonds he'd given her: she wanted to kiss him. To kiss him and see if the promise in his eyes was real. To kiss him and forget the past hurts in creating new memories. He rose to take her hand and was about to draw her into his arms when Durwood shoved open the dining room door, Cecil Rhodes at his side.

"My dear, Cecil wishes to be first. . . ." Durwood trailed off. He smiled, delighted. "We'll wait." He backed out, pulling a less-than-delighted Cecil with him.

As Devlin reached for her again, Charlaine said breathlessly, "The guests are arriving. Shouldn't we go to the foyer?" She almost ran to the door and flung it open, her light steps tapping a frantic rhythm of escape.

Any other man might have been upset, left unsatisfied and aching. Devlin Rhodes smiled. An anticipatory, very male, very French smile.

The Ice Princess was about to melt.

* * *

The reception line stretched out the long ballroom, wrapped around the hall and ended in the foyer. A galaxy of jewels glittered on unlined and wrinkled necks alike, most of it purchased at Kimball's. A few of Devlin's clients were there, however, and it was these newly rich who laughed loudest and ate heartiest.

And why not, Elizabeth thought, smiling at their hearty enjoyment. Then, for the tenth time, she scanned the crowd, looking for a certain short, elderly man. She scowled. Coward. He was so afraid of her that he would let this important milestone in the life of his partner pass him by. She peered through her lorgnette at the head of the line, trying to see how her niece was bearing up. Charlaine looked composed, polite and heartbreakingly lovely. Only Elizabeth knew her well enough to read the confusion behind the facade.

Poor child. She was uncertain whether to be happy or glum at the congratulations spouted to her left and right, seeing as she had not yet accepted her own union. But with time she would. Elizabeth smiled at the attentive, striking figure of young Devlin. Indeed, any red-blooded female couldn't live long in intimate contact with that handsome scamp and remain indifferent.

"Good evening, Your Grace."

Elizabeth's lorgnette slipped comically down her nose. She peered through one lens, her world cockeyed, half in and half out of focus, but she would have recognized that solemn tone anywhere. "Good evening, Mr. Levitz."

The formality almost made her choke, but if this was his game, far be it from her to break the rules. An energetic waltz played in the background. People in every shade of silk and satin imaginable twittered in all corners of the room like exotic birds.

Yet, buffeted as they were on every side, for one timeless moment Elizabeth and Mordecai stood alone, staring at one another. Elizabeth read the regret and yearning in his eyes. The lorgnette slipped from her hand, making his beloved face a blur. She reached out to him. "Mordecai," she whispered.

The tips of his strong fingers brushed hers; then, with a rare curse, he turned and stomped off. The Duchess of Kensington reddened under the curious stares and hurried in the opposite direction. For the first time since her debut over fifty years ago she'd been routed from a ballroom by a man.

Charlaine sighed with relief as she saw the end of the receiving line. If she had to bear one more hearty male laugh, or fend off one more snide female glance, she would scream. Her tension returned as she saw who brought up the rear. She felt Devlin's hand tighten on hers.

What was that witch doing here? She could not believe Devlin had invited her.

Cecil held the brassy beauty's arm as he said loudly, "Congratulations, Charlaine." When those nearby were staring, he added, "But it was so *hasty*, dear child. And, as Shakespeare would say . . ." He trailed off.

"*Hasty marriage seldom proveth well*," Charlaine filled in mentally. Somehow she managed not to wince at the insult. She should have known Cecil would not let her own treatment of him pass unanswered.

Putting his arm about her shoulders, Devlin paraphrased, "We wooed in haste, wed at leisure . . . and now love for all time."

Murmurs at the clever response rippled from the

onlookers. While Cecil scrambled for a retort, May-bell, garbed in sapphire silk to match the expensive jewels at her throat, smiled wickedly. "So ye said to me once, ducky."

The whispers died away. Only the orchestra could be heard as all eyes turned to Charlaine. She tilted her chin higher and tried to pretend her face had not drained of color.

Devlin's arm tightened about her shoulders as he said, "Delusions of grandeur again, Maybell? Pity. Must be your choice of company." Devlin stared pointedly at Cecil, then swung his bride away. "Now excuse us, all. We have a ball to open."

For the first few steps, Charlaine was clumsy. She had never been so humiliated. Her hand was stiff in Devlin's and all her warm feelings for him had frozen to ice in the pit of her stomach.

"I did not invite her, Charlaine. Another of Cecil's ploys to humiliate me. Though how he found her, I cannot guess."

Some of the ice melted. Charlaine remembered Henry's passion outside Devlin's shop. He was conspicuously absent tonight. She had a strong feeling that he had followed Maybell. Still, even if Devlin did not deliberately humiliate her, if he found such women attractive, what chance had she?

"Did you . . . care for her as she says?"

Devlin didn't answer until he pinioned her evasive gaze. "No. My relationship with her lasted only a few months, when I was new to London, and lonely."

And starved for female companionship. A pang pierced Charlaine as she wondered how long he had been without a woman now. Her father's words reverberated in her ears, making her stumble.

He swept her up, stopping the pace long enough for her to recover. Those blue eyes that haunted her dreams held hers as he said, "The only woman I want in my bed, or my heart, is in my arms."

The words were too ragged, too spontaneous to be false. She melted against him, believing them because she wanted to. She pressed her cheek against his shoulder, treasuring the beating of his heart against her own.

Everything would be all right.

And so it seemed as the party wore into the wee hours. They had cut the enormous cake and consumed gallons of champagne, yet few of the guests left. The music was too lyric, the food too good, the wine too fine. Devlin was off in a corner with Durwood and his cronies while Charlaine spoke to an old school friend, when a footman handed her a note on a silver tray. Charlaine opened it.

Please meet me in the garden. I am not dressed for the ball, but I have information of interest to you. Henry Dupree.

Frowning, Charlaine crumpled the note and tossed it on a side table. She should ignore the fellow, she really should. Yet . . . what information did he promise? She wavered.

Her friend asked, "What is it, Charlaine? Do you wish me to get Devlin?"

Charlaine stared at her bridegroom. He was regaling the gentlemen with some tale. They hung on his every word. He wouldn't even notice if she slipped away for a moment. She wiped her damp brow. Besides, it was devilishly stuffy in here.

"Nothing of import. I shan't be but a moment. No one will miss me." And Charlaine briskly walked out of the ballroom.

She was wrong on all counts.

*   *   *

Devlin saw her go. He broke off the story he was telling about a fight he'd seen between two diamond miners and said, "Excuse me, gentlemen, for a moment." Where was she heading in such a hurry?

He'd almost made it to the ballroom door when a firm hand landed on his arm. "Lord love a duck, but ye are always in a hurry these days. Take a moment to share a word with yer old sweetheart, won't ye?" And Maybell pulled him outside the ballroom into a small antechamber set up as a coatroom.

Short of physically pushing her away, Devlin could not avoid her, especially as she planted her lush backside against the door.

From opposite corners of the ballroom, the duchess and Mordecai watched the young couple leave. Elizabeth hurried out, with Mordecai not far behind her.

And from his seat against the wall, Cecil Rhodes checked his pocket watch and smiled. He rose in leisurely fashion and approached the elderly set of ladies who gossiped in a corner. "Would you care to join me outside for a breath of air, ladies?"

Charlaine peered through the dark at the Diana fountain. The moon flirted with clouds, casting enough light for her to see that Henry was not there yet. She sat on the edge of the fountain and trailed her fingers in the water. Diana watched her dispassionately, with a haughty composure forever frozen in stone. Charlaine reflected that she had once been like that, fearful of the pain emotional attachment brought. She'd spent a childhood grieving for the mother she'd never known, and an adulthood resenting her father for his distraction with business.

What wasted emotion. She was still staring up at Diana, vaguely realizing that now was neither the time

237

nor the place for this revelation, when Henry said, "You put her beauty to shame."

Charlaine stood. "What did you wish to see me about, Henry?"

Henry whipped a familiar oilskin-wrapped rectangle from behind his back. He was dressed in simple black pants and a white shirt with flowing arms that made him look romantic and handsome.

Charlaine's attention was fixed on one thing—the book. She grasped it and opened the wrapping, holding her breath as she ran trembling fingers over the binding, the back, and flipped through the pages. He had kept it safe, as promised. But . . .

"Where did you get this?"

Henry shrugged. "Does it matter? All that matters is that what was stolen from you is safely returned. And what a beautiful object it is. Now I understand why you always look like a princess from some fairy tale. Your family has lived its own legends for generations." Henry went down on one knee and took her free hand. "Please, my dearest Charlaine. Come away with me. Let us add our own romantic story to this book. We can get your sham of a marriage annulled."

Pulling away so quickly that Henry almost fell off balance, Charlaine retorted, "Are you mad? I will not dishonor my name so."

For a long moment Henry was still. Then he jumped to his feet. The clouds chose that moment to cover the moon, so Charlaine didn't realize he was so close until it was too late. He clasped her in a passionate embrace, ignoring her gasping protest, and lowered his mouth over hers. At first she was too stunned at his presumption to struggle, and then, for one curious instant, she waited, wondering if this handsome young man who obviously desired her could arouse her passion as easily as Devlin could.

She lay quiescent, but the passionate suckling of her lips left her cold. Her heart rate did not quicken, as it did with Devlin, nor did her loins tighten, nor did her mouth tingle. She was about to pull away when a familiar voice said, "Goodness, we are apparently de trop. Come along, ladies."

Charlaine wrenched away, but it was too late. The gaggle of old women with Cecil Rhodes were already honking like geese. Charlaine gave Henry a furious look and scrubbed at her mouth, wondering what excuse she could make, but a movement behind the staring ladies caught her attention.

A very quiet, very still Devlin stood there. The moon made its grand entrance, and they stared at each other's disarray. His collar was crooked, and, as he slowly approached, she saw lip rouge on his lapel. That voluptuous blond harlot traipsed after him into the garden, the telltale smearing at her lips speaking volumes to Charlaine's outraged sensibilities.

The excuse for her own behavior died stillborn. Pain made her sway in her light dancing slippers, but it was the look in Devlin's eyes as he stood in front of her that made her chin go up. How dare he condemn her for something she did not invite, when proof of his own unfaithfulness lurked there on his person?

Quiet drifted over the peaceful garden like a fall of snow, deadening Charlaine to everything but Devlin. The ladies watched, all agog, as the delicious scandal unfolded before them like a lurid play. And Cecil? His glee at the humiliation of his erstwhile relative glowed in his gray eyes. Mordecai and Elizabeth hurried down the terrace, Durwood hot on their heels.

But the young couple knew nothing but each other. When Devlin stepped closer, his fists clenched, Charlaine stiffened, wondering if he was going to hit her. He brushed her aside, wrenched the book Dupree had

239

picked up out of the man's hands, tossed it aside, and gave the clerk an uppercut.

Henry fell sideways, caught himself and barreled forward, his arms about Devlin's waist. The two men went sprawling next to the fountain. The moon hid again, but the grunts and furious curses gave the listeners clues to who was winning. Charlaine made to hurry forward to stop them, but a strong arm pulled her back. She tried to wrench herself away, but Cecil would not allow it.

"Every woman wants to be fought over, my dear," he whispered into her ear. "Let them settle this as men should."

"I'd expect that of you, you . . . tyrant." Charlaine kicked his knee. He winced, but let her go.

By the time she rushed forward, the fight was over. The moon came back out to show Henry propped drunkenly against the side of the fountain, his clothes wet in the spray, half-conscious. His nose was bloody, one eye bruised.

Devlin stood over him, his chest heaving, his fists still clenched. The only mark on him was a small cut at the edge of his mouth. His breathing slowed as he looked at his wife. She refused to hang her head, and gave him back as good as she got. He bent, picked up the book and tossed it at her. "This is yours, I believe."

She caught it, realizing vaguely that he was going to leave her. The book was proof of that, for he had always said he would keep it until he won. His suit was at an end because she had disgusted him with her apparent infidelity. A thousand excuses came to mind, but she voiced none of them. *Let him go*, whispered the heiress. The more vulnerable Charlaine trembled with despair.

Wiping at his cut lip, Devlin turned on his heel—toward the estate gate.

Help came from an unexpected quarter. "Now you can add rank thievery to all your other flaws," Cecil drawled. He glanced at the book Charlaine cradled to her breast.

Devlin froze. Slowly he turned. "Oh, yes? Well, one might ask where you found this, ah, supposedly stolen item."

Cecil smirked. "In your flat."

Gasps circled the growing crowd of onlookers. Mordecai followed as Elizabeth hurried to her niece and drew her under a protective arm.

Cecil's smile faded. "I did not find it, of course. I believe a certain Pinkerton agent, who is aware of your, er, reputation from when you lived in America, was determined to see justice done." Only Cecil Rhodes could make breaking and entering sound like a virtue.

Charlaine pulled away from Elizabeth and stood on her own two feet, as she had done for as long as she could remember. "Did I report anything stolen to the police?"

"Not to my knowledge. But that doesn't change the facts," Cecil blustered.

"I beg to differ." Charlaine handed the book to Devlin. He hesitated, then took it. "A gift can hardly be construed as being stolen."

Some of the tension eased from about Devlin's mouth. Carefully he wrapped the book.

The whispers that circled this time were not critical of Devlin Rhodes. Cecil realized he'd lost the advantage, and was fumbling for a response when Mordecai stepped forward.

"And I may just contact the police myself. I wondered why my window was broken. Most unsporting of you, Mr. Rhodes."

Cecil glared his particular brand of intimidation from his much greater height, but it bounced off the

Colleen Shannon

stony countenance of Mordecai Levitz.

Durwood joined Mordecai. "My butler will see you out, Cecil. Now, ladies, we have put out some fresh champagne. Do join me." Durwood put his hands on the backs of two of the ladies and led them away.

Humiliated, Cecil then tried to glare Jeffries down, but that worthy looked down his nose with a distaste only a Scot could convey with such silent eloquence. Henry had struggled to his feet, cradling an obviously aching head. He looked from Charlaine to Cecil, but he stared at Devlin longest. A shiver went through Charlaine at his expression, but then the young clerk stomped off, ignoring Cecil's call to wait.

Cecil went back up the steps, pausing only slightly at Devlin's sarcastic, "Thank you for your kind congratulations on my marriage—cousin. And thank you for bringing Maybell."

Mordecai caught Elizabeth's arm. "We have not waltzed yet, my dear. Shall we remedy that?"

"I should be honored, sir." And the duchess, with a last worried look at the young couple, followed Mordecai back into the house.

Now, when Charlaine needed darkness most, the moon stubbornly held sway over the clouds. She swallowed, trying to ease the pounding of her heart, but it seemed caught in her throat as she quavered, "Well, our ball shall be talked about for a long time to come, at least."

He did not laugh. He merely continued to stare at her as if he'd never seen her before. Finally he said, "And should this make me happy? I have done my best to live respectably, and you dishonor me—"

"I? Dishonor you? You have it backward—husband." She glanced disparagingly at the lip rouge on his lapel. "At my own ball you have a tête à tête with your old inamorata."

"And you swooned in the arms of your new one."

Charlaine flounced past him toward the steps. "Ooh! Leave it to you to see a perfectly natural reaction in such sordid terms."

He caught her arm and shook it slightly. "Natural? Natural that a wife denies her husband his rights, only to grant them to a rank stranger?"

"Henry is no stranger." She jerked away. "And the only thing rank around here is your hypocrisy. You deny me kisses until I am molded to your will." She flicked at his lapel. "Well, if ever proof existed that my decision was right, here it is. Now excuse me. I have had enough of this . . . celebration."

She ran up the steps, hoping to keep the tears at bay until she reached her room. To her relief, Durwood stood at the door escorting out the last of the ladies. He saw her run past, as did the women, and said to them without missing a beat, "We hope you will visit us again soon." When the door was closed, his composure cracked. He took two steps toward his daughter, but stopped when Devlin burst through the door, rage flushing his face.

"Now, Devlin, I am certain Cecil orchestrated that embrace. Do not—"

"He did not orchestrate her response. She lay still and let him kiss her while she denies me. Well, no longer." Devlin took the stairs three at a time.

The sound of Charlaine's door slamming punctuated his rage and quickened his steps. Durwood hovered at the bottom of the stairs, indecisive, but Mordecai said from the door to the ballroom, "He will not hurt her, Durwood. Perhaps this is what they need to clarify their relationship."

"Clarify? What a peculiar way to put it."

Mordecai arched a brow. "Actually, I would compare a marriage to a diamond's clarity. Some are

243

cloudy and cluttered; others are pure and clear. But it sometimes takes a telling blow to see how well they're structured. Tonight Charlaine and Devlin's marriage will either become a thing of beauty or . . ."

"It will shatter into bits."

Gently Mordecai nodded. "It is in God's hands now."

Devlin gritted his teeth as he reached the door to Charlaine's bedchamber. He paused, his hands on the sill, trying to calm his raging male instincts. For the first time in his life, he understood jealousy. Many times the various women in his life had grown possessive and clinging, which only made his interests stray further. He'd never understood their behavior.

Until tonight. The fury that had surged through him at the sight of Charlaine letting Dupree kiss her had almost taken off the top of his head. It still surged through his veins in a primitive rhythm answered by the beat of his heart. One urge, one need so deep-seated that cavemen must have felt it too, made his hands shake as he reached out to Charlaine's doorknob. Primitive it was, this need he'd never known, this urge for conquest. He battled it for a moment longer, knowing that he risked all on this one night.

And then, with a simple movement of her wrist, she routed his struggling chivalry—she locked her door.

The sound of that bolt going home steadied his hands. No more indecisiveness or misplaced gallantry. She'd teased him, denied him for the last time. She would be his, this night. They were wed, and if she sent him on his way after he had bedded her, so be it. At least she would never forget him. He lifted his leg and kicked at the doorjamb. The damned English oak splintered a bit, but it held.

Her voice quavered at him through the door, "I have my gun!"

He kicked again. The jamb split. The last kick sent the door reeling back on its hinges. He barreled through.

Indeed, she stood there, still shrugging into a dressing gown. A sense of déjà vu almost overwhelmed him as she finally, awkwardly, managed to tie the garment while still holding the weapon on him. Her hand trembled, but at this range she could hardly miss.

Hauling the sofa before the door to hold it shut, he said through gritted teeth, "Shoot me if you wish, for I swear I'd as soon be out of my misery as spend another night on this damned sofa."

Her mouth made an O of surprise as he straightened to face her and began to take off his clothes. First the cutaway coat, then the vest, finally the shirt. That strong bare chest made her eyes widen. The pistol trembled so that she looked in danger of dropping it.

"I suggest you use it, or put it away. No more maneuvers, no more bluffs, no more excuses. Tonight you are mine." And he approached her.

She ducked behind the table holding the flowers, obviously expecting him to spend time in an undignified game of tag. Again he proved that tonight was different. Tonight the soundrel, the libertine French frog, held sway. He kicked the table aside, sending flowers and books scattering.

Her grip tightened on the pistol as he came closer still. She nibbled at her lip, sobbed something unintelligible, and tossed the pistol aside. It skittered over the floor, landing behind the drapes. She tried to run, but strong, hungry male hands caught her midflight.

She struggled, kicking at his legs, trying to pry his arms free, but he was as strong as steel and equally rigid. As he pulled her inexorably closer, he knew she felt that he was rigid below the belt as well. Her angry color left in a rush. She went still.

His grip eased. A rush of French battered at her wavering defenses: *"Ma petite, s'il te plait, surrendre. Je t'aime."*

He saw from her uncomprehending expression that she didn't speak French. It was just as well. He had not meant for the confession to slip out. He preferred to show her.

He swept her up in his arms and carried her to the bed.

Downstairs, Mordecai and Elizabeth still swayed dreamily to the strains of the sleepy violinist who had agreed to play a bit longer. The rest of the musicians were gone. The servants had almost finished cleaning up, and Durwood had long ago sought his bed, with a last worried glance at his daughter's door.

"Why did you not ask me to dance earlier?" asked Elizabeth.

Mordecai ran a hand over her silvery, disarranged coiffure. "I do not wish to subject you to the gossips, Lizzie. Why, your own servants disapprove of me. Do you think this gathering would look favorably upon our relationship?"

She raised her head to glare at him. "Do you think I give a fig? I have never been sought after by the sticklers of society. I do not intend to begin now, in my twilight years."

Running a tender finger from her indignant nose to her stubborn mouth, he whispered, "Twilight? My dear Lizzie, you will be forever young, even if you live to a hundred. And you make me feel . . ."

She smiled wickedly. "Show me how I make you feel." She stopped dancing, caught his arm and drew him to the foyer. To the sleepy Jeffries she said, "We shall see ourselves out. Good night, Jeffries."

"Good night, Your Grace, Mr. Levitz," Jeffries said

without the least hint of disapproval. He remained to help Elizabeth with her wrap, opened the door for them and bowed them out, closing the massive portal with a yawn.

"See?" Elizabeth said. "He's a sensible fellow, and does not care that we leave together so late."

Mordecai followed Elizabeth to her coach, but he paused with his hand on the latch. He was about to sin grievously. He was too old to disobey the God of his ancestors so lightly. Mordecai looked up at the moon, which had won its battle with the clouds. He swore it smiled a blessing on him. He would attend Temple twice on Saturday. Sighing in surrender, he opened the door and helped his dear Lizzie into the carriage.

Tomorrow was soon enough for regrets.

I will regret this tomorrow, warned Charlaine's last rebellious instinct as the soft mattress cradled her. She fidgeted as he lay down beside her, knowing she should move away, but unable to. Once he made her his, she would be forever stamped his possession. There would be no annulment, no escape.

The knowledge was not strong enough to break the spell of desire. From their first meeting, when they had shared that single, passionate kiss in this very bed, part of her had known she would end here, this way. But the primitive feelings they'd vented tonight transformed this moment into a reward, not a punishment.

She was a woman; he was a man. By the laws of God and state, they were wed, and their union, and others like it, insured the survival of human kind. As she visualized the child that could come of this night, her last rebellious instinct died. She opened her arms to her husband.

Devlin stiffened. Simultaneously all the male aggression seemed to flow away from him on the riptide of her surrender. Slowly, carefully, he embraced her. Holding her eyes, he said, "*Chère*, I have wanted you for a lifetime, it seems. I am sorry I broke your door. I will fix it myself tomorrow."

A giggle escaped her. She had held a gun on him and he apologized for breaking into her room? She covered his mouth with a fingertip. "That's what we have servants for." Closing her eyes, she tilted her head back and whispered, "Never mind that now. Kiss me."

Nothing happened. His arms were just as tender, but when she peeked at him through half-closed lashes, his blue eyes had darkened to navy. Surely he didn't mean to hold to that stupid vow?

"Do you love me, Charlaine?"

Both her eyes opened fully. Indeed, that was the question. "I . . ." She licked her lips. His eyes tracked the movement hungrily. He wanted to kiss her as badly as she wanted to be kissed, yet his stupid male pride must be fulfilled first. Well, she had her pride too. Love required total trust and total fidelity and total surrender. Too many unanswered questions remained in their relationship. "Does it matter?"

Apparently it did, to him. His arms withdrew. He sat up on the edge of the bed, his back to her.

Charlaine admired his sleek power. The slightest movement made his muscles ripple. The thought that he might walk away from her, and leave her aching yet again, was more than she could bear. Quickly, before her nerve could fail, she shrugged out of the dressing gown and tossed it to the floor. Even as he tensed to get up and walk away, she slipped up behind him, circled him with her arms and kissed the nape of his neck.

He stiffened as if she'd stabbed him with a poker.

Indeed, she gasped herself at the feel of his flexing muscles against the sensitive tips of her breasts. A harsh groan escaped him as he rubbed his back against her.

Her breath quickened as her nipples hardened at the caress. "*Vraiment*, on your stubborn head be this, my darling." And he turned around so quickly that she almost fell over, hauled her into his arms and lowered his lips to the throbbing hollow at her throat.

A sigh escaped her as her bones turned to porridge. She lay draped over his arm as his mouth strayed from her neck, across each collarbone to her upper arms. He lifted each arm and planted a tiny love bite in the sensitive hollow of her elbow, where blue veins pulsed with life and passion. She stiffened as a thrill ran like lightning down to her toes. How did he know her pleasure points better than she knew them herself?

His lips trailed down her arms to her wrists, circled them with more tiny nips, then kissed the palms of each hand. Finally he said huskily, "Open your eyes, my darling."

She obeyed, but the way he looked at her as he slowly, gently, pulled her forefinger into his mouth made a strange moistness grow between her thighs. The dewy warmth spread as he suckled her. Dear Lord, was that what he felt when . . . No wonder men were always frantic for sex. And so he prepared her, with a skill she would not recognize until later. Without touching a single more salient part of her anatomy, or kissing her lips, he had her squirming with desire beneath him. When he'd suckled her opposite finger, he caught her ankles and pulled her flat on the bed. Then, for a long, breathless instant caught between eternity and a dream, he leaned back on his heels to touch her only with his eyes.

The action was as erotic as the act that would follow. Starting at her ankles, blue flames lapped at every pore, heating her passion with every touch. He savored the strong arch of her calves, the pretty dimpled knees, the perfect thighs and . . .

When that heated gaze touched her like a brand at her most intimate spot, she could not avoid the instinctive reaction to cup herself in embarrassment. He did not pull her hands away; he did not cover her with his long, powerful body to sap her will.

He merely whispered, "Please, my wife. Let your husband look his fill upon you."

How could she deny him after that? She took a deep breath and moved her hands. Some bold instinct she would not have credited an hour past even gave her courage enough to watch his reaction.

He stared at the auburn curls that glistened with the dew he had incited. His own eyes closed briefly. His teeth gritted; his hands clenched. Somehow she knew he was squelching the urge to take her then and there.

Taking a deep breath, he opened his eyes, finished his appraisal with an admiring look at her breasts, and then straddled her. The position made his own arousal even more apparent. She could hardly ignore the bulge straining at the front of his breeches. She had still not seen that impressive part of his imposing person.

Fear tingled through her, but it didn't survive the sensual onslaught that followed. She bore the physical evidence of how well he had prepared her, so the seductive power that had been leashed for her pleasure was slowly loosened for his own.

In one swift movement, he pulled her legs wide and covered her. She cringed, expecting to hear his breeches open. Any second he would take her, as men were rumored to take their brides the first time: for their own pleasure, in haste. She should have realized that her French frog was not as other men. For the moment, he rested against her, content to rub that covered hardness against the sensitive vee between her legs.

By degrees, her fears faded as a strange sensation grew. The primitive friction incited an equally primitive instinct. She acted on that instinct, wanting, needing, no barriers between their flesh. She pulled at his waistband. "Off. Now."

A smile stretched his sensual mouth. He lowered it to her ear, crushing her into the soft mattress with a weight that was somehow not too heavy. "In a moment. When you are ready."

Ready? She blinked at him, wondering what more she could do to show her own need for him. When he finally lowered his mouth to her breast, she found out how naive she was. There was more desire to feel, more to give. This was her first taste of a bountiful cornucopia that would sustain them their whole lives long.

He savored every taste like one who had known too many tidbits and was now offered the nectar of the gods. His breathing quickened as he kissed, lapped and nibbled at her breasts, cupping their round weight with his free hand to bring them each to his mouth. His other hand was equally tender as he brushed though the damp curls and found the source of her strange throbbing.

Oh, God, she would melt beneath him if he did not stop. . . . *Oh God, don't let him stop.* Not for the first time in her relationship with him, and certainly not for the last, Charlaine felt torn in twain by the conflicting emotions he inspired in her. She had never known that pleasure could verge so close on pain. But surely she would scream if he did not stop brushing her, pulling away, suckling at her nipples, then returning to his deep caresses. She began to squirm beneath him, moaning, "No more. Too much."

"Not enough. Not yet." His voice, so deep and husky she almost didn't recognize it, rasped her aroused sensibilities like velvet. "Now, my darling, you are mine, every perfect inch of you."

And he finally unbuttoned his breeches to pull them off.

She heard the rustle of his clothing, felt him removing his nether garment, but she was beyond protest, or even fear. The virginal instincts had died as the woman inside showed her the meaning of desire. At the first touch of that satin steel against her belly, her eyes popped open. She had to see.

Gasping, she gripped the silk bedcover with restless hands while she stared at all that made him man. His tower of flesh trumpeted its own desire, throbbing against her. The clarion call of her response kept her still even as she wondered how she would hold him all.

The tender laughter in his eyes made her blush as he obviously read her thoughts. "You are made to fit me, *chère*, as you will shortly see. But first . . ." He gently caught her hand and brought it to that tumescence. He groaned at the first brush of her fingers, scattering the last of her hesitation on the winds of his pleasure.

The knowledge that she could make him weak with desire as well gave her confidence. She gave in to her curiosity and learned the texture and weight of him. Dear heaven, he was strong; he was virile male personified as if they were Adam and Eve knowing each other for the first time, as God had decreed. And yet he was vulnerable too. His aroused wand of flesh was vulnerable in her hands. He was so needful that he pulsed in her grip, yet, stiffening every muscle in his body, he waited and let her know him.

Her heart thundering against her ribs, she pulled at him gently. He blew a long breath between his teeth, brought both knees between her legs and spread her thighs wide. "Pull me into you, *chère*. Show me you l— want me."

Blindly she obeyed, spreading her legs wider still. Only this mysterious flesh she held could soothe her raging fever. She brought the tip of him to bear on her damp curls. After that, she did not know what to do.

He did. The head of his desire nudged her once, twice. She bowed beneath him, biting her lips, as the throbbing grew painful. A final time he brushed her, using his manhood in the most intimate caress there was. She screamed and arched beneath him. The throbbing built and built—and burst, flooding her like a broken dam that drowned her in pleasure so intense that she died a little. Over and over she tumbled, unaware if she were right side up or upside down, but knowing that somehow he supported her and kept her safe.

Devlin felt her little death beneath him. His exultant manhood found the right angle and drove deep, penetrating the virginal veil so cleanly and swiftly that she barely felt it. Indeed, as the one stroke brought him deep inside her, he felt her spasms grip him and urge him on. The breath left his lungs in a whoosh as he finally knew the ineffable pleasure of lovemaking.

For this act was not mere sex, or even healthy desire. This was love, the only love he had known since his mother, the last he would covet. He luxuriated in her, watching her lick her lip where she had bitten it, waiting for her to come to herself again.

A shuddery sigh shook her end to end, making her tighten around him. He gritted his teeth, forcing himself to be still in the intimate clasp of her body. When her eyes finally opened, they were green, greener than he had ever seen them. She finally seemed to realize the intimacy of their position, for she blushed under his intense stare.

Her embarassment would not last long. Tenderly he pulled out of her, and then returned his gift inch by inch, letting her feel its entirety as he sought the tip of her womb. She gasped at the sensation. "See what you have denied us?" he whispered. "Come with me again."

And he was patient, as patient as if his own desire had not grown so acute that he ached with it. He lifted her knees and drew them over his shoulders, holding her open and helpless before the hungry thrusts. But he was careful to reach high on every outstroke, and it wasn't long before he felt her throbbing again. She began to follow the primitive dance like one born to it, pushing vigorously with her hips on every instroke.

He cupped her breasts in his hands, quickening the tempo, afraid to close his eyes lest this be a dream. But with every thrust he knew her better, and not only in the biblical sense. Her passion was all the more urgent for the years she had stifled it. But only he would know this sweet desire, for she loved him. She had not said the words yet, but her body was a violin tuned to vibrate only at his touch.

The thrusts grew longer, more primitive. He was fully embedded in her, but it was still not enough. Her eyes fluttered shut again, but that he could not allow. "Open your eyes, Charlaine," he growled. "Look at me."

Panting through her passion-swollen mouth, she obeyed. His gaze fixed on that lush mouth. He wanted it, wanted to taste it, consume it, almost as much as he wanted to fill her with the fruition of his desire.

She licked her lips. A tremor shuddered through him, passing from him to her and back. He felt himself swelling inside her, felt the orgasm growing until he knew nothing but the need to fill her with the seed that would bear good fruit. She tensed beneath him, her silken purse opening and closing around him. She gave a shuddering little sigh and died again.

He buried his lips in her breasts, pulled her legs higher around him and shoved deep. Only when he felt the pulsing tip of her womb did he allow himself release. And for the first time in his life, he arched his back and screamed his own pleasure as the spasms arrowed through every atom of his body like a starburst. He filled her, and filled her, his body as helpless before the onslaught of pleasure as hers was. Somehow he kept his eyes wide, her gaze a tender prisoner to his, holding her feelings as open to him as her body lay open to his male pleasure.

The green depths were dazed, yet fully aware of what they shared in this mingling that was more than an exchange of bodily secretions. He held her gaze even as the spurts slowly died. He prayed that they would find fertile ground, for after this night he would die rather than lose her. A child would cement this bond so that nothing, not even her own strong will, could break it.

When she went limp beneath him, he gently withdrew, fetched a small damp towel and cleaned the evidence of their union away from her thighs and womanhood. She was so tired that she mumbled only a token protest, curled against him when he was done and slept.

For a long time, despite his own exhaustion, he stared into the darkness, savoring her bare silken skin against him. He could not help worrying what the dawn would bring, for he knew all too well that passion was like a drug: it either made you want to indulge again and again, or it made you sick and vow never to take another drop. Charlaine had enjoyed herself, no doubt about that, but she was not a woman to be ruled by her instincts.

Unless she grew to love him as he loved her, this joy would be only temporary. He would not allow that. A last smile stretched his lips as he followed the sandman.

She had her treasure back. He had shared her soft bed; now he had only to eat from her golden plate. Surely soon the love would follow so he could kiss her. . . .

Chapter Ten

Dawn came as uncertainly as Charlaine's feelings. The pearly glimmerings of light foretold a brighter day, but for now night was dominant. Charlaine blinked sleepy eyes, felt something warm, large and hard brush against her, and almost jumped out of her skin. Devlin Rhodes, her husband, and now, as she abruptly recalled the night past, her lover, slept with one possessive arm about her. His bare torso snuggled against her side. He slept peacefully, like a man who had been satisfied more than once through the night.

Easing from under his arm so as not to wake him, Charlaine blushed as she slipped out of the covers. In the pinkening light, she looked at her mirrored reflection. She had two love bites on her neck, remnants of that last coupling, when she'd turned to him before dawn. His beard had grown enough to scratch her tender bosom. And yet at the time, that sensation had merely made what he was doing to her more pleasur-

257

able. After a quick glance to assure that he still slept, Charlaine went to her full-length mirror. Wonderingly, she stared at herself.

From lips to ankles, she seemed different. Her skin had never been so rosy, nor her mouth so full and content, nor her eyes so clear despite a limited amount of sleep. Torn, she turned away from the evidence that the men in her life, damn them, had been right. She had wanted him, wanted him as much as Devlin had said, and she had enjoyed the consummation of her marriage as much as her father had predicted.

If they were right, that meant she must have been wrong. She had always viewed marriage and its incumbent responsibilities, from the matrimonial chamber to the birthing chamber, as largely a pleasure for the husband and a grim duty for the wife. Yet last night she had learned that in bed, at least, mating could be equally as pleasurable for the female, when the male was skilled. She tied her dressing gown about her slim waist with a tight twist, but the modesty came too late.

Some of the fullness left her mouth as she speculated where Devlin had learned those skills. Skill? Art, or witchcraft, more like. For nothing she had ever known, from viewing a completed necklace of her design to her presentation to the queen, had given her as much sheer, goose-pimpling, spine-tingling, gut-wrenching pleasure as becoming one with Devlin Rhodes. Therefore, shouldn't she set aside her ambitions, concede defeat and admit him to her heart as she had already admitted him to her bed?

"No."

The denial slipped out instinctively. The love her mother bore her father, literally, in the form of her daughter, had killed her. The few friends Charlaine had ever known had changed from vivacious young debutantes to grim and anxious matrons, dominated by their husbands. No, as powerful as Victoria was, as good an example as she tried to set for her subjects, her way of life was not for Charlaine.

Like her great-great-grandmother Callista, and her grandmother Chantal, Charlaine had to set her own destiny. Their husbands had, over time, learned to let their wives handle their own affairs, and they had not fought the female line of succession as so many of their ancestors had. Not because they were not strong men, not because they did not value the estates and growing wealth daughter passed to daughter, but because they loved their wives. Deeply, completely, to the point that the happiness of their spouses had been more important to them than their own superficial male pride.

Finally, as she had been longing to do since she awoke, Charlaine turned to look at the sleeping man in the bed. Would he be so generous?

Sweet memories of his generosity lingered in the very scent of her skin. How many times had he delayed his own male pleasure to assure hers? And yet, inexperienced as she was about men, she knew that the way men acted in bed, and the way they acted when money was involved, were very different. Still, Devlin had not protested overmuch when she'd demanded that he relinquish all rights to her estate. And even last night, when she had been completely vulnerable to him, he had not tried to change her mind about that.

Perhaps, just perhaps, her reluctant choice of husband could be the right one.

When a tap came at her door, Charlaine started.

"My lady, your tea is ready," said a serving maid.

"Come in." Charlaine sat down on her couch, waving at the sofa table. The maid set the tray down with a clatter when Devlin moved. Her eyes huge, she stared at the bed, at her mistress, then back at the bed. A big smile stretched her face.

"You may go," Charlaine said tartly. She would be the subject of much speculation in the servants' quarters today, but then, she was accustomed to that.

Bobbing a small curtsy, the maid backed out.

Charlaine was pouring tea steadily until a husky voice said, "Good morning, *chère*."

Tea splashed into the saucer. She pretended not to notice as she set the pot down and picked up a scone. "Good morning."

His wicked, contented smile was not so easy to dismiss. "And how do you feel this fine day?"

Tired. Confused. Exhilarated. "I am well, thank you."

His smile went lopsided. With a flourish he tossed back the covers and stood. He stretched, his magnificent form bare.

Despite herself, she tracked his every movement as he casually walked to the armoire and pulled out his own dressing gown. In the brightening light, she was amazed that he had not crushed her, or even hurt her. How had she managed to hold him there . . . ? Blushing, she put a napkin in her saucer to absorb the spilled tea and drank the reviving brew. When he joined her, she poured him a cup. He sipped, grimaced, and set the dainty cup down in his saucer. His large hands looked too tough to hold the bone china without breaking it, but she could attest to their dexterity.

The words popped out of their own accord. "Are you always so gentle with fragile things?"

His gaze leaped to her face. Those blue eyes darkened. "Always." His voice softened to a whisper. "Especially when I treasure them."

Whispered love words of the night past lingered in

the air between them, sweeter than the scent of the jam pot cozily ensconced amid the scones. She swallowed and looked away. She heard dishes rattle, and the next thing she knew, he had cut some fruit and sausages in bites, moved close to her on the couch, and now held a tempting morsel of pear before her on a silver spoon. She glanced down at the plate. It was gilded.

I shall eat from your golden plate, share your silver spoon and your soft bed. . . . he had vowed weeks ago. Was it only weeks? She felt as if she had known him all her life. She reluctantly opened her mouth, took the bite of pear, and chewed. He used the same spoon to dip his own bite of pear, his lips lingering over the implement, as if he tasted her essence too.

She swallowed hastily, coughing. Another of his vows fulfilled. She had the book back; now he had only to kiss her to make his transition complete. She glanced at the rumpled covers, felt her own tender aches, and abruptly knew she could not spend another night in that bed with him. The last of her own identity would be usurped by the power of this frog she was beginning to realize was more of a prince.

She rose so quickly that tea sloshed on her dressing gown. She hid behind her screen, sensing his frustration in his utter stillness and quiet as he tried to figure out what was wrong, but even when she was dressed he said nothing. He only watched her with understanding dawning, as if he knew the loss of her virginity troubled her.

When she made a hasty excuse and turned toward the door, he finally said, "Will I see you later today?"

She stopped, her back to him, and answered lightly, "Of course."

Of course not. She felt suffocated, threatened on all sides. She had to get away. She hurried down the stairs, her stomach queasy, and hid in the study until she heard his voice speaking to Jeffries at the front door. The door closed.

She ran back up the steps, hastily packed her own bags, and carried them down the stairs herself. By the time Devlin reached his store, she was gone.

Across London, Henry Dupree knocked on Cecil's door. "There is a Duchess of Kensington to see you, sir."

Cecil frowned. He was still brooding over his humiliation of last night. To be actually evicted from the Kimball estate, as if he were some common criminal, while the real criminal was honored . . . "Tell her I'm busy."

Henry turned to do exactly that, but a walking stick shoved the door open, preceding an imposing figure in blue lace and white swansdown. Only a woman of the duchess's presence could so easily wear the youthful style. To Cecil's eyes, however, she looked ridiculous.

"I am busy, Elizabeth."

"One should never be too busy to see an old friend, Cecil." She met Henry's glare with a haughty toss of her head. When Cecil nodded toward the door, Henry left reluctantly, shutting the portal with a definite snap.

Elizabeth sat down in the chair before his desk without being invited, but then, she seldom did the accepted thing. They had known one another for years, for her husband had graduated from Oxford and encouraged other young men from the college. When Rhodes came to the duke seven years ago, shortly before he died, the lord had not hesitated to invest in the new De Beers Mining Company. Her late husband had believed that Rhodes was an unusual man, of simple tastes and heritage, who would one day be rich beyond dreams, and those lucky enough to associate with him would prosper equally.

The pair exchanged a glance that acknowledged this history. Tacitly, Elizabeth nodded her thanks that her own lavish lifestyle was partially due to her shares in De Beers.

Elizabeth reflected aloud, "You know, I have never forgotten the way my husband described you to me shortly before he died, a description he attributed to Barney Barnato. Would you like to hear it?"

Cecil was annoyed at the reference, for he was currently involved in a fierce struggle with his Jewish rival for control of the richest diamond fields in Africa. When she shrugged and leaned back, he said, goaded, "What?"

"Barnato said he tries to avoid contact with you because when he is with you half an hour he not only agrees with you, but comes to believe he's always held your opinion."

Pleased surprise widened Cecil's gray eyes before they hardened to granite again. "A great exaggeration, given how volubly and openly he opposes me. Beside, it is an opinion you obviously do not share."

Elizabeth shrugged. "Nor is it a trait you find admirable. Would Cecil Rhodes, vicar's son, be one of the richest men in England if he did not hold to his own opinion?"

"Probably not."

Casually, Elizabeth twiddled with her walking stick before she pinioned him with bright blue eyes. "Then surely you should respect that trait in a man who shares your blood."

Cecil scowled. "If you came here to beg for mercy for that blackguard, you waste your time. He is a thief, a liar and a bastard. I want him gone from my country."

"Any second now you will use the royal *we*. Odd, I thought Victoria was queen."

"England's greatness is best propagated by educated men who serve her interests, not guttersnipes who—"

"Refuse to share your dreams of empire. Did he really abuse you so when he spoke against you in Kimberley? From what I understand, it was you who started the fight at the assembly. I'm told you grabbed him by the throat when he called you a fool and an egotist."

Cecil's mouth snapped closed, but he would not give her the satisfaction of asking how she had learned that. The little Jew, no doubt. "He may have greater physical strength, but he is no match for my intelligence. He fled Africa shortly after he humiliated me, literally selling out when there were those in my opposition who begged him to stay. He is basically a weak man." He had the grace to flush when Elizabeth lifted a brow. "Morally, at least. He may have fooled you and the Kimballs, but I saw him for what he was while we were in Africa."

Elizabeth shook her head sadly. She rose. "I can see it is pointless to appeal to your common sense. It is not like you to let feelings rule your reason, Cecil. But this time I give you fair warning: Charlaine loves this young rogue, as I freely admit he is. She will not stand by and allow you to ruin him, even if she has to go to the queen. I remind you that Victoria is extremely fond of her."

"Are you threatening me, Elizabeth?"

"Why no, Cecil. No more than you threaten. Merely, ah, sharing my opinion. Good day to you." With a regal nod, she exited. She noted that Henry seemed to sit down at his desk hastily in the next room, but she didn't care. If Cecil let his help listen at keyholes, why, he was a bigger fool than she'd thought him.

Cecil bellowed, "Henry, get in here!"

Henry rushed in, his ascot askew. "Yes, sir?"

"I want you to fetch that Maybell woman for me. Immediately."

"Yes, sir." He hurried back out, waiting until he was outside to sneer at the closed door.

"It's I who will be giving orders soon enough, you arrogant bastard," he whispered. But for now, he hurried off to do his employer's bidding.

The second she drove through Summerlea's gates, some of Charlaine's disquiet eased. She hung out the window, appraising the fresh stucco and new cross timbers she'd ordered for the small but elegant Tudor mansion. Every time she came here, she had only to close her eyes to visualize Callista, and her grandson Vincent, walking through the chess hedge hand in hand. Like those from the more famous Hever Castle, the home of Anne Boleyn, the gardeners of Summerlea had painstakingly trimmed the tall hedges in the shapes of chess pieces, forming a giant board-maze. But Charlaine could walk through the maze with her eyes closed.

"Stop!" Charlaine shouted to the coachman. The carriage was still rolling when she leaped down at a dead run. She rushed inside the maze, following its tortuous twists and turns to the center, where a rose garden basked in the sunshine, along with a marble bench and a fountain. She sagged down on the bench, listening to the sound of the water. Slowly, slowly, resolve firmed her mouth again.

Summerlea was the most tangible symbol of why she had vowed never to marry. Give it up at the stroke of a pen, or at the utterance of a two-word sentence?

Never. And what she feared had come to pass. Even though Devlin had signed away all rights to this estate, she could not sit on her own property without wanting to share it with him. Guilt marred her pleasure in this perfect summer day, for her longing to share all with him, even this sacred trust, had grown with her feelings. How could she be his love and not trust him with the thing she loved best?

She did not love him, could not dare love him. Why, she had seen the evidence of his nature, that he had once escorted that blond harlot, and felt his experience in the most personal way. How could she trust him to be faithful, much less to share her wealth without squandering it?

The answer was undeniable: she could not. Quite simply, she had too much to lose. And he made her weak, made her want all the things she'd scorned. As to what she had to gain, well, of that she did not allow herself to think. Decisively she rose. With a much calmer gait, she went to the main house and ordered a hearty lunch. She'd need fortifying for the battle to come, for Devlin would not be happy when she told him of her decision.

After work that day, Devlin was whistling when he entered the Kimball home. He still could not call it home himself, and somehow thought he never would. As soon as Charlaine was ready, they'd move into a little house he'd been eyeing near Grosvenor Square. It was expensive, but tasteful, and especially since the jubilee, with all the recent brisk jewelry sales, he could afford it. There they could build a new life together. As to her precious estates, he had neither need nor want of those. It was Charlaine herself he wanted, not just as she had been last night, purring beneath him, but even deeper, truer. He longed to be the only man for her, as she was the only woman for him, her heart's mate, and nothing less.

He grinned. And if he didn't kiss her soon, he'd go mad. He bounded up the stairs when he didn't see her. "Charlaine? I finished the necklace today. I want to show it to—" He broke off when he entered their chamber to the sight of gaping drawers and scattered clothes. She'd obviously packed and fled.

He sagged down on the bed, closing his eyes in despair. If she could run from him after the night they'd shared, it was hopeless. Then the anger began, an insistent little whisper, finally trumpeting so loud that it drowned all else. How could she? He had veritably worshiped her last night, saying with his touch and body all he longed to express by kiss and deed. He could have taken her before last night, but he'd feared precisely this result. She had to come to him willingly, completely, or there would always be barriers between them. Even last night, if she had not made it obvious she wanted him, he would have somehow found the strength to pull away.

"Very well, little miss coward," he said through gritted teeth. "You wanted to see how far you could push me? Well, I've just reached my limit."

Surging to his feet, he changed his clothes to more appropriate attire for his mission, bolted back down the stairs and called for his horse.

The clock struck six. Charlaine started, forcing herself to concentrate on *Macbeth*. It had been years since she'd read this particular play, but the brooding tale was not a good choice for her nerves. When the exterior door to Summerlea opened and closed, she almost jumped out of her skin. But when no other sound came, she relaxed slightly.

The door, recently oiled, opened on silent hinges.

Even quieter feet approached. It was only when a shadow blocked her light that she looked up. She gasped a small scream. An apparition from her past gazed down at her. Her husband wore the same black garments he'd favored when he climbed up her tower such an age ago. But this time he was not smiling.

He pulled the book from her lax hand and glanced at the title. "Hmm, how appropriate. Have you come to the good part yet?"

She had never seen him thus. Rage seethed under the calm; his eyes were almost black with the torment of his feelings. Her voice shook. "What part?"

He leaned over her chair, trapping her with his hands on the arms. "Why, 'Double, double, toil and trouble. Fire burn and cauldron bubble. Eye of newt and toe of frog—' " With a repressed rage that terrified her, he kicked the footstool away from her feet and hauled her up into his arms, concluding in a sibilant hiss, " 'When our actions do not, our fears make us traitors.' "

That gave her strength enough to pull away. "I am traitor to nothing. Rather, it is my loyalty to my ancestors that aggrieves you now."

"Have I threatened you? Did I refuse to sign your little paper? Have I forced myself upon you?"

Reluctantly she shook her head to all of the queries. "But if you do not have any of that in mind now, why do you come to me dressed as you are?"

He bowed deeply, sweeping a hand down himself. "To make your choice simple. Two men stand before you: the French invader you despise, and the lover you turned to last night. Choose whom you want, Charlaine, for I cannot bear another instant of your ambivalence."

And he stood tall, daring her with his eyes, the bold Frenchman incarnate. But was he frog or prince? She sensed that this moment was pivotal in their relationship, but the choice was not that simple. She felt torn in twain, for she could not reconcile the tender lover who made her glory in all she feared with the frog who threatened her very identity as she knew it. "I . . . I . . ."

His eyes closed in pain. When they opened again, they were black voids. He spoke in French. *"Tres bien, chère. Au revoir."* And he turned toward the door.

Something snapped in her. She raced to the door, blocking him. "You've had your say. Now I wish to have mine."

He cocked his head in that inquiring way that she usually found charming. Not this time, for his eyes, those beautiful blue eyes that always sparkled with life and vitality, remained dead.

She scanned the room for inspiration, anything to calm herself for what had to be said. She went to the sideboard near the door, and poured them each a burgundy with a shaking hand. She went to him, offering a glass.

He took it politely and brought it to his lips, but she could see that he neither tasted nor felt it. Panic almost overcame her as she realized she was losing him. If he walked out that door, he would never come back. But wasn't this what she'd wanted when she fled here? She was no longer so sure.

Nervously she wet her lips. Finally a spark banished some of the darkness in his eyes as they fixed on her mouth. He seemed to have forgotten the glass in his hand, but he did not move or speak. He was watching, waiting.

"I wish I could make you understand how responsible I feel to this estate and the wealth passed down to me by the Kimball women," she began. "I am not owner of it; I am keeper of it."

"Until what? If the Ice Princess remained a virgin to

her death, who would you pass it to?"

Leave it to a male to put it in such practical terms. "I never intended to die a virgin. One day, I hoped to wed. But only to a man who would love me for myself, on my own terms. Not to one who colluded with my own father to force me into marriage." That still stung. She knew now that her father was mostly to blame, but Devlin had not exactly protested the hasty wedding. And she still suspected that his true goal was her wealth and property. He had enslaved her in bed, and if she continued on that path, she would say anything, sign anything, to keep him close.

She was so caught up in her own feelings, and his footsteps were so stealthy, that he towered over her before she knew it. "Would you have preferred that I leave you dishonored, scorned by society?" he asked quietly. Too quietly.

Put that way, how could she answer yes? "No, but I would have preferred a choice, not an ultimatum."

"You mean a choice like I gave you today? Bah, woman, you don't know what you want. Well, when you decide, you know where to find me." He reached out to move her aside so he could exit.

At the touch of his hands, she cringed. Not because she didn't want him to touch her—because she wanted it too much.

The spark in his eyes died. His hands dropped. He walked into the room to set his glass down, and, for a long moment, he remained still with his head bent. "I will grant you an annulment, if you wish it."

She scarcely credited her ears at first, for she had not asked for, nor expected, this. Of a sudden, her confusion fled under a glorious burst of rage. And they said women were fickle! "You barge into my life, steal my most cherished possession, maneuver me into wedding you, seduce me, and now you want to wash your hands of me?" Her voice grew in volume with every word until she was shouting. "Well, you do not get rid of me that easily!"

"But I thought it was what you wanted." Now he looked confused.

"You know little of what I want," she began, but he interrupted.

"I know all I need to know," he said quietly. And he waited for her to ask.

Almost, she didn't, but she had to know if he truly understood her, for no one else did. Even her father. "And what is that?"

"That you want to be loved, and to love. But you are too afraid of being hurt to admit it, even to yourself."

The truths hit home like blows. Indeed, he understood too much. Defensively, she reacted as she used to. She picked up the wineglass she'd discarded and threw it at him.

It landed squarely in his chest, not breaking, but spewing its almost full contents over his face, torso and arms. He closed his eyes at the shock as wine dripped down from his eyebrows onto his lips. Then he opened his eyes. The wineglass rolled, unbroken, under the drapes.

For a frozen moment she was still, like a hunted creature about to be pounced on, for menace gazed at her. With a squeak she turned to run, but she was too late. In three great strides he caught her, kicked the door closed and hauled her around to face him.

She kicked and writhed, dimly aware on some primitive level that she'd wanted this even as she fought him. She could not bear that cold hardness, not from him.

She needn't have worried. There was nothing cold about him now. His cheeks were flushed, his eyes sparkled with rage, and his breath was hot upon her brow. As for hard, well, she knew what that thrusting fullness against her abdomen meant as he pulled her even closer. He stuck his face into hers. Burgundy dripped from his shirt onto her dress, transferring the heat of his skin to hers.

Tingles started at her hairline and grew as he bumped his hips into hers. "Incite me further at your peril. I want you so much now that I—" He broke off, staring at her mouth with such hunger that the tingles spread to the pit of her stomach and lower. When she licked her lips, tasting him and the burgundy, he inhaled sharply.

His lips lowered over hers until she could almost feel them. She stared at that strong mouth, the slight indentation in the middle of his lower lip, the pure curves that sang to her blood when they laughed—or yearned, as now. She had never wanted anything in her entire life as much as she wanted to kiss him. Without thinking of the consequences, she parted her mouth and raised herself on tiptoe. Their lips brushed, but iron hands caught her waist and kept her from deepening the embrace.

"You want to kiss me, *chère*?" he whispered.

Her lips burned under the temptation of his breath. She felt him hardening further as he stared at her lush mouth.

God, yes. Now. Often.

"Tell me you want me. That you will be mine, now and forever, so we can add our own story to your family heirloom." He touched his straight white teeth with the tip of his tongue.

The tingles had centered between her legs now. *Give in. Love him, for he will never hurt you.* Had she been anywhere but Summerlea she would have given in, but she had spent too many years dreaming of her ancestors in this room. Trust was unfurling within her like a flower, but it had not yet reached full bloom.

"I . . . I . . ."

With a groan that she echoed, he wrenched his arms away and turned blindly for the door.

She sensed that his control was about to break, but she cared not. With a smothered little sob, she wrapped her arms about his waist and buried her nose in his back. He stiffened, and then, with a bitten-off curse, he turned and crushed her in his arms.

She closed her eyes with a sigh of gladness, but he did not kiss her, as she expected. He buried his nose in the sweet hollow at her throat and inhaled deeply. She caught his ears and hauled his head up, but again he evaded her seeking mouth.

His voice was so husky she barely recognized it. "Kiss me then. Kiss the wine away and help us both forget the morrow."

The morrow? What would happen then? Before she could question him, he gently pulled her face into the strong curve of his neck. She kissed it, tasting the wine on him, and an even more seductive sweetness. The taste of man, aroused man, the only man she had ever known this way, or ever could. She kissed every inch of his neck, and when she reached the hollow where his pulse beat like a hammer, she licked him.

He swallowed harshly, and she tracked the movement with her tongue, her head whirling with a need she was just beginning to understand.

But he, her French lover, understood fully. He locked the study door with an adroit flick of his wrist. With the other hand he caught hers and pulled her to the rug before the fireplace. She was so intent on licking the rest of the wine away from his face and neck that she barely realized her dress was open until it dropped to her waist.

She merely shrugged her arms out of it hurriedly,

uncaring of anything save the moment. The morrow and its truths to be faced would come soon enough. She tugged at his shirt so impatiently that two of the buttons popped off.

A husky laugh swirled above them, heady as the wine. "Patience, *chère*. This is like a dance—slow is better."

Too busy shoving his shirt off his shoulders to heed him, she buried her nose in his soft chest hair. Shyly she licked one of his nipples. A strangled groan escaped him. He tugged at her chemise, but the tiny hooks held. She heard him mutter something uncomplimentary about women and their gewgaws, and she smiled against his smooth, tempting skin.

"Patience, remember?" She drew back with a teasing smile.

Her smile slipped as she saw the look in his eyes. A stormy passion roiled in the deep, dark blue, a hunger so deep she wondered if she could ever fill it. It both frightened her and heightened her own desire until she didn't know whether to flee or to pounce on him.

As usual, he soothed her fears by the simple means of a shaky fingertip that traced the outline of her mouth. "Ah, *chère*, you are my penance for a misspent youth. Never has patience seemed less a virtue than when I am with you."

Her mouth burned where he touched it, but she had to smile at the raw male honesty. "I am told the flamenco is a sensuous dance. It is fast, I believe?"

He froze at the subtle invitation, and then his arms went around her. With a tug, he popped the hooks off her chemise. The ripped fabric slipped away, leaving her bare to the waist. He shrugged out of his shirt and pulled her close, rubbing their torsos together.

Her eyes fluttered shut at the sensation of his hair prickling her exquisitely tender breasts. Again she raised her mouth; again he eased her away.

"Stand," he ordered softly.

She obeyed, though she wondered how her shaky knees held her weight. He pulled her dress and petticoat down until she stood before him in stockings and underdrawers, and soon those were gone. When she was bare of all but a blush, he rose and began removing his own remaining clothes with measured intent, his gaze never leaving her.

Somehow this intimacy was more poignant in the full light of the late afternoon. Even the heavy drapes could not keep out the curious sunlight, as if Nature herself wanted Charlaine to know the full import of what she was about to do. Frenchman or no, frog or prince, this man was about to come inside her body and perform with her the most intimate act two people can do. But, as she watched his beautiful form reveal itself in all its fully erect glory, not a whisper of warning sounded from her usual instincts.

This was right, this was good, this was needed. With a blazing smile of sheer joy, she opened her arms to him.

He grabbed her as if he'd never let her go, running his hands up and down her back, her hips, her thighs. Desperation hummed from him like a mournful tune, but her heart was too full of happiness just then to heed it. Later, when it was too late, she would remember. Her heart pounded too hard in her ears to hear anything but the surging of her own hot blood. She began to run her hands over him, starting at his strong shoulders, down the arrow-straight spine, ending at his firm buttocks. She kneaded them.

With a choked little sound of surrender, he picked her up, carried her to the rug and laid her down. She held her arms up for him, but for a long moment he sat back on his heels and just looked at her. Looked at her as if he could never get his fill. Slowly she sat up. With a boldness he had taught her, she picked up his hands and brought them to her breasts. He cradled her tenderly, his thumbs circling the smooth globes but not touching the erect centers.

She caught his arms and ran her hands over his biceps. For a long, sensuous moment they sat facing each other, luxuriating in their differences. But when her eyes wandered down to his groin and fixed there, his touch became more urgent. He lifted one of her breasts to his mouth and sucked the nipple inside, his other hand feeling for the moist readiness between her thighs.

Patience was not a virtue he sought anymore. With a growl of primitive male need, he shoved her flat, separated her knees with his hands and drove deep between them. With one stroke he brought them both home, to a place they could only find together. Instinctively Charlaine thrust back at him with her hips, knowing only that she could not get him deep enough to sate this ache. Over and over his taut maleness dipped into her, as if he sought the essence of all that made her the one woman he needed.

Even as her body shook beneath his hungry lunges, she knew it would never be enough, that this hunger he inspired would last her whole life long. The hunger grew, and grew, until it became a raging need that only his fruition could satisfy. He brought her legs around his waist, giving her hoarse instructions of how and where to move. Blindly she followed, the empty ache spreading from her center to her extremities. Then, with an abrupt satiation that made her go limp, she was filled with him. His own guttural cry of triumph accompanied the potent splashes into her womb, inciting a pleasure she'd never known. She shook with it, somehow knowing this ambrosia was a banquet they could share any time they pleased.

She went limp, her limbs heavy and laggard, as he collapsed upon her. She ran her hands over his back and shoulders, tears coming to her eyes. When he eased back, she turned her head into the rug, hoping he wouldn't see how he moved her. For a long moment they were silent.

Then he rose, carried her petticoat to her and helped her put it on. She said nothing, somehow more embarrassed dressed than she had been naked. He seemed to understand, for aside from a strange smile, he did not tease her. Instead he pulled on his own breeches, then went to his shirt and fetched something.

He shook the black velvet pouch. Pink fire plopped out and glittered in his hand. She gasped. He held the necklace proudly before her. Reverently she took it and draped it over her hand.

The heart-shaped central stone and the complementing rose diamonds along each side of the heart-shaped woven gold chain were set on tiny springs. They bounced and sparkled with every muted ray of light. Charlaine could only speculate what they would look like in broad daylight. The accompanying white diamonds were the purest in color, clarity and cut she had ever seen, and they perfectly accented the fiery heart of the pink diamonds. It was without doubt the loveliest piece of jewelry she'd ever seen. She wanted to believe the significance of this heart-shaped gift, but he did not kiss her or proclaim fidelity.

He shoved her petticoat off her shoulders until she was bare to the waist and clasped the necklace about her neck. With a contented sigh, he draped her heavy red curls over her shoulders and sat back to drink her in with his eyes. "I knew you would look like this."

"Like what?" She had to clear her throat, her voice was so husky.

He hesitated, but the words seemed torn from him. "Like a woman born to love the man who gave this to her."

The words sparkled between them, precious and significant as the stones she wore. Indeed, as she stared at the pride of possession on his face, the heavy weight between her breasts felt somehow as if it belonged there. As she belonged to him.

The traitorous thought frightened her. He had spent weeks making this necklace, and she knew that he had created it for her. Was this a labor of love, or a cold, calculated seduction, the last design to bring her to heel? Surely, if he loved her, he would say so.

Frantically she pulled at the delicate clasp. "Take it off."

He frowned at her obvious panic, but brushed her hands away and removed the necklace, putting it back in the sack.

"You do not intend to enter this in the competition, do you?"

He shook his head. "I cannot bear for anyone to wear it but you. Consider it my second wedding gift."

"But can you afford to pay Father for the stones?"

He waved an uncaring hand. "Do not worry about me. I shall contrive quite well without your father's help. Despite what you think, it is not your money that I want."

She pulled her petticoat back up. Armored slightly, she stood, poured herself another glass of burgundy, and sipped. When she could speak steadily, she asked, "What do you want?"

He stared at her with disbelief. Then, impatiently, he rose to dress in the rest of his clothes. His head was bent over his shoes, which might have accounted for his odd tone when he answered. "If you truly have to ask me that, then what we shared just past was as big a lie as your wedding vows to me. Well, I will no longer live a lie. I am moving back to my flat, Charlaine. It is obvious you will never care for me." He rose and faced her.

The warmth was gone from his eyes again. She wanted to shiver and mourn, but she tilted her head and tossed back, "You too promised to love and cherish, I believe." He'd gotten what he wanted from her, and now was off, like a man too embarrassed to linger with his light-o'-love.

He finished buttoning his shirt. Then, with a wrench, he jerked open the drapes. The sun was setting over Summerlea. In the distance the lake danced with fire. Swans glided there, while wildflowers bobbed at the water's edge. The maze lurked on one side, the rose garden on the other. He looked from the lovely but solitary scene outside, to the woman who owned the grounds and everything on them. "You are right. You belong here, the Ice Princess dreaming of what could be while what is slips through her fingers like melting ice." He bowed formally, as if he had just met her and would never see her again. "Dream on, lonely little princess. Maybe Summerlea can embrace you when you're sad, and remember you after you're gone." And he turned for the door.

The words to call him back rose up in her throat to choke her, but they would not come.

As if in afterthought, he pulled the necklace from his pocket and tossed it on the table beside the door. "Keep this. Enter it if you wish. I have no need of it any longer." And he closed the door quietly behind him.

Charlaine remained erect until she heard his horse gallop off; then she collapsed where she stood. The hot torrent of tears melted the last that remained of the Ice Princess, but for the life of her, Charlaine did not know who remained in her stead.

Those last two weeks before the jubilee were the longest of her life. She stayed at Summerlea, refusing her father's increasingly demanding notes that she return home. She rode during the day, read at night, and tried to recover her usual happiness in her solitude, but she knew it was hopeless. Everywhere she turned she saw Devlin, heard his laughter. He even followed her into her dreams.

Each night, as she finally drifted off to sleep in the wee hours, she thought she heard her great-great-grandmother Callista saying sweetly, "You have chosen well, my daughter."

Yet when she awoke, she felt no comfort, for he was not there. The long days and longer nights were dreary, but clarifying. Before the two weeks were out, she knew one thing, the only thing that mattered: she would never be happy without him. Whether she loved him or not, she needed him; she wanted him. She would have to chance his sincerity and fidelity.

On the morning she left for London, she took the short odyssey she'd been avoiding and climbed to the highest hill on her estate. Here, giant oaks sheltered the small family graveyard. Simple gravestones marked the ancestors who had fought to leave her this legacy. There, an angel marked her grandmother Chantal's grave. Charlaine wished she could remember the lady as well as Aunt Elizabeth obviously did. She'd heard the many stories of how Chantal, a poor girl of good birth, had loved her handsome young lord too well, and had had to flee in shame, pregnant with his child, when he went away to fight Napoleon. But Chantal had been too young to understand the depth of his love for her, or how steadfast was his devotion. Years later he'd found her, but she denied knowing him, fearing he would take her son. They would suffer the flames of torment together before they finally risked all for love of each other, and finally found joy and truth. To celebrate it, he had given her an exquisite ruby heart ring that Charlaine's father had had made into a stickpin.

But it was at the foot of the old oak, where two simple markers seemed snuggled against the oak's knobby old knees, that she knelt. Lovingly she brushed the ivy away and read, *Callista, most beautiful one. Beloved of Drake.* And his matching stone read, *Drake, beast tamed by beauty. Beloved of Callista.*

The oak had twined about the two markers, as if even in death the lovers clung to one another. Tears dripped hot and fast onto the fertile ground of this sacred place as Charlaine sought a peace that eluded her. Usually when she came here she felt fortified, and knew she did the right thing in doing all she could to protect the gift they'd given her. Yet Callista would not have wanted her to die alone and childless. And she could not shake the gut instinct that her great-great-grandmother would have adored Devlin.

However, that knowledge made her choices no easier. Her resolve to live her life on her own terms had been her bedrock, but her feelings for Devlin had shaken her to her moorings. She truly did not know what to do. She was on the verge of losing him, she knew that, yet she could not take that final step toward wifely duty, as everyone, from her queen to her father, even to Aunt Elizabeth, wanted.

The decision should be easier, especially now. Charlaine's hands slipped to her abdomen. Her menses were a week late. Her fears of dying childless were quite probably moot at this point, but that, too, merely added to her confusion. The father of this child made her weak and giddy with a glance, or the lightest touch, yet she had only kissed him once. How much more enslaved would she be when she cast off the last of her reserve and admitted that she . . . ?

She surged to her feet and ran back down the hill to her carriage. Her muddled thinking accomplished nothing. It was time to act.

As she began the short drive into London, she passed a small pub with a pretty little garden. Here several men sipped ale and gossiped about the quality. One man sat off by himself, watching the road that led to Summerlea. When her carriage passed, he sat up straight. He tossed several coins down on the table, set his bowler hat firmly on his head and mounted the horse, saddled and ready, waiting at the hitching post. Sticking a booted heel in the animal's side, Lewis Temple took off across the countryside for London.

Those two weeks were also the longest of Devlin's life. A thousand times he almost called for his horse to gallop back to her and beg. Always something held him back. It was nothing so simple as pride, or even anger, that kept him working in his shop from dawn to dark. It was the solid conviction that he had done all he could to woo this stubborn woman, and that if they were ever to find happiness together, the next step was up to her. He sensed she cared for him, but doubted she knew the deep, consuming passion he felt for her. Not yet.

Maybe she never would. His fingers slipped as he mounted a stunning sapphire, and he bent one of the delicate prongs. He cursed roundly.

Mordecai glanced up from the shipping schedules he was perusing. "Why don't you go see her? You will never be happy without her."

With measured care, Devlin set aside the ring he was working on. "A homily you should look to yourself. And you might as well quit studying those shipping tables. You know you're not ready to return to New York. Not yet, anyway."

Fiddling with his yarmulke in a sure sign of his distress, Mordecai pretended not to hear.

Devlin pressed, "Elizabeth's called here several times, ostensibly to look at my new wares, but we both know what she was truly shopping for."

Mordecai reddened but did not respond.

"Given how late you returned the night of the ball, I do not need to ask how, ah, deeply your relationship with the duchess has progressed. I say to hang with propriety. It will not be the first time a Jew wedded a rich Gentile, nor the last. I do not doubt that Elizabeth will even attend temple with you, if you ask."

Mordecai folded the schedule with a snap. "I find a lecture on propriety quite hilarious, coming from you."

Shrugging, Devlin pulled the ring back toward him again. "I should think that you were past the age when you cared what the world thought, Mordecai. If you let Elizabeth slip away, you will regret it." When Mordecai glared at him, Devlin held up an appeasing hand. "That's all I will say on the matter. But I believe you should accept her invitation to attend the jubilee with her. She has some of the best seats in Westminster."

"And you? Do you go with Durwood?"

Devlin's fingers quivered a little as he answered steadily, "That is up to Charlaine. If she asks me, I go. If not . . ." He shrugged, but the flippant gesture was not matched by the brooding look in his eyes.

*   *   *

283

From her carriage, Charlaine stared at the door to Devlin's flat. It was almost dark. She really should wait until tomorrow to see him. Sensible or not, she'd had her coachman drive straight here so she could try to coax Devlin back to the estate. They could never come to an accord living in separate houses. She wanted him by her side, day and night. She knew it was but a matter of time before she gave in, but at this moment, she did not care. She missed him.

She walked up the short walk and banged on the knocker. She thought she heard a scurry of movement, and then the door opened. "Devlin, I—" She broke off with a startled gasp.

Maybell stood there. To say she was dressed was an exaggeration. Her brassy locks fell over her shoulders in waves that still could not disguise the large breasts almost exposed by the low neckline of her sheer dressing gown. She looked like what she was: a slut. But a sensual, beautiful slut. She opened the door wide in invitation. "Devlin isn't here, dearie, but ye be welcome to come in and wait."

Charlaine stumbled back down the steps, almost falling. From somewhere, she found strength enough to force the words out. "N-never mind. It c-can wait." And she ran back to the carriage, almost blinded by tears.

Devlin rounded the corner on his way home just in time to see her get back in her carriage. He called after her, but the coachman had already pulled away. However, he saw the tears on her cheeks as the carriage passed. Her head turned. Their eyes met. He was shocked at the disgust there, and wondered what he had done to deserve it. Then she was gone.

Stunned, he walked slowly to his flat. Why had she come to him at last, only to leave in obvious distress? He pulled out his key, and then frowned when he realized the door was ajar. He shoved it wide. His stomach dropped to his shoes at the sight he beheld—Maybell, up to her old tricks. She lounged on his sofa as if she owned it and drank his wine as if she'd selected it. He slammed the door behind him and leaned back against it, his mind racing.

"What a surprise, Maybell. I do not recall inviting you here."

She licked her lips in a gesture that once would have excited him. Now she left him cold, for she was as avaricious and ruthless as the men who hired her. He wondered what he'd ever seen in her.

"Lord, lovie, ye ain't livin' with that frozen lady no more. I thought ye could use a real woman to warm ye."

He looked about the apartment, and finally spied her discarded clothes in a pile by his bed. He took them back out to the sitting room and tossed them to her. "You have five minutes to dress and get out. Then I throw you into the street as you are."

"Ye can't talk to me like that. Why, I know who ye are and what ye've done. And I know two gents who'd love to hear me sing down at the Yard. I still got them jewels ye stole fer me when ye first come to London."

Devlin raised an eyebrow. "Are you threatening me, Maybell?"

Immediately the hard expression on her face softened. "No, lover. I ain't had no one like ye before or since. Them fancy gents tells me ye can get an annulment or somethin', and be free to take up with me again." She reached out to embrace him but he sidestepped her neatly.

"I will never be free. It's too late for that, even if I don't live with Charlaine Kimball. Go, Maybell. Please." Abruptly, he was tired. Not just tired, but bone-deep weary. A few weeks ago he might have run to Charlaine with an explanation, but now he just pulled off his shoes and collapsed. Let her think what she pleased. She always did anyway.

Gathering up her clothes, Maybell turned away in a huff. When she was dressed, she came toward him and propped her hands on her generous hips. "Ye ain't actin' normal, lover. Ye'll change yer mind when she don't give ye the time o' day no more."

Devlin waved her away.

Scowling, she turned for the door, promising over her shoulder, "Ye ain't seen the last o' me."

Her voice grated on Devlin's nerves. He looked her up and down contemptuously. "Indeed? I thought I'd seen all of you, as have half the men in London."

Her mouth dropped open at the insult. Her full lips worked helplessly for a moment; then she screeched, "Ye dirty bastard! I—"

She broke off when he surged out of his chair, flung open the door and pushed her outside. She was still staring at him in shock when he slammed the door in her face.

Blessed silence descended. He sat back down and propped his elbows on his knees and his head in his hands, wondering what the hell to do now. Maybell scorned was dangerous. She could indeed go to the authorities, and they might be able to trace the two stolen necklaces he'd given her, but it was essentially the word of a whore against a respectable jeweler.

Still, he had a feeling Temple was behind Maybell's involvement more than Cecil was. Cecil was ruthless, but he had a prudish snobbery that would have made his use of Maybell in this manner distasteful. Devlin rose unsteadily. He had not been sleeping well, but now was as good a time as any to beard the lion in his den. This vendetta the two men had against him had to end, or by God maybe he would leave London as Cecil obviously wanted so badly.

He went out, locked his door, and hired a hansom to take him to Cecil's hotel.

Chapter Eleven

Elizabeth, Duchess of Kensington, strode imperiously into the foyer of the Kimball home. If her coiffure was a bit more mussed than usual, the lines in her face slightly more pronounced, no one, least of all the impeccable Jeffries, remarked upon it. He opened the door to her and sighed his relief. "Thank heavens, Your Grace, you have come. Lady Kimball just returned, and she . . . she . . ." He broke off, obviously mastering his emotions. "We need your help."

"So I apprehend from Durwood's note. Do not announce me, Jeffries. If this chit is so anxious to make others dance to her tune, then she has some music of her own to face." She marched upstairs.

However, she held on to the banister more than usual. She'd hardly slept a wink since the wedding ball a bare two weeks ago. Since that last night with Mordecai, she'd been convinced he was going to give in and admit he loved her, but he'd been gone from her little summer cottage when she awoke. Every time she went to Devlin's shop, Mordecai disappeared with a weak smile.

Rejection was a new feeling for Elizabeth, and it did not sit well with either her temperament or her years. She'd never once set her sights on a man and lost him. But then, Mordecai Levitz was not like most men. Well, lose him or win him, one thing she knew: Charlaine could not be allowed to throw away her own chance at happiness because of some infantile fear. She'd given the girl her head long enough.

When she rounded the corner to Charlaine's door, she heard the sobbing. Her firm step checked, and her even firmer countenance softened. But she collected herself, knocked briskly, once, on Charlaine's door, and shoved the portal wide.

Her niece huddled on the sofa, her arms wrapped about her knees as she rocked herself in pain. She had to blink the tears away to focus on her aunt. "P-please, Aunt, n-not now—"

Elizabeth sat down beside her and put an arm about Charlaine's stiff shoulders. "Hush, child, you have brooded enough. If you had seen fit to confide in me, we could have avoided all this."

A desperate shake of her head was Charlaine's only response.

"Tush, you silly goose, think you that slut was at Devlin's flat by invitation?"

Charlaine's eyes widened.

"How do I know, you wonder? Why, your coachman, child. When you came home so upset, Durwood questioned him. Your loyal retainer, who is, apparently, as fond of you as the rest of the staff, saw this Maybell woman answer Devlin's door, dressed, shall we say, scantily."

Charlaine closed her eyes as her face twisted in

pain. "And he has the gall to call *me* fickle. Why, it's been only a fortnight since—" She bit her lip.

Elizabeth smiled. "Ah, I knew it was only a matter of time. Why, the room fairly glows when the two of you are in it. But if that is the case, why did Devlin come back to London with a brow like a thunderclap, while you stayed alone at Summerlea?"

"Because I will not give in to his domination." Charlaine snapped her lips closed, as if she regretted saying too much.

"Are you sure you are not related to Mordecai, my dear? You are both of similar minds, it seems." Elizabeth's full mouth had a wry slant, but then she smiled again. "How frightening it must be, to both of you, to know the full fury of love for the first time. I wish I could impart some of my own life experience to you, my dearest niece. Your grandmama Chantal would know how to convince you, for if ever there existed a more loving, giving woman, I have never met her."

"But do you not see, Aunt? It is precisely out of loyalty to her, and to Callista, that I cannot give in. If I love him, how can I deny him my estates? And I am haunted by the fear that that is what he is really after. And if . . ." She cupped her stomach, biting her lip.

Joy flickered in Elizabeth's hazel eyes. "Aha, so that's the way of it, eh? It is more important than ever that you put aside these girlish fears and take your rightful place." She caught Charlaine's hands. "Has Devlin asked you to revoke the agreement he signed at your wedding?"

She shook her head.

"I predict that he will not. I have known Devlin Rhodes for some years, child. He's a scamp, a rogue, but he also has his own sense of honor. And most important, he loves you, child."

Hope quickened Charlaine's breathing, but it was

short-lived. Her lungs collapsed in a depressed sigh. "He has a peculiar way of showing it. He will not even kiss me. And why did he have Maybell there if he loves me?"

"I suspect Maybell was there the same way she was here at your ball. By invitation, yes, but at the behest of one Lewis Temple. You remember him, no doubt? Mordecai told me that he hates Devlin because of something that happened in America, and he's been working with Cecil to discredit Devlin. They will do anything to drive a wedge between you and your husband." Elizabeth leaned forward until her nose almost brushed Charlaine's, to emphasize her next words. "While you think on all this, I want you to ponder two things. One, reformed rakes make the best husbands, for once they love, they love well. And two, Devlin Rhodes, for good or ill, is your husband. He deserves the benefit of a doubt. If you do not support him and go to him, you may lose him. Mordecai told me Devlin is so upset at this, ah, conflict, that he is considering returning to Africa."

Charlaine covered her mouth with one hand, but her little moan of pain still slipped out.

Complacently, Elizabeth rose. Indeed, from the look on her niece's face, she'd given her much to think about. "And lastly, unless you want to cause more talk than there already is, I suggest you invite Devlin to be your escort to the jubilee. It is Victoria's day, and she will not enjoy celebrating fifty years of rule by seeing you gossiped about." She patted Charlaine's hand. "And I promise not to tell anyone your news until you are ready. But I counsel you to settle your future, for you have only a few months at best before the world knows that the Kimball line has been sustained."

Elizabeth stumbled a bit as she turned for the door, but she caught herself. Her head swam, and it took a

Colleen Shannon

second to clear. Had she taken her powders today? She couldn't remember. When she was steady again, she turned for a last word. "I love you, my dear. Your grandmother would be proud of you, but she would counsel you to trust your husband. Love can hurt, it is true, but it also gives the greatest joy. It is worth the risk." She exited, closing the door quietly behind her.

Charlaine lay down, clutching the pillow to her middle. Aunt Elizabeth's words had the ring of truth to them. Almost, she had come to this conclusion herself during those lonely weeks at Summerlea. But the pain that seared through her every time she remembered Maybell's smug expression would give any woman pause. And if the woman had sneaked in, as Elizabeth believed, then why had Devlin not rushed here to make excuses?

Because she had hurt him too. The certainty came with a sudden assurance that nothing, not even her own fears, could deny. As Devlin would say, it was her move.

Now what?

Devlin nodded haughtily when Henry Dupree backed away from the door, obviously stunned to see him. Devlin stepped into Cecil's suite and closed the door behind him. "Tell your employer that I wish to see him." He tendered one of his calling cards.

Limply, Henry took it. He scanned it, then tossed it contemptuously on his desk. "He will not see you."

"That is not your choice to make, is it? Tell him I am here, or I shall announce myself."

Henry sputtered for a moment, but when Devlin turned, Henry blocked Cecil's closed office door, gave Devlin a last glare, and then knocked softly.

"What do you want?" asked an irascible voice.

"Ah, sir, Mr. Devlin Rhodes requests an audience."

292

Henry put sarcastic emphasis on *requests*.

Dead silence answered, and then the door opened from the inside. Cecil filled the portal, as much with his formidable presence as with his bulk. "What the devil do you want?"

Devlin wondered wryly if a white flag would do any good. He glanced at Henry, then said only, "A private word, if you please."

"Whatever you have to say to me, you can say in front of Henry. He is intimately familiar with all my current business affairs."

"I daresay. However, unless you wish him to be equally familiar with our past, ah, contretemps, I suggest you let me in." Devlin planted his feet firmly and crossed his arms over his chest, giving a sturdy imitation of an oak tree. One way or another, even if it meant fisticuffs or pistols at dawn, he was having this out with Cecil Rhodes. Sending Maybell just as Charlaine came to him was the last straw.

Cecil's gray eyes narrowed to slits; he was obviously not used to being threatened. Finally, with a powerful hand, he slammed his door open against the wall and waved Devlin in. "Henry, fetch me the latest financial newspapers. I shall call you again when I need you."

Henry looked between the two men, seemed as if he might argue, but finally he turned in a huff and slammed out, so obviously angry that he forgot his hat.

The two cousins stared at each for a long moment, and then Devlin sat down without being invited and pulled his mother's necklace from his pocket. He tossed it on the desk before Cecil.

Cecil picked it up and handled it curiously, as if he'd never held a locket before; finally he opened it. He sucked in a shocked breath as he absorbed the two pictures. Finally, his expression inscrutable, he offered the locket back. "Your parents, I presume."

Devlin pocketed the keepsake. "Yes. My father gave this to my mother shortly before he died. He intended to marry her, you know. Tell me, does he resemble your father?"

Cecil nodded reluctantly. "Yes, somewhat. I never knew him, but I have heard my father speak of his brother."

Smiling wryly, Devlin deduced, "Not flatteringly, I would guess."

Cecil shrugged his broad shoulders before he said flatly, "This changes nothing. If this little artful move was an attempt to invoke some familial bond, you failed. Your father was a scoundrel up to the very way he died." And Cecil's expression concluded, *Like father, like son.*

"Did you know that the man who killed him lusted after my mother, and that my father was defending her honor? Your own sainted father would disapprove of this?"

Surprise spoiled Cecil's poker expression, but he recovered quickly. "If that is what your mother chose to believe, I will not deny you the same comfort."

Devlin ground his teeth together, counting to twenty in French. Somehow, in his emotional moments, the tongue of his birth was most comforting. It was a good thing Charlaine did not speak French, or she would have no doubt of his feelings for her. Devlin forced his thoughts back to the matter at hand. "And how does your competition with Barnato progress?"

"That is none of your concern. You sold out, remember. To Currie, I might add, who sold to Barnato. Barnato is so determined to ruin me that he cares not if he wrecks the entire diamond market."

"Is he selling at a loss again?"

"No, but almost. And he, damn him, can produce

more cheaply, even since I have put my workers into compounds. Since I did this, the cost of a carat has been reduced, but his costs are still less."

Devlin looked away to hide his distaste. Cecil's innovative business concept of virtually imprisoning his workers in compounds to lessen the problem of theft had been successful, but at what cost to the men's families and lives? This last tactic had driven Devlin to sell to Currie at a lower cost than Cecil had offered, on a matter of principle. But he knew Cecil would not understand his reasons, so he didn't bother arguing.

"It will be healthier for us all to end this divisive competition, ally into one amalgamation, and exercise prudence," Cecil continued. "In my years in this business, I have learned one thing—men will not buy an unlimited number of stones for their wives and sweethearts; when the price of diamonds is low, they buy more, but never have I calculated a year wherein they exceed four million pounds worth of stones. If we wish to succeed for years to come, we must adapt to this market, not fight it. But my way of thinking shall prevail. You shall see."

No doubt. Devlin had heard rumors that the house of Rothschild was the latest ally of De Beers. With those deep pockets behind him, Cecil would crush the competition. Devlin looked at the man opposite and thought how much he resembled the South Africa he loved: rugged, uncompromising and ruthless. He was also complex, but honest in his business dealings. Which made his behavior in the matter of Maybell all the more inexplicable.

"Tell me something, Cecil. Do you dislike me because I am your baseborn relative, because I sold to your rival, or because I bested you at fisticuffs in front of your allies in Kimberley?"

"All of the above." The flat response took on a bit

more life as he added, "But I wish to see you gone from here for none of those reasons. You and your kind are not good for England."

"And you will use any means to that end, even hiring a harlot to discredit me with mý wife?"

A red flush colored Cecil's broad cheekbones. He shifted on his chair. "That was not my idea, but if it succeeded . . ." He shrugged.

"Ah, your inimitable assistant, no doubt. He hates me even more than you do because he lusts after my wife."

Shock rounded Cecil's elongated eyes.

Devlin shook his head wryly. "For an intelligent man, you certainly have your blind spots, especially where women are concerned." He stood, put his hands on Cecil's desk and leaned forward to emphasize his words. "But know this: No matter if you feel any loyalty to your uncle and his son. No matter if you feel no empathy for a fellow jeweler. No matter if your ally Durwood Kimball welcomes me into his family. But your grudge against me has upset my wife, and this I cannot allow. Leave off your underhanded schemes to discredit me, or I will take action of my own. Clear?"

Slowly Cecil rose. "You should know better than to threaten me, given our history."

Devlin straightened too. "I do not react calmly either, when I am backed into a corner. I love my wife, Cecil. Her happiness is important to me, and we have enough problems without your interference. Please, for all our sakes, leave off your investigation. You will find nothing, and you will go to great expense only to be embarrassed."

Eye to eye, the two men confronted one another. They were of a height, and more alike than either would ever admit, but they were also dissimilar. And it was these differences that made them each crack a reluctant smile.

"Do you truly love Charlaine?" Cecil asked curiously.

"Truly. Deeply. As only a scoundrel can love. I never would have married her otherwise. I promise to treat her well, and to be an upstanding gentleman. My word as a Rhodes."

Closing his eyes for a moment, Cecil contemplated this news. When his gray eyes opened, they were clear, and softer than usual. "Every man deserves a second chance."

Delvin went weak with relief.

"But I caution you, Henry and Lewis Temple dislike you even more than I do. I shall discharge Temple, but I suspect he will continue his, ah, grudge, as you put it, against you."

As if cued, the outer door opened. A tentative knock came. "Sir, Mr. Temple is here to see you."

"Send him in."

Temple burst in, saying, "Success at last! This woman has agreed—"

"—to go to the authorities and swear I'm a thief and a liar? What else? A raper of women or murderer of children?"

Temple whirled. In a measure of his strength, his shock did not last long. "The latter two would not surprise me. I know for a fact that you are a defiler of women. My sister died because of you."

Devlin blinked in shock. "Wha—"

As if now that the truth was out, only the whole truth—as he saw it—would do, Temple swept forward on a tide of righteous indignation. Henry Dupree gave up all pretense of not listening and shoved the door wide to observe the confrontation. Cecil frowned at him, but shrugged as he too watched this reckoning that had been too many years in the making.

"Remember Sally Temple? She was my half sister," Temple said bitterly.

Recognition and regret flickered on Devlin's features. "Now I understand. But I had nothing to do with her death."

His face reddening, Temple reached out to grab Devlin's throat, caught himself and made brutal fists instead. "Nothing? You bastard! She was so miserable because you gave her the heave-ho that she scarce knew what she was doing that day when she stepped into the street."

"I agree, she scarce knew what she was doing, but it had nothing to do with me. It was her opium addiction that—"

Temple's hands were about Devlin's throat before Devlin could finish. "She was too good for you, and you cast her aside as if she were trash." His hands squeezed until Devlin's face began to turn purple.

Cecil half rose, but sat back down again when Devlin flashed a knee up into Temple's groin. Temple stumbled back with a scream, clutching his privates. Devlin coughed for a moment, but straightened and fixed an inimical eye on his declared enemy, his voice slightly hoarse.

"Think what you like, but I grieved for her, and I still think of her. Even if she was distraught over me, that's not my fault. I did my utmost to keep her away from the opium dens, but the addiction was too strong. I had already decided to go to Africa. What did you expect me to do? Drag her with me? Besides"— his anger began to fade until he finished in a dull monotone—"we did not love each other, despite what she told you." Devlin nodded briefly at Cecil. "Thank you for the audience, Cecil. I hope to see you at the jubilee." Pivoting, he stalked out, brushing past Henry, who recovered his balance quickly and sent a hateful sneer after him.

When Temple had his wind again, he came forward—gingerly—to face Cecil. "What is this? You've made peace with the wastrel?"

For the presumption, Cecil looked Temple up and down with a scornful stare that had made lesser men tremble. Temple didn't budge. "That is none of your concern. Be good enough to know that your services are terminated. I do not believe, whatever his earlier flaws, that Devlin Rhodes is still a thief. He genuinely loves his wife, and I am not God, to persecute him for his sins. Every man deserves a second chance." Cecil pulled a check up and began writing. When he was finished, he blew on it to dry the ink, then offered it to Temple.

Temple didn't even glance at it before he tore it in two. "Money cannot substitute for conscience. You, sir, are as big a scoundrel as your baseborn relative if you quit now."

Slowly, with the power of a man in his prime who knew his own destiny and intended to forge it, Cecil rose. "And you, sir, are a fool if you think to speak to me like that with impunity. I have let myself be swayed to use every underhanded trick we can think of against this man, to no avail. Devlin Rhodes"—and for the first time he said the surname without wincing—"could have used similar tactics against me, and at the very least could have asked his wife to complain to the queen. Instead, he came here today, face-to-face and man to man, like one who truly has nothing to hide. For the sake of his father—my uncle—and my own father, who taught the virtue of forgiveness, I can only give him this chance."

"But, sir," protested Henry, "I thought you wanted him out of England—"

A big, commanding hand shushed Henry with a slicing motion. "Even I can change my mind. For the moment, at any rate. Now return to your work, Henry."

"But, sir—"

"Now." Cecil did not shout, for he didn't need to.

Gnashing his teeth, Henry reluctantly returned to his desk in the next room.

Temple looked as if he might say something else, smashed his bowler hat down comically over his big ears, and stomped out, slamming the door behind him.

Wearily Cecil sat back down. His buttocks had barely touched the chair before another knock sounded, this one even more imperative than the last. Cecil closed his eyes and counted to ten, but asked calmly, "Yes?"

The Dowager Duchess of Kensington swept in like the aristocrat she was. "Cecil, we need to talk." She closed the door gently behind her. "You must discharge that unpleasant fellow Temple. He's not serving your interests, but only his own. I have had him investigated, and he blames Devlin for—"

"Yes, yes, I know all about that. Get to the point."

The duchess reared back in affront. "Well, plain speaking indeed. If that's what you want, listen to this." She swept the few hairs bold enough to escape her pompadour back up into her big picture hat. Then her hand fell, and she stood to her full, imposing height. "Devlin Rhodes will be good for my niece. Leave him be, or you will have me to reckon with—a certain little gray-haired lady who is not known for her timidity."

Cecil folded his hands neatly before him on his desk. "This seems to be my day for threats before lunch. They do not sit well on my stomach."

" 'Tis not your stomach you should worry about—
'tis your pocketbook."

That got his attention—as she'd intended. "Would
you care to elaborate?"

"Certainly. I hold ten percent of the De Beers shares.
What would happen to your plans to amalgamate all
the Kimberley mines into one conglomerate if I
should, say, sell my shares to a certain Barney Barnato?" The duchess raised an eyebrow at him.

Fury roiled like tempestuous seas in Cecil's gray
eyes, but then a queer calm descended. "Be my guest.
I have other plans." That he and Barnato were working on an alliance at this very moment, he did not say.
Partners, even old enemies, could work together much
more effectively than competitors.

This time her surprise showed. "I see."

She obviously didn't, but he had to admire how
quickly she regrouped. Cecil's feeling that he'd under-
estimated his young cousin increased. He could finally
admit, to himself at least, that he'd let bruised male
pride at being bested in business and fisticuffs affect
his judgment. The Duchess of Kensington was obviously very fond of the young scamp, if she was willing
to risk her own lucrative shares in his defense. Fur-
thermore, she was as astute a judge of human nature
as Cecil knew.

He hid a smile as she stood even taller and threatened, "Be that as it may, if you force me, Cecil, I shall
go to the queen. She will not be happy at your perse-
cution of the husband of one of her favorites."

His amusement grew. "Indeed? That I should love
to see. You know how our queen detests scandal."

His nonchalance obviously began to concern her.
She fumbled for words, and the lines of worry deepened in her face.

Finally he left off teasing and rose to face her. "Had

you arrived five minutes earlier, you would have seen young Rhodes leave my office with a smile on his face. He can be most persuasive, when he chooses." Cecil recalled the two young faces in the locket. Now that he'd seen his uncle as a young man, he saw the resemblance Devlin bore to his father. That alone dictated that he give Devlin another chance. There could be no question that the man was, indeed, related to him.

Hopefully she asked, "Do you mean . . . ?"

"Indeed I do. We have made our peace, after a fashion. I have discharged that unpleasant American Pinkerton fellow, but I suspect he will continue his mission, with or without pay."

She shrugged. "He will find nothing."

Cecil remembered Maybell's expression as they both left the wedding ball, escorted none too politely by Jeffries. But he spread his hands expressively as if to say, *Who knows?*

The duchess cocked her head and raised her lorgnette to see him better. "And why, pray tell, did you lead me on and let me make a fool of myself with empty threats?"

He smiled gleefully. "If you had survived African politics as long as I have, you would know never to bluff unless you've the grit to follow through. Sell your shares you might have, but you would never humiliate Charlaine by acquainting the queen of our, er, family squabbles."

She crinkled her nose at this masterly understatement, dropped her lorgnette on her ample bosom and said, "Well, I shall slink home, my opinion of myself fairly ruined." But she dropped a sly wink, and it was apparent nothing daunted her. At the door, she paused. "Cecil, I never knew your father, but somehow I think he would approve of your forbearance."

"For once, my dear Duchess, we are in complete

agreement." He held the door for her. "Will I see you at the jubilee?"

"In that crush? Probably not. But I will be there." An odd expression descended over her face, a mixture of determination and longing. "Along with my chosen escort. But at least now, if I see you, I will not have to give you the cut direct."

And she swept out, as regal as if she had won their little battle of wills.

Smiling wryly, Cecil sat back down. He thought of something, went to the door and began, "Henry—"

Henry had left without so much as a by-your-leave. Now where had the young fellow gone to?

Henry hurried after Lewis Temple. "Wait a minute!"

Temple turned with a scowl. "What?"

"Do you intend to leave for America?"

"Not yet. Not until my mission is finished."

Henry sighed deeply. "I thought so. May we talk?"

Some of Temple's hauteur eased. "For a moment."

Charlaine nibbled at the tip of her pen, scribbled something, then crumpled the note. The floor around the little desk in her chamber was littered with clumps of expensive paper. She'd been trying for the past hour to compose a note with just the right touch of pride and politeness to invite Devlin to be in their box for the jubilee. She'd not spoken to him in weeks, and it was obvious he had no intention of coming to explain why Maybell had been attired so scantily in his flat. Her father and Elizabeth had both tried to make her believe that Maybell had been brought there by Temple rather than at Devlin's invitation, but Charlaine wasn't so sure.

And until she was sure, she could not relax her guard enough to invite Devlin home. She certainly could not tell him that he was going to be a father. *Typical French frog*, she tried to sniff to herself, *love them and leave them*. But her own criticism did not ring true, for that second time, at least, had been as much at her initiation as his.

Thus, here she sat, trying to do her duty as a wife. Everyone from the queen down would be scandalized if the newlyweds attended the jubilee in separate boxes. Finally she settled on a bald, *"We shall expect your escort to the coronation tomorrow. Please fetch us two hours early so we can get there through the streets in time. Your"*—she hesitated, then finished with a flourish—*"obedient wife."* She gave the note to a footman with orders to deliver it; then she fetched her carriage for the ride to the dressmaker's. She would do her best to see that, after tomorrow, her husband could ignore her no longer. And once she was reassured about Maybell, they had to have a long talk. For the child's sake, they had to come to an accord of some kind. Prince or frog, he was going to be a father.

She tried to visualize this momentous occasion, but the only image in her mind was of Devlin's perfect mouth hovering over hers, and the kiss that would forever change their lives.

Across London, a very different lady struggled with a very similar note and a like dilemma. The Duchess of Kensington looked out the window above her exquisite Chippendale secretary. Even this dignified section of London was atwitter over tomorrow. The next house over, footmen polished the marble steps. Across the street, she could see maids washing windows in preparation for the grand party to come after the coronation.

Durwood's own party would be small but select. Elizabeth's decision whether to attend rested on the shoulders of one man. One small, stubborn jeweler with a heart as big—and as guarded—as his mind. Swallowing her unusual nervousness, Elizabeth forced herself to finish the note. *". . . I should be grateful for your escort. It is amazing how few people think of including aging duchesses in their invitations."* There, it wouldn't hurt to appeal to his chivalry. She concluded, *"Please reply forthwith. I have missed you."* This last slipped out of its own accord. She considered striking it out, but she sighed and left it in. She suspected he felt the same, but he was just too stubborn to admit it.

Signing with a flourish, she folded the paper and stuck it in an envelope with her embossed seal. Her heart beat faster as she watched her liveried footman carry it out the door. She had promised herself that she would quit acting like a schoolgirl with a fetish if this last tactic proved futile. If Mordecai were really so opposed to a long-term relationship with a rich Gentile, then she could fight him no longer. She would go back to the loneliness of her golden years and try to live with the regret.

Still, the thought brought tears to her eyes. She turned down the gas lanterns to watch the night collect itself and wondered if her former peace with herself would ever come again.

After its busiest day ever, the Rhodes jewelry store was about to close when two liveried servants arrived. Each offered his note with a respectful bow to the clerk who answered the door. The clerk took the notes with a promise to deliver them.

The two servants stared at each other as the door was locked behind them. "Queer state o' affairs, hain't it, when a duchess has to beg audience with a Jew."

The Kimball servant agreed with a toplofty, "Or a

Kimball has to run after a husband who ain't good enough fer her." Shaking their heads in equal disgust, the two men went about their business, having proved the old aphorism that there's no one more snobbish than an aristocrat's servant.

Inside, the clerk knocked on the office door, set the two missives down on the desk, nodded, and left by the back entrance.

Mordecai and Devlin looked up from tabulating the week's take, barely glancing at the two notes. Even the usually stern Mordecai smiled his glee as he drew a bold line beneath the profit column. "Fifty years of Regina Victoria has certainly made three years of Rhodes and Levitz profitable."

Devlin nodded, but the shadows under his eyes made his own grin seem halfhearted. Devlin had known great poverty, and now was about to know great wealth, for since his appearance at the queen's ball, and the wedding ball, some of the bolder, more curious of the quality had begun to patronize his stores. The irony would have made him smile, had he felt like smiling.

Charlaine forced him to sign away all claims to her estate even as she gave him the means to acquire greater wealth merely by wearing his ring about her finger. Devlin closed the account books with a snap. Pity his newfound prosperity couldn't buy him happiness. He stared out the window at the revelry. London would not sleep tonight, nor the next, as it celebrated the reign of one small, imperial little woman who had brought her country to world dominance in the short space of fifty years.

Devlin tried to find joy in his heart, as so many native Englishmen obviously did, but he had seen too much of the seedier side of life to revel in Victoria's conquests. For every territory claimed by England, some other way of life was lost. Maybe it was a less civilized way of life, maybe even less worthy in God's eyes, as Cecil believed, but it was a way cherished equally by the people who lost it, whether they were Indian or Zulu or Irish.

Again, Devlin felt that pull to go back to Kimberley for the uncomplicated grind of hard work, thievery and greed. How much easier to guard his back than his heart. As a lover, despite his French blood, he was a total failure. All he knew was that he could not bear to be in the same city with Charlaine, much less the same house, and have her continue to treat him with this icy politeness.

Mordecai watched him brood, but then he noticed the notes. He picked them up. His already pale complexion went gray at the bold feminine hand that had written his own name. He picked up the other note and handed it to Devlin. "Something for you from Charlaine."

Devlin started and grabbed the note. He ripped it open eagerly, his hands trembling, but when he was done he crumpled it as he read her signature. Obedient indeed. If she were obedient, she deserved a whipping. He had a good mind not to attend. Let them talk. Pretending all was well between them in front of so many curious eyes was beyond him at the moment.

A little sound caught his attention. He looked up. Mordecai stared at his invitation with an expression that could only be termed tormented. Devlin tossed his own invitation in the garbage and went to his old friend.

He glanced over Mordecai's shoulder. At least the duchess said she missed him. Devlin gently squeezed Mordecai's arm, feeling his tenseness. "She is not used to rejection, Mordecai. If you refuse her this time, she may not ask again."

Colleen Shannon

Mordecai stared blindly at the note and did not respond.

Devlin sighed and said louder, "I have never seen you so grim as these past weeks. Forget what people say, or the complexities involved when your main domicile is New York. You can both work things out, if you want to."

Finally Mordecai said quietly, "But I cannot give up my religion, even for Lizzie."

Devlin frowned. "Has she asked you to?"

"No. But if I do not, and we wed, she a Gentile, me a Jew, what do you think her friends will do? I can answer that." He tossed the invitation across the office as if the simple act could vent his frustrations. "They will ostracize her, and she will be miserable."

"I do not believe she cares a fig what others say. It will not be the first time people of different religions have wed. From what I understand, she is not a devout Protestant anyway."

"But at our ages, we should know better."

Devlin smiled slightly. "Exactly. At your ages, you should know that happiness is too fleeting to throw it away without a struggle. You have never loved a woman in your life, Mordecai. Does it not occur to you that God is giving you a gift to honor you for your years of unswerving devotion?"

"But why couldn't he make it a nice Jewish lady?" Mordecai blurted.

"Now you disappoint me." Devlin released Mordecai and stepped back. "Maybe it is you who is prejudiced and does not want to wed a Gentile."

Mordecai blinked his shock, and then bit out, "You should not speak to anyone so blithely about females when your own marriage has been less than successful."

When Devlin looked hurt, Mordecai swallowed.

308

"Sorry, Devlin. I just cannot speak calmly about Lizzie." He nodded at the paper Devlin had tossed away. "Do you intend to go with Charlaine?"

Devlin started to shake his head, nodded, and then he shrugged.

With a sad little smile, Mordecai said, "We are a silly pair, are we not? Glooming around here like two lonely bears going into hibernation." He stared blindly into space, but then color returned to his face. He walked briskly to the desk and pulled out two sheets of notepaper. He shoved one across the desk to Devlin. "I know what my response will be." And he began to write.

Devlin's hand reached out to pick up a pen. And then, with a life of its own, it too began to write.

The missive was curt but precise:

> *I shall call for you at the appointed time. Your devoted husband.*

Charlaine crinkled her nose, knowing his appellation of himself was a jab at her purported obedience. But she breathed a sigh of relief, for he had been so distant, literally and figuratively, that she had begun to think she'd never see him again.

Eager to check her attire for the morrow, she rose so quickly that her head spun. She had to sit back down, rest her head on her knees and breathe deeply to stem her abrupt nausea. A knock sounded at her door.

Durwood peeked in with a mild, "My dear, have you heard if Devlin attends wi—" He broke off when he saw her sweaty upper lip and pale skin. He rushed in to kneel at her side. "What's amiss, child?"

A telltale hand stole to her stomach before she could stop herself, but she tried to bluff it through anyway.

"Something I ate, no doubt." The mere thought of food was enough. Her eyes widened as her stomach gurgled. With a hand to her mouth, she jumped up and ran into her water closet.

When she came back out some minutes later, her father was leaning back—sprawling, more like—in utter contentment, a silly grin on his still handsome face. For a moment, father and daughter stared at one another, both of them thinking the same thoughts, with a slight gender difference, for he thought of a rough-and-tumble little boy with black hair, she of a luminous little girl to leave her estates to.

"When do you intend to tell him?" he asked softly.

It was too late to lie, but she was not ready for Devlin to know yet. Not while there were so many unanswered questions between them. She still had to know why Maybell had been at his flat; she still had to coax him into kissing her. Lately, that last intimacy he denied her had become symbolic of the incompleteness of their entire relationship. How could their hearts link as one when their lips had not?

The thought made roses bloom in her cheeks, for her nightly dreams were weakening her daily reservations. Somehow, since melding with Devlin in that most intimate of ways, a gentle certainty had grown that he was a good man, that he would never hurt her, and that it truly was she, and she alone, who appealed to him, not her wealth. But how could she tell him these things when he refused even to see her?

Finally she answered, "In my own good time."

He frowned. "He will be extremely hurt if he discovers on his own."

"Do you intend to tell him?"

He hesitated, and then shook his head with a wry smile. "I have interfered in your life quite enough, I believe."

A burst of laughter escaped her. "Now that, I never thought to hear you say."

The merry sound made his eyes mist over. "How much you remind me of your mother when you laugh like that," he murmured.

Her smile faded. "Did you truly love her that much? So much that you can never wed again?"

Wordless, he nodded.

Her shoulders lifted and fell in a deep sigh. "Then such is probably my fate."

"Yes, my dear. Exactly as I've been trying to tell you. Make your decrepit old father happy and honor the memory of your mother by embracing your new family and passing on the legacy gifted to us."

The manipulative words would have angered her a month ago, or even two weeks ago; now, despite herself, she saw the sense of them. "I will think on it."

He rose and pulled her up into his arms for a tight hug. "And whatever your decision, I want you to know that I am proud of you. You have made me a very happy man." That silly grin stretched his face again. "I am to be a grandfather at last."

She hugged him back, feeling at peace with her father for the first time in years.

But he had not changed that much, as he proved with an autocratic, "Now come along to dinner. You will feel much better after you eat."

And for once, she did not argue.

The day of the jubilee dawned bright and clear. Charlaine looked out the window as she sipped tea and ate biscuits to settle her stomach. But the flutters there owed as much to whom she was to see this day as to her nausea, and she was not thinking of the queen. When her queasiness had quieted, she rose to dress.

Even she, who had known only the finest silks and velvets since infancy, gasped when she saw the gown the designer had made for her. It could be only one color, the color that matched the necklace Devlin had made for her with such loving care: pink.

The hint of a bustle accented the beauty of silk chiffon so fine that pink air seemed to float about her feet with every step. The gown was embellished only with a deep frill of the finest lace at hem, leg-o'-mutton sleeves, and a low-cut bodice. The tiny nipped-in waist was accented by a band of brilliants that matched the bows on her pink silk slippers. It was a plainer ensemble than most would wear to this grand occasion, owing its elegance to the form of its wearer and the fineness of its construction. However, when the maid reverently set the rose diamond necklace about Charlaine's neck, it glittered and bounced with every move, her perfect complexion and pleasing shape accented as never before. The maid set a rose diamond comb at the side of Charlaine's upswept hair and stood back.

"Miss, I ain't never seen ye lookin' better," she said reverently.

Charlaine peered in the mirror. Even she was impressed by the vision gazing at her. Delicately she touched the necklace. She could no more enter this thing of beauty into something so crass as a competition than he could. It fit about her neck as if it would suit no one else. And surely he would know how she felt about him when he saw it around her neck.

She closed her eyes and clutched her stomach, for she was not certain she could admit those words to herself, much less to him. But when she opened them, it was not the Ice Princess who gazed at her. It was the woman, the expectant mother, who had been born and molded at Devlin's touch. It was not he who had been transformed; it was she. It did not matter whether he was a French frog or a prince, she loved him for what he was.

The revelation still whirled in her head when her father knocked. "My dear, Devlin is downstairs with the carriage. Are you ready?"

Suddenly joyous, she trilled, "Yes, Father!" and ran to her destiny.

Downstairs, Devlin ran a finger between his tight shirt collar and his neck. How would she look? Would she be angry, or distant, or . . . His heart beat faster as he hoped that, somehow, she would have missed him as much as he had missed her. He was still speculating when the door opened and his bride swept in on her father's arm. He gasped at the sight of her. His resplendent new black silk jacket with tails, his gray silk waistcoat and black top hat suddenly seemed too constricting, most especially his breeches. God, she'd never been so lovely.

He swept her head to foot with a hungry gaze, so caught up in drinking her in that he didn't hear Durwood close the door to give them a moment of privacy. There was something different about her, a vibrant life and energy she'd never had before. And yet there was something else too, some strong feeling emanating from her that he'd never felt.

She met his gaze full-on, performing her own earnest search. He only wished he knew what she searched for. His gaze settled last on the necklace at her throat. What was he to make of her wearing it on this most august of occasions? Was she proudly displaying the sign of his possession, or advertising the elegant offerings of their joint jewelry houses?

Or, worst of all, taunting him with what he could not have? The Ice Princess was capable of that. But surely the woman staring at him was too warm and glowing to be so calculating. He cleared his throat, wondering why he felt so awkward. "I have never seen you more lovely, *chère*. I am proud to be your hu—ah, escort."

A winsome smile stretched that lovely face. "Husband will do. For we are wed, are we not?" She wiggled two fingers together so that her wedding ring glittered in the light.

Some of his tension eased. "Indeed." In name, anyway. But this was a start. "I have missed you."

She started to retort, swallowed and replied, "I have missed you too. You . . . should make me very happy if you moved back in."

"I cannot live as we were." *All of you, or nothing.* He tried to say the forbidden words with his eyes, but she looked away, a flicker of hurt spoiling her glow.

Maybell lurked between them in all her bosomy glory, but now was not the time, or the place, for that subject. He offered his arm. "We must go, or we will never make it to Westminster in time to view the procession." She accepted his arm.

A tingle spread from his arm to his extremities even at that light touch. In a daze, he nodded at Durwood, said all the right things, and then politely helped his wife into the carriage, but all the time, inwardly he brooded. Had it really been only two weeks since that time at Summerlea? It felt like forever. But he would not accept that stolen bliss again, even if she initiated it, unless it led to something more substantial. This woman whom no man had claimed had changed him to a man none of his former lovers would recognize. While Durwood and Charlaine stared out at the streets packed with every imaginable conveyance filled with gaily dressed revelers, Devlin watched his hands pull his gloves through his fingers over and over again.

Where before he had wanted freedom, now he

wanted roots. Where before he had desired many women, now he wanted one. And where previously he had called no place home, now he felt alone and adrift when she was gone.

He glanced at Charlaine's face, alive with curiosity and good spirits as she leaned forward to wave at an acquaintance in an adjacent carriage. She had turned an independent tomcat into a lapdog panting for her slightest touch, and he did not like it one bit. Especially as he had given up so much of his own independence, while she held fiercely to her own.

Durwood said something.

Devlin blinked and focused on his father-in-law. "I'm sorry, sir, I didn't hear you."

"Do you know if Mordecai attends with Elizabeth?"

"I believe so, yes."

Durwood nodded without a trace of disapproval. "They will come to our little dinner party later?"

"If Elizabeth can convince Mordecai, no doubt."

"And you will stay the night this time." This was not a question, but Devlin felt Charlaine's abrupt interest and answered carefully.

"Perhaps, if it fits into my plans." Devlin pretended not to notice the way she leaned back, deflated.

His confused ambivalence grew with every mile. Why was he here? Why had she invited him? Most likely to quiet the gossips. Yet she had obviously never cared overmuch for the opinion of the ton. He felt more and more at a loss.

By the time they finally pulled up in the long line of carriages leading to the procession area before Westminster, he was in a positive stew. Even as he helped Charlaine down, he felt the urge to flee this exalted company and surroundings for the things he knew and cherished. But for the moment he was trapped, so he tried to behave as expected.

They stood on the raised platform set high beside the street to allow the onlookers to see the procession. The masses surged below, some climbing roofs, others streetlamps, the better to see. Even from this lofty perch, they had to strain to see over the elaborate coiffures and top hats of the quality in front of them. The towering buildings blocked the breeze, and the rising sun had become bold. They waited, but still no rattle of coach wheel came. The heat grew oppressive, the crowd restless.

Charlaine began to swallow rapidly and wave a gloved hand before her face. Solicitously, Devlin took out his kerchief to wipe the beads of sweat from her brow. She nodded her thanks, but her face had taken on an ashen hue.

"Perhaps you should retreat to the carriage, my dear," Durwood said. "All this standing about is not good for you."

She gave him a quelling glance that Devlin noted, but did not understand, responding only, "I am fine. They shall be along directly."

But another thirty minutes passed before they finally heard carriage wheels rattling on the newly paved street. By then Charlaine was leaning heavily on Devlin's arm. She recovered enough to peek over the crowd as the first of the long column came into sight.

Soldiers in every conceivable uniform made a solemn vanguard to this solemn occasion. British, Scottish, Indian and German troops were present. Nations from all over the globe had sent representatives to honor this tiny woman and the vast hegemony she'd helped create and maintain.

The kings came in covered carriages, dressed resplendently in their own crowns and royal raiment. The Indian princes wore turbans that glittered with

316

jewels. Some sported jeweled daggers and swords. A couple looked ludicrous in rented hansoms, and Devlin could only wonder who had failed to procure them properly elegant carriages as instructed. The crown prince of Prussia elicited gasps from the onlookers, so resplendent and regal was he in his snow white uniform. He deigned to nod from side to side, but he did not permit himself something so crass as a wave.

And finally, at last, came the simple but elegant carriage bearing their monarch. Regina Victoria nodded and waved occasionally to her subjects, but even at this distance, Devlin had to wonder if she hoped her guards could shield her in the event someone shot at her again. When the procession was past, following the rigorously designed plan of the streets nearby, the masses began to pour into the abbey.

Again Devlin was helpless to shield Charlaine with more than an arm and an occasionally well-placed elbow. They had to enter through a dark tunnel to get into the lofty cathedral, but once inside, it still felt claustrophobic owing to the gigantic tiers of galleries over the west door. The floors and walls surrounding them were covered with an ugly red carpet centered with stars. The intent had been to maximize the seating, but Devlin could only wonder how the queen could make a grand entrance through this airless cubbyhole.

"Excuse me," Devlin said crisply, grinding a heel sharply into the toes of the man leading a common-looking woman up the aisle, who would have run them down in his eagerness to find a seat. He winced and fell back.

Doggedly Durwood continued upward. Finally, at the top row where the view was best, he stopped and indicated their seats. Devlin helped Charlaine into hers, wiping her brow again. She seemed positively ill. What was wrong?

"Charlaine, do you wish to leave?" he asked in growing concern.

She shook her head. "I shall be fine in a moment. It is just the crowd, and the heat."

He suspected something else was wrong, but he let her excuse pass without argument.

Again they waited. As soaring as it was, even Westminster began to feel hot with so many people packed so close. Charlaine fanned her face continuously with her hand. Finally Devlin took his coronation brochure, folded it into a fan, and gave it to her. She accepted with a smile of thanks.

The time dragged; the coronation chair far below covered in gold cloth seemed to shimmer in the heat. Finally, with a blare of trumpets, the members of the procession began to file into the abbey in the same order in which they'd driven.

Despite himself, Devlin leaned forward for a view of that tiny, majestic figure. It seemed anticlimactic when she finally appeared, coming slowly from the gloom of the tunnel, walking in the hushed silence to the seat both birth and training had molded her for. At some distance, facing her, the foreign kings and princes sat in solemn homage.

On the queen's right stood her royal princes, on the left her princesses, each bearing the insignia and crown or diadem of his or her rank. When the service finally began, the chattering in the galleries stopped, for the poorest among the thousands of witnesses still felt the significance of this moment.

Fifty years was a long time to reign. And no one could doubt that this tiny woman, despite her flaws, had done her best to rule fairly and well according to her own strict sense of values. In all she did, she tried to be a good model for her subjects.

Even Devlin felt a bit awed as he bowed his head in prayer, along with representatives of every peerage in England. Through the long service and many prayers, Devlin looked about for Mordecai. He never saw him in the crush, but he did see Lady Jersey aiming her opera glasses down at the coronation. Other lesser notables joined in the rudeness despite the scandalized looks sent their way by the more circumspect.

Finally, the crown upon her regal little gray head, the queen rose to accept the homage of those who had come to pay their respects. They filed before her, and she kissed each of them, except for the crown prince of Germany and Prince Louis of Hesse. When they had all passed, she seemed to realize the slight and called these two worthies back to kiss them as well.

Devlin smiled, for the true Victoria was apparent in that moment. She was autocratic, selfish and shrewdly intelligent, it was true, but she was above all a mother. She seemed like a proud hen clucking over her chicks as her progeny settled about her.

Charlaine wiped a tear away. "This day will be long remembered," she said simply.

"Do you attend the garden party at Buckingham Palace?" Devlin asked.

Durwood answered, "No, we sent our regrets. After this exhausting day, I want my own walls about me." When the queen had left with proper pomp and circumstance, the crowd began to leave. The pushing and shoving behind the bottleneck at the tunnel made those in front rush even faster.

Devlin took one look, glanced at Charlaine's still pale face and said, "We shall wait until things clear."

Durwood nodded his agreement. They had to wait almost an hour, and finally, as they began to file down,

Devlin heard a familiar voice. "Devlin, my boy! Over here!"

And there she was, Elizabeth, Duchess of Kensington, properly regal in her favorite lavender, Mordecai in tow. Devlin rose to accept her proffered hands.

"Did you enjoy the ceremony?" she asked.

She took in Charlaine's halfhearted nod and sweaty brow, but the concern that flickered in her eyes did not last long as Charlaine gave her a look Devlin did not understand. The conviction grew that something was going on here that he was not being told about.

Mordecai said, "Poor little lady, I felt the weight of the world bearing down on her under so much scrutiny. I have never before considered the burden it must be to be a sovereign."

"Or a queen's coachman," Elizabeth inserted with a last glance at her niece. "I am told that the queen's coachman was asked if he'd be driving any of the royal guests about from Buckingham Palace. His response was, 'No, sir, I should say not. I am the queen's coachman. I do not drive riffraff.' "

The hearty laughter this elicited from the party helped lighten the atmosphere, but it did not dissipate the hint of stormy weather to come. Even as Devlin helped his bride down the many steps to the floor, he was wondering. . . .

Why did he sense a conspiracy of silence between Charlaine, Durwood and Elizabeth? What had happened that they weren't telling him?

Chapter Twelve

By the time the blessed walls of her estate came into view, Charlaine was so tense she felt as if she'd snap. She sensed Devlin suspected something was different about her, and her stomach was so violently disagreeable now after the long, hot day that she wasn't sure she could hide her condition much longer. Indeed, from the intent way he watched her, it might already be too late.

"I wish to lie down for a moment," she said the moment they walked in the door.

"Certainly, my dear." And Devlin took her arm to escort her up the stairs.

A frantic search for an excuse yielded nothing but a weak, "I nap better alone." But she hadn't the nerve to look at him as she said the lie, for she wanted nothing so much as his arms about her again.

"I shall merely make you comfortable, then go on to my flat."

"No, please stay." This time, when she said the words, they were not ambivalent. She didn't want him to leave again, that much she knew, even if he discovered her secret.

"I shall only change for the party this evening and return forthwith." He opened her chamber door.

She opened her mouth to call for her maid, but he put an intimate finger over her lips and caressed the soft surface, whispering, "There are some advantages to being married. Let me act as your maid." And he turned her about to unfasten her dress.

Protest never even crossed her mind. She stood meekly before him, even when he undid her petticoats and chemise. Even when he pulled her drawers and stockings off. Even when he gently led her to the bed, pulled back the down comforter and laid her down. She waited for him to join her, but he merely stood back and appraised her as she lay there naked, wearing only the necklace of his design.

She let him drink his fill, for it was too late to do otherwise, nor did she want to. A sense of belonging and rightness grew every time he looked at her thus. Yes, lust lurked in this rakehell's eyes, but there was also tenderness and a deeper, truer emotion that she was slowly beginning to trust. Could it truly be that he loved her?

"Ah, *chère*, you are more lovely even than the necklace," he said softly. "No matter what comes later, I will always remember you best at this moment." And he moved, with visible effort, toward the door.

The words came of their own accord. "Don't go."

His back stayed rigidly turned to her. "Do not tempt me again beyond bearing. I cannot continue this half relationship with you, Charlaine. You are my wife, and I want us to live together in our own household, or not at all."

She looked about at her tower, where she had known much joy—and much loneliness. The choice was not difficult. "If you wish."

His shoulders lifted in a sharp gasp. He whirled. "When? I've found a suitable little place—"

She held up a hand. "We have some things to settle first."

His wandering eyes proved how difficult he found it to concentrate on her words. Smiling, she pulled up the sheet to her neck and nodded at her safe. "You know where the book is, as I recall. I should love to watch you retrieve it."

A black eyebrow raised. "I thought you did not encourage me in my former, ah, hobby."

"But how can you steal something that we jointly own?"

Both eyebrows rose at this, but a guarded shutter descended over the hope in his expression. However, he went to the bookcase without argument and twisted the hidden spring. He had the safe open in five seconds flat. He took out the book and brought it to her.

"It is much faster when one knows the combination," he said.

"So I should imagine." She propped pillows behind her head and patted the mattress beside her.

Still wary, he sat down, looking as if he might flee at any moment. She opened the book that she had memorized from beginning to end, wondering why she felt a warm glow at being able to share this intimacy with him at last. Never in her life had she felt the urge to divulge her family history to any man, but they could not progress in their relationship without a foundation to build on. She carried his child. God willing, their own story would be added to this book someday, and she owed it to her ancestors to see that

323

he honored them as much as she did.

She pointed at the picture of the red-haired beauty picking a yellow rose. "This was my great-great-grandmother, Callista Raleigh." And she recounted the strange tale of a woman swept away by a masked man masquerading as a beast, only to find that her abductor was actually the only man she could ever love.

Next she pointed at a picture of a petite young woman with raven hair and huge eyes of a grayish lavender. She was dressed in a diaphanous dress that fell to her ankles in triangular pieces of purple chiffon of every shade, accenting a tiny waist and graceful legs. She stood on tip-toe, her arms gracefully extended in longing toward a handsome young man dressed in the bright red British regimentals of a captain. He watched her with steadfast devotion all the more striking in this cynical Victorian age. On the palm of his hand, extended toward her, was a fiery red ruby heart.

Her voice was husky with emotion as she again visualized the tragedy and heartache this pair had suffered; yet they had loved each other all the more because of it. "This is my grandmother Chantal. She was Aunt Elizabeth's friend when they both danced in the ballet."

His eyes narrowed. "Chantal, eh? I believe that is a French name."

Her smile deepened. "Indeed, as I just discovered. My father never told me of her heritage, but my aunt recently did. So you see, we are even more suited than you suppose, for she too, was, ah, born on the wrong side of the blanket."

He traced the lovely heart-shaped face in the portrait with his fingertip. "And no doubt his parents were opposed to their match."

She nodded. "But my grandfather never loved any-one else and he persisted until he won her."

He smiled, but there was a tinge of sadness on his handsome face. "I knew I had much in common with your ancestors." They shared a long look that brought a flush to her cheeks and quickened his breathing.

Those heated blue eyes caressed her form in the clinging sheet. "Why have you shared this book with me at last?"

To avoid looking at him, she wove her fingers in and out of the sheet, but if their marriage were to progress, she had to be honest. "I wanted my husband to learn the history of my ancestors and why I am so loyal to them." *And I wanted the father of my children to know this, too, so he can recount the tales to my children, as my father did to me.*

Hopefully, he took her hands. "Since we are being honest with one another at last, there is another sub-ject we must address. *Chère*, about Maybell—"

It was her turn to put a finger on his lips. "Don't. Not now. We can discuss her later." She yawned. "Now I need only to sleep." She peeped up at him through sultry eyes.

He smiled at the feminine ploy and sat down beside her at her wordless invitation. When she puckered her lips and raised her arms, he sighed and gently drew her to his breast. "Difficult as it will be, I will only hold you." When she made to kick the sheet away, he pulled it back up to her neck with a tight smile. "Let's not make it impossible, mmm?"

A yawn aborted what began as an argument. Meekly she lay back, her cheek on his strong shoulder. It was so good to have him hold her. She could stay like this forever.

He stroked her bare upper arm until, within minutes, her breathing evened out. Only then, when she was unaware, did he draw back enough to look at her as he never dared when she was awake. With a hunger that shook him to his boots, and, even more harrowing, to his soul.

Why, he wondered despairingly, had his heart picked this independent, prickly, stubborn woman instead of the good, obedient wife he'd always believed he'd want? Despite her new openness, he wasn't certain she would ever come to him, or truly love him as he loved her. Even now, sleeping peacefully in his arms, she held something back. Instinctively he knew she had changed somehow, but how, he could not yet define.

How different are the motivations of a man in love, he thought wryly. Not so long ago he had not much cared what any woman felt, save that they knew pleasure in his bed. But Charlaine was different. Oh, the sex, yes, they obviously had that, but even that joy was temporal compared to the steadfast devotion that only love can bring. And to realize that he, the French frog libertine she always named him, now pined for the same emotion other women had claimed to feel for him, well, there was a rough justice in that. Perhaps he truly had been cruel to Sally, as Temple obviously believed.

He laid Charlaine back down and slipped out of bed, unable to hold her without wanting her. Troubled, he quietly walked out of her room, the certainty growing that he could never be satisfied with half of her. Which left them with—what?

Pregnant black clouds bore down upon the estate by the time the clock was nigh on seven. They seemed to labor toward a painful delivery as the fleeter winds urged them on. Durwood cast a wary eye out the window as he awaited his guests. "We're in for the deuce of a storm, I should say."

Devlin didn't answer. He'd been brooding since the coronation. Now he looked splendid in his severe formal attire, but he had a drawn, desperate mien Durwood had never seen in him. "What's the matter, lad?" Durwood had grown genuinely fond of the young scamp. Devlin had shown great restraint with Charlaine, but how he would react to his impending fatherhood, especially given that he was the last of the family to know . . . well, Durwood only hoped Charlaine told him before he figured it out himself.

"Nothing. Nothing new, anyway." And he sipped his port indifferently, as though Durwood had not paid a good ten pounds sterling for every ruddy bottle.

Durwood scowled. Something was badly wrong. Before he could question Devlin again, however, a regal figure swept into the male domain of the study without so much as a knock. Durwood opened his mouth to give a blistering dressing-down to the interloper, but when he saw who it was, he shut it and said calmly, "Hello, Elizabeth. I am glad you came after all."

Glancing around her, Devlin arched an eyebrow at the duchess. She tilted her chin even higher, as if daring him to remark that Mordecai had obviously decided not to attend.

He shook his head. "We are a sore trial to the women of this household, are we not?"

"Trial? I should say not. Nuisance is a better term." But her well-shaped hand quivered slightly as she fiddled with her immaculate coiffure, a sure sign of her distress. "Never would I have believed that such a stable personality as Mordecai Levitz could be positively flighty."

Devlin spewed a sip of port back into his glass. "Flighty? Mordecai?"

The duchess took to pacing. "How else would you describe a man who kisses me one moment, then refuses to take me to a party the next?"

With an uncomfortable clearing of his throat, Durwood rose. "Excuse me, but I will check on Charlaine." He left quietly.

The duchess barely noticed. Her cheekbones were flushed and she fanned a hand before her face. "Goodness me, but it's hot."

Hot? Devlin had just thought how chilly it was with the approaching storm. In concern, he rose to escort Elizabeth to a chair. Most uncharacteristically, she didn't even protest. "Why is he so determined to hold me at arm's length? He loves me, I know he does. And at our age, we should grasp whatever happiness comes our way."

"I agree with you totally, Your Grace, as I have told Mordecai on more than one occasion." Devlin knelt on one knee before her to take her hands. He frowned, rubbing them, for they were clammy. "Do you feel well?"

She jerked her hands away. "I am fine, you young scamp." She took a deep breath, and her rapid breathing slowed somewhat. "It's your wife you should concern yourself with."

It was his turn to move away. He stalked to the window to watch the glowering skies, reflecting how perfect they were for his mood. "That is up to her."

Elizabeth was raising her lorgnette to peer at him when the door opened. A thrill of awareness ran up Devlin's spine, and he knew who stood there even before he turned. Charlaine, love of his life, stood in the doorway with a winsome smile that went straight to his head. God, she was lovely. This evening she wore red, as if she wanted to celebrate the vibrance of life and passion with him. The red dress had tiers and tiers of gold-spangled lace, starting at the hips in a fall that made a short train behind her. The short sleeves were trimmed in more lace that made the bodice fall off her shoulders, emphasizing her attributes. A yellow diamond comb held her hair up atop her head. At her throat glittered the Yellow Rose.

Devlin was so busy absorbing her through his very pores that it took a moment for Elizabeth's distress to penetrate. She made a gasping sound, her hand fluttering.

Charlaine dragged her gaze away from Devlin's heated stare. Her eyes widened. She ran to Elizabeth and placed a hand on her aunt's forehead. "No fever. Devlin, we should fetch the doctor."

But a strong grip caught Charlaine's hand. Elizabeth shook her head emphatically, made a hoarse gasping sound, then air whistled through her lungs again. Huskily, she said, "I am fine. It's just that you remind me so much of Chantal in that dress. Your grandfather had it made for her to match the necklace when he carried her off to make love to her." And she sat up straighter, sipping the sherry Devlin had poured for her.

Ah, no wonder the dress had such an old-fashioned air. It was a dancer's costume. If one looked close, one could see a slight difference in the pattern of the lace at the hem, and Devlin realized a talented seamstress had lengthened it for Charlaine's taller height. Now what did this mean? That Charlaine wanted him to carry her away, or that she wanted to dance, or that she was showing all present that she was a woman grown, passionate about her husband? Devlin's head whirled, and he had to turn away and catch himself against the windowsill. Her motivation could be any of those, or others, but one fact superceded all else: she still held something from him. What was it?

A soft hand landed on his shoulder. "Devlin, our guests are arriving. Come with me to greet them."

He took her hand with a polite smile, hoping she couldn't sense his turmoil. "Certainly, my dear." He offered his other arm to Elizabeth.

With a grand nod, she put her fingertips on his sleeve, and off they went to the front portico, where Durwood was already welcoming a former prime minister. The next hour passed quickly for Devlin, greeting and meeting the upper echelons of the ton.

One older woman wearing a diamond necklace so gaudy that it would have bought his flat and two like it twittered, "Such a crush at the garden party at Buckingham, Durwood. You should be glad you did not attend. I declare, the queen was positively mobbed. It was disgraceful."

Her stout husband agreed with a distinctively British harrumph. "Embarrassing, what, with all those heathen statesmen in attendance."

The next woman in line positively simpered at Charlaine. "You sweet child, I do not believe I have ever seen you in better looks, though your dress is a bit, ah . . ." She coughed delicately.

"Daring?" Charlaine arched a wicked eyebrow. She caught her husband's arm even more closely. "I am a married woman now. I may dress as I please." And she looked up at her husband, her expression plainly stating that she wanted to please only one man.

Devlin had to shift his feet, hoping the quick surge at his loins did not show in his tight formal trousers. He had never seen Charlaine like this. He didn't know whether to rejoice or to hold his breath in fear. Something of import would happen this night. He felt it.

Looking vaguely scandalized, the woman passed

on. For another twenty minutes, Devlin and Charlaine circulated the room, but he left most of the talking to her. He was content just to watch her, but, inexplicably, the empty feeling in the pit of his gut grew. He kept watching the door, expecting Mordecai to break down and arrive. Elizabeth sat against the wall in a chair, talking intimately with another elderly lady, but her color still worried Devlin.

The guests were milling about like excited magpies, all atwitter over the recent event, when Jeffries came to the dining room door in his best livery and announced, "Dinner is served." En masse, the guests streamed into the dining room just as an imperative knock sounded at the door. Lightning flashed outside, followed quickly by a boom of thunder.

Devlin's sense of unease crested as the footman opened the door to a burst of rain and wind—and to two other elemental dangers to Devlin's new place in the world.

Alone in the foyer, he and Charlaine stared at Maybell and Lewis Temple. Durwood had already taken his place at the head of the dining table, but Elizabeth paused in the act of rising, saw who it was and came over to them. If her step was a bit unsteady, no one else observed it.

"I do not believe you were invited here," Charlaine said coolly. She waved to get the attention of a footman, but they all appeared busy.

With a preemptive bang, Temple closed the front door with his foot. "I do not believe you should be so hasty as to evict us, unless you would rather your dear devoted husband spoke to Scotland Yard instead of to me."

Charlaine's hand dropped.

Devlin said calmly, "I shouldn't wonder if they

wouldn't be interested in speaking to Maybell, as well."

Temple blinked in shock and glared down at the woman hanging on his arm.

Maybell was dressed a bit plainer than usual, in a green high-necked ball gown, with her bounteous locks restrained. She paled slightly, but tossed her head. "Cor, if that ain't a kettle callin' a pot black, ye threatenin' me with me own past."

Elizabeth raised her lorgnette with hauteur, as only a dowager duchess could. Even Temple was uncomfortable enough to run his finger under his collar as severe hazel eyes, enlarged in the lorgnette, first looked him up and down, then proceeded to Maybell. That woman was brazen enough to wink.

With a disdainful sniff, Elizabeth said, "What we do in the past has no more bearing on our present than we allow. Tell me, young woman, is this to be a sample of your future—blackmail, slander and revenge?"

Temple swallowed, but Maybell retorted, "It's better than livin' a lie, that it is." Pure malice twisted her beautiful face. "Why don't ye tell this sainted laidy and yer even more sainted wife how we met—lover?"

Devlin felt Charlaine start at the adroit stab. He tightened his grip on her hand as he replied, "Why, at the home of a mutual acquaintance."

A bold, brassy laugh that matched her looks issued from Maybell. "Ain't that a fancy way o' saying ye come to the home of my provider to rob 'im, and I caught ye, but kept quiet when ye promised to share some of the loot with me."

Elizabeth and Charlaine gasped. Devlin felt his wife pull away at the same time that thunder struck so close that it rattled the windows in the house. Devlin turned to face Charlaine, feeling vaguely that the elements roiling outside were also boiling within him.

Now was a good test. Either she believed him or not. He was either a husband, or a frog acting the part of a prince.

"That's one way of putting it, true," he agreed quietly. "But my perspective might be different in that this man had insulted me, and tried to cheat me, and that you were about to leave him anyway."

Everyone looked toward Maybell for her response. "So it's true, ye admit bein' a thief?"

Devlin bowed shortly. "An accusation I have never denied."

Temple's gleeful smile froze under Devlin's icy stare. "Again, in my checkered past. I have not thieved in some time, nor do I intend to again."

"Leopards never change their spots." Temple made to turn for the exit.

A door opened and closed loudly. Durwood advanced into the foyer. He fumbled in his pocket. "The trouble with personalities who live for vengeance is that they are so unbending that they have probably erred greatly somewhere in their own pasts." Durwood pulled out a piece of paper and read:

"Sir, pursuant to your recent inquiry, Mr. Lewis Temple is no more in our employ. He disobeyed direct orders to return to America. We have reason to believe that he is involved in some illicit activity. We cannot recommend him for employment. The Pinkerton National Detective Agency."

In the dead silence, Durwood folded the note back and put it neatly in his pocket. "I thought it peculiar that you continued to work this erstwhile case after Charlaine and I discharged you, and I did a bit of investigating of my own. Now, would you care to elaborate on what you intend to say to Scotland Yard?"

Maybell glanced at Temple scornfully, obviously disgusted by his silence. "Aw, fights like a man. He's just bluffin'." She strode forward and stabbed her finger in the air before Charlaine. "Ye think jest because ye're a laidy that I ain't good enough fer him. Well, as far as I can tell, ye don't want him none, anyways. Why don't ye jest step aside and—" She broke off with a screech when Devlin caught her arm, shoved Temple away from the door and opened it.

"I have never liked being discussed as if I were not present," he said. With the rain drifting in on the violent wind, Devlin leaned forward into Maybell's face to emphasize each of his words. "Now. For the last time. I do not want you, Maybell. Regardless of what happens in my marriage, it is over between us. Now go. Straight to Scotland Yard, or to hell, it matters not to me, but you should be aware that I will have a deal to say to the constables in my own defense and that a great portion of it will not reflect well on you." And shoving her out into the rain, he turned on Lewis Temple.

Actually, Devlin felt slightly sorry for Temple. Lewis obviously blamed himself for his sister's death, even as Devlin had blamed himself for not earning more money for his ill mother. Emotions. They made everything difficult. Somehow he managed not to look at Charlaine, though he felt her full attention as he said to Temple, "Lewis, if I could lose both my arms and legs and bring back Sally, I would. I swear it. I cared for her as only a young man can, but she would not have been happy in Africa. She might well have died in a far less . . . quick manner, as I almost did on numerous occasions."

Under the barrage of condemning eyes, Lewis was recovering his self-confidence. He stood tall. "That does nothing to excuse your coldhearted rejection. If she had not been so upset that day—"

"And if you had spent more time with her . . ." When Lewis swallowed, Devlin sighed. "See? Recriminations solve nothing. Sally died because she could not overcome her addiction to opium. It had little to do with me, and less with you. You've nothing to blame yourself for. And when she was sober, she was a delight. She would not be happy to see what you've done to your life in this futile search for vengeance. That said"—Devlin hesitated, then went on—"recent circumstances have made me see things I never saw before. I was probably a bit cruel to her—"

Charlaine gasped and took a step back. Devlin glanced at her, then returned his gaze to Temple, who was listening intently now. "I make no excuses for myself save that I was young, and ambitious. Perhaps, if I had married her and tried for several years, I could have helped her overcome the addiction. But, to be blunt, I did not love her enough." Devlin held out his hand. "Please, can we let bygones be bygones? I will not pursue any inquiries against you if you agree to leave me alone. Deal?"

Temple looked from Devlin's hand, to Charlaine's still, white expression, to Elizabeth's raised lorgnette and Durwood's cautious face, then back to Devlin's hand. Slowly he reached out to shake it. "I cannot wish you well, Rhodes, but I will pursue you no longer. As you say, I am not without my own sins." He tipped his hat to the ladies. "Good evening." And out he went into the rain.

With a mental dusting of his hands, Devlin turned to his wife. *Uh-oh.* She looked extremely upset, and he could only attribute that to his story about Sally. Dammit, did she think he'd grown up in a cabbage patch, as she had? He took two urgent steps toward her, but she stopped him with an outflung hand.

Colleen Shannon

"No! I fear if you come close, we will be bombarded by your old lovers."

He stopped cold. "That is unfair. Yes, I was involved with other women before you, but none since. I swear it. Besides—" He broke off as he noted, out of the corner of his eye, that Elizabeth was swaying on her feet.

She began fanning herself again. "What excitement! I thought we were having a simple little—" She gasped and clutched her chest.

Charlaine reached out to her just as she gave a queer little cough and fell.

Diving, Devlin managed to catch her before her head struck the marble. "Send for the doctor," he barked, carrying Elizabeth into the study and laying her gently on the sofa.

He rubbed her hands. She stirred and said softly, "Mordecai," before subsiding again.

Charlaine rushed in and fell to her knees beside the sofa. She felt frantically for her aunt's pulse, and then sat back on her heels, sighing her relief.

Devlin saw her swallow several times, and her face took on a greenish hue, but she only said, "I've sent a servant for her physician."

"Stay with her," Devlin ordered. "I'll be back shortly." And he stalked out. Durwood was seeing his guests hastily out. More than a few of them looked offended, but he didn't seem disturbed. Devlin had to ease through the throng at the door, but finally he achieved the drive, where he'd left his carriage.

The ride to his flat had never seemed longer, for the streets were still thronged with merrymakers. He shoved open the front door to his flat so hard that it banged against the wall. Mordecai, his shirt collar and tie askew, sat alone in the dark, his elbows on his knees, his head bent in his hands. He wasn't even wearing his yarmulke, which said more to Devlin of his old friend's distress than anything else could have.

Devlin took a couple of deep, calming breaths, wondering why Mordecai's ambivalence to Elizabeth upset him so. He suspected it was because he badly wanted his mentor finally to know the joy of giving and receiving love, and because he was envious of the duchess's obvious deep feelings for this man so far away from her social status. Sometimes Devlin wondered if Charlaine would be so guarded with him if he'd come from her rarefied world.

Shaking off the gloom, he slammed the door behind him with equal force. Mordecai looked up, bleary eyed, as Devlin turned up a gas lantern and began mildly, "Why didn't you come to the party with Elizabeth? She was disappointed."

"I did not want all her snobbish acquaintances to see us together."

"Oh, yes? For her sake or your own?"

Mordecai leaned back slowly, apparently deducing something was wrong from Devlin's tone.

"Besides," Devlin pointed out, "you'd just come from as public an event as one could imagine."

"There were too many people there for anyone to notice us. This small, intimate party is different."

"I see. Well, far be it from me to sound like a disapproving father, but for Elizabeth's sake, I must ask— what are your intentions toward her?"

Bending his head again, Mordecai mumbled, "God help me, I do not know myself."

In a burst of rage, Devlin strode directly in front of Mordecai and hauled the smaller man to his feet.

"Wha—" Mordecai protested, but Devlin interrupted.

"As you have done to me many times over the past, it's time for you to listen to a few home truths. You're a coward, pure and simple. You do not like coming out of your comfortable little world to one where you feel persecuted, even with the love of a very worthy woman at stake."

Mordecai fell back two steps, his face ashen, as Devlin finished softly, "Or maybe it's worse than that. Maybe it is you, the Jew, who is prejudiced against a Gentile. Well, if you do not intend to marry the duchess, then leave her be."

Devlin turned, then stopped as if in afterthought. "Oh, by the way, I came here to let you know that Elizabeth has collapsed at Charlaine's. We are as yet uncertain of her ailment, but it looks serious." And with a last blistering look at Mordecai's bug-eyed, dazed face, Devlin opened the door.

"W-wait!" Mordecai ran after him. "I'm coming."

Devlin kept his back turned so Mordecai couldn't see his little smile. He suspected Elizabeth had just collapsed from exhaustion, but Mordecai didn't need to know that. And, on the ride back to the estate, Mordecai, the cautious pragmatist, kept urging the coachman on to reckless speed.

In the study, Elizabeth waved away her hovering doctor, who was listening to her heart. "I am fine, confound it, Theodore. Now leave me be." Charlaine watched from a chair, her expression still pained. She rubbed her stomach.

Wincing as her loud voice reverberated in his newfangled stethoscope, he dropped it and looked over his half glasses severely. "I have told you time and again, Your Grace, that you must rest more. A woman your age—"

Now she positively bristled. "My age has nothing to do with it. I am just fatigued, that is all, from all you hangers-on and poppinjays who try to tell me what to do—" She broke off when she heard a familiar voice outside in the foyer.

"Where is she?"

The duchess gave her doctor what might, in any other woman, have been a pleading look. She whispered fiercely, "I am at death's door, understand?"

That poor man looked confused as Devlin led Mordecai in. His Lizzie lay back in a veritable faint, one arm limply hanging over the couch, the other folded over her bosom as if she readied it to hold a funereal lily at any moment.

Mordecai gave a frightened bleat and dropped to one knee beside her. "Lizzie, Lizzie, what have you done?"

She didn't answer, but she tossed her head restlessly, moaning.

Frowning, Devlin glanced at his wife. She smiled slightly.

Grinning now, he offered his arm to her. "My dear, shall we retire? We've had enough excitement for one night. Good evening, all." They exited.

Neither Mordecai nor Elizabeth answered him, or even noticed them leave.

She finally fluttered her lovely hazel eyes open. She stared blankly at Mordecai, as if she didn't recognize him. "Oh, woe is me, never have I felt this way." She clutched her heart.

Surging to his feet, Mordecai glared at the doctor. "Help her, you fool."

The doctor stuck his hands in his conservative frock coat. "I fear she has an ailment I cannot treat," he responded dryly, and truthfully. When Elizabeth winked at him behind Mordecai's back, he coughed into his hand.

"What do you mean? Are you a man of medicine or

not? Do something!" Elizabeth made a gesture that Mordecai didn't see.

With a resigned air, the doctor offered his stethoscope to Mordecai. "Listen to her heart for yourself. There's nothing I can do."

More ashen than ever, Mordecai accepted the stethoscope with obvious dread. Awkwardly, he slipped it about his neck and stuck the earpieces in his ears.

With a last indignant sniff, the haughty doctor said, "You shall receive my bill, Your Grace, and it will include the price of a new stethoscope. I suggest you get more rest." And he stalked out, obviously not pleased at being used as a pawn in the power struggle.

Mordecai approached the duchess, bent and set the listening device against Elizabeth's chest. He started, his head rearing back. He frowned in suspicion, then stuck the piece more firmly against her breast. When her heart rate accelerated, he said through his teeth, "Lizzie, open your eyes."

He tried to move his hand away, but her own came up and caught his. "Forgive me, but I had to know how you felt about me." And she opened her eyes to give him a smile that chased his scowl away.

He teetered on his feet for one perilous moment, like a man standing on an unknown precipice; then, with a strangled groan, he sat down beside her and hauled her into his arms for a passionate kiss. For a long moment no sound came from either of them, but finally, with a little sob of joy, Elizabeth pulled away and sank her head onto his shoulder.

He stroked her hair, then pulled the last of the pins from her still thick silver locks and ran his hands tenderly through them. "You frightened the life out of me."

"Or the fear," she whispered. "I know you're about to do something that scares you, Mordecai, but I swear we will overcome the whispers and the condemnation. I will spend part of the year in New York with you"—he blinked in surprise at this—"as you can spend part of the year here with me. We shall stay so busy with Charlaine and the baby that—" She broke off, covering her mouth with her hand.

Mordecai froze. He glanced at the door, as if fearful that Devlin had heard. "He obviously doesn't know. Does she intend to tell him?"

"I have encouraged her to, but she's stubborn. She seems to want things settled between them before she lets him know."

Sighing in resignation, Mordecai drew her close again. "If he finds out on his own, there will be hell to pay. He's already talking about returning to Africa." Then, as if he wanted nothing to spoil their hard-won happiness, he buried his lips in her neck. "Marry me by special license, Lizzie. I do not want to wait."

"Happily, my darling." And they kissed again, more passionately than before, pledging their troth in the age-old way that knew no boundaries of youth, or religion.

And, if their hair was gray, their hearing a bit faulty, and their skin wrinkled, their hearts still beat in perfect synchronized delight like those of the younger couple.

But it was not delight that quickened Devlin's heartbeat, or made Charlaine retreat to her bed.

Devlin hovered by the door, growing concerned as she lay back, cradling her stomach. She gave a distressed little burp. He eased closer to the bed, wondering what ailed her. "I did not see you eat a bite. Shall I fetch you a plate?"

She winced at the mere mention. "No, thank you. I shall be fine in a moment." She took deep breaths.

When she seemed a bit easier, he took another step closer and cleared his throat. "Ah, Charlaine, about Maybell . . ." He waited for her to interrupt, but this time she looked at him with a waiting expression, apparently willing to listen.

"Do you believe what she said about me?"

"Yes."

When he looked disappointed, she added hastily, "But despite your somewhat checkered past, I still believe you to be a basically honorable man."

Devlin grew even more depressed. After weeks of the most persuasive wooing of which he was capable, he was rewarded with a milquetoast epithet. Honorable. And basically honorable at that. He turned away to fiddle with her dressing table mirror, hiding his expression. "And the other? Do you believe that I have, ah, strayed from you?"

When she was a long time answering, he turned to face her. This he had to know.

She nibbled at her lip, but finally said, "No."

His relieved sigh stopped in a gasp as she added softly, "Not yet, anyway."

Closing his eyes, he rubbed his throbbing temples. "I see. Well, since you still cannot trust me fully, then we have but one more question to settle." His hands dropped, and he straightened, trying to prepare himself. He suspected her answer, but still, he had to know. "Madam wife, do you love me?"

Her eyes widened at this plain talk. She turned her head aside on the pillow and pretended not to hear.

That only made him more determined. He strode to the side of the bed, gently turned her chin and looked down into her lovely face. Ah, how could any woman be both so beguiling and so stubborn? He leaned so close that their breaths mingled. "I say again, *chère*— do you love me?"

She nibbled even more uncertainly at her lip, but when his gaze went hungrily to her mouth, she stopped. "I . . . maybe."

His heart lurched. At least it wasn't outright rejection, as he had feared. Lying down beside her, he leaned even closer, until the heat from their almost touching mouths caused a conflagration that seared from him to her, and back. "When will you know?"

Please, let her ask me to kiss her. This time I have not the strength to deny either of us.

Restively she squirmed beside him, but she only managed to bring her dress up about her thighs. He set one hand on a long, silken leg and stroked the length of it. Perhaps he was being unfair, but the power of sex was the only advantage he had over her. And he was near the end of his rope. For weeks he'd slept in this room, aching with need. For weeks he'd pretended to go as usual about his daily tasks, but the empty feeling in his heart was satisfied only when he was with her. Even then, his heart was only half full, for he could never be happy with the part of her she allowed him. He could have been a Kimball himself, for he knew in his bones that he too would love once and well, and never again.

And so here he was, staking all on one bold gamble. That, too, was nothing new to him. "*Chère*, I must know."

"But why? Can we not go on as—"

"No." His hand wandered higher. "We proceed as man and wife, finding our own home, starting a—" He broke off, for they had never discussed children, and surely it was far too early for that. Still, he hungered for a red-haired little girl to cuddle and a dark-haired boy to tumble with. His wild bachelor ways only made him yearn the more for the stability of family life now, with the one woman who had lured him to it.

Colleen Shannon

She caught his hand and set it firmly away. "I see. You wish an heir too. As much as my father. Well, what if I am not ready?"

He felt the chill in her tone. Was she so opposed to children, then? He struggled to appease her. "We can wait as long as you wish for that aspect of our relationship to bear fruit."

She gave a weird little chuckle that ended in another bilious burp, but she didn't contradict him.

Warily he continued, "But without love we cannot be happy."

"On that, sir, we agree." She pushed him aside, stood, wavered, clutching her stomach, and then gasped out, "But do you love me?"

Why did she always reverse everything? He stared at her, wondering if the truth would send her fleeing or bring her close. Recklessly he opened his mouth. "I—"

She swallowed harshly, ran past him to the water closet and threw up.

Devlin rushed in after her. She was bent over the receptacle, heaving with spasms. Only phlegm came out, however, as she had eaten nothing for dinner. He wet a soft cloth and bent on one knee beside her. She was ill. This was no time to force the issue. "Poor *petite*. Here, let me help." He tried to wipe her brow, but she swatted him away.

"You've done quite enough, thank you." She looked as if she regretted the retort, and he saw the fleeting expression cross her face.

Guilt. Fear that he would find her out. Stunned, he sat back on his heels, the cloth sagging in his hand. No wonder everyone had sent him surreptitious glances over the past few days, as if they knew something he didn't. She was pregnant. She knew she was pregnant, had known it for days, and Durwood and

344

Elizabeth obviously also knew. The surge of elation was inundated by an even more primitive emotion: anger. This deliberate slight spoke more truly of her feelings than any platitude could have.

Still, he courteously helped her to her feet, escorted her to the bed and then went to the door, all without a word.

"Devlin, I—"

"I shall be back in a moment."

Still moving briskly, as though only then could he prove to himself he still functioned, he went back to the kitchens, raided the cupboards, heated the kettle and made a tray. When a scandalized scullery maid tried to take over, he sent her about her business with one warning, blistering look. She backed away and fled.

Then, his hands rock steady, he carried the tray back up to his wife. She searched his face with wide eyes as he went to the bed, propped pillows behind her back and poured her a cup of tea. What she was looking for, he didn't know. And, in truth, he was no longer certain he cared.

"Devlin, you're not angry that I didn't tell you?" She sipped the tea he'd poured her.

"Angry? Why should I be angry?" He took one of the biscotti he'd fetched her and gobbled it down in one bite.

Slowly she set her cup down beside the bed, bracing herself.

Good, she knew him well enough by now to be wary. She should be wary. She should be shaking in her shoes. He didn't know whether to turn her over his knee or kiss her senseless. Or leave her flat. This last alternative increasingly seemed to be the only reasonable one. He knew that he could not continue this way.

"Devlin, I did intend to tell you, truly I did."

Colleen Shannon

"When? When you could not wear your clothes any longer?"

"No. When we got everything worked out between us. I did not want your devotion out of duty, or because of the child." Reluctantly she nibbled at one of the biscotti, then ate the cheese and crackers he'd cut for her.

Only when the greenish look about her mouth had gone away did he vent his true feelings. "How can we work anything out when you will not be honest with me?"

"I would have told you soon."

"About something even more important than our heir." He pulled the cup out of her clasp, set it down, tamped down his own primitive feelings of pain and anger, and cupped her face in his hands. "One last time I ask you, *chère*, do you love me?"

She closed her eyes. "Please, Devlin, I do not feel well. Can we have this conversation later?"

The pain grew unbearable then. He stood and bowed formally. "As you wish. Good evening." He went to the door, feeling every step rattle his bones, as if he would turn to dust the minute he was out of her sight. But no, the closing door might have aged him, and it might have left a chasm between them that nothing now could breach, but he still breathed, he still walked, he still saw.

But felt? Ah, a train could have run over his foot at that moment, and he would not have noticed it.

Elizabeth and Mordecai came out of the study holding hands. Devlin smiled courteously, his numb heart feeling a tinge of gladness at their obvious happiness. "Congratulations are in order, it seems."

Mordecai nodded, watching him closely.

Elizabeth chirped, "We intend to wed by special license tomorrow. You and Charlaine will be our witnesses, of course."

Carefully, Devlin responded, "I hope the weather holds for the ceremony. Congratulations to the two of you. Now, please excuse me." Bowing again, he quietly left the house.

Even Elizabeth stared after him in concern, but Mordecai said grimly, "Something's wrong. Go see what Charlaine talked to him about."

A few moments later, Elizabeth hurried back down, white faced. "He knows. And Charlaine said he acted most oddly."

"Do not alarm her, but I'm going after him. When he's like this, he's like a wild horse with a broken bridle. Nothing will stop him." And he disappeared out the door.

Slowly Elizabeth walked back up to Charlaine. It was time that young miss had a talking to.

Mordecai burst into the flat, panting from his haste. He was too old for this. "Devlin, where are you?"

"In here," came the flat response.

With foreboding, Mordecai hurried into Devlin's chamber, knowing what he'd see. Sure enough, Devlin was throwing clothes into a portmanteau.

Enervated from his own emotional epiphany, Mordecai sagged down on the bed. "You cannot leave now. Not when Charlaine is so close to loving you."

A wild laugh preceded Devlin's bitter response. "Indeed, she loves me so much that she tells two others of her condition and doesn't tell me."

"She told no one. Lizzie figured it out, as did Durwood. And Lizzie just told me."

Devlin stopped packing, contemplating this. "It doesn't matter. A woman in love would have been

347

overjoyed at the news, would have hurried to share it with her beloved."

"If Charlaine were a little homebody, you would not want her. She is used to her independence, and it is hardly surprising that she doesn't know how to deal with such a quick pregnancy." Mordecai watched Devlin closely, having a shrewd suspicion that Devlin was a bit ambivalent too. "A child will complicate an already complex relationship. Surely you do not dispute that."

Wadding up one of his best shirts, Devlin tossed it into the bag. "No. But she just lost one of her biggest irritants. A husband she does not want."

Mordecai rose to fetch his yarmulke so he could think clearly. Devlin was packing even faster now, and when he was like this it was hard to reason with him. With the skullcap on his head, Mordecai went to Devlin's side, pulled his hands away and said simply, "If you leave her now, you will lose all you've suffered for. Lizzie believes Charlaine already loves you deeply; she just wants you to say it first."

"I have. In bed." Devlin's eyes clouded over at a hurtful remembrance.

"All men say it in bed. Besides, did you speak French?"

"Yes."

"Charlaine doesn't speak French. Lizzie was informed that you've vowed not to kiss Charlaine until she admits she loves you. Is this true?"

"Yes."

"Love is not a contest, my boy. It's a gift, as you've so often reminded me. Toss it away, and you will regret it."

Devlin slammed the portmanteau closed. A cravat and a shirttail poked out, but he only hefted the big case to the ground. "I cannot toss away what I do not have. I have done all I can to win her, and still she will not soften. I cannot bear more, Mordecai. I long for the simpler life, before I had so many material things and so little satisfaction. In Africa, at least, I am taken for what I am, not where I came from. I will always be a French by-blow to Charlaine, which is why she cannot love me. That is why I would not kiss her. Sex and kisses, she wants with me, but I will not win her in a moment of weakness. She must come to me, truly, and admit she loves me with full honesty and awareness, or we have no hope of happiness. And she will not." Devlin carried the portmanteau to the living room.

Trailing him, Mordecai tried his last ploy. "So you would reward Charlaine's and Durwood's faith in you by leaving her to raise your child alone?"

The composed mask slipped, and for the first time Mordecai saw how deep was Devlin's anguish, but he stood tall and said, "I should imagine Durwood will be delighted to raise the child as his own, considering how badly he's wanted an heir. And Charlaine, well, she will make an excellent mother. The child will want for nothing."

"I hope that little lie comforts you the whole long journey, and every day in the diamond fields. A child, boy or girl, always needs both parents. I am ashamed that you, of all people, cannot see that, Devlin."

The mask slipped further. Tears gathered in those bold blue eyes that were not so bold at this moment, and it was plain to Mordecai that Devlin did not really want to leave. His only defense was a weak, "I will come back one day. Maybe if I am away awhile, Charlaine will grow to appreciate me."

Gently Mordecai gripped the strong young shoulders in his hands. "Devlin, I have watched you grow from a wild young orphan, to a tough young laborer,

349

to a businessman and finally, to a settled married man. You know you are like a son to me, and I have always been, and will always be, proud of you. But if you desert your wife and child now, I tell you plainly that you will regret it. You will probably never win Charlaine's trust then. All I ask is that you wait another couple of days before you do something rash. The trains run the next day, and the day after that. But a decision like this should not be made in the heat of the moment, when you are hurt and angry. You have given me wise counsel; now listen to mine."

Devlin's mask fell away entirely. He gave a shuddering sigh, dropped into a chair and fell back against it, his eyes closed.

Mordecai held his breath, easing it out when Devlin finally whispered, "Very well. I will wait until after your wedding. But if she does not soften then, I am leaving."

Knowing better than to argue further, Mordecai merely nodded. "Now, what shall we have for dinner? I am starved, and my stomach growls every time I think of all that wasted food at Durwood's house."

Devlin ate when Mordecai brought him some meat and cheese, but the white look about his mouth never went away.

Lizzie, do your best, Mordecai pleaded inwardly, as if she could hear him across the miles. And across town, Lizzie was, indeed, doing her best to talk sense into the girl who was like a daughter to her.

Chapter Thirteen

"That's nonsense," Elizabeth retorted. "Devlin does love you."

"Then why did he leave? He doesn't seem pleased about the child." Charlaine sat quietly in her dressing gown while Elizabeth brushed her hair, but her lashes were wet, and she'd been crying when Elizabeth came up. Marched up, in Charlaine's opinion, to do battle with her niece. Yet her aunt's expression had softened when she saw how upset Charlaine was.

Charlaine gave another little hiccup, wishing her stomach would settle. So far, this joyous event had brought the two most interested parties naught but misery. The only ones pleased about this baby were not intimately involved in either its creation or its rearing. But then, from the beginning, her relationship with Devlin had suffered precisely because so many well-intentioned friends and relatives had done all they could to throw the young lovers together.

Would she be sitting here now, pregnant with his child, mooning over a man who apparently no longer wanted her, without that intervention? Charlaine's body flushed with warmth as she remembered the two wondrous couplings that had led to this nausea, but that heady delight was easily won and even more easily lost. It was the quiet smiles, the caring hand, the shared thoughts, that had bonded her irrevocably to this man. Now, with so much at stake, she realized how tender and gentle he had been with her. How could she deny either of them the union they both wanted? Yet once she admitted she loved him, how could she withhold anything from him, including the legacy she'd spent her life safeguarding?

Abruptly Charlaine rose, Elizabeth's soothing brush tangled in her hair. Charlaine pulled it free so hard that several strands of hair came out. She tossed the brush onto the dressing table and strode to her safe.

Elizabeth watched her, frowning. "What's amiss, my child?"

Charlaine pulled the book from its protective covering and cradled it in her hands. "Aunt, did my grandmama Chantal love Grandpapa even when he forced her to wed him?" Hers too had been a forced marriage, and she identified even more strongly with her ancestor now that they had lived the same experience.

"Ah, so that's it." Elizabeth sat on the edge of the bed and patted it. "I have often wondered why you have never asked me very much about those days."

Charlaine hung her head, but nothing but the truth would do. "Because I feared the reality was very different from the pretty pictures and the pretty words."

Crooking an imperative finger at her niece, Elizabeth said, "Come, sit, and we shall try to make sense of this muddle."

Charlaine sat down beside her aunt, still cradling the book.

Elizabeth opened the pages to the picture of Chantal and Vincent. A tender smile deepened the well-used laugh lines on her still lovely face. "Now there was a stormy union. Even more stormy than yours. Chantal had been on her own since she was seventeen, when she had fled England, pregnant with Vince's child. She was not accustomed to anyone ordering her about, and she had become a great dancer who made a comfortable living by the time your grandfather found her again. She feared losing her son to him, so she refused to admit that she was his youthful love, though of course he didn't really believe it. Quietly, he had her investigated. When he discovered the truth about his son, he carried her off and made her wed him."

Elizabeth smiled tenderly. "Ah, things were simpler in those desperate days. Women could not own property, or run a business, as they can now. It was a rare woman who could survive on her own talents, and your grandmother gave up her independence no more easily than you have. Chantal taught me how to dance, how to be strong." She squeezed Charlaine's hands. "Most important, she taught me to how to love."

"And Chantal? Did she wed him because of the boy?"

"Partly. Of course, at the time, she was angry with him, as he was with her."

Charlaine sighed. "And so I feared. They wed for purely practical reasons, neither caring for the other."

Elizabeth raised her lorgnette to subject her niece to a piercing stare. "I declare, you know more of human nature than that. You come naturally by the passion that led you to the only man in the world who is perfect for you." When Charlaine bit her lip, Elizabeth

353

dropped the lorgnette and moderated her tone. "At any rate, neither of these two strong-willed individuals would admit the true reason they married, a reason that had little to do with the dictates of society. If you are honest, it is the same reason that you wed Devlin." Elizabeth stopped and looked at her niece expectantly.

Blushing, Charlaine whispered, "Lust."

Elizabeth smiled. "So some call it. In actuality, the kind of attraction between you and Devlin, the same kind that Chantal and her soldier knew, has far deeper and more complicated roots. What is there to be ashamed of in an instinctive, primitive recognition of one's mate?"

Charlaine grew still. In her inimitable way, Elizabeth had made it all so clear. Charlaine's heart surged in her breast. Again, she stared at the picture of her ancestors. "So she loved him, then?"

Elizabeth patted her niece's cheek. "Yes, my child, beyond reason, as he loved her. It was a love so strong that it survived a decade-long separation, lies, pain and anger. I only hope that you do not make the same mistake she did, and hurt the one you love the most."

Charlaine tried to visualize her life if Devlin left her and went to Africa. Her mind went blank. Her life would be a black void without him. Such had been her life before him, had she only had the sense to realize it. The agonizing choice, in the end, was easy.

Like the Kimballs before her, she had lived her own fairy tale and not even realized it until it was almost too late. This French frog had crept slyly into her world, charmed her father and aunt into his allies, and slowly taken over her life. As he had promised, he'd shared her silver spoon and golden plate, he'd slept in her soft bed, and now he made her swoon with love of him. And he loved her in return; she knew he did.

With a sudden burst of joy, she sprang to her feet

so fast that the book fell. She picked it up and set it back in the safe, planning all the while. The time for prevarication and pride was past. It had not been in her nature to gamble, but that was before she had so much at stake. What better way to end their stalemate than to go to him and declare her love? Charlaine waited for the usual reflexive independence to surface, but she felt only a peaceful certainty. She could not wait to make love with Devlin now that she finally knew the meaning of the word. And dear Lord, the kiss they would share would surely shake the very ground under all of London.

"Aunt, would you help me dress?"

Again Elizabeth raised her lorgnette and observed Charlaine's brilliant smile and determined chin. With a little nod of satisfaction, she dropped the lorgnette. "I knew you had too much of your forebears in you to let him get away. You are a sensible chit, just like your grandmama was. Now, what do you wish to wear?" Elizabeth bustled to the closet.

The choice was easy. "Something pink." And Charlaine went back to the safe to pull out the rose diamond necklace, which had twinkled at her, stating Devlin's feelings in a very tangible way, if she hadn't been too stubborn to see it.

As she began to dress, Charlaine added, "Would you please ask my father to fetch my barrister? I need him to draw up some papers."

"I shall be glad to, my dear." Elizabeth went to the door. "Oh, and I hope you will also celebrate my own happiness with me."

Charlaine whirled, her hands behind her back fastening her dress. "You and Mordecai?"

Elizabeth nodded, that lovely smile stretching her face again.

Her dress falling to her waist, Charlaine ran across

to give her aunt an ebullient hug. "I am so happy for you. I knew he would not be able to resist you long."

Tears sparkled in Elizabeth's eyes. She sniffed, hugged her niece hard, then released her. "And let this be a lesson to you, young lady. Men are stubborn, but they cannot resist a determined woman."

Regret and pain twisted Charlaine's lovely face. "I have hurt him, Aunt. I did not mean to, for he's always been so confident and bold, but what if he refuses me?"

Elizabeth smiled conspiratorially. "Use your primary advantage against him." She opened the door. "The same advantage I used with Mordecai."

"You mean?"

"Seduce him, you silly child. Now hurry up. You've amends to make."

And, for the first time in her life, Charlaine was so eager to dress that she managed the complicated affair without her maid, thinking one thought, dreaming one dream.

The kiss. The kiss that would change an Ice Princess into a woman. For the frog would not be transformed into a prince for one simple reason: Devlin had always been a prince. A prince of kisses, a prince of dreams.

Charlaine hurried even faster after that.

Without a glance at the antechamber, Cecil Rhodes strode into his office. "Henry, fetch your notebook. I've a letter to send." When there was no response, Cecil looked back out. He stared at the empty desk. It was not merely empty of an occupant; it was literally empty. No ink blotter, no nibs or ink pot, or even paper. Cecil opened the drawers to find the ledgers and accounts records also gone.

Stunned, Cecil sagged against the desk. He could not believe the evidence of his own eyes. Henry Dupree had obviously left abruptly for parts unknown, taking everything he could with him. Cecil's face took on an ashen hue. He rushed into his office and quickly opened the massive safe. Henry was the only person other than himself who knew the combination, but surely he would not actually . . .

Cecil stared at the empty shelves. The last diamond shipment, in its entirety, was gone. Over a million pounds' worth of stones. Cecil had to lean against the wall, he felt so weak and sick to his stomach. He was not typically such a poor judge of character. Devlin Rhodes's face came into his mind's eye, and he had to amend hastily, at least not of those men in his employ. This was a trick he could have far more easily believed of his cousin than of his trusted assistant.

Swallowing several times, Cecil forced his wavering steps toward the door. Scotland Yard, immediately, though it was doubtless too late.

The sun was dancing a tarantella of fire and magic when Charlaine set a dainty foot on the carriage step put down by her coachman. She cast an eager eye on Devlin's door. She'd not sent word, as she was so excited and anxious to see him that she couldn't wait. She twirled her parasol and smiled at her expectant coachman. "You may leave. I shall not need you again this evening." Charlaine intended to follow her sage aunt's advice to the letter.

The coachman looked about doubtfully at the crowds surging in the streets. "I should wait and see you safely in, my lady."

Charlaine smoothed her hair back, trying to calm herself. "Nonsense, I've only to cross the street. Go on. I shall see you all tomorrow at the wedding."

Reluctantly he put the carriage steps back up and clucked to his team.

Colleen Shannon

Charlaine watched him disappear; then she started to step down from the curb. A hired coach rattled up and stopped before her, forcing her back to the walk. She started to skirt it, but paused when a familiar voice spoke.

"Good evening, Charlaine. What a pleasant surprise to see you." Henry Dupree stepped down from the coach, a charming smile on his handsome face.

Charlaine offered her fingertips to his outstretched hand, but drew away when he brought them to his lips. Why did he always seem to be lurking about when she least wanted to see him?

"Good evening, Henry. Now if you'll please excuse me." She tried to walk past him, but he caught her arm.

"I've a problem with the ring you sold me. I fear the stone is loose. Would you mind looking at it for me? I have it here in the carriage." Henry opened the carriage door.

Charlaine hesitated. Even a moment of delay was difficult, but if the stone were loose, she owed this man a look at it. She knew Henry was infatuated with her, and from her newfound softness she discovered compassion for his unrequited love. Surely a moment of kindness would not delay her happiness enough to matter. Charlaine accepted his hand up into his carriage.

From his tiny back porch, Devlin watched the sun mark the end of another day of futile longing. Almost, he wished to hold it back, for by the time it set on the morrow, he would be on his way to Africa. He tried to find peace, if not joy, in the thought, but the emptiness in his life yawned before him like a chasm. Fill the days as he might with grueling work, his thoughts would never be far away from his wife and his child.

Why go, then? part of him demanded. But he knew that he could not stay under the circumstances. This burning need for her would eat at him day by day, growing worse with every dawn, until he did something, said something, that gave her such a distaste for him that she would send him away. Far better to go now, while his dignity and memories were intact, than to watch their relationship wither on the vine of resentment. As he had told Mordecai, maybe when he was gone, Charlaine would learn to miss him. One day he would return.

Devlin dragged himself back into his flat to help Mordecai prepare for his big day tomorrow.

The next morning Elizabeth fluttered about her dressing chamber like the blushing bride she was. She shoved away her maid's encroaching hands. "Touch that ribbon again and I shall slap you!" Elizabeth tried yet again to set the riband woven through her lovely, shining silver locks. It was gold, to match Mordecai's heart, and gold to match their years, and gold to match their value to one another. Another simple gold satin ribbon adorned the waist of her cream-colored lace dress, but aside from an ancient but lovely woven gold necklace and earrings to match, which Mordecai had purchased years ago from an Egyptian, she wore no other adornment. She did not look like a wealthy duchess. She looked like what she was: a woman in love, going into her union with a full heart. And somehow, she knew she had never looked lovelier, even in her youth.

The woman reared back with a huffy, "Really, Your Grace, this agitation is most unlike you."

Elizabeth barely heard her. She glanced at the clock on her mantel. Only thirty minutes to go. Where the devil was Charlaine? She always had such a delicate touch with confounded things like balky ribbons. Be-

Colleen Shannon

sides, Elizabeth was dying to know how her niece's meeting with her obstreperous husband had gone.

A knock sounded at the door. The maid opened it and blinked in shock at the man who stood there.

Durwood Kimball rushed inside the bedchamber, for once uncaring of the proprieties. His usual composure was in tatters as he said in a shaky tone, "Elizabeth, I cannot find Charlaine anywhere! The coachman said he set her down yesterday evening at Devlin's, but I've just come from the church, and he has not seen her."

The ribbon dangled half in, half out of Elizabeth's hair as her hands fell. "But that's impossible. She told me herself she was going there."

Their eyes met in her dressing table mirror, considering the ramifications of Charlaine's disappearance. All the lovely color left Elizabeth's face, and Durwood's already furrowed brow twisted into a terrified grimace. A commotion below made them both leap hopefully toward the door.

Side by side, they rushed downstairs into the salon. Their faces fell when they found no one but Devlin, Mordecai and Cecil. Both men were holding Devlin by an arm as he struggled between them, saying between gritting teeth, "I'll kill him for this!"

Mordecai said in his usual logical way, "We have to find him first, and this fury does not exactly allow for calm thought."

And from his other side, Cecil said grimly, "No one wants to find him more than I. But thrashing about like an enraged bull accomplishes nothing but the breakage of valuables."

Elizabeth scarcely spared a glance at the Sevres vase Devlin had apparently knocked over in his fury. "I presume this person we speak of is Henry Dupree. He is behind her disappearance."

Mordecai took an instant to smile at her and sweep her with a loving gaze before he replied, "As usual, my dear, you are exactly right. Cecil came to us at the church when Durwood sent word to ask if he'd seen Charlaine. Cecil deduced, correctly, I believe, that Henry kidnapped Charlaine literally upon our doorstep."

Elizabeth collapsed into her favorite chair. "Oh my, how I wish I was wrong this time."

Durwood said, "Did Henry leave you a note, Cecil, anything that might give us a hint of his intentions?"

Cecil smiled bitterly. "Something much more eloquent than a note. An empty safe. I've contacted Scotland Yard, but so far they haven't picked up a whiff of him."

Durwood fell back a step at this revelation, terror flickering in his eyes. "Dear God, he's taken her out of England. He can never stay here after a theft of that size, and he knows it."

Shaking off his friends, Devlin stood straight, his chest heaving like a bellows. Finally he spoke, his voice as dark and calm as any of them had ever heard it. "Let me guess. No one matching his description has boarded any of the public trains or ships."

"No, I'm afraid not, at least not those we have yet investigated. However, I did not know at the time that Charlaine accompanied him. They were not looking for a couple, but for a man alone."

"Charlaine would not go quietly," Durwood said with certainty. "He could not risk taking her out in public."

They were all silent, thinking, when Devlin said with a fixed look, as though some unheard voice called to him, "I believe I know exactly where he's taken her. The last place anyone would think to look."

With one movement, all turned to him. Devlin

smiled grimly. "Summerlea."

An excited babble of conversation broke out as they all debated this unlikely possibility.

Devlin held up a commanding hand for silence. "Summerlea is near the coast, is it not?"

Durwood nodded. "And Cecil and Henry have visited us there several times in the past. He knows how far it is from any of the main roads, and that we keep our yacht berthed in a private cove not far from the estate."

"Summerlea, I was informed by Jeffries," continued Devlin, "is vacant at the moment since Charlaine left a week or so ago. She told the servants they all had the summer off as she did not plan to visit again."

"But how would Henry know this?" Mordecai asked.

"The same way he knows everything else."

"By his insidious eavesdropping." Elizabeth shook her head in disgust.

If possible, Cecil looked even more disgusted. "Am I to infer that this degenerate has been listening in on my important conversations?"

Rolling his eyes, Devlin let Elizabeth respond.

"It astounds me that you never noticed, Cecil. Every person who ever visited your office knew of his propensity, save you. For such an astute man, you can be positively blind at times."

"Why the devil didn't someone tell me?" He glared at each of them in turn.

"We have all noted how well you take advice," Devlin said dryly.

Cecil's beetling brows lowered ominously, but then he gave a wry laugh. "Given our history, I have to admit I deserved that." He grew serious again. "But I shall never forgive myself if mishap comes to Charlaine because of my obtuseness."

"On that we can agree, at least." Devlin's scowl made

him bear, for just an instant, an uncanny resemblance to his cousin. Decisively, he turned. "I'm for Summerlea."

Elizabeth, Mordecai and Durwood started to follow, but he blocked their exit. "No. She is my wife, and I can protect her better if I work alone."

A big hand caught Mordecai's shoulder and pushed him gently aside. "And he is my former employee, and I have a great deal at stake here as well. I go, either as your ally or alone, if need be, but I go."

The two cousins, of a height, glared at each other. Devlin gritted his teeth, but finally, with a bitten-off epithet, he strode out the door. Cecil dogged his heels.

The other three trailed them to the foyer and wished them Godspeed. The two men paused only for a nod, and then the door slammed behind them.

Biting her lip, Elizabeth held her tears at bay. "I fear for them all."

Mordecai cradled his wife-to-be with a protective arm. "Nonsense. When Devlin wears that look on his face, no one can stand against him, least of all a little weasel like Henry Dupree. In fact, this may be a blessing in disguise."

Elizabeth jerked herself away from him with an appalled look.

Durwood rebuked, "Thought you were a more sensible fellow than that."

"I am a sensible fellow, and I know Devlin Rhodes as well as anyone on this earth. His instinct for flight has been replaced with a much more productive one. He will protect his mate, and the last of their lingering doubts about each other will be settled in a kiss long overdue."

Durwood looked much struck by the notion. "Indeed, you may be right."

But Elizabeth didn't seem so certain.

Mordecai turned to her with a smile, saying, "Well, my dear, shall we proceed with our own wedding, or do you wish to wait?"

Rubbing her elbows, as if she were abruptly chilled, she said, "We wait. I cannot marry without my niece present. As for your deduction, I would agree with you, Mordecai, save for one thing." Her lovely hazel eyes were worried when she ended, "Henry Dupree is obsessed with Charlaine. I believe he stole the diamonds largely to make himself worthy in her eyes. If he thinks he's about to lose her irrevocably, he may do something desperate."

For the tenth time in the space of the last twenty hours or so, Charlaine tried to speak reasonably to Henry Dupree. So far her logical arguments had won her nothing but pats on the head and kisses on the cheek, but she was even more determined than he was. "Henry, please listen. I cannot go to the continent with you because I am a married woman."

He smiled gaily, pouring her a second cup of tea and carefully sweetening it as she liked. He'd never poured tea her before, so he must have observed her tastes closely. If she had not been so frightened, she might have been touched at his obvious devotion, but her fear grew still greater when he said with satisfaction, "That will not serve, my dear. We shall obtain you an annulment easily enough when we reach Italy."

She bit her lip and accepted the teacup, not quite able to tell him about the child. He'd always been a strange man, with his sweaty, grasping hands and his passionate speeches. She had no way of knowing what he'd do if he knew she was pregnant by the rival he detested. For the second time, she looked at the sun, which had passed its zenith and was starting the long, slow slide to afternoon. And to her ruin, for she knew he expected her yacht to be supplied and ready to sail with the evening tide.

She closed her eyes yet again, trying with all her heart and mind to call to Devlin. *Come to me, my love.* She felt Henry sit beside her and take the cup from her hands. Yet again he tried to pull her into his arms. Yet again she resisted, turning her head aside from his descending mouth. So far he'd taken her rejections calmly, but this time his handsome brow furrowed a bit when he leaned back to appraise her. "Really, I deserve better than that. I have risked everything for you, and I should like to see a bit of gratitude."

She stifled a wild laugh and hung her head as if in shame. "I am just tired, Henry. Might I be allowed some privacy to rest? My night was not precisely rest-ful." What an understatement. He had pulled the car-riage he'd hired into a copse far off the main London road, rested his head against the only door and told her to sleep.

She'd watched him drop off and eased over to the window, hoping to squeeze through, but it was far too small. When she inched toward the door, he awoke with a start. "Try that again and I shall tie you up." When she shrank at his tone, he sighed and took her hands. "I'm sorry, my love. This is not the way I would have chosen to woo you, but you left me no choice. I know you do not love that wastrel your father forced you to marry. In time you will grow to care for me as much as I care for you." And he'd tried to kiss her.

She'd turned her cheek aside into the upholstered seat opposite. "Please, just let me sleep."

A silence followed, then a bleak, "As you wish. Good night. Things will look better to you in the morning, as will I."

Tears came to her eyes at the confident prediction. This was her comeuppance. The Ice Princess had waited too long to thaw, and now she would be carried away on the deluge of another man's passion, wanting only the arms of her husband. What poetic justice.

That night was the longest of her life, but eventually dawn came, as it always does.

Charlaine had been astonished to recognize the road they traveled next. She'd assumed he would take her directly to the outskirts of Bath, for some hired ship, but his intentions were even bolder. Her mouth dropped open when Summerlea came into view from atop the rise before it. For an instant, joy rang in her heart like church bells. She was safe and free, for she was home!

But then she recalled giving all her servants the summer off. She glared at Henry, unable to hide her resentment this time. "How did you know it was safe to bring me here?"

"I have my ways." And he'd pulled the carriage to a stop before her very doorstep, helping her down with all the courtesy of the suitor he obviously considered himself.

Kidnapper! Somehow she kept the insult to herself, for she realized antagonizing him would avail her nothing except perhaps bonds. He escorted her to the front door, watched her open it and then gave a peculiar whistle.

A chill ran up her spine as two seedy-looking individuals slunk around the corner of an outbuilding. They gazed avariciously at the tiny diamonds glittering on Henry's palm. He gave one to the tall, skinny one and one to the short, stocky one. "And another to each, when you have us safely in Italy." They pocketed the small diamonds and disappeared as quickly as they'd arrived.

Italy? Charlaine's despair grew. They would expect Henry to make for France, which was precisely why he'd decided to go the long way about.

Henry consulted his pocket watch. "We should be ready to sail by evening, if all goes well. Meantime, would you care to show me about Summerlea? I confess on my previous visits, I was too busy yes-sirring to notice how fine this little estate truly is." He sniffed with obvious hauteur.

And he'd trailed her about like a man interested in inspecting his newly acquired property. Charlaine deduced that he, at least, would never sign away all rights to her estate as Devlin had. By the time they made it back to the salon for tea, she was wilted with tension, wondering if she were truly the subject of his obsession, or merely the tool he'd selected to get back at Cecil and Devlin, or his golden entrance into a way of life he coveted.

However, their conversation at this moment put that speculation to rest, as he made it clear what it was exactly that he coveted. He gently lifted her chin and stared at her with darkening blue eyes, inching closer to her on the sofa. "I have loved you from the first moment I saw you."

Loved me, or my possessions? she wondered cynically even as he held her chin firm for his descending mouth. This time she stayed quiescent, her hand groping for the heavy silver teapot. His lips moved passionately upon hers, evoking nothing in her save distaste. She was lifting the teapot when his iron clasp twisted her wrist. With a gasp of pain, she dropped the heavy pot. He merely twisted harder as tea sloshed over the tray onto the fine Oriental carpet, staining the side of the satin sofa.

"You are spoiled, my dear, always wanting your own way even when you do not know your own mind," he said in a too-pleasant voice. "But I shall fix that soon enough. Now kiss me, kiss me as a lover should."

And he caught her face in his hands and covered her mouth with his own greedy, grasping lips that matched his heart and mind.

She bore it as long as she could, but when he tried to thrust his tongue in her mouth, she pulled away, gagging. The tea surged in her stomach. She covered her mouth with her hand and ran for the water closet.

He followed, keeping her in arm's reach even then. She slammed the door in his face and barely made it to the receptacle before she threw up the tea and biscuits she'd had for breakfast.

When she leaned back, exhausted, her brow clammy, he opened the door and towered over her. She took one look at the disgusted realization in his face and closed her eyes in despair.

"You carry his seed, don't you?"

She did not deny it. In truth, she was so sick and tired that she didn't much care what he'd do. But fear was a welcome jolt to apathy when he caught her arm and hauled her to her feet. "The leavings of a by-blow." He sneered into her face. "How appropriate, save for one thing." He shook her slightly. "You belong to me!"

Pretense was beyond her. Even if he killed her for it, she could no longer bear his hypocrisy. "I belong to no one but myself." She shook him off and stood tall. "But I choose to bed and wed but one man, and it is not you. Now let me go, or I swear I will make your life as miserable as you have made this last day. . . ." She trailed off at the look in his eyes, wishing she'd phrased the retort differently.

"Last day. If that be your wish, then far be it from me to deny you." And he caught her by the hair and dragged her from the water closet toward the stairs, forcing her up them. He shoved her into the first bed-chamber, slamming the door behind them.

Finally she feared for her life, but he released her

abruptly, closing his eyes as he obviously struggled for control. When they opened, the black rage had changed to a cold calculation that frightened her even more. "Speak to me like that again, and you will regret it." Backing out, he took the key and locked her in.

Immediately she ran to the window, but the drop from the second story was sheer, with nothing to hold on to. She caught the sill with longing hands, watching the sun lower ominously. She only had an hour or so until sunset. She measured the drop with a glance. Twenty feet, at least. If not for the child she would have risked it. Hanging her head, she wept, fearing that she would never see Devlin again.

Devlin almost screamed with frustration as he turned the carriage back around to seek the first inn he came to. Why did the only road between Summerlea and London have to be blocked by that ghastly carriage accident? Fear gnawed at his innards like a giant tapeworm, for the sun told him noon approached, and the estate was still several hours' travel away.

Cecil hung on to the side of the fast curricle, cursing, as Devlin steered them through the crowded streets. "What rotten luck. I wish these damned foreigners would leave as quickly as they came."

Devlin scarcely heard him. From some primitive source, he felt Charlaine's fear and despair, and his own fear urged him on to reckless speed. He turned a corner too quickly, spying an inn with horses for hire, and caught their wheel against a curb. Sparks flew. Their vehicle teetered on two wheels, then slammed back onto the cobbled street with a jolt that made them throw a wheel.

Cecil's hat went flying, and he would have fallen from the cockeyed curricle if he hadn't caught himself.

Colleen Shannon

He gave Devlin a fulminating look, saw the white set of his cousin's mouth, and said with a sigh, "You go on. I'll deal with the mess here and follow as quickly as I can."

Devlin didn't need a second urging. He jumped lithely from the tilted vehicle and ran to the inn as if wings were attached to his feet. Cecil climbed down more carefully, wondering where the bobbies were when one needed them.

By the time she heard footsteps outside the door, Charlaine had wiped her eyes, blown her nose, and from somewhere pulled the tattered rags of dignity about herself again. Devlin was constantly in her thoughts, but unless he was clairvoyant, he'd never figure out where Henry had taken her. Only memories of him, the child they'd created and the life they could still share, kept her calm when Henry strode inside as if he owned the place—as he would shortly own her.

What was wrong with her, that she had once viewed Henry as safe but boring, and Devlin as dangerous? Would she pay for her poor judgment with her life?

"Come along, my dear. The yacht is ready." As punctilious as if he offered an outing instead of a kidnapping, he extended his hands to her, smiling.

The urge to slap them away and pound the smile off his face with her fist was overwhelming. From somewhere, she found the strength to give him a weak smile in return. However, as she accepted his arm, her feet were unwontedly clumsy. Numerous times he had to steady her. Once she almost fell, but for his arm about her shoulders. They hadn't yet reached the stairs when he gave an exclamation of disgust and hefted her into his arms, carrying her toward the stairs.

No expediency could have kept her still then at his

370

hateful, invasive touch. No one touched her so but Devlin. She struggled, kicking her feet, pounding his shoulders with her fists. "You hateful, disgusting little man, let me go!"

His impatient glance down at her changed to something much more malevolent as he stalked to the top of the long, curving staircase. "I should be careful of that sharp tongue, lest you startle me into losing my grip." And he made to stumble, almost dropping her over the top step.

She grasped wildly at him, fear for her child overcoming even her antagonism.

His throat worked with his emotions as he said through gritted teeth, "I confess I much prefer that we begin our new life together without the burden of the brat you carry."

She bit her tongue until it bled, helpless and hating him even more for it, as he dangled her over the edge. From somewhere, another world perhaps, the prince her dreams had conjured came to rescue her, slamming the heavy entrance door against the wall, and standing there indomitably, the vermilion sky behind him painting him in hues of glory lessened not a whit by the little pistol he brandished. Charlaine recognized it as the same pistol she'd held on him on two separate occasions.

"Dupree! Set her down gently. If you drop her I will shoot you where you stand," came that blessed, longed-for voice.

Before she could stop herself, Charlaine flung her arms longingly toward him, struggling yet again to be free to go to him. Henry's clasp only tightened. She went still and let her brilliant smile say the words she dared not utter, lest they literally send Henry over the edge.

Henry's arms began to tremble, whether from the

strain of holding her so long or from hatred, Charlaine could not say. But her eyes widened in fear as she felt his clasp begin to loosen. She reached out wildly to grab at anything, but the newel post was too far away.

In a rush so fast she would not be able to believe it later, Devlin ran up the stairs three at a time as Henry dangled her over the edge of the first step. "If I cannot have her, neither can anyone else, least of all a scoundrel like you!" And Henry opened his arms and tossed her down the stairs.

Charlaine screamed, feeling the hard wooden stairs rushing up to meet her with terrifying force and speed, flailing her arms and legs, but she could not get her feet under her. Then, with a last burst of effort, Devlin dove, stretching his length out across the width of six stairs, stretching out beneath her like a human mattress. She landed on his back, feeling the breath leave his lungs at the impact. She grasped a stair balustrade and caught herself, and then hastily scrambled off his back. Wincing, he turned to face her.

She gasped and cradled his bruised cheek and swollen eye, running her hands over him, looking for broken bones. "Are you all right?"

He kissed her palm passionately. "I am now." He helped her to her feet. "Come along. I'm not letting you out of my sight again." He paused only to pick up the pistol he'd dropped in his dive.

She thought he stumbled once, but his expression didn't change as they mounted the last of the stairs in time to see Henry disappearing down the far end of the hallway.

"Where does that lead?" Devlin asked.

"To the servants' stairway," she responded grimly.

"Stay here! Lock yourself in a room and hide." He hurried down the hallway.

When Charlaine followed without a word of argument, he didn't pause as he cast her a glare. "For once do as you're told, please?" His point lost its impact when he stumbled again.

She had to catch his arm to keep him from falling. "And leave you to face that madman alone? I have learned my lesson, Devlin. We belong together. If necessary, we will die together."

His face changed, softening, as he stopped cold. His lips descended. She stared at his mouth, aching with the need to feel it, to revel in it, and forget that Henry Dupree had ever kissed her.

A slamming door below brought them back to the moment. They jerked apart and ran to the servants' stairs. Devlin's limp grew more pronounced when they finally reached the bottom. Charlaine started to burst outside to the rear courtyard, but Devlin shoved her aside, hid against the wall with her and shoved the door wide. A pistol exploded, sending a bullet through the door, where it left a small hole marking its power, and then careened into the wall, sending plaster showering over them, before it finally lost its impact.

Devlin counted to three before he barreled outside, stooped over, gesturing to her to do the same. Charlaine obeyed, thankful she did when another shot came, whizzing over her head. They tumbled to the ground together, rolling behind the shrubs next to the door, their breathing fast. Devlin peeked over the bush, but the fire this time came from a different direction, ricocheting over his head against the stucco wall. He ducked back down again.

"Does he have allies?"

Charlaine nodded, unable to speak. Had they come so far, through so many misunderstandings, only to die like this? Another shot came from the other side, passing so close she felt the heat of it.

Devlin poked the little pistol out of the bush, aiming

it in the direction of one of their assailants, but its retort sounded puny compared to the firepower leveled on them. In the deepening gloom, Charlaine knew he couldn't see what he aimed at, much less hope to hit one of them. But then, their enemies labored under the same disadvantage. Never had Charlaine wished for utter darkness more than at this moment.

A few more potshots came, but the couple were too well shielded by the greenery and the darkness. Devlin tried a more potent weapon than the pistol: his voice. "The local magistrate is on his way, Dupree. You might as well give up. You'll still go to jail for thievery and kidnapping, but if you stop now, at least you won't hang for murder."

A wild laugh answered them, along with a barrage of gunfire. Devlin pushed Charlaine down, covering her with his body. "That was not exactly helpful, was it?" he said grimly into her ear.

Even under the circumstances, the feel of him against her after so long brought a warmth and longing that gave her strength. Shoving him off, she boldly rose, ignoring his efforts to pull her back down, and said, "Henry, I give you leave to take my yacht. I regret that we have come to this, but I truly wish you well. Please go, while you still can."

A long silence; then a cynical voice said, "How magnanimous of you, my dear. I knew there was a reason why I loved you so."

Charlaine was warned by his past tense and flat tone. She dove back down just as a bullet winged above her head, lodging in one of the Tudor staves of Summerlea. Vengeance, it seemed, was even more important to Henry Dupree than self-preservation.

The standoff dragged on. Finally they heard one of the hired men whine, "This ain't gettin' us nowheres,

guv. Let's get out o' here fore we gets too well ac-
quainted like with the inside of a cell. I've had my fill
of those."

"Shut up and do as you're told," came Henry's response. "These two don't leave here alive."

Despairing, Charlaine sank against Devlin. "What
can we do? There must be something!"

Even in the darkness, she could see the shine of his
smile. "After I've melted the Ice Princess, defeating a
vengeful suitor is a bagatelle. Stay here." And slowly,
quietly, inching his way, he began to slither out of the
shrubbery.

Charlaine longed to follow him, but she knew her
many petticoats would rustle. Not for the first time she
cursed the silly encumbrances society decreed she
wear. She could only lie still, hoping Henry couldn't
hear her thundering heart, and pray for Devlin's
safety.

He was halfway across the courtyard, to the stand
of trees where their assailants hid, when Henry's hateful voice came again. "Damn you, I said be still, if you
want to be paid!" They heard running footsteps; then
a shot made Charlaine fear for Devlin until she realized it was aimed in a different direction. She heard a
heavy weight fall, and a new voice she hadn't heard
before bleated in fright.

"I ain't done nothin'."

"Precisely. Now we sit, and we wait, or you can be
a coward like your friend and suffer the same fate."

"But don't ye hear it? It's too late!"

A new sound caught her attention, the same one the
hired men had obviously heard first.

Hoofbeats, furious with purpose, pounding over the
bridge leading to Summerlea. The other man's voice
began to fade as he obviously retreated. "There's too
many of 'em. Ye got any sense, ye'll get to that ship,

rich and alive, or stay, brave and dead." His footsteps stumbled over something, then beat a hasty retreat.

Charlaine was emboldened enough to follow Devlin's example, knowing that the sounds of the approaching riders would hide her movements. She squinted. Devlin had made it to the first tree now, but where was Henry hiding?

She heard a grunt, then made out two figures grappling over a pistol. Rising, she ran to help Devlin.

But a rider burst through the trees first and launched himself from his still trotting horse. He landed on the two men. Charlaine froze when the pistol went off, but breath wheezed through her lungs again when she realized it had harmlessly hit a tree.

She hurried up, wondering who their savior was, just as torches blazed into the courtyard, carried by a motley assortment of bobbies, workingmen and servants, a few of whom Charlaine recognized. Cecil Rhodes's grimacing expression was thrown into vibrant, determined relief as he said through gritted teeth, "Leave him to me, Devlin. He's mine."

Devlin stepped aside and let the former employer and his trusted employee battle out their frustrated rage against one another. He favored one leg, but his clasp about Charlaine's shoulders as she crept up to him was strong and loving.

They both watched the uncertain battle, for though Cecil was bigger and more powerful, Henry was fueled by rage. He tried to knee Cecil in the groin, but their close contact made the dirty move impossible.

Still, Cecil was so enraged by the ploy that he found strength enough to fell his opponent with an elbow to the chin. Henry stumbled back into the waiting arms of the bobbies. He struggled against them, his expression virulent with frustrated hatred. "This is what you always do, Rhodes. Let other people do your dirty work for you, yes sir, no sir, whatever you say sir. Well, not this time." And, with a gleeful sneer, Henry stuck his hand in his pocket and pulled out a pouch, opening it. He tossed it as high and far as he could, aiming for the artificial pond off to the side.

Diamonds sparkled in the torchlight like fireflies, sprinkling over the lawn as they flew back whence they'd come: to the earth and its embrace. Several men made ineffectual grabs as the pouch flew over their heads, but Henry had thrown it too hard. It plopped into the pond, sinking rapidly.

"There you are, Rhodes. Try losing all you care about, and see how it makes you feel."

Unable to hide his grimace, for Cecil Rhodes knew the cost and effort required to wrest the stones into the light of day, he still said with remarkable calm, "Yet again, you err in judgment. There's only one thing I care about at this moment." And he nodded at the bobbies. They clapped Henry in irons. "Take him away. It makes me sick to look at him." And, his head still set proudly on his broad shoulders, Henry Dupree stalked away. Anyone watching him being led away would not have believed the things he'd done in the past two days, so dignified and handsome did he look.

His chest still heaving with his fury, Cecil came over to Devlin and Charlaine. "Are you two all right?"

Devlin nodded. "I'll help you recover the stones, Cecil. It shouldn't require more than a few weeks of digging."

Cecil smiled wryly as he watched the men with him stealthily digging in the grass. "Too late, old chap. Serves me right, I guess. Perhaps I was too demanding of Henry, but no treatment deserved this. Besides, it's high time Lloyd's pays me back for some of those outrageous fees I've been paying all these years." He shook himself like a dog shaking off water, then

Colleen Shannon

smiled at the couple. "It appears perhaps the outcome will be felicitous for the two of you, anyway." Cecil nodded at a servant. "Take them back to London. Slowly." And he smiled, waving them away, before the great Cecil Rhodes bent and began digging in the dirt. This was, after all, how he'd begun.

Charlaine rested her head against Devlin's shoulder as he limped around to the front of the house and tenderly handed her up into the hired carriage. Following his master's instructions to the letter, the coachman eased them into motion.

But he needn't have bothered. The pair were so close to one another that a galloping pace couldn't have made any difference. His chest heaving with the emotions about to demand free rein, Devlin turned up the carriage lantern to look into the dark green eyes staring trustingly up from his shoulder. "Well, wife, what have you to say for yourself?"

The fleeting thought came that they were both filthy and aching from their ordeal. The Ice Princess would have been too fastidious to share such an emotional moment while so dirty. But Charlaine Rhodes, beloved of her prince of kisses, merely opened her arms with a smile that made her more lovely than she had ever been. "I love you, my husband."

His quick breathing stopped. Then, with an iron clasp that made her head swim, Devlin lay back on the carriage seat and pulled her atop him. For a long moment they remained thus, their hearts beating as one, their gazes locked as they shared their emotions in an intimacy more poignant than any they had yet known, but less so than many they had yet to experience.

"And I love you," he finally whispered shyly. "I have loved you almost since you first held a pistol on me, certainly long before we wed."

378

Charlaine closed her eyes in pain. "Why didn't you tell me?"

"Because you always held me at arm's length. The more I was with you, the more I wanted you, but my best wooing seemed to be ineffective. Finally my longing grew so great that I could not bear it, especially when you wouldn't tell me about the child." A warm hand settled on her abdomen.

"Would you really have left me?" She leaned back to pout at him reproachfully.

A heated blue gaze fixed on her mouth. "Not for long. I was kidding myself about that. I would have come back before the month was out. And now, my dearest, sweetest princess, I have a promise to keep."

Joy surged through Charlaine, invigorating enough, despite her overworked emotions, to make her playful. He had made her wait so long, but the yearning was about to be richly satisfied. She pretended to pull away. "Oh? And what is that?"

Strong hands pulled her back. He gasped when she settled her hips upon him. "Kiss me, wench, and tell me when we're done if I'm frog or prince."

She cradled his strong cheekbones in her hands. "I do not have to kiss you to answer that. You have always been a prince. I was just too scared to see it. I kiss you, my darling, but it is I who am transformed." And softly, gently, she lowered her mouth upon his.

They shared a little gasp at the electric current that seemed to pass from her lips to his. She pulled back, startled at the tingling sensation, but he buried his hands in her hair and hauled her head close. His mouth locked on hers in a kiss that rocked them to their moorings. His lips were so hungry, and so eager, that at first he seemed awkward, uncertain, but when her lips opened over his, he accepted her invitation and licked the corner of her mouth, teasing her to

379

open wider. She gasped at the sensation, and then her eyes opened wide as she felt the thrust of his tongue. It dipped inside, retreated, then came insatiably back, as if he explored her deepest essence and made it his own in that most evocative of ways: by giving her his own.

She had never known intimacy so great, no, not even in his bed, for this feeling was so heady and so intense that her eyes teared. *I love you, I want you, I will die happy in your arms,* he said wordlessly, in that ineffable French way that she could have enjoyed all along if she hadn't been so stubborn. For minutes on end they kissed, the miles passing, the years stretching before them like a gift. Occasionally they surfaced for air, but only for a moment, for the hunger so long denied could not be so easily filled.

And with every thrust of tongue and caress of hand, they healed the hurts and formed a future that did, indeed, make a fitting legacy to pass on to the child they'd created.

A week later, Charlaine and Devlin hurried out to the step of their new home to meet the newlyweds back from their quick honeymoon. Charlaine and Devlin had arrived in London in time to bathe and be witness to a delayed candlelight ceremony, all the more moving for its shadows. Mordecai looked ageless, strong and calm, as if the last of his ambivalence had died, as he set the wedding band about Elizabeth's finger.

And she, well, she could only be described as radiant. Now, in the broad light of day a week later, the pair seemed bonded at the hip as they entered Devlin and Charlaine's tiny but tasteful salon. They sat down, holding hands, and smiled at the couple opposite.

"I do not need to ask how you are, my dear niece,"

Elizabeth teased. She pretended to shield her eyes from a bright light. "Joy veritably emanates from you."

Charlaine sank comfortably against Devlin's strong shoulder. She was glad to see the couple, but it was getting late, and their marriage bed, despite its frequently rumpled covers, called to them both. Devlin jumped when she placed her hand on his thigh.

"And how was Europe?" he asked his old friend.

Mordecai shrugged. "Old and decrepit. I understand why my father emigrated to America. I shall always prefer New York." He patted his wife's hand. "Lizzie and I have booked passage there a month hence. We stay for two months before we return."

Devlin nodded, but his next question was interrupted by a knock at their door. Their only servant, a pretty young maid, answered it and ushered in a mousy-looking little man in a top hat that kept rocking over his ears so badly that Charlaine wanted to reach out and catch it. Still, she was too glad to see him to mind his obvious awkwardness when he bowed low over her hand, his hat toppling off, knocking over a picture on the small table next to the sofa. Blushing, he caught the hat and set it back on his head.

"I have the papers drawn up, madam. Do you wish to sign them now?"

"Yes." Charlaine stood, pulling Devlin to his feet.

Mystified, he looked from her to the papers the man spread on the table. "What is this, Charlaine?"

"Something I should have done long ago. A wedding gift, if you will. Read, dearest."

He was only one paragraph into the legal document when he froze. His eyes, navy blue and soft with love, met hers. "You do not need to do this, you know."

Mordecai was puzzled, glancing between the two, but Elizabeth's frown cleared in a joyous smile.

Colleen Shannon

"You've changed that cursed marriage document, haven't you?"

Charlaine nodded. "All I own I share with my husband, and our children."

Moved, Devlin swallowed, scanned the rest of the pages, and smiled. "I see that you leave Summerlea only to our eldest daughter."

She held her breath. "Do you object?"

He shook his head, but he teased, "No, but I pity the poor fellow who tries to win her away from this legacy." And he signed with a bold stroke.

The man, who was obviously an attorney, blew on the ink, then carefully folded the document and put it in his coat pocket. "I shall keep this with your other papers, my lady, as you requested." He tipped his hat, and set it back down at a comical angle. "Good day."

Devlin lifted Charlaine's chin up with a loving hand. "Thank you. It was not necessary, for I would cut my arm off rather than leave you, or cheat you, but I appreciate the gesture. Now I have something for you."

He left, returning quickly with a familiar object.

Charlaine caught her breath as he handed her the Kimball book. He opened it to the pages after Chantal and her soldier. Charlaine stared at the skillfully painted picture, so moved that she couldn't speak.

Elizabeth tugged Mordecai up and came to peer nosily over Charlaine's shoulder.

A man wearing a crown of laurel leaves stood hip-deep in a pond, bare to the waist. In his arms he held a beautiful, red-haired princess who wore a necklace of pink diamonds. Their gazes and their lips were poised, forever frozen in that most treasured moment when two people admit they love one another. A frog sat on a lily pad, his head cocked approvingly as he watched.

The caption read, "Charlaine, beloved of Devlin, for-

382

ever bound to her prince of kisses."

Charlaine's gaze wavered. How had he known that this had been her lifelong dream? To write her own love story here, to read to her children, and to her children's children. She tried to speak, couldn't, and let her swimming gaze express her gratitude instead.

He pulled the book from her hands, set it on the table and said, "Excuse us, please, Mordecai and Elizabeth. We are glad you are back." Smiling their understanding, the Levitzes made their hasty good-byes and departed.

An intimate silence lingered in the air as Charlaine and Devlin stared at one another. There was a time when one of them would have rushed to fill the quiet with talk, but in the past week they had progressed so much in their relationship that each expressed his thoughts with a glance.

Charlaine wiped her tears away and took his outstretched hand, whispering, "Yes, my love, I am tired." Devlin paused only to kiss her passionately. Then, with a joyous laugh, he swept her in his arms and carried her up the stairs.

And, from its place of honor on the table next to the sofa, the book of dreams and fairy tales sparkled in the sunlight, beckoning a new generation to celebrate, and learn the lessons of love.

SPECIAL SNEAK PREVIEW!

A Faerie Tale Romance

The Steadfast Heart

By Colleen Shannon

Theirs was a love meant to last forever. She was his ballerina, he her steadfast soldier. But then an unexplained twist of fate sent the lovely Chantal de Montand into the dark English night, leaving Vincent Kimball heartbroken. Now, years later, the handsome earl can't believe his eyes when a reluctant trip to the ballet reveals an exquisite new dancer. With her raven tresses and lavender-gray eyes, she can only be his Chantal, his true love, dancing her heart out once again. And though the determined beauty denies it, Vincent swears that this time around he'll uncover what made her run—and prove to the gentle beauty the power of their steadfast love.

An extraordinary retelling of Hans Christian Anderson's classic, *The Steadfast Tin Soldier,* by the bestselling author of *The Gentle Beast.*

Don't miss *The Steadfast Heart*!
On Sale in 1998
At Bookstores and Newsstands Everywhere

Read on for a preview of Colleen Shannon's sizzling faerie tale romance, *The Steadfast Heart*, coming in 1998 from Love Spell!

Few of the ton attended the King's Theater on that balmy London night. Most found the Duchess of Derbyshire's masque far more interesting than this London debut of a little known ballet and lesser known prima ballerina. But of the two events, this performance of *La Vestale*, a tragic tale of forbidden love, would be remembered in the years to come.

In one of the most exclusive boxes, a man stood surrounded by people. He had a confidence in his bearing, a discreet elegance in his person that drew admirers and detractors alike. He wore a yellow rose diamond stickpin and an emerald signet ring with a casual grace that said much of his heritage. When he spoke, he did so quietly, as one accustomed to being listened to.

Still, it was not his obvious nobility, nor even his pleasant face one noticed first. His appeal was derived from the spirit within—a serene strength and gentle wisdom, an interest in those around him of whatever station. His smile conveyed the confidence of one born to rule, and the initiative to do so wisely. He was not a man to stand out in a crowd, yet the men and women squeezing into his box to offer their greetings gravitated toward him.

Some were hangers-on, eager to be seen with this most elite member of an elite circle; others were admiring acquaintances hoping to further their friendship; and a bare few were genuine friends who wondered why he had attended the ballet this night.

They knew what it cost him.

The eleventh Earl of Dunhaven, Vincent Anthony Kimball, smiled warmly at interloper and well-wisher alike. "In truth, had I known I'd stir up such interest, I'd have rented a larger box! Have I become so bookish that it's an event for me to enjoy an evening out?"

Only two people remained when the crowd had left. A tall, red-haired man and a small, imposing dowager wearing a tiara bright enough to illuminate Westminster at dusk. "Robbie, tell him it's past time I coaxed him into attending a ballet," said the earl's mother.

Vince snorted. "Coaxed, is it? More like coerced, madam."

"Talk to him, Robbie. Tell him how foolish he is to hold sacrosanct a boy's memory and condemn me to loneliness because of it." When Vince's mouth tightened, she said more insistently, "It's true. Were it not for that French chit you'd be married with a brood by now. . . ." Robbie's tightening fingers gave her pause less than the anguished flash of blue eyes before they looked away.

There was an uncomfortable silence before Robbie said tactfully, "I've yet to meet a woman who would be happy to play second fiddle to John Bull, ma'am. As long as Vince is so devoted to politics, perhaps it's best he not marry."

Vince shot him a grateful look. "So I've tried to tell her. Some people were not meant to wed, and I, I fear, am one of them." As the lights began to dim, he relaxed into his seat as if the issue were settled.

Adeline, Countess of Dunhaven, gave a disgruntled sigh and turned her attention to the stage, but Robbie still watched his friend. He knew Vince better than anyone, and he worried at the white look about his friend's mouth. Adeline had no idea how much Vince had loved Chantal, so she didn't know how it strained her son to attend a ballet, any ballet, because of the memories it revived. Robbie was more admiring of his lifelong friend than ever.

Vince's unfailing charm and tact even when he was not in the best of humors himself never ceased to amaze Robbie. He'd kept himself sequestered for too long. It had been over ten years since Chantal's disappearance. For his friend's sake, Robbie hoped Vince would lay Chantal's memory to rest. Thus, Robbie had added his persuasions to Adeline's to attend the ballet tonight—for a different reason.

He'd heard from a friend who attended this same ballet in Milan that the prima ballerina was of uncommon beauty. She was a wisp of a thing, as delicate and graceful as her namesake, Papillone. If she was as charming as rumored, then maybe here, at last, was a woman who could interest Vince longer than a night or, at most, a week. Robbie knew of no quicker relief for the dismals than a new mistress. As for the reports that Papillone rejected all admirers, Robbie dismissed them as rumors planted by the little danseuse herself to entice more bees to her honeypot. Who ever heard of a virtuous ballerina? he scoffed inwardly, settling back as the curtain opened.

Vince gritted his teeth to still the gorge rising in his throat and told himself he was being ridiculous. Adeline and Robbie were right. It was high time he exorcised the ghost that had haunted him for far too long. Chantal was either dead or married by now. If she had cared as much for him as she claimed, she never would have disappeared without a word.

And so he forced himself to watch, trying to deny the tearing anguish in his gut as the first dancers floated on stage. But the memories persisted. It should be Chantal on that stage, dancing for him, only for him, as she had so many times before. He was too busy grappling with himself to pay much attention to the stage as the first act began.

A mock Roman circus had been set up, complete with chariots, horses and spectators draped in togas. The games at an end, the Vestal Virgins entered to a slow, measured rhythm from the orchestra, bearing the palms and crowns for the victors.

They wore the briefest of togas, baring a graceful shoulder each, a golden cord tying the white gauze about their waists. The material had been so cleverly draped that, though each dancer was covered to her ankles, details of each supple figure were quite apparent. So in tune were they as they arched, dipped and swayed that at first, none stood out. Like a sonata, they blended into a harmonious whole, no figure crescendoing apart from the others. But then the corps de ballet faded into the background, leaving two people in the forefront.

Vince's wandering attention sharpened. He leaned forward.

Center stage stood Decius, the winning gladiator, clad in leather jerkin and helmet, with Emilia, the smallest Vestal. Unlike the other dancers, who wore their hair up, her long, blue-black tresses were braided with a golden cord, the braid falling over one delicate shoulder. Her waist was tiny, her hips as curvaceous as the legs that could be glimpsed through the thin gauze. She lifted slim arms to place the crown on Decius's head. The lamplight centered on them, highlighting the emotional moment of two people falling in love at first sight. For the first time, the prima ballerina's face was clearly lit.

Vincent groaned as blood rushed to his head. He fell back against his seat, oblivious to Robbie's "My word!" or Adeline's shocked gasp. He mouthed then the very name his companions had hoped tonight would erase from his lips. "Chantal." And finally, in a hoarse shout, "Chantal!"

Vince bolted out of the door. He leaped down the stairs three at a time, his pulse keeping time with each frantic step. He ran to the stage door, a prayer mumbling through his lips, "Dear God, let it be, let it be, please. . . ."

His way backstage was blocked by the stage manager. "No one is allowed backstage during a performance, me lud."

Vince threw a desperate look at the stage, which he could barely see. He saw nothing of Chantal, and panic filled him. What if she left before he had a chance to see her? What if he'd imagined her, conjured up the image he most wanted to see in the stress of attending his first ballet since she disappeared? He couldn't wait until the performance was over. He must find out NOW.

He looked at the manager's angry face. He looked back at the stage. For only the second time since reaching maturity, he acted on instinct, emotionally rather than logically. As if defeated, he turned and retreated a few steps. When the manager followed, he darted around the corner of the wing and stuck out his foot.

The man fell headlong. Vince leaped over him and ran out on stage, aware but uncaring that he would become the cynosure of all eyes. Uncaring that he, who assiduously guarded his good name so as to set the example he espoused, would make a spectacle of himself in exactly the way he abhorred in others.

The Vestals were pirouetting when Vince burst onto the stage. He searched frantically for that haunting face. A dancer noticed him and faltered to a halt, drawing the attention of the others. One by one they stopped and stared as this obvious gentleman walked slowly through them, searching, searching.

Vince didn't feel the shocked, fascinated gazes as even the orchestra whined to a stop, the musicians, too, pausing to stare. The audience buzzed as Vince wended his way to the front, his eyes riveted on a gleaming black head.

He pushed through the stunned troupe, clasped the girl's arm and turned her to face him. The air left his lungs in a whoosh as the eyes he would never forget looked at him, a miasma of emotions in their lavender-gray depths. They were enormous eyes, vaguely slanted and fringed with thick, black, curling lashes. Eyes he'd despaired of ever meeting again.

Utter silence prevailed as every person in the theater, from maid to mistress, from footman to Duke, stared. And as the earl put up a shaking hand to touch her face, every person present caught the hunger and familiarity in that touch.

Vince knew nothing but the lovely, distressed face before him. With every pore of his body he absorbed the features that still haunted his dreams: high cheekbones, pointed chin, dainty nose, full mouth and pearly teeth just visible between her panting lips. He would have been content to stare at her for hours, but when Chantal flinched away from the caress at her cheek, he was galvanized into action.

He jerked her to his lean frame, groaning at the feel of her against him, substantial rather than the wraith he'd reached for in the interminable dark, lonely nights. He sensed the shocked gasps from the audience, but his only concern at the moment was Chantal.

He forced her averted chin up and looked into the eyes that were now veiled. "Why do you deny me, Chantal?" he whispered tenderly.

She bit her lip, refusing to answer, so he did then what his body had been urging him to do since he touched her. He lowered his sun-streaked head over hers and kissed her, swallowing her gasp. For the barest instant, she melted against him, as if familiar with the touch and taste of the mouth seeking hers so urgently. Then she stiffened and tried to push him away. He lifted his head and looked down at her, his blue eyes moist, but he would not release her.

She closed her eyes, a pained look twisting her porcelain features, but when she looked at him again, her steely gaze matched her tone. "You mistake, m'sieur. My name is not Chantal. I insist you release me."

He did so, reluctantly, but kept within easy arm's reach. "Then why did you respond to my kiss?" His little smile deepened when a blush tinged her cheeks.

She patterned her worldly smile after his own as she

looked him up and down. "You are a handsome man, m'sieur."

As they led him off stage, he frowned, for the Chantal he had known could never have been so bold. . . .

Someone's Been Sleeping In My Bed

A Faerie Tale Romance

Linda Jones

**WHO'S BEEN EATING FROM MY BOWL?
IS SHE A BEAUTY IN BOTH HEART AND
   SOUL?
WHO'S BEEN SITTING IN MY CHAIR?
IS SHE PRETTY OF FACE AND FAIR OF
   HAIR?
WHO'S BEEN SLEEPING IN MY BED?
IS SHE THE DAMSEL I WILL WED?**

The golden-haired woman barely escapes from a stagecoach robbery before she gets lost in the Wyoming mountains. Hungry, harried, and out of hope, she stumbles on a rude cabin, the home of three brothers, great bears of men who nearly frighten her out of her wits. But Maddalyn Kelly is no Goldilocks; she is a feisty beauty who can fend for herself. Still, how can she ever guess that the Barrett boys will bare their souls to her—or that one of them will share with her an ecstasy so exquisite it is almost unbearable?
_52094-X   **$5.99 US/$6.99 CAN**

BESTSELLING AUTHOR OF
LONGER THAN FOREVER!
FOUR WEDDINGS AND
A FAIRY GODMOTHER

Only a storybook affair like the marriage of Cindy Ella Jones and Princeton Chalmers could lead to three such tangled romances— and happily ever after endings:

BELINDA

Kidnapped from the wedding party, the lonely beauty will learn how a little love can tame a wild beast—even one as intimidating as Cain Dezlin, the handsome recluse.

LILITH

Thrown together with Frank Henson, a seemingly soft-spoken security guard, self-absorbed Lilith will have to learn that with love and respect, there's a prince waiting behind every toad.

ROBERTA

The shy redhead's heart has been broken by a wicked wolf once before—and now that Maximilian Wolfe has shown up at the wedding she is determined to get to her grandmother's before the big bad Frenchman can hurt her again.

_52114-8 $5.50 US/$6.50 CAN

A Faerie Tale Romance

Big Bad Wolf by Linda Jones. Big and wide and strong, Wolf Trevelyan's shoulders are just right for his powerful physique—and Molly Kincaid wonders what his arms would feel like wrapped tightly around her. Molly knows she should be scared of the dark stranger. She's been warned of Wolf's questionable past. But there's something compelling in his gaze, something tantalizing in his touch—something about Wolf that leaves Molly willing to throw caution, and her grandmother's concerns, to the wind to see if love won't find the best way home.

__52179-2 $5.50 US/$6.50 CAN

The Emperor's New Clothes by Victoria Alexander. Cardsharp Ophelia Kendrake is mistaken for the Countess of Bridgewater and plans to strip Dead End, Wyoming, of its fortunes before escaping into the sunset. But the free-spirited beauty almost swallows her script when she meets Tyler Matthews, the town's virile young mayor. Tyler simply wants to settle down and enjoy the simplicity of ranching. But his aunt and uncle are set on making a silk purse out of Dead End, and Tyler is going to be the new mayor. It's a job he accepts with little relish—until he catches a glimpse of the village's newest visitor.

__52159-8 $5.50 US/$6.50 CAN

Dorchester Publishing Co., Inc.
65 Commerce Road
Stamford, CT 06902

Please add $1.75 for shipping and handling for the first book and $.50 for each book thereafter. NY, NYC, PA and CT residents, please add appropriate sales tax. No cash, stamps, or C.O.D.s. All orders shipped within 6 weeks via postal service book rate. Canadian orders require $2.00 extra postage and must be paid in U.S. dollars through a U.S. banking facility.

Name _____
Address _____
City _____ State _____ Zip _____
I have enclosed $_____ in payment for the checked book(s).
Payment <u>must</u> accompany all orders.☐ Please send a free catalog.